*To Red, who opened the first door,
and to Meredith, who opened the second*

# Exile from Eden

PART ONE

# Exile from Eden

# PRAISE FOR
# QUEEN OF SHADOWS

"Sylvan's powerful debut is packed with startling action, sensual romance, and delightfully nerdy vampires. [Her] compelling take on vampirism, its underlying characters, and a comfortably unabashedly feminist plot will have readers hungry for a sequel."
—*Publishers Weekly* (starred review)

"*Queen of Shadows* pulled me in . . . Sylvan's rich, dark, sexy reimagined Austin is filled with people I want to visit again and again . . . Sylvan's got voice, doesn't miss a beat, and rocks it all the way to the last note. Sit down. Shut up. And enjoy the show. It's intense, dark, sexy, with just the right touch of humor. Looking for a new addiction? Go no further."
—Devon Monk, author of *Dead Iron*

"Grabbed me on the first page and didn't let go. Miranda, the heroine, is vulnerable and gutsy, with magical abilities even she doesn't suspect. Vampire David Solomon is as powerful and heroic as he is deliciously seductive. Dianne Sylvan has created an original take on vampires that I thoroughly enjoyed, and I'll be looking for her next book with great anticipation. She's a skilled and talented storyteller who definitively knows how to deliver one hell of a book!"
—Angela Knight, *New York Times*
bestselling author of *Master of Shadows*

"Dianne Sylvan is an incredibly talented writer. She draws the reader not only into the story but into the very marrow of someone who is starting to question [her] grip on reality. If you aren't familiar with the Austin area, you will be once you turn that last page . . . *Queen of Shadows* concludes with a great flourish, leaving the reader euphoric."
—*Sacramento Book Review*

*continued . . .*

*Ace Books by Dianne Sylvan*

QUEEN OF SHADOWS
SHADOWFLAME

# SHADOWFLAME

## DIANNE SYLVAN

ACE BOOKS, NEW YORK

**THE BERKLEY PUBLISHING GROUP**
**Published by the Penguin Group**
**Penguin Group (USA) Inc.**
**375 Hudson Street, New York, New York 10014, USA**
Penguin Group (Canada), 90 Eglinton Avenue East, Suite 700, Toronto, Ontario M4P 2Y3, Canada
(a division of Pearson Penguin Canada Inc.)
Penguin Books Ltd., 80 Strand, London WC2R 0RL, England
Penguin Group Ireland, 25 St. Stephen's Green, Dublin 2, Ireland (a division of Penguin Books Ltd.)
Penguin Group (Australia), 250 Camberwell Road, Camberwell, Victoria 3124, Australia
(a division of Pearson Australia Group Pty. Ltd.)
Penguin Books India Pvt. Ltd., 11 Community Centre, Panchsheel Park, New Delhi—110 017, India
Penguin Group (NZ), 67 Apollo Drive, Rosedale, Auckland 0632, New Zealand
(a division of Pearson New Zealand Ltd.)
Penguin Books (South Africa) (Pty.) Ltd., 24 Sturdee Avenue, Rosebank, Johannesburg 2196,
South Africa

Penguin Books Ltd., Registered Offices: 80 Strand, London WC2R 0RL, England

This is a work of fiction. Names, characters, places, and incidents either are the product of the author's imagination or are used fictitiously, and any resemblance to actual persons, living or dead, business establishments, events, or locales is entirely coincidental. The publisher does not have any control over and does not assume any responsibility for author or third-party websites or their content.

SHADOWFLAME

An Ace Book / published by arrangement with the author

PRINTING HISTORY
Ace mass-market edition / August 2011

Copyright © 2011 by Dianne Sylvan.
Cover art by Gene Mollica.
Cover design by Annette Fiore DeFex.
Interior text design by Tiffany Estreicher.

ISBN: 978-0-441-02065-2

ACE
Ace Books are published by The Berkley Publishing Group,
a division of Penguin Group (USA) Inc.,
375 Hudson Street, New York, New York 10014.
ACE and the "A" design are trademarks of Penguin Group (USA) Inc.

PRINTED IN THE UNITED STATES OF AMERICA

10  9  8  7  6  5  4  3  2  1

# One

Autumn that year came in like a lion and devoured the last few straggling moments of an endless, scorching summer. Storms swept through central Texas and scoured the world clean of dust and dried grass. The entire city seemed to come alive once the burden of heat was lifted.

The nights were already chilly the first week of October when the last known member of the Blackthorn gang sprinted in terror through the streets of Austin, searching for someone, anyone, who would shelter him.

Door after door slammed in his face. No one in the Shadow World was stupid enough to take him in . . . not tonight. Bars closed early, windows went dark, and the wind's icy fingers snatched all hope of escape from the city's empty streets. Only a fool would look outside tonight. Only a fool would get involved.

The Signet was on the hunt.

Desperate, he ran for the heavily populated areas of downtown, hoping to get lost in the mortal crowd, unaware that across the city his low body temperature and preternatural speed were being tracked by a bank of computers that sent out his coordinates every five seconds. There was nowhere he could go now without a target flashing on his every move.

"Status report."

Faith's voice was fierce even through the digital ether.

*"Rabbit is approaching the eastern corner of Fifth and Trinity. Move to intercept?"*

From her perch atop the restaurant across the intersection, the Queen of the Southern United States watched the streets with her eyes narrowed, sweeping the area with her senses. She stood with one foot up on the low wall around the roof's perimeter and held her hair back out of her face with one hand. Her breath came in smoky clouds, slow and calm, as she waited, patient, unhurried.

Human traffic was high even for a Thursday. Their quarry had no doubt come this way precisely for that reason, believing that the Elite wouldn't want to cause a scene.

"Hold your position," she replied into her com just as a thin shape darted around the corner, weaving his way among the people on the sidewalk, trying not to look like he was on the run.

He crossed Trinity against the light, narrowly avoiding a bus, intent on reaching the side nearest her, which was far less busy, darker, and located conveniently near an underground access point. She let him cross and waited.

Finally, when he thought he might be safe and slowed his pace, she vaulted over the side of the building. The air rushed past her for two stories, and she twisted in midair to land, her boots striking the pavement solidly.

She straightened, tossing her hair back over her shoulders, the wind catching her coat and whipping it back to expose her throat. When the rabbit saw what was around her neck he froze and went ghostly white.

He spun around to run back the way he had come, but he was surrounded. Behind him Faith crossed her arms and smiled.

He faced Miranda an inch away from panic.

"Would you like to beg?" she asked.

Mindless survival instinct gripped him and he threw himself at her, snarling.

She laughed, stepped to the side, and caught him in the face with a fist. He landed sprawling with an animal cry of fear and pain and scrambled back to his feet, trying to gain some kind of advantage when there was none to gain. He took a swing at her, and she blocked it easily, twisting to punch him in the gut and again in the head.

He stumbled but didn't fall; he was no weakling, though it clearly surprised him that she wasn't either. Obviously he hadn't listened to the whispers that had rolled slowly through the Shadow World like an oncoming storm for the past three months . . . or he'd heard the stories and dismissed them, as no mere woman could be so strong.

He was learning differently now. She ducked another hit, this one more reckless. His fear was beginning to show.

She liked that.

She spun around and kicked him in the head, and he went down but immediately forced himself back to his feet despite the blood flowing from his nose and mouth. He was clearly dazed, but desperation drove him to try again and again, only to be beaten back by a laughing Queen who hadn't even broken a sweat.

There were humans nearby, approaching from the east. Distractedly she bent her will toward them and gave them a mental nudge to turn left instead of right. By the time they realized they were headed in the wrong direction, there would be nothing to see.

She moved closer to the rabbit until she was only a few feet from him, allowing her power to swell around her. He let out a whimper and fell back.

"Kneel before your Queen," she hissed.

He dropped to his knees, sobbing incoherently in her shadow.

"A fine display from a man who killed two of my Elite during the war," she said. "You were a key player in the gang, Jackson. We know who you are and have a list of your crimes. You've eluded capture this long only because you hid like a coward while your friends died in your place. But not anymore."

At the sound of her sword being drawn from its sheath, Jackson fell down on his elbows, clapping his hands over the back of his neck. Now he decided to beg; he blamed the others in the gang, especially Ariana and Bethany Blackthorn, for forcing him to kill. He wasn't responsible, they were; he was only following orders.

She'd heard it all a dozen times in the last few months, and she knew every time, as she did now, that it was a lie.

"You disappoint me," she told him. "Worse? You bore me." She kicked him again, this time in the side, so he instinctively moved his arms down to protect his stomach and left his neck exposed. With a single graceful swing she beheaded him and leapt back in time to avoid the gush of blood that bathed the sidewalk scarlet as his body toppled over.

Dark, grim satisfaction warmed her as the body twitched into stillness. The head had landed faceup, its eyes gaping open in shock, mouth slack.

She leaned down, seized the edge of Jackson's jacket, and used it to wipe her sword before sheathing the blade. She would need to clean it thoroughly when she got home; Sophie had taught her never to let a blade go to rest still bloodied . . . not to mention that the sword itself had once belonged to Sophie, and Miranda could practically hear the diminutive vampire's acerbic voice every time she was tempted not to treat the weapon with the respect it was due.

She looked up at Faith, who was smiling ferally. "Cleanup on aisle three," Miranda said.

Faith gestured to the rest of her team. They knew the procedure: Take the body and the head up on the roof of a nearby building where it would be exposed to the sun at dawn but not likely found by any passing mortal. Tap into the hydrant nearby to spray off the blood. Hopefully after tonight it would be the last time they'd have to go through the routine for a while.

She stood watching for a moment while they worked, and Faith joined her. "You're getting disturbingly good at this kind of thing," the Second said quietly. "I'm still not used to seeing it."

Miranda smiled. "What's even more disturbing is that I'm not disturbed at all."

Faith shrugged. "I recall you saying that first night: This is your work now."

The Queen thought back to the battle at the Haven and the long night of cleanup and casualties that had followed. Faith had wanted her to go and rest. She had declined and instead stepped into her role without hesitation, organizing the Elite to burn the dead and patch up the wounded, leaving the Prime to restore the network and deal with the damage to the building itself. It had been nearly sunrise before either of them had stood still.

"Where is our Lord and Master tonight?" Faith asked. "Shouldn't he have been out here, too?"

"No," the Queen replied, eyes on Jackson's headless corpse as two Elite maneuvered it onto a plastic sheet to carry it away. "He had an appointment. It's best if I handle this anyway—I want my presence known."

"I think you've succeeded there." Faith nodded toward the scene. "We've got this if you need to go."

"Good. I'll see you back at the Haven. Have the night's final report on the server before you code off shift."

Faith bowed to her, as did the others. Miranda nodded, then turned and walked off into the darkness.

The standoff took place in a back corner booth at Kerbey Lane Café.

A woman with a shaved head and multiple facial piercings stared down a blue-eyed man in a long black coat as he drank a Corona with lime and she ate a plate of black bean nachos. Around them the café bustled as always, the patrons blessedly ignorant of what might be unfolding among them.

They could have been any two people—albeit an odd couple—on a date getting to know each other over Tex-Mex.

"So . . . you're a vampire."

He gave her a measured nod.

"And you're officially the most badass vampire in Texas."

"The Southern United States, yes."

Kat stared at him hard, and he couldn't help but be impressed; she wasn't afraid of him, at least not yet. Most humans could feel something of what he was, and it made them uneasy. Either she couldn't feel it, which made her as dumb as a bag of hammers, or she was strong enough to stand her ground.

His money was on the latter.

He knew he could terrify her if he wanted to. All he had to do was let his shielding slip or will his eyes to silver or his teeth to extend. He could fix her with a certain facial expression—that of a panther watching a deer from a tree overhead—and she would instinctively seek an escape, any escape.

He didn't do any of those things. This was too important for such childish play.

For the first time in a long time, David Solomon had something to prove besides how frightening he was.

"You turned my best friend into a vampire," Kat said, her stare unwavering. "Why should I have anything to do with you?"

"Because you care about her," he replied reasonably, "and you know that I'm not going away."

"I know this story," she told him. "Hot mysterious guy sweeps in right when she needs someone, isolates her from her life, pulls her into something dangerous. You know how those things end up? In bruises and hotline phone calls. Restraining orders. Best friends with concealed handgun permits showing up at the guy's house and shooting his balls off."

He looked down at her messenger bag. "Let me guess . . . a Sig P232?"

"Not the point, Count Pretty Boy." Her eyes narrowed. "Although, if I shot your balls off, would they grow back?"

David smiled. "I think you and I are going to get along fine, Kat."

"Speak for yourself. Tell me what makes you the kind of guy that deserves Miranda."

"I don't," he said. "But she and I are bonded and will be so until our death. Nothing can change that now. She's stuck with me . . . and so are you, if you want to keep her friendship, and I sincerely hope you do."

"Why?"

"Because she's going to need you. In some ways she's as old as I am, but in others still so young . . . she still has ties to the mortal world that she wants to hold on to. Whether that proves possible will depend on the kind of support she gets from that world, namely you."

"Then you're saying I'll help keep her human."

"No." He sat forward, holding her gaze. "She isn't human, Kat. She never will be again. One day she'll watch you grow old and die, and she'll stay the same, ageless, eternal, until someone murders us both. What she is, is your friend, and the fact that she wants to stay your friend despite the pain inherent in loving a mortal speaks very highly of you. You should be honored."

Kat nodded slowly, almost smiling. "So should you."

"I am."

She nodded again, and then said, "You're buying, right?"

"Absolutely."

"Then let's talk about dessert."


Five minutes before curtain—just as her agent, Denise, was about to have a coronary—Miranda Grey strode into the club with her hair tangled from the wind and her eyes bright with the thrill of the hunt.

She could hear the crowd on the far side of the stage, one low murmur of three hundred voices, their collective expectation a living thing crawling up the walls. She took the flight of metal stairs up to the wings with a grin on her face and drank in their emotions on a single deep breath.

She gave Denise a thumbs-up. Denise made a forehead-wiping motion of exasperated relief in return. Flipping her hair back and shrugging her coat into the tech's hands, Miranda turned toward the stage manager and nodded.

A hush fell as the house lights lowered and the spotlight trained on the mike and the single object behind it: her guitar, on a stand, gleaming black.

Applause erupted when they saw it.

Miranda smiled and walked out into the light.

There were three things that Miranda wanted after every show: blood, chocolate, and a hot shower.

Before she could have any of those, however, she had to get backstage and run the press gauntlet, then somehow sneak out the back to either drive herself or wait for Harlan to take her somewhere more private to hunt.

There were a great many vehicles at the Signet's disposal, but the one the Prime favored was the Town Car that Harlan piloted through the city streets; if he and the Queen needed to be in separate places or ran on different schedules, as often happened these days, they had to coordinate Harlan's trips or, as she preferred, she had to bring her own car into town.

Although David had serious misgivings about her being alone in the city, Miranda loved her car, and she loved taking the winding road that led up to the Haven through the Hill Country. She liked being independent. So most nights after she was finished at her gig and had found herself someone for dinner, she slid behind the wheel of her little silver Toyota and took Loop 360 out of town.

She was almost ready to escape the club's heat and noise when Denise knocked on the dressing room door and said, "Hey, do you have a minute?"

"Sure," Miranda called, double-checking that the mirror was still covered with a towel. "What's up?" she asked, gathering her sweaty hair back out of her face and securing it with a stretchy band.

Denise MacNeil was a strikingly beautiful black woman who radiated competence and confidence, two things that

Miranda had discovered were vital for a woman in the music industry. Denise carried herself like a warrior, and in fact she reminded Miranda strongly of Faith, except instead of a sword Denise was armed with a briefcase and BlackBerry and hunted opportunities, not lawbreakers. Miranda would have continued to play the bar circuit without much thought if Denise hadn't come along, but in the short time she'd been the Queen's agent she had already set the wheels in motion for a recording contract and doubled her bookings. It would have been easy for someone so ballsy to be a bitch, but Denise still had a warmth to her that seemed to bring her even greater respect.

"There's a woman here from the *Statesman* who wants an interview for their weekly entertainment supplement," Denise was saying. "Nothing drawn-out, just a few questions. Are you up for it?"

Miranda sighed. She had played hard, and worked hard, holding the audience's attention pretty easily, but it was still draining, and she hadn't fed tonight. Her teeth were starting to ache and her insides felt like they were drying out. She took a quick internal inventory and judged she had about half an hour before things got unpleasant. "Sure."

"Great. Also, don't forget next week we have a meeting with the guys over at the Bat Cave."

"Got it."

Denise grinned at her. "And one other thing. They have these weird little devices now that you can talk into so your voice comes out the other end—that way if you're going to show up, say, two minutes before curtain, you can keep your agent from pissing her designer pants."

Miranda smiled back. "Not once have I ever been late," she pointed out. "But I'll try not to cut it so close next time."

Denise shook her head and left, saying, "I've been in this business fifteen years and I've never adjusted my watch to Musician Standard Time."

Miranda closed her guitar into its case, running her hand along the Martin's gleaming neck. "That's Vampire

Standard Time," she said quietly to the instrument, "but we won't tell her that."

A moment later, there was another knock, and a woman poked her head into the dressing room. "Ms. Grey?"

Miranda looked up from her phone, where she was checking to ensure there were no texts waiting from the Haven, and gestured for the human to enter.

The reporter was completely average looking, with mousy brown hair in a rather severe cut with bangs and glasses that made her look like a librarian. She was wearing a nondescript suit a year or two out of style and was clearly nervous. "I'm Stacey Burnside with the *Austin American-Statesman*. Denise said you had a moment for me?"

"Come in," Miranda said with a smile. Her Signet had come with a set of new and strange instincts, one of which was to put humans at ease whenever possible; she felt almost maternal toward them, especially the awkward young women so unsure of their place in the world who could barely make eye contact with the glamorous rising star who seemed to have it all. "Have a seat."

Stacey almost knocked over the folding chair as she sat down and rummaged for her recorder. Miranda could sense the experience of an educated reporter—and Stacey was no amateur, she could feel that much—warring with awe.

Miranda got that a lot . . . at least, from humans. She was trying to get used to it.

"I won't keep you long," Stacey said, fiddling with her digital recorder until a red light came on. "We're just doing a piece this week on emerging artists who do their recording here in Austin."

"Well, I'm happy to support the local music scene," Miranda told her, taking the other folding chair and crossing one leg over the other. She had her coat on, but her Signet peeked out from her collar, and she caught the young woman staring at it for a moment. That also happened a lot. Most of the time people had the same look on their faces: *Is that thing glowing?*

"Austin has been very good to me since I started

performing," the Queen added. "I'm hoping to work with the guys at the Bat Cave on my upcoming CD."

Stacey pushed her glasses back on her nose. "That's the studio founded by Grizzly Behr, the father of Mike Behr of Three Tequila Floor, right?"

"Yes."

"I hear it's impossible to get into the Bat Cave these days."

Miranda smiled. "They were as excited about the prospect as I was." The music business was all about influence . . . and Miranda had that in spades. There was no door that was closed to her, no velvet rope to keep her out no matter how exclusive the club. The Signet held sway in every level of government and the Prime a hand in every game in town, legal or otherwise. It wouldn't take much effort to have her first single on the *Billboard* charts the day it was released.

She didn't want that. She had every intention of making it on her talent . . . but she wasn't so naïve as to think the industry cared about talent as much as it cared about power. She was quite willing to kick down the door to success with one of her brand-new knee-high boots.

"You recently debuted a new song, 'Bleed,'" Stacey said. "Critics are having trouble categorizing it—what influences gave rise to its sound and lyrics?"

Miranda toyed with her com, considering her answer. "It's a deeply personal song," she replied. "The lyrics were some of the first I wrote after a particularly difficult time I had last year. I felt that the shift in tone, from pain to triumph, was something that would resonate with audiences. It definitely has the feel of an early Tori Amos track, but the studio version will have more electronic elements. The vision we have for the album as a whole is a lush, dark sound that still leaves room for the rawness of some of the lyrics."

"You tend to play your personal life close to the vest. Recent rumors have you married—is there any truth to that?"

She smiled. "Yes, actually." She held up her left hand,

showing the platinum band around her finger. "I've been married for about two months."

Stacey's eyes lit up—a scoop! "Can you tell me anything about your husband?"

"Oh, I could tell you a lot of things, but he's a very private person, as am I. I will say that meeting him absolutely changed my life, and that we make a perfect pair."

"Do you live in the Austin area?"

"Yes."

"In the city itself, or a suburb?"

Miranda chuckled. "In the area." She checked her watch, rose, and said, "I'm sorry, but I do need to head home."

"One more question, please, if that's all right?"

She looked so eager Miranda couldn't help herself. "Fire away," she told the woman as she folded her chair and leaned it back against the wall. She tried to leave things tidy for the band that came in after her, though they rarely saw fit to return the favor.

Stacey reached into her bag again and dug around for something. "Um . . . hang on . . ."

Miranda refrained from rolling her eyes, but the gnawing feeling in her stomach was starting to become a serious issue. She was still learning to manage her hunger; unlike skipping a meal back when she was mortal, waiting too long to feed could impair her judgment and lead to unfortunate incidents . . . and had, more than once, the first few weeks. If David hadn't insisted on hunting with her for a while, she might have killed someone. She had an emergency pack in her car, kept safely on ice in the trunk, but her car was a block away and there were usually people milling around outside so she couldn't just pop it open and slurp it down.

"Okay," Stacey said, straightening. Miranda noticed she had something in her hand, something metal with the flash of wood—

"How stupid are you for being caught without a bodyguard?" Stacey asked, and lifted her hand.

Miranda's body reacted before her brain could register

what was happening; she threw herself backward as the gun went off, twisting sideways a split second before the stake bit hard into her shoulder. The impact threw her backward into the wall, and she snarled, springing forward toward the woman, who had already turned on her heel and bolted from the room.

Miranda missed Stacey by mere inches and flung herself after the woman, her vision gone scarlet with rage; Stacey sprinted through the narrow backstage passageway, knocking people over as she ran. Miranda snaked through the crowd, ignoring the pain and the feeling of blood running down her torso. She heard gasps behind her as she closed the space between herself and the would-be assassin, but Stacey reached to the side and hauled a stack of speakers on wheels out behind her to block Miranda's path.

The Queen kicked them out of the way and resumed her pursuit, but by the time she burst out the backstage door there was no sign of Stacey, no sign of anyone; the alley was empty.

"Goddamn it!" Miranda snapped to the empty air.

Immediately, the alert on her com went off. *"Emergency team to Mel's Bar and Grill, code Alpha One!"* she heard Faith's voice command in broadsend-mode, then, *"Star-two, Star-two, Miranda, are you all right?"*

Miranda took a deep breath. "Star-three, this is Star-two, and I'm fine. I'm injured but not severely. A woman posing as a reporter staked me in the shoulder. She had some kind of spear gun. I lost her but I'm heading out to track her now—"

"Like hell you are," came a voice.

Miranda turned in time to see the shadows beyond the edge of the building grow dense and coalesce, the substance of the night twisting on itself, resolving into the shape of a man in black with a glowing stone at his throat.

The Prime was at her side in seconds, and the look on his face, though extremely attractive to her, would have made a human's blood run cold. "What happened?" he asked, taking hold of her shoulders.

When he saw the stake he hissed and his eyes went silver.

"It's not bad," she insisted. "If we hurry, we can still—"

"You're hurt," he replied tersely. "That takes priority. Now, hold still, and brace yourself . . . take a deep breath in . . . now breathe out slowly . . ."

She did as he said, and on the out breath, he took hold of the stake and pulled it.

Miranda cried out; she felt the wood sliding through her muscles as if every splinter of the stake were jagged and tore the flesh around it. It was as if the wood left behind something oily and poisonous that seeped into her body and stole her strength away.

Her vision swam, and she sagged into the Prime. "Oh, God . . ."

"Easy, beloved," he said, considerably more gently. "Easy. Close your eyes . . . breathe."

Miranda clamped her eyes shut and dragged her awareness to the feel of his hands on her arms, the sound of him breathing, the rhythm of his pulse that she could feel, always, beating in her own veins. She felt him drawing power up out of himself and feeding it along the connection between them, and her shoulder grew unbearably hot for a moment, then itched horribly before fading into numbness.

When she opened her eyes the wound was gone, though there was a gaping hole in her coat.

"Shit," she murmured. "I love this coat."

With that, she passed out, thankful he was there to catch her.


Faith managed, somehow, to keep David from tearing the building apart in search of the attacker, but it wasn't easy. The half-dozen Elite who reported to the scene were obviously frightened by his anger. Who wouldn't be? A black cloud of seething energy surrounded him as he stood cross-armed and watched the team sweep the club for evidence and another team followed the fading traces of the assassin's flight. The few humans who were aware of the situation had no idea what they were really dealing with, but they knew Miranda had been attacked and that her security personnel were handling it. The look on her husband's face was enough to keep everyone, human or otherwise, at a distance.

She joined the Prime once the team had things in hand and took her usual place at his side—his left, as the Queen's place was his right. The Queen herself was unconscious in the car.

"This is unacceptable," David said darkly. "She is not to go anywhere without a bodyguard. Understood?"

"Fine by me, Sire, but you'll have a hard time convincing her of that."

"I'll have her followed if I have to."

Faith merely nodded. She had already learned not to take sides. "Aside from the stake itself, which we'll bring in for analysis, there's nothing," the Second said. "No one has any recollection of what this woman looked like, except of course for the Queen. Somehow the bitch managed to convince Miranda she was human, and that's . . . disturbing."

"Agreed."

"Best guess, she was a vampire with a hell of a shield, but there's no way to know for sure."

"Here's a better question," David said. "Forget what she was and let's ask ourselves *who*."

"Obviously it was a planned hit. She had fake press credentials and even a dummy phone number. I'll put out feelers for anyone buying an ID by that name, but I doubt we'll get anything." Faith nodded to Elite 33, who was carrying Miranda's bag and guitar out of the club to the car, and asked the Prime, "Didn't the network register something was wrong?"

David's expression went from dark to hellfire. "Interestingly enough, no. There wasn't even a blip."

"How did you know to call us here, then?"

"I felt the stake." His eyes were fixed on the car at the

end of the alley. "Either the attacker was human and faster on her feet than a Queen, or she was a vampire who somehow doesn't show up on the network. I don't like either of those possibilities, Faith. I'm counting on you to find this person and bring her to me."

Faith didn't mention how difficult, if not impossible, that would be. The Elite had expert trackers, but so far the team had come up empty-handed; this woman had vanished into the crowded city without leaving a single footprint or energy trace. Even the strongest psychic they had—Miranda—had lost her, though if she hadn't been injured chances were the Queen could have hunted the woman down in minutes.

A planned attack. Specific, focused . . . which led Faith to believe that this Stacey had known exactly who and what she was trying to kill. The Shadow World was aptly named; very few humans knew of its existence, and few vampires would associate with the human world enough to connect Miranda Grey the singer with Miranda the Queen. Even fewer vampires would be stupid enough to go up against the Signet after the example that had been made of the Blackthorn. Someone had known that Miranda would be alone—if she'd had even a standard Elite security detail, the guards would have been right outside the door to block the assassin's escape.

Harlan appeared at the Prime's elbow. "Sire, the Queen is asking for you."

David nodded to Faith, who followed him to the car, where Miranda was sitting with the door open, looking disheveled and seriously pissed off.

The Queen's Signet was glowing brightly and there was dried blood all over her coat and jeans and some in her hair. Her heart-shaped face held a look even scarier than David's had.

She looked up at her mate and spoke very deliberately. "Blood. Shower. Chocolate. *Now.*"

David actually smiled, bowed, and said, "As you will it, my Lady. Harlan, start the car. Faith, finish up here and

have a report on my server ASAP. I'd like you to drive the
Queen's car back to the Haven yourself when you're done.
I want a full patrol sweep of the city with a description of
the suspect—have the description sent to APD as well, just
for laughs. Also, inform the owner of this establishment
that he will need to double security for all of her shows;
money is no object. I want a short list of bodyguard candidates by morning."

"Yes, Sire."

He met her eyes. "This doesn't happen again, Second."

Faith bowed. "You have my assurance, Sire."

He gave her a nod, then got into the car with his Queen,
and a moment later they were on their way back to the
Haven.

Miranda wanted to punch someone, but she settled for
sinking her teeth into someone's throat.

Blood, hot and salty-sweet, flowed into her mouth, filling
the sandpaper emptiness in her belly and veins, soothing the
need to claw and kill. She drank deeply, her hand wrapped
around the woman's neck to hold her still, her power
wrapped around the woman's mind to keep her calm.

The girl was a jogger, very healthy, her heart rate up so
her blood was fully oxygenated. She tasted faintly of coco-
nut, meaning she'd probably had Thai at her most recent
meal, and her skin had the warm scent of youth and rasp-
berry body wash.

Miranda released her, holding her steady for a moment
while her awareness returned but impressing strongly on
her mind that nothing out of the ordinary had happened.
She'd been out for a jog and tripped.

"Are you all right?" Miranda asked her, giving her voice
silvery tones of concern.

The girl blinked. "Um . . . yeah. I guess I tripped."

"You should get home. It's late."

"Yeah. Thanks."

The girl pushed her earbuds back in place and started

her iPod again; Miranda heard the Black Eyed Peas as she ran away. The wound in her neck would close by morning, leaving what looked like twin mosquito bites, and those would be gone a few hours later. The stronger the vampire, the faster the bite healed; it was usually the young and weak who were discovered because they were unable—or too stupid—to cover their tracks.

Relief moved through Miranda's body and she sighed, rolling her head to the left and right before turning back to the car where her Prime was waiting for her.

She knew that look. He always got it when he watched her hunt.

Deliberately, Miranda licked her lips and smiled.

Prime and Queen stared at each other for a long moment before she walked back to the car, stepping into his arms and kissing him hard.

He made that purring noise she loved and pulled her against him, letting her suck on his tongue and dig her nails into his shoulders, the contact banishing the last of the lingering anger from the attack and replacing it with an entirely different kind of intensity.

Still, the events of the night had drained her, and she eventually drew back and laid her head on his chest, eyes closing.

"That was stupid," she muttered.

He didn't say anything, but of course she knew what he was thinking; he had protested her desire to go anyplace alone for months now, insisting that something like this would happen the second she let down her guard. She felt guilty—it wasn't just her life she was gambling with by traipsing around the city by herself. If that stake had hit true, if her reflexes had been slower, they would both be dead now. And whoever it was, having failed, might very well try again.

"Let's go home," he said softly.

She nodded and sank back into the car, leaning on him after the door was shut and they were on their way again. "All right," she said. "You win. Bodyguards it is. But they can ride in their own damn car."

He put his arm around her and kissed the top of her head. "Deal."

"Is this kind of thing going to happen a lot?"

"Oh, yes," he replied, not reassuring her in the slightest. "My first year I had at least a dozen assassination attempts. Most of them were lone nutjobs or Auren's old cronies. They waited until the transition was secure, a few months, before trying anything, thinking they'd lured me into complacency."

"But you don't travel with bodyguards now."

"No . . . but I did for a long time. It takes a while to establish a reputation, Miranda. Right now you're being tested in the eyes of our kind. They want to see how you handle yourself, how tough you are. The longer we stay in power, the fewer fools will try to take us down."

She wriggled as close as she could, not caring that she was probably getting his clothes as filthy as hers. "Thank you for not saying 'I told you so.' "

He shrugged. "I understand that you value your independence. I don't want you to lose it. But now you see that we have to be careful. The more you're in the public eye, the harder it will be to keep your two lives from colliding. I want you to live the life you want to live for as long as you can, but you have to be realistic. Plus . . ." His voice darkened, and despite the words the sound caused a low current of electricity through her body. "Lone nutjob or not, I intend to find whoever hurt you and tear the skin from her bones with my bare hands."

She looked up at him and said wryly, "You're such a ball of sunshine, baby."

As she'd hoped, he laughed and kissed her.

Miranda settled back against him and closed her eyes, the vibration of the car beneath her and the heartbeat at her ear lulling her as much as the thought of what she had to look forward to: a steamy, hot shower; a Snickers bar; and most important, a long morning spent in the arms of her Prime.

# TWO

Midafternoon, while the human world bustled around in its frenetic race, was a time of peace at the Haven. The halls were dark and silent, except for the footsteps of the half-dozen diurnal guards. There were no training sessions in the Elite quarter, no patrols checking in and out, and the sensor network powered down partway to conserve energy. Throughout the complex of buildings and the mansion that made up the Haven, 126 vampires slept.

Today, it was 125.

David lay on his back with one arm up under his head and the other wrapped securely around his Queen, who slumbered with her head on his chest and her hair spilled out over his bare skin. His hand moved in absent circles on her back, and though she often tossed and turned throughout the afternoon, today she was tranquil. Indeed the radiating heat from the fireplace, the weight of the comforter, and the pull of Miranda's exhaustion should have drawn him along into dreams himself, but his mind simply refused to be still.

He'd had many sleepless days during his tenure as Prime. There was always something to worry about, the night-to-night welfare of his territory an endless equation to solve . . . and the last three months had added a new variable.

She could have been killed.

The memory of seeing her blood running down from the stake wound made him clench his hand into a fist so hard it shook.

He had never feared for his own life, and he didn't now, but having Miranda complicated matters—he could no longer discount the ever-present threat of assassination. As he had pointed out to her, more than one life was at stake. If he died, she died. That was reason enough to be more careful.

Eventually Miranda grunted and rolled away from him, and he gave up trying to sleep. He got out of bed, pulled on his robe, and sat down at the computer to run a few quick checks.

Situation normal. The city was quiet; it was rare to have any sort of vampire activity during daylight, and then it was confined to the indoors and there wasn't a whole lot he could do about it. He knew there were about two dozen vampires living belowground in the sewers and old tunnel systems, but unless they made a nuisance of themselves he saw no reason to bother with them. They were followed on the sensor network like everyone else; in Austin—and eventually every metropolitan area of the South—there was no such thing as privacy for vampires. If they didn't like it, they could leave. The Shadow World's denizens weren't known for their good behavior toward humans, and it was his job both to keep their people safe and to keep his people safe from discovery.

So far it was working. The vampire population of the South had actually increased since the network had gone up, and vampire-on-human crime had dropped. Other Primes who opposed his ideas had prophesied a mass exodus of vampires unwilling to be followed around, but they'd been proven wrong . . . and nothing pleased David more than proving the Council wrong.

The Haven's various computer systems were all running happily. There was nothing to worry over. Out of curiosity he did a diagnostic of the solar panels that supplied the entire complex with power; there had been a few glitches with the subsystem that charged the cars, but he'd debugged them and so far this week there'd been no additional problems.

Yawning, he checked his e-mail, then opened his schedule to have a look at the week's events. There at least something interesting was happening.

When a new Prime claimed the Signet or took a Queen, his allies and those wanting to curry favor paid state visits as soon as they could. Pairs from all over the world as well as powerful vampires from his own territory came to offer their congratulations and get to know the new administration. Of the twenty-six other Primes, nineteen had made overtures toward visiting, and four had already come and gone. They arrived in style, stayed a few days, and went home to spread the latest gossip among their Court.

Faith had dubbed the whole tradition the Magnificent Bastard Parade.

So far things had gone smoothly. The four Primes—and two Queens—had all been friends of his and had taken to Miranda immediately, though Tanaka of Japan had observed to David privately that the others might not be so . . . open-minded, as he put it. Tanaka, an expert diplomat who managed to keep up good relations with all but about three Signets, hardly ever gave bad advice, and though David's first inclination was to insist that Miranda could handle herself . . . he did have a few misgivings.

The Signet system was thousands of years old. The youngest living Prime was over two hundred, and Miranda was one of a handful of Queens in history to take a Signet just after coming across. Primes weren't known for their forward thinking or progressive politics. In other words, most of them were sexist pigs, and Miranda . . . well, she wasn't the type of woman to keep her mouth shut when angry. She spoke her mind, was smart and observant, and David knew that the very qualities he loved about her were going to get them in trouble if she didn't learn quickly that these old, hidebound men of privilege were not all going to like the fact that David treated her as an equal.

Primes and Queens were meant to function as two halves

of a whole. History, however, had not been kind to women, and neither had vampire politics. Queens were powerful, yes, and certainly had a reputation of their own, but they usually took a backseat to their mates. For the most part the Queens were perfectly content with the way things were, as were their husbands, and because they were bound at the soul the Primes tended to give their Queens as much or as little responsibility as they wanted—but some were outright subservient to their Primes; a mystical relationship didn't always mean a healthy one.

David was already considered something of a maverick for his love of technology and got plenty of stern looks and raised eyebrows thanks to his history with Prime Deven. He was used to it, and he knew when to ignore it. Miranda had not yet learned to pick her battles.

In the coming week she would have to. They were due a visit from Prime James Hart of the Northeast; his territory included New England as well as the most densely vampire-populated metropolitan area, New York. He had ruled a hundred years with no Queen, and five minutes after meeting him it was obvious why—but his sexual appetite was well-known, and it was rumored he kept a harem of vampire women whom he terrorized into obedience.

He was not a friend to David. In fact David had no idea why Hart was so keenly interested in coming to Texas so soon; generally a Prime's allies came first, and it took months for everyone to make the arrangements. Pairs were mostly anchored to their territories, and leaving even for a few days was a major undertaking. Allies made the effort as soon as possible as a show of support. Usually neutral parties or antagonistic ass-kissers waited until the rush was over. David hadn't expected Hart to come at all, and that would have been just fine.

Obviously Hart wanted something. That alone was enough to make David uneasy about the visit. The thought of Hart and Miranda in the same room, while wickedly amusing to Faith, set his teeth on edge.

As he was closing his schedule—Hart was set to arrive

on Tuesday—he looked over at his contact list and noticed that only one other person was online at this ungodly hour.

"What are you doing up?" he typed.

*"Painting my nails & watching porn,"* Deven answered promptly.

David grinned and replied, "Right. What color/kind?"

A pause, then: *"Black/Midget."*

David snorted quietly. "Couldn't sleep?"

*"No. You know how it goes."*

David glanced over at the bed, where Miranda was still blessedly asleep. Yes, he knew how it went. At least once a week, sometimes more, she fought her way out of nightmares, and once she'd been so inconsolable that the only thing he could do was mentally knock her unconscious.

It bothered her that she wasn't "over it" already. Her life was so different now, last year seeming so far away that she expected herself to have healed and moved on, and she refused to be seen as weak or needy no matter how much it hurt.

He had tried again and again to tell her that it wasn't that easy. Old scars persisted into immortality. She wasn't the first person he'd had to watch cope with a traumatic past.

"When are you coming to Austin?" he asked.

*"Still working on it. Maybe next month?"*

"Just let me know so I can stock the house with good whiskey and dancing boys."

David imagined Deven in his private study at the Haven in Sacramento, a cozy room with leather couches and a small part of the Prime's impressive weapons collection on display. Even if he was in nothing but a bathrobe, Deven would have a knife on him somewhere and a sword within easy reach. He even kept a blade hanging on the back wall of his shower.

And all of that was after seven hundred years. David thought about telling Miranda that, but he had a feeling she'd find it more depressing than reassuring.

*"Have to go,"* Deven said. *"Meeting."*

David wished he could communicate "quizzical" over the Internet. "At two in the afternoon?"

*"Talk to you later. Kisses, sugarblood."*

David chuckled. Dev signed off before he could reply, but that wasn't unusual; the Prime of the West wasn't much for online communication, preferring to size people up face-to-face.

David stretched, closed his computer, and stood up, going over to put another log on the fire before he tried sleeping again. Then he returned to the bed and drew the curtains so that only the foot was exposed, allowing and keeping more heat in.

He smiled at Miranda, who had in the space of thirty minutes managed to sprawl out so she was taking up the entire bed. One of the pillows seemed to have vanished completely and the comforter was tangled around her legs. But even with her limbs akimbo and in a rather inelegant position, with the firelight casting a golden glow over her skin and catching the jeweled highlights in her hair, she was a breathtaking creature to behold.

A moment later she made a noise that might have been a word, then blinked and opened her eyes, their green a bit dull with sleep. She didn't ask why he was up; it was hardly the first time. She simply extended a hand to draw him back into bed.

He was quite happy to comply. He took the opportunity to unwind the covers and shuck his robe, then slid in next to her with a sigh.

She resumed her former position with her head on his chest, lifting a hand to touch first his Signet, then his lips. "Love you," she murmured, eyes already closed.

He kissed her almond-scented curls. "Love you, too."

This time he fell asleep.


The nine candidates for the Queen's personal guard stood at attention, each impeccably uniformed and waiting expectantly for judgment. They ranged in appearance from a huge tattooed bald guy with enormous holes in his ear-lobes to a petite blond pixie who according to Faith was actually older than David.

Miranda walked along the line slowly, looking each one up and down; only one looked visibly cowed by her gaze, and she crossed him off the list in her head immediately. She didn't need someone following her around who was terrified of her.

She had met a few of them before. One was a new recruit since the war and had moved up the ranks quickly. Two had experience as the Prime's guards, and two others had stood guard at their suite door. All had been vetted by Faith for their ability as warriors, their stealth, and their dedication. David had done extensive background checks when they were new to the Elite, of course, but he'd rerun them all. All that remained was for Miranda to choose four; they would work in pairs.

"What do you think?" Faith asked.

Miranda went to stand beside her, crossing her arms. "I don't know. I mean, we're not going to hang out or any-thing—they're going to follow me around and make sure I don't get staked. You vouch for their fighting skills, so what else is there?"

Faith shrugged. "You have to pick them, my Lady. I've done my part."

"All right . . . let's see." She took Faith's clipboard and pen and crossed off the timid man. "Four is scared of me. Six is so tall and gangly he'd stand out in a crowd. Three looks bored. Two more? Hmm . . ."

She walked back over to the line and did another slow circuit of the guards, this time extending her empathic energy toward them, not intruding but just testing the waters for anomalies.

Two was too ambitious. He was more interested in impressing his superiors and moving up through the ranks than protecting her. That didn't bode well; if the situation was dire he might make some stupid hero move to show off. She crossed him off.

She stepped back and addressed the guards. "Raise your hand if you like Nickelback."

The guards exchanged glances, and reluctantly the blond pixie raised her hand.

Miranda crossed her off the list.

"Numbers two, four, six, three, and nine, you may go. One, five, seven, and eight, please remain for your briefing. Thank you all."

The four who remained were consummate professionals and kept their happiness to a brightening of the eyes and a relieved sigh. The others departed with varying degrees of grumbling or head shaking. That was all right; if they really were worthy of the post, they'd have another chance. There was always a need for the true Elite and the truly loyal.

Miranda handed Faith back her clipboard and addressed the guards. "Welcome to my service," she said. "As you know, I am in need of bodyguards to accompany me into the city for regular performances, meetings, and other appointments. If we're all very lucky, your job will be extremely boring. I'd like you each to introduce yourselves briefly—Elite designation, name, and favorite musical genre or artist."

As each one spoke she shook his or her hand, taking a moment to do an extra psychic sweep of each.

"Elite Seventy-two, Aaron Sawyer, jazz."

"Elite Twenty-six, Jake Verona, Johnny Cash."

"Elite Forty-four, Minh-Li Tsai, trip-hop."

"Elite Sixteen, Lalita Madhavi, anything with a violin."

Satisfied, Miranda nodded to them. "Again, welcome. I'll leave you to Faith for the rest of your briefing. I look forward to working with all of you."

With that she looked over at Faith, who bowed; the four guards echoed her motion, and Miranda nodded again, then walked away with a sigh.

Bodyguards. She still didn't like the idea . . . but there really wasn't much choice, at least not right now while she was so new to the Signet. David couldn't be with her every minute of every day, and though her combat skills were already excellent—and improving continuously as she kept training—she still wasn't as quick on the draw as the Elite could be. The extra eyes looking for threats would be invaluable the more she got out in public; most humans would have no idea what she was, but any vampire who wanted her dead would have a great many opportunities to come at her while she was onstage or in a crowd.

She left the Elite training building and headed toward the left; in her mind she could sense a low-burning spot of energy that she recognized as David, over near the pasture where the horses were kept. She could find him anywhere with a thought, and call him to her side almost instantly, but still, even someone as strong as David couldn't be everywhere at once. If she wanted her own life beyond the Haven and beyond their marriage, she had to get used to the idea of bodyguards.

She didn't have to like it.

"I know this is hard for you to accept," Faith had noted mildly before bringing out the candidates, "but there are some things your Prime and I know that you don't. Diplomacy, for example . . . and security for another. You have to trust us, Miranda. Not everything is going to be instinctual for you."

Sighing again, Miranda left the path and angled toward the long white fence beyond which stood a single structure, the stable.

Inside the building smelled of hay and alfalfa and horse, though it was as scrupulously clean as everything else at the Haven. All but two of the stalls were usually empty; David's two prized four-legged friends were housed at opposite ends of the stable. Miranda passed by Isis, the female, but didn't go any closer.

Isis pointedly ignored her.

The Haven had staff to work in the stable, seeing to the night-to-night care of the horses and keeping the place clean, but David preferred to manage them himself as much as possible and always took care of them after a ride.

The two horses deferred to him readily but mostly seemed to think Miranda was beneath their notice or, at least, viewed her the way she imagined a lion would view a hamster: harmless, possibly delicious.

The Prime entered the stable leading Osiris; the Prime was sweaty and dusty and so was the horse, though Osiris clopped along with his head high and proud, his tack jingling. They had no doubt taken the long course around the Haven's extensive grounds, which had its own system of programmable lights.

Miranda didn't like horses. They were big and dangerous and strange. But she had to admit that David looked astonishingly hot next to one, and even more so on the stallion's back. She'd watched him ride a few times from the safety of the fence and then dragged her Prime into an empty stall to put him through his paces.

David knew she was there, but he smiled when he saw her. "Fair warning," he said. "I stink."

"I know. I can smell you both from here."

The smile became a grin. "Didn't bother you last time."

She grinned back. "It's not my fault—it's all the leather and sweat. The boots alone are worth a good shag."

He brought the massive beast to a halt and set to removing his tack, a lengthy ritual she'd sat through before; there was a lot involved in the care and feeding of a horse, and Osiris stood placidly and let himself be pampered. The grooming process involved several kinds of combs and brushes, a rag, a hoof examination, feeling along the legs—as far as pets went, cats were so much easier.

"You don't have to stand quite so far away," David told her. "He's about as fierce as a puppy."

Miranda stayed where she was. "A thousand-pound puppy that could kick my brains in."

"Osiris," the Prime said to the horse, "are you going to kick the Queen's brains in?"

To Miranda's surprise, the horse snorted and shook his head, his feathery mane flying to either side. He looked for all the world like he understood every word.

David rubbed Osiris down with sure strokes. Miranda had learned that grooming his horses, along with debugging code and taking apart complex circuitry, was like yoga for the Prime.

She climbed up onto a rail and let her feet swing, trying not to bother him while he was so immersed in what he was doing; instead she took the time to admire how he moved, how his hands followed Osiris's muscles to check for injuries or other problems, how he murmured to the animal as if they shared a secret. She could almost understand the attraction some women had to horses, watching them like this.

"You shouldn't be uncomfortable around powerful beings," David said. "You're a powerful being, too, remember?" He led Osiris into his stall.

"It's not just that," Miranda replied. "They look at me all sideways like they're trying to decide whether to eat me."

"That's because their eyes are on the sides of their head, not the front," he explained. "They have a nearly three-hundred-sixty-degree range of vision. They need to be able to see all around them in the wild, both to keep tabs on herdmates and to watch for predators. That's how they look at everything—don't take it personally."

She hadn't really thought much about it. "Oh. Makes sense, I guess."

He gestured for her to come closer, and after a moment's hesitation she came to stand next to David, ready to jump back out of the stall, examining the enormous nostril that was entirely too close to her face. The horse's ear flicked toward her, but he made no sign of agitation and turned his attention to the hay hanging in the back of the stall.

"It's safe," David said gently. "I promise."

Tentatively, sure that Osiris was going to turn and bite her hand off, she reached out and lightly touched the side of his neck, her heart pounding in her throat.

Osiris suffered the touch without comment and didn't so much as bat an eye when she tried again, this time laying her hand on his neck and gingerly stroking the hair and the powerful muscle beneath.

"Isis and Osiris are Friesians," David told her, no doubt to distract her from the huge wall of animal she was touching. "They're very showy and proud, but usually pretty docile. Osiris's dam—his mother—was a handful, though."

"How many generations have you owned?" she asked, running her hand along the horse's side, amazed at how solid and strong he was.

"Three, counting him. I had his mother and grandfather."

"What about Isis?"

He smiled. "She was a bribe. The Prime of Eastern Europe was trying to get on my good side. It worked."

Miranda, quite done with her experiments, moved back out of the stall, crossing her arms, grateful to put distance between them again. David gave her a look that held more than a little pride; he knew how much she hated being afraid of anything. The first month she had refused to even go in the stable. He was hoping one day she'd want to try riding, and though she'd snorted openly at the suggestion, it wasn't as if they would run out of time for her to overcome her fears.

"I've still got a while here," David said, taking a metal thing—a hoof pick, she remembered—from the wall and gingerly lifting up Osiris's front left foot. "Why don't you go on inside and I'll finish up, shower, and join you?"

She nodded. "Sounds good. I'll be in the music room."

Another smile. "You're kidding."

Miranda stuck her tongue out at him. "I have songs to finish," she said. "I'm in the studio in a few days."

"By the way, how did the bodyguard roundup go?" he asked as he inspected the hoof in his hand for rocks and, she guessed, small mammals.

"Fine. I guess we'll see tomorrow. After the latest Magnificent Bastard gets here, I've got a show."

"Right." David's voice and expression altered very slightly, and she frowned, catching the subtle hardening of his tone.

"What's wrong? Are you still worried about Hart?"

"I want to know what he's up to, but there have been no rumors or intelligence suggesting why he's coming here. The only thing I can think of is that he wants Kentucky back—there's a full Council in three years and we have to rebid for it, but there's zero chance I'll be outvoted. I've got representatives from Louisville ready to testify that they want my continued leadership, and Hart can barely hold his own territory without constant threat of revolt. So, yes, I'm suspicious. Not even Dev has any idea, and if anyone would know, he would."

Miranda had been hearing about Deven for months now, and she was both anxious to meet him and on the verge of rolling her eyes every time she heard his name. According to both David and Faith, Prime Deven knew all, saw all, and had never lost a fight; he was old and smart and powerful and apparently shot unicorns out of his ass. "Don't worry," she told David. "We can handle him, can't we? He'll be on our turf, after all. You have the right to toss him out if he misbehaves."

"Not if," David said. "When. And it's not that simple. Hart has allies in the Council who aren't known for their fair-mindedness. They're a minority, yes, but they can still make life very unpleasant for us if they want to. It's in our best interest to maintain good relations on the surface."

Now she did roll her eyes. "If you say so. Personally I don't see the point in playing nice. You're David Solomon. Everyone's scared shitless of you."

David shook his head. "Not everyone."

"Well, they should be." Miranda moved just close enough to kiss him on the cheek—he did smell rather horsey, after all—and said, "I'll see you after you've showered, Lord Prime. Have fun giving your pony a pedicure."

The Prime chuckled and swatted her lightly on the ass as she walked away.

Faith met her on the steps to the house. "I've got Lalita and Jake scheduled for tomorrow night, if that's all right with you."

"Any particular reason you matched them that way?"

"I ran them through some scenarios in various pairs, and they seemed to work well together, as do Aaron and Minh. Also Lali and Jake have run patrols on the same team, so they're comfortable with each other. I have them as your primary guards for now, but we can change that if you find you prefer Aaron and Minh."

Faith walked beside her down the hall; as they passed, the guards at each station bowed, and Miranda gave them an acknowledging nod. "I'm in for the night," Miranda told the Second. "The Prime will be soon, too—I'm sure he'll want you to check in before you log off."

Faith nodded, then slowed down. "My Lady . . ."

"Yes?" Miranda turned to her.

"I know what you're going to say to this, but . . . I just feel like I need to say it."

Miranda sighed. *Here we go again.* "Go on."

"I'm just wondering if it's safe for you to continue playing in public." At Miranda's expression, Faith added, "Someone tried to kill you, Miranda. I'm not being paranoid. And having a Prime like Hart in town . . . well, it tends to bring out the crazies. I'm perfectly willing to give you as big or small a security detail as you and the Prime think is best, but I just . . . I just want you to think. Think about how many lives depend on you."

Miranda made a face. "Faith, nobody but David depends on me. If we die, there will always be another Prime."

"Maybe. But I don't think you get how important you are to all of us. What do you think it was like in this territory before Auren was deposed? Vampires killed at will, and no one even tried to stop them. Hunters were starting to flood the major cities of the South, and the entire Shadow World was almost exposed. Right now the Council majority sides with David that no-kill laws are the safest thing for all of us, but Hart is one of the ones who disagrees. What if he's got some hotshot vampire friend willing to start a war for your Signet?"

Miranda crossed her arms and faced the Second. "What do you want me to do, Faith? Give up everything that matters to me? I can't do that. I can't live forever—and more-over, I can't be the person David needs as his partner—if I can't be who I am. I'll take guards, I'll have Harlan drive me, I'll do what I can to put your minds at ease. But I can't give this up. Music is . . . it's who I am, Faith."

Miranda hated the note of pleading in her voice, but it had the desired effect, as Faith looked stricken by the intensity of her tone, and her whole demeanor changed from "second in command making battle plans" to "wor-ried friend." Miranda tried hard not to take advantage of Faith's friendship, but it was hard sometimes to know where to draw the line between Faith-her-friend and Faith-her-Second, especially given how much older and wiser Faith was.

"We're all on your side, Miranda. But we have to be realistic. You're a vampire now, and not just any vampire. You are Queen. You'll never be like the others. Ever."

Miranda stopped outside the music room door. She nod-ded to Faith—not in agreement, but in acknowledgment that she had been listening to her Second's concerns and wouldn't automatically dismiss them. "I hear you, Faith."

"Thank you, my Lady. That's all I ask." Faith was clearly not satisfied with the conversation, but she said only, "I'm logging off for the night, then, after a quick check-in with the Prime. Send out if you need me after that."

"Thank you, Faith. Dismissed."

Miranda slid inside the music room and shut and locked the door behind her, standing for a moment with her back against the door, eyes closed, trying to breathe.

When she opened her eyes, she smiled with relief.

The room was her refuge, more important to her than any other place in the Haven. Here she could lay down her responsibilities—which she was already having trouble carrying—and just be Miranda for a while.

From the moment she'd first set foot inside the room, she had known it was hers. She was meant to be there. Her hands were meant to touch the keys of the magnificent instru-ment that took up a third of the space: her Bösendorfer

Imperial Grand, a gleaming black empress holding court over the room. There was also space devoted to her other instrument of choice, the Martin guitar she had bought after her old one was destroyed. It had its own stand and its own area for her to practice in.

Miranda took off her coat and hung it and her bag on the rack by the door. She approached the piano, as always, as if walking into a church.

Then she laid her hands on the piano's lid, exposed the keys, and sat down, leaning her head sideways on the keys for a moment, closing her eyes.

With her eyes shut she felt along the keys with one hand and gently touched a few, the barest hint of a melody almost too quiet to be heard. She hummed with the notes, letting her energy sync with the piano's; it wasn't alive by any stretch, but it sort of reminded her of the Signets in the way it responded to her. The stones' light flared or dimmed to match the bearer's emotional state, and it felt like the piano's strength rose up to meet her own, or lay down beneath her sorrows. She couldn't believe she had ever lived without it.

On the far wall hung a portrait of the woman who had bought the Bösendorfer and set aside this room for it: the seventh Queen of the South, Elizabeth Jensen, who had been murdered, with her Prime, by Auren in 1914. Bess, as she'd been known, was the first African-American Queen in the South, and had been a slave in her human life. She was known all over the territory as a wildly intelligent woman who spent her immortality becoming as educated as she could, studying music, medicine, history, art, and several languages. And though like most Queens she'd taken a backseat in Signet politics and had been the subject of scorn and derision from several other Pairs, she had been a noble woman, greatly respected by many.

Miranda wished she could have met Bess, if for no other reason than to thank her for her devotion to music. Bess was the only Queen so far to whom Miranda felt any kind of real connection, and she wasn't even alive.

Gradually Miranda applied more pressure to the keys and more notes to the melody, raising her head until it leaned against the piano's lid. She let her fingers find their own way, channeling the pile of confused emotions in her heart into sound where they could be lifted up and turned into something beautiful.

The Prime tended horses and worked equations. She made music.

Sometimes she played songs that she already knew, and sometimes she just improvised or combined both— without even thinking, it always ended up dark and complex, the lines of melody doubling back and twisting around themselves like Celtic knotwork. Certain themes repeated on certain days.

More than once she'd woken up here with David sitting nearby keeping watch over her as she played in her sleep. Her arms would ache for hours afterward, but it was better than having nightmares.

As if the thought had summoned him, she felt a warm presence flood through her mind, and she knew without looking that David was there, taking up his usual seat in the small audience section of the room. She still remembered the first time she'd seen him there, back when she was human, back before either of them had been ready to admit what they had, deep down, already known about the connection they shared. He'd be sitting with his hands folded, elbows on the chair's arms, carelessly regal and infernally attractive. She could feel the comfortable weight of his gaze.

She reached along their bond, drawing the gentle surety of its power into the music, creating two streams of melody and twisting them around each other so that the chord was stronger than the sum of its notes. Together they were a natural harmony, and she followed it deeper until the room and the Haven and the world disappeared and there was nothing but one song, breathtakingly beautiful and intense beyond words.

She brought the piece to a winding conclusion, and by the time the last chords rang into the air, pain had begun to assert itself in her hands. She lifted her eyes to the clock and realized with some surprise that she'd been playing for almost two hours.

When she lowered her eyes, David was beside her, sitting down on the bench and taking her hands in his. "Silly woman," he chided affectionately. "You could burn yourself out doing that."

She leaned against his shoulder, all the tension gone from her body. The piano wasn't quite as good as sex, but it came damn close. "Only way to fly," she murmured.

He was smiling, and she felt the heat of healing energy pass between them again, soothing the cramps in her fingers. It was a handy thing in some ways, being Paired; they could heal each other of anything short of a mortal wound almost instantly, even faster than a vampire's natural regenerative speed. Either of them could draw from their combined power, and there were supposedly ways they could work together to become even stronger, but David had said that must wait until she wasn't so new.

She was dimly aware that he threaded his arms around her and picked her up. She heard the faint clunk of the piano lid closing, followed by the sound of the lights clicking off, and turned her face happily into his chest, inhaling the scent of his shirt. There was something in the way he smelled—some undertone of great age that would never have registered to her mortal senses—that she found deeply comforting, like leaning against a mountain or redwood or some other nearly eternal thing.

Doors opened, doors closed; the guards at the suite door gave their greetings. Inside the suite was warm from the hearth that Esther had stoked before they arrived.

David deposited her on the bed and sat down, taking one of her legs and removing her boot, unconsciously running his hand along her shin as he had Osiris's. She chuckled.

"I'm not a horse," she said without looking up.

"I'm well aware of that," David answered wryly. "Horses are far less stubborn than you."

"That's why you love me."

She could hear him smiling. "As a matter of fact, it is." He pulled off her other boot and then set to removing the rest of her clothes with deft, practiced hands. "That, and about a thousand other reasons."

"Such as?"

"You're willful, smart as hell, courageous, and you look good in red," he said, touching a finger to her Signet, then lifting a tendril of her hair from her forehead. "You also have a tremendous heart, and, if I may be so bold, absolutely perfect breasts."

Miranda's eyes popped open, and she saw the wicked glint in his. "Flattery will get you seriously laid, Lord Prime," she said.

"I was hoping you'd say that."

She sat up long enough to put her hand around his neck and pull his mouth to hers, and then she rolled back, hauling him onto her with a growl. He braced himself on his hands to keep from knocking the wind out of her, then tore his lips away and leaned down to kiss a slow line from her throat to her breasts, still bound in black lace.

She arched her back to let him unhook the offending garment, then shifted her shoulders from side to side to strip it off and toss it aside. Meanwhile her fingers ventured in between the buttons of his shirt to find the muscle underneath and, with only a little fumbling, managed to push the shirt off. She moved her hands up his back, feeling the slightly raised lines of the hawk etched into his shoulders.

She loved the sensation of sliding her hands down into the waistband of his jeans and around to the front to unzip them. His skin was like silk over stone and warmed under her palms and lips.

She would never have expected in a thousand years to *want* so much, to crave both the taste of his blood and the deep aching pleasure of their bodies wrapping around each other and joining. That first second of contact when they could finally touch without barriers of space or fabric was the same every time: a shock to her system, like coming in from freezing rain to the edge of a volcano. Her body was still surprised at how badly it needed his.

The first time after the battle had frightened her. She hadn't realized just how much he'd been holding back that night in her apartment. A human body was so easy to break . . . and two vampires without restraint could easily break furniture, her screams practically peeling the paint off the walls. The intensity of it had been almost too much, but the trust between them was so complete, and the joy of being reunited so overwhelming, that her fear had evaporated.

He alone could touch her. In all of eternity, all the world, there would never be another. She had no desire to ever look at another man—she didn't even feed on them. Her time in hell had made sure of it, and the amulet around her neck sealed it. He alone . . . he alone.

Forever.

# Three

Tuesday evening began with the arrival of a blustery cold front that swept through central Texas leaving frost in its wake . . . followed by the arrival of a black stretch limousine and a black van.

Because Faith was Second in Command, it was her job to show the visiting Prime to his rooms, see that he was comfortably installed, then come and let the Pair know when it was time for the formal introduction. Meanwhile David and Miranda waited in David's workroom, where he was taking apart the newest-generation Apple gadget to see how it worked. He had an abiding love for the technical poetry of circuits and chips, and elegant design, whether in a phone or a beehive, was his idea of porn.

Miranda knew by how intent he was upon the task that he was, if not nervous, deeply uneasy about the meeting.

She sat with her feet up on an empty chair, trying not to let his emotions affect her. That was a consequence of their connection: She could not shield herself completely from him, ever, and the best she could do was learn to gently nudge his presence to the back of her mind, where it wouldn't overtake her own. Most of the time she liked having him there. There were times, however, when the whole thing was a pain in the ass.

"It's been over an hour," she said. "This is getting ridiculous."

David made an irritated noise. "He's doing it on purpose. Throwing us off schedule asserts his control over the situation."

"I'm supposed to be in town in two hours. Why don't we just go meet him now?"

He looked up at her and smiled. "Because that's not how we do it, beloved. I know, I know—to hell with custom and rules—but these protocols have been in place a lot longer than you have. These silly little niceties keep order among the Signets. Besides, watching the way someone navigates the system teaches you a lot about him."

"If this guy is as big a dick as everyone says, I don't think I want to know more about him," Miranda pointed out, but he did have something when it came to the value of observing others; she had been watching her husband since the onset of the Magnificent Bastard Parade and had learned quite a bit about him that she hadn't been aware of before. There were areas where he was perfectly happy to flout custom and others where he was a stickler; if he felt the Shadow World was better served by following the rules he did so, but if he believed something was hampering their evolution as a society he ignored it, taking the flak from the others without batting an eye.

"You mentioned you'd met Hart once before," Miranda said. "What happened then?"

David set aside his toy and sat back, crossing his arms. "I dropped a dead deer on his head."

She blinked, sure she'd misheard. *"What?"*

A nod. "It was his state visit after Deven and Jonathan Paired. He waited nearly a year to come, then proceeded to abuse the Haven staff, belittle the Elite, and treat the Prime like a cockroach. He didn't say anything to Jonathan because Jonathan would have cheerfully crushed his skull, but I heard him in the hallway calling Deven a degenerate faggot, and lo and behold this hideous old deer head that had been hanging on the wall for seventy years fell down. The antlers almost put his eye out."

Miranda laughed so hard she nearly cried.

It was widely known that David was powerful; he had almost all of the higher abilities attributed to the most powerful of their kind, including the power to Mist, basically a form of teleportation that could be performed only by a Signet bearer. His telekinesis, however, wasn't common knowledge. It was entirely possible Hart had no idea there was any malicious aforethought in Bambi's suicidal leap.

Before she could compose herself completely there came a knock at the door, and Faith joined them, looking more agitated than Miranda had ever seen her.

The Queen sobered immediately. "Faith, what happened?"

The Second shook her head, her mouth set in a tight line. "Your guest is ready for you," she said.

Queen and Prime exchanged a look. "Faith, tell me," David said. "I want to know exactly how that bastard behaves while he's here."

Faith's eyes were like two slivers of flint ready to spark off any available tinder. "He brought his women," she replied. "Four of them. They're . . . the rumors are true, Sire."

David closed his eyes and sighed. "I was afraid of that."

Miranda looked from him to Faith. "What rumors?"

"Everyone knows Hart has a harem," Faith told her. "There's been speculation for years over whether the women he keeps are there of their own free will, and over how he treats them. The prevailing thought is that he turns them himself and keeps them weak, nearly starving, so they can't fight him."

Miranda felt the first stirrings of molten wrath forming in her stomach. "And it's true?"

"Apparently. You should see them . . . they're skin and bone. None of them make eye contact. They just shuffled into their room and one of his Elite shut the door and stood guard."

The Prime rarely displayed anger, even to his Queen, but she felt it flare up inside him and saw the subtle change in his expression that few other people would recognize as carefully controlled fury. When he spoke he was deadly calm. "All right. So he brought them into my Haven knowing perfectly well how I would feel about it. I think it's safe to assume his intentions in coming here are not pure."

David stood, straightening his shirt and reaching for the suit jacket he had hung over the back of his chair. They always dressed to the nines for these things, and although some Primes reinforced their reputations with old-fashioned wardrobes or stereotypical Goth-esque vampire attire, David opted for impeccable hand tailoring from the finest local shops so that everything fit him perfectly and only added to his allure.

Miranda was still working out her own style as far as that went. She had her stage clothes, lots of leather and jewelry, and a variation thereof that she wore into town when her presence was required. So far she'd had the most success with what she called "neo-bitch goddess," and tonight she'd worn black pants and heeled boots, a long coat, and a bloodred lace-trimmed top that perfectly matched the stone of her Signet. It was definitely not casual wear, but still wasn't a frilly cocktail dress or Hillary Clinton pantsuit. She wanted to look impressive but be able to breathe, fight, and slouch when necessary.

"Let's go, beloved, and get this over with," David said. He turned to her, arms out slightly in the universal vampire gesture of *I have no idea how I look—what do you think?*

Miranda ran her hand down the front of his jacket, resting her palm over his heart. "Gorgeous as always," she said fondly.

"You, too," he replied, leaning in to kiss her on the forehead before taking her arm.

Faith looked like she'd rather eat a live scorpion than go anywhere near Hart again, but she was nothing if not a professional; she held the door open for them, but as Miranda passed she heard Faith mutter, "We're going to need another deer head."

*   *   *

David was immensely proud of Miranda for not drawing her sword and decapitating Prime Hart five seconds after meeting him.

In fact, his fears about her reaction were completely overblown; he realized she had been observing him the last three months, and though she was friendly and somewhat relaxed with the first three Pairs who came to visit, when confronted with a notorious man like Hart she did the same thing David did and slipped on a mask of cordiality coupled with professional disinterest.

He loved it when she surprised him. It reminded him that though she was young and a little rash, the Signet never chose wrong. He could only imagine her in twenty or so years when she had stepped fully into her power and authority and was every inch the Queen . . . no one, not even Hart, would dare cross her then.

Or, it seemed, today.

"Welcome to our Haven, Prime Hart," David said, bowing, extending his hand. "Our home is your own."

Hart gave a slight bow. "I bring you greetings from the Northeastern United States," he said smoothly, and reached out to shake David's hand.

Hart was a handsome man; he had a polished look and demeanor that would not have been out of place debating on the Senate floor and appeared to have been in his early forties when he came across. He had silver hair and ice-blue eyes; the overall effect was that of a man who presumably would have had no trouble landing women . . . willing ones. If David hadn't known about the actions behind the suave façade, he might even have called him charming.

David turned to Miranda. "Allow me to introduce Miranda Grey-Solomon, Ninth Queen of the Southern United States."

Hart looked Miranda up and down, then bowed a bit less than he had to David. Still, he smiled when he said, "A pleasure. Prime James Hart."

Miranda bowed. "Welcome to our Haven, Lord Prime. I hope you enjoy your stay."

Hart had already returned his attention to David. "I look forward to the next three days," he said. "I think it's time the Northeast and the South renew their friendship, with a Council meeting coming up soon."

Having fulfilled the requirements of Signet formality, David nodded. "Perhaps we could retire to the study to discuss matters of state."

Hart nodded curtly, then gave Miranda a faintly dismissive look. "I'm sure your young wife has other matters to attend to and is quite busy with her household duties."

David wasn't quite quick enough to change the subject.

"I am neither a housewife nor a servant," Miranda said coldly, staring daggers at Hart. "I am Queen of this territory and I don't require a man's permission to stay or go."

Before Hart could reply, David interjected, "She does, however, have a performance in town tonight, which I'm sure she would much rather attend."

Silently he willed Miranda to let it go this time—he wanted to know what Hart was up to, and if he stormed out now in a fit of pique they might never find out.

Miranda shot David a poisonous look but merely turned on her heel and walked away.

David gestured down the hall. "This way, please, my Lord Prime."

The study David had chosen for their meeting was not in the Signet wing; he wasn't going to let Hart anywhere near their private residence. It was a somewhat neutral venue with a square of identical love seats that put no one more in the spotlight than any other and was tastefully decorated to show off the Haven's wealth without ostentation. There was a map of the U.S. Signet territories on the wall in their current configuration with Kentucky firmly in David's grasp . . . just as a little reminder.

As they sat, one of the servants came forward to pour their first glass of whiskey. David hoped they'd brought up a very large bottle.

"Ice," Hart said shortly to the servant without looking at her.

David felt himself bristle at Hart's officious tone but said nothing. He couldn't let every little thing Hart did aggravate him, or they'd be at war before the hour was up. Hart came from a different world and time than David; the rumor was he'd been a Crusader, son of a noble family somewhere in Europe. He'd been ordering people around his entire life. David had spent his childhood covered in soot at his father's side, and as a vampire he had worked his way up through the ranks of the Western Elite. Plenty of Primes were disdainful and dismissive of their servants. He couldn't let it get further under his skin just because it was Hart.

Not to mention it would be hypocritical to lecture Miranda about diplomacy and then start trouble himself.

"Why don't we get down to business," David said.

Hart actually smiled, though it wasn't a particularly friendly expression. "And what business is that, Lord Prime?"

"Cut the crap, Hart. What are you doing here?"

Hart regarded him silently for a moment before saying offhandedly, "You're going to have your hands full with that woman."

"She has a name."

Hart lifted his hands. "All right. Pardon my tone. I'm just saying, you know how the others talk. You have a reputation to protect—my advice would be to rein her in before that shrewish tongue gets you in trouble."

David didn't bat an eye. "The only person in this building about to be in trouble is you. And if you think I don't notice that you're dissembling, you're a fool." He took a sip of his whiskey, then asked, "Are you after Kentucky again, James? Because you're not going to get it."

The Prime made a noise something like a snort of derision. "I have more important things to worry about than a state full of vampires swilling home brew and fucking their sisters, David."

"Then what do you want?"

His pale eyes narrowed and he said, "You're telling me you don't know?"

"If I did, trust me, you would be on the first plane back to New York."

Hart's gaze turned speculative, and for just a moment David saw something in his face—not quite fear, but very close, and equally astonishing. Then, even more surprisingly, Hart was perfectly honest.

"You and I aren't friends," Hart said, his tone almost becoming amiable; it wasn't as if how he felt about David— or vice versa—were any big secret. "I've opposed you at every turn, and frankly I think you're a limp-wristed, bleeding-heart child with no business playing at the grown-ups' table."

"And I think you're a relic of an age best left behind," David replied, "and also an arrogant, raping, pretentious swine. Your point being?"

"Call off your dogs," Hart said. "Whatever you want from me, name it. I'm done with this game."

David felt his eyebrows shoot up. "My dogs?"

"The Red Shadow, David. Whatever reason you sent them after me—a vendetta, to prove something, I don't give a damn—name your price. I've lost five of my Elite in the last four months and my Court is scattering to the winds. There's unrest in every state. You know damn well what happens then—some little deviant upstart like you slips in and has my head."

"Deviant," David said, rubbing his chin. "I haven't heard that one in a while."

"I'm serious. Everyone knows it's the Shadow. You're the only Signet with ties to the Shadow. What little intel we've gathered points toward you or someone here in Austin as the Alpha. Insult my belief in our supremacy, insult my virility, but don't insult my intelligence."

David leaned forward, frowning. "I have no idea what you're talking about. I don't know any more about the Shadow than you do. How do I have ties?"

"That girl, the one who trained your Queen. My sources say she was one of them. She had to have been working for you."

Finally something made at least a little sense. "Sophia Castellano? I didn't even know she knew Miranda until later. She was acquainted with my Second, and she told Faith she had left the Shadow."

"No one leaves the Shadow. How do you think they've maintained their secrecy for so long? Either they die on assignment or the Alpha kills them. There's no retirement plan. This Castellano woman was either trying to get inside your Haven for something or lying about ever being an agent."

"But I thought they only worked alone," David said. "How could more than one be in your territory causing problems? That doesn't sound like their tactics."

"Oh, it's them all right. Elite disappearing, not even a second's static in the line, no witnesses, and their bodies reappear after obvious torture—but there's no evidence whatsoever on the bodies or anywhere else. No mere gang is capable of that kind of ghost operation. Then there's this . . ."

Hart reached into his coat pocket and tossed a small object to David, who caught it and held it up to the light. "The hell?"

"You're the technomancer. You tell me. I recovered it near the corpse of one of my Elite."

David frowned and examined the tiny device in his hand. It was some kind of wireless communication device, obviously, but he'd never seen one quite like it. It was made of silver metal, the same size and shape as an in-ear hearing aid, and completely seamless except for the hole that sound came through. The metal was the same color and sheen as the coms his Elite wore, but it was much harder and there were absolutely no markings on it.

"You checked this for fingerprints?" David asked.

"Of course," Hart snapped. "You're not the only Prime with resources."

David smiled. "Oh? Then you had this sent to a lab and analyzed?"

"Why? Obviously it's one of your little inventions."

David was itching to crack the thing open, but he feigned indifference as much as he could. "Given that I have my own intelligence network and my own Elite, why would I need an organization like the Shadow at my beck and call? As I understand it, they hire out to humans as assassins and spies, to go where human spies can't go. That's why the Council has never bothered tracking them down—they're no threat to us." He turned the device over in his palm again, considering it, and said, "Besides, they predate me by at least a century. Prime Deven heard about them as early as 1500. He'd heard that the Alpha was an Italian connected with the Medici family."

"Surely the organization has changed hands by now."

"Not necessarily. It's difficult to maintain that kind of secrecy if you have to hand over control to someone else. From what little I know about them, they sound like the kind of network that was created by one person who trained each agent individually."

Hart let out a slow breath and downed his whiskey in one long swallow. "Then you give me your word that you are not involved in this."

David stared at him for a moment, then down at the device, then back up. "I will do you one better, Lord Prime. Leave this thing with me. If you give me a chance to tear it apart and analyze it, see what makes it tick, I can learn more about its manufacture and send you all my findings. Knowing how it's made and where it came from might help you track down your killers."

For a moment Hart looked dubious, but finally he agreed with a nod. "Done."

Then Hart set his glass down and stood. "If you don't mind, then, Lord Prime, I shall retire for the morning. We can meet again after sunset to discuss anything else—there are a few finer points I'd like to go over with you about the upcoming Council, but I think that's best saved for later."

David stood as well and bowed. "I bid you good morning, then, and good rest."

Hart nodded, still curtly, but with a slightly less dismissive edge than before; David could hardly believe it, but it almost seemed like he'd won some grudging respect from the Prime in the last hour.

Hart was escorted back to his suite by one of the door guards, and David sat back down in his chair still holding the earpiece. He was madly curious about it. Was it really Red Shadow technology? Or something else? Whatever it was, it wasn't his.

David had considered using earpieces for the coms, but in the end he'd gone with the wristbands because they were harder to lose in battle unless the wearer's hand was severed. He'd never been entirely happy with any of the in-ear models he'd tried, and their reception of outgoing speech was iffy. Plus, he'd created the coms with the DNA sampling system, and that would have been much harder on a piece a tenth the size. For his purposes wrist coms worked just fine.

Depending on what he found when he got the earpiece open, however, there might be some new tech inside that he'd want. He didn't much care about Hart's problems, but there were plenty of reasons to want the earpiece in his possession.

He hadn't lied to Hart—he knew little of the Shadow because there was little to know. They worked for insanely wealthy humans, not vampires; they were mercenaries with no moral code, and they never worked in groups. It was highly unlikely that they were involved in this . . . but still . . . whoever was clearly had advanced tech, and that could pose a problem.

He lifted his com. "Star-three."

*"Yes, Sire?"*

"Report to the first-floor study, please."

*"Two minutes, Sire."*

Faith joined him, still looking a bit frazzled, and he gestured for her to take Hart's vacated seat and pour herself a drink.

"What did you learn?" she asked.

David held up the device. "We have work to do."


Miranda was angry that night.

Kat couldn't help but think back to the night she'd seen her friend onstage months ago, back when the worst thing Kat could imagine was that Miranda was strung out on drugs, and she had walked offstage and fainted. Kat had had no idea what was really going on—the possibility would never have occurred to her in a thousand years.

And despite everything she'd seen, Kat still wasn't totally sure she believed it.

She'd seen Miranda change . . . seen her teeth . . . seen her bite Drew . . . and she'd felt the change in her friend from some deep place in her gut that knew a predator when it saw one. She'd watched David from across a table, all the tiny alien things about him making a disturbing kind of sense. And yet . . .

Vampires? Really?

Kat hung out in the wings as she often did during Miranda's shows, leaning sideways against some kind of rigging, one hand steadying her and the other resting on her stomach. Funny how having a vampire Queen in her life made all her own problems seem a bit smaller.

That wasn't comforting.

Something had Miranda fired up, though, and not in the same way as she had been that night months ago—then she had been emerging from years of slumber and shaking off her old life to find herself powerful. Tonight she was just plain old pissed off. Kat could see it. She didn't have to be an empath to read her best friend.

Kat didn't bring it up until after the encore, after Miranda had stalked off the stage to her dressing room and changed, after the house lights were out and the applause was no longer making Kat's ears ring.

When, finally, they were sitting in the café—at the same table where Kat had squared off with David, it turned out—Kat stirred sugar into her decaf and said, "Okay, spill it."

Miranda was no longer fuming but she was still gravely irate, and she lacked her husband's ability to put on a poker face. "It's nothing."

"Oh, bullshit."

Miranda smiled. "Yeah, okay."

"Come on, Your Majesty." Kat took a drink of her coffee and made a face; without caffeine it just wasn't the same. "This is a no-crap zone, here at this table. I am officially your No-Crap Friend."

A sigh. "I told you about all the other Pairs coming to visit, right? The one that's here now is a complete dick. He has slave girls, Kat—what do I do about that?"

"Slave girls? For real?"

"Yes. They're being kept against their will—at least Faith thinks so. I could offer them asylum, but that could cause a rift between the South and the Northeast, and David says that would come back to haunt us—this bastard has powerful friends. But I can't just sit back and do nothing, can I?"

"Wow." Kat sat back, staring at her friend. "Your life is just fucking weird now, you know that?"

She grinned. "Yes, I do. And I have this feeling it's just going to keep getting weirder."

"I can guarantee that," Kat replied, slowly turning her coffee cup in her hand. "Look, Mira, I've counseled runaway teens and battered wives. I've taught English to Afghani women fleeing the Taliban. But when a vampire Queen comes to me and says some vampire bastard is keeping slaves, I have to be honest: I have no idea what to say."

Miranda chuckled and shook her head. "Remember when the worst thing that could happen was getting knocked up at a frat party?"

Kat swallowed hard, looking down at her cup, her insides knotting up before she could force her emotions back down again. Damn it, if—

Too late.

"Hey," Miranda said, staring at her keenly, "what's wrong?"

Kat still didn't meet her eyes. "Quit doing that psychic thing on me."

"I'm not. I promise. I've just gotten a lot better at reading people. It's . . . part of the job, I guess. You've been weird all night, not just now. It's your turn to spill it."

"It's not important," Kat said, surprised at the spark of anger in her own voice. "Just a human problem."

Miranda didn't snap back at her or even show that she heard the last statement. Kat remembered what she'd said about being empathic, that words didn't always matter and she could feel the truth underneath them, even without trying. It was what had driven her crazy before.

Miranda reached over and grabbed Kat's hand, then sucked in a breath. "Holy shit."

Kat snatched her hand back. "I told you not to do that!"

"I'm sorry," Miranda said. "I just wanted to be sure. I keep myself shielded and I'm not used to picking things up from mortals, but you're different. You're my friend."

Kat did something completely out of character and also completely embarrassing. She burst into tears.

She felt Miranda shift from the opposite side of the booth to sit by Kat and offer her shoulder. Kat buried her face in Miranda's neck, and Miranda murmured to her, stroking her back. It was as if she were putting off gentle waves of soothing heat, and if that was part of her mojo, well, Kat wasn't going to argue with it right now.

"Does Drew know?" Miranda asked.

"Not yet. He's in Beaumont at a conference. Due back in a few days." Kat wiped her eyes on her napkin and sat up, but Miranda stayed where she was, a solid presence that Kat wanted desperately to cling to until she wasn't so scared of drowning. "I don't know what I'm going to do."

Miranda didn't say anything at first, and Kat went on, "I have an appointment at the women's clinic Thursday for a consultation. I can go back a week later for the big suck . . . but . . ."

"You aren't sure," Miranda said. "Kat . . ."

"I mean, I have a house, and I've got money from Dad's estate—not piles of it, but I do okay. And Drew might be a good dad. But I'm . . . God, Mira, how could this happen? I'm on the fucking pill!"

Miranda had an odd look on her face, at once gravely attentive and miles away, as if she were listening to two conversations at once. Her fingers were still curled around Kat's arm, and they were suddenly hot as she stared off into space.

"Kat . . ." she said softly, "cancel the appointment."

"Wait, I'm not just going to—"

"I'm not telling you to keep it." Miranda cut her off gently but insistently. "I'm saying wait. Give it two weeks. Talk to Drew. You've got a little time to decide . . . I know what you've always said you'd do, but just wait. Just a little while. I promise it will be okay."

Kat gaped at her, her panic momentarily forgotten. "What the hell are you looking at?"

Miranda's eyes cleared, and she blinked and took her hand away. She looked, and sounded, as rattled as Kat felt. "I don't know. Nothing like that has ever happened before."

She moved back across the booth, and Kat was able to breathe again. "Well, it was creepy."

"Yeah." Miranda looked a little dizzy and leaned her forehead in her hands for a minute before looking up at Kat. "But take my advice, Kat. Wait. Nobody's going to force you to do anything you're not a hundred percent sure about . . . but make sure you're a hundred percent sure."

Kat swallowed and nodded, grabbing her glass of water and gulping down half of it out of sheer nerves. "Okay."

Miranda nodded. "Good." She pushed her hair back from her face, seeming a little nervous about the whole thing, but when she spoke again it was with conviction. "No matter what happens, Katmandu, I'm here for you. We'll figure this out."

Kat mustered a smile for her. As weird as Miranda's psychic fade-out had been, there was still something

incredibly comforting about having gotten the truth out—
just knowing someone else knew was a load off her shoulders. If it had been a year ago, Miranda's reassurance
wouldn't have been very reassuring, because she had been
batshit insane and teetering on the edge of oblivion, but
now . . . Kat might not know much at the moment, but she
knew that if Miranda said something would happen, God
himself would buy a ticket to watch it go down.

She was the Queen of Shadows, after all.

A woman's duty was to serve her man. She must be quiet
and dutiful, obedient, accommodating. She must defer to
him in all things, for he knew best, as was ordained by God
Almighty when Adam first bade Eve to lie beneath him in
the Garden.

Cora stared up at the unfamiliar ceiling of the Haven
while Prime Hart grunted and swore above her, her mind
in the soft dark corner she had long ago created for it, a
place where she was dimly aware of what her Master was
doing, but it was only her body that he was invading, and
she, Cora, was safe, watching from far away. There was
only so far she could go, but every inch of distance was a
treasure to her, and there she waited once again while he
shuddered and burst hot and cruel into her body.

Sated, he rolled off her, and the cool air of the room
intruded; she felt it most on her damp thighs and the
forever-trembling skin of her fingers. All the girls shook.
They shook because they were weak . . . because they were
women, and women were weak. Cora imagined Eve trembling as Adam ground his hips into hers, wondered if the
first woman had felt the shame of it as she gathered her
scattered fig leaves and stumbled to the stream to wash that
first fallen seed from her. Did she feel dirty afterward, as
the earth was dirty, fallen, made of dung and the sticky
leavings of men?

There were nine women—girls, he called them, and
not ever by name, only as "you" or "girl" or "whore"—in

Hart's harem, and they had been gathered as thoughtfully as a collector might gather works of art; each one was chosen for specific attributes, so that when he wanted a buxom blonde, he had one, and when he wanted an exotic African slave girl, he could dress Naomi in silks and make her dance for him.

Cora had been chosen for her dark hair and her olive skin, neither of which she really had anymore. She remembered, sometimes, the feel of the Italian sun on her arms, the wind lifting her hair as she ran, laughing, through her father's fields, past the lemon trees, among the twisted olive branches.

So long ago.

Hart pushed himself up off the bed and walked out of the room without a parting word. He had his own room for sleeping and came into the smaller room of the suite only when he wanted a girl. He had brought four this time, and though the servants at his Haven acted like it was some kind of honor, all the girls who got to stay behind were relieved and grateful for a few days' peace.

Cora wasn't certain they all understood what they were. They were so young when he brought them in, and he forced his will upon their memories as he forced himself into their bodies. Few of them remembered where they had come from. All they knew was the stabbing pain of penetration, the burn of knees too long on the floor and a jaw cramping from being held open too long. They knew pulled hair and bruises, bite marks, whips, costumes. Hart was creative in his lusts. He'd dressed her as a nun more than once and defiled her while she recited the Hail Mary to him.

She turned onto her side for a moment, eyes closed, listening to the furtive movements of the others where they were all positioned around the room on the floor waiting to join her on the bed they would all share to sleep.

There was a routine to this. Hart came into the room and pointed at one of them. He gave his orders. The girl of choice did as she was told for however long he lasted, and when he was done, he would leave them alone. The others made sure she fed first when the bottle came around. They tended to each other, not out of any particular kindness, but because they were glad it wasn't them this time.

No one spoke of this. It was possible Cora was the only one who thought of anything more than the gnawing hunger that was as much a part of them as the length and thickness of the Master's shaft. Perhaps they even enjoyed it; she didn't know. They didn't talk about it. They didn't talk much at all.

She was making them uncomfortable lying there, not moving. More than once he had killed a girl and they'd had to wrap her body in the soiled sheets and lay her in the hallway for the servants to burn. But this was not their Haven, and the Master would be more discreet. There was something he wanted here.

Cora slowly, painfully climbed off the bed and drew herself erect, refusing to lurch and hobble. There was so little dignity for them, she clung to whatever shreds she could catch. There, too, she was strange to the others. She walked to the bathroom, coaxing her legs through the steps it took to get there, and closed herself in silently to wash away any trace of her Master.

The new girls usually cried the first few times. Not yet suffering the effects of having too little blood, they still remembered enough about life to know that they were being violated. No one offered them comfort; there was no point. They might as well learn to bear it. It was going to happen again, and again, in a hundred different ways, until they were so used up that they simply lay down and died. Cora had seen it.

In fact, she had seen it two days before they left their Haven. The long-limbed redhead, Shannon, had been there longer even than Cora, surviving continual starvation and abuse until one night when the Master had been dissatisfied with her and beat her until she was still. Cora had tried to feed her, but she refused to drink. Even so, it took two days for her to die, and the last day she was moaning, delirious with fever, her body rotting from within. Their kind could not sicken unless they were so incredibly weak that their healing ability shut down.

Cora cleaned herself up and brushed her once-abundant hair, which had started falling out this past year. She imagined that she had perhaps another decade before she followed Shannon. She could always stop feeding, but he would notice. The ones who died were permitted to do so because he was tired of them. He had yet to tire of Cora. In fact, sometimes it seemed he reserved a special kind of viciousness for her, as if he had noticed her strangeness and wanted to punish her for it.

She left the bathroom and took the garment that had been thoughtfully left for her on the chair by the door. The others had curled up on the bed. The bed here was larger than the one they had at home, with a mattress that was new and soft, comforting to joints that had no layer of fat to protect them. She curled up on her side again, running her hands over her body, cataloging how many ribs she could count, how far her hip bones protruded.

There was a knock at the door, and she watched the Master's servant, Jones, pass through the room. He was a eunuch, and mute—whether his silence was the result of a natural disability or the Master had cut out his tongue for some perceived offense, Cora would never know.

He opened the suite door and one of the Haven servants, a plump woman in the livery of this territory, smiled generously and said, "Good evening. I've brought the blood you requested . . . are you sure it's enough?"

Jones nodded and took the tray from her; on it were a single plastic bag of blood and four glasses. The servant looked perplexed but didn't make an issue of it, and left.

Jones was fed on a different schedule, and as a man, he was given more. He set the tray down and poured out their servings, then came around and handed each a glass.

The new girls always guzzled, but then they realized there was no more coming, and Cora watched the hunger drive them slowly mad until it simply ceased to matter. It was one way in which the Master brainwashed them; the haze of starvation was a mind killer. Sometimes if they performed well he would give them extra as a treat. The veterans learned to sip tiny bits over the course of an hour or more, savoring it, making it last.

Cora dipped her finger in her glass and touched the blood to her lips, then licked. It was human, which was nice. They didn't always get human. If the Master thought they were being too energetic, he switched them to rats for a while.

She looked over at Naomi, whose eyes were huge and white in her dark face. Cora remembered Naomi when she was new, before her eyes had sunken. She had been so beautiful. Stunning, even. Cora had stared at her for hours, just loving the way she moved and the liquid brown of her eyes. Twenty years later it was all gone and there was a skeleton left . . . all that remained after the girl had decayed.

*Why am I different?*

She'd first started seeing it about five years earlier. She'd begun to have thoughts . . . sinful thoughts, violent thoughts. Once, as the Master shoved his dick into her mouth, she imagined biting down hard enough to sever it. She imagined him screaming in agony, and her stomach clenched with hatred. It had been so long since she had felt anything, she had been sick afterward.

She began to question things. She began to think about Adam and Eve. Had Adam beaten his helpmeet? Used her body whenever he'd liked—whether or not she was a willing participant? That first creation of God . . . the truest example of what a man should be like, fundamentally, before culture and history had even come to be . . . had Eve been free to speak? God had commanded her to lie beneath him. But had he commanded her to let him grind her beneath his heel?

Cora knew another story.

Once, when she was a child, a man came to her father's house—her father had called him a Jew. He had told fanciful, even blasphemous stories to the children when there were no adults in earshot. The land he had come from was rich in stories, overflowing with stories, and she drank them deeply.

In his land there was another woman, one before Eve. She was flawed, sinful, proud. She refused to lie beneath her husband. She wanted him to lie beneath her. She left the Garden and became a demon, eating the souls of young boys, causing men to think lustful thoughts. The Jews made signs against her, said prayers. She was evil and to be feared.

Cora liked her.

She had forgotten that story, and that wicked woman, for a great many years. But something had made her remember . . . only hours ago. Something had brought that story, the story of the Lilith, back to her.

No, not something. *Someone.*

Cora had seen the Lilith. She had beheld that terrifying beauty, mother of serpents. She had seen her walking the halls of this very place. She walked with purposeful steps, clad in black, and the wild snakes of her hair were the color of blood. She did not lower her eyes to men. She was not obedient or quiet. Men followed her, bowed to her.

Here, the Lilith was named Miranda, and she was Queen.

Cora had seen her for only a few seconds, but her image was burned into Cora's mind, a study in fire and iron.

*Queen.*

Every time Cora thought of her, she began to shake inside, sometimes so hard it made her head hurt. That thought made Cora remember those long-ago days in the fields, running, laughing, her muscles pumping hard and her cheeks rosy with health. What would this Queen do if the Master commanded her to lie down? Cora knew she would not obey. But how could that be? How could a woman simply . . . say no? Did her Prime let her feed whenever she wanted? How did she not go wild, then, and lose her soul to the devil?

Perhaps she already had. But damnation, Cora realized with a spinning feeling in her mind, would almost certainly be better than this.

She would never know what changed. She would never understand how, in that moment, lying there with her finger in her mouth sucking the last traces of blood from beneath her nail, she would suddenly look around the room at the pathetic bones of what had once been sweet young girls and her heart would throw itself around the inside of her chest with so many emotions she couldn't breathe. She would never recall precisely what it was, what wanton thought passed through her mind, that pushed her up off the bed, ignoring the screaming pain in her joints and muscles, and to her feet.

The others were staring at her as if seeing her for the first time. In a way that was true. They all so rarely looked at each other; it had taken her a decade to realize that Suzette had blue eyes. But they were looking at her now, frightened that her bizarre behavior would bring the wrath of hell down on them.

Cora didn't stumble, nor did she hesitate. She went to the door and opened it.

There was a guard outside, a tall man with coloring not dissimilar to her own. He was dressed in the uniform of the Signet warriors of this territory, so different from the see-through wisp of gauze she had worn every day for eighty-one years.

"May I help you, Miss?" the guard asked in English.

She knew little of the language, but she had picked up enough from the other girls that she could say, haltingly, "Please . . . please help me. I . . . please . . . I must see the Queen."

# Four

When ordinary couples fought, they stood face-to-face in kitchens and living rooms. They started out discussing, then moved on to arguing, then shouting. Even in a reasonably healthy relationship sometimes tempers flared and things got broken: A dish might be slammed thoughtlessly on the counter, a pillow thrown into a vase, or, on rare occasions, a fist put into a wall.

When David and Miranda fought, swords were involved.

Faith watched the whole scene with a morbid fascination akin to watching Mt. St. Helens erupt on television in 1980. She was standing at a safe distance on the edge of the practice ring, and thankfully there weren't any other Elite hanging around this time. Usually at least a few liked to eavesdrop on the Prime and Queen sparring, to see if they were really as good as rumored to be.

They were. Obviously the Prime had at least a hundred years' practice as a warrior over his mate, but the Queen was no slouch and had already doubled her speed and agility since taking the Signet. It was the Queen, in fact, who had decided they should learn to fight as a team, two coordinated halves of a damned scary whole.

"So what am I supposed to do, then?" Miranda asked, swinging her blade in a smooth arc toward his head.

David parried easily and drove her back. "I told you," he said calmly. "Stay out of it."

"I can't stay out of it," she snapped. "He's starving and raping those girls to death." She leapt out of the way of the sword that barely missed her sleeve and spun sideways, bringing her sword up hard and almost knocking his from his hand with a loud ringing strike. "He's been here two days—I can't just look the other way while that's going on under my own roof!"

"Unless those girls come out and say that they want to be rescued, we can't assume that they're unhappy," David shot back. "Intervening without an accusation of abuse from one of them would be tantamount to a declaration of war against Hart. No doubt he has them too scared to speak up for themselves. Chances are that's why he brought them in the first place—to try to goad us into acting."

"Then why all this 'let's be allies' crap?"

David made a disgusted noise and ducked her blade, spinning around to slam his sword back into hers. Sweat was running down Miranda's face, her hair and T-shirt were soaked, and even David had beads appearing on his forehead—a first, Faith thought, since she'd last seen him fight Deven. Miranda's fighting style was similar to David's already, so she knew a lot of his moves, and her only disadvantage other than inexperience was her tendency to let emotions get the better of her. That, too, would take time to overcome.

"That's exactly what it is—crap," David said. "As soon as he gets what he wants, he won't need to kiss ass anymore. But I'll have the analysis of that earpiece and he'll have only what information I want to give him. He thinks he used me, I keep the device, everyone wins."

"Not everyone." Miranda dropped flat to avoid being cut, then swung her leg around and knocked David backward off his feet; he hit the ground in a roll and was up again in a blur of motion, already driving the Queen toward the edge of the circle. She dove in to counterattack, but all she got was her sword clattering to the ground several feet away, just out of reach.

David paused, glanced at her sword, and the blade rose into the air and zipped over to his outstretched hand. "Now what are you going to do, my Lady?" he asked politely, swinging both in circles.

"How can you be such a coldhearted bastard when you know what's happening to those women?" she demanded, crossing her arms. "After what happened to me?"

He gave her an annoyed look. "Oh, were you turned into a vampire as a teenager against your will and taken to be part of a harem?"

"You know what I mean!" The Queen's anger flared and she pushed it outward—Faith could feel it starting to boil in her own blood. The nerve of the Prime, refusing to help . . . what kind of man was he, anyway, to . . .

Faith caught herself and bolstered her shields before her thoughts became violent. This was one of Miranda's weapons; it was hard to defend against and most people would have no idea how. Luckily she did. So did David.

His power-aura expanded, her wave of wrath bouncing off him harmlessly, and he gave her a stern look. "Remember the rules, Miranda. I don't throw things at you, and you don't try to heart-spank me."

"Maybe you deserve it," Miranda said. Even if her anger wasn't affecting them anymore, it was still a palpable force in the room, and Faith knew, from seeing this sort of thing before, that if she didn't ground it out it would make her do something impulsive and foolish—

—like throwing herself to the ground, rolling under the Prime's spinning blades, and crashing into his feet, which worked well enough at first, sending both swords into the air and the Prime to the floor on his stomach. Miranda got up first and flung herself sideways in time to catch one of the swords, and David rolled right and caught the other.

Then they were back on their feet, Miranda attacking with unrestrained fury, exactly the kind that got rookie Elite killed. For a few minutes there was nothing but the sound of blade and blade hitting each other so hard it was a wonder neither broke. Faith watched, smiling, feeling proud of the Queen for having learned so much so quickly. Sophie had been a good teacher . . .

. . . whoever she was.

Faith frowned, her attention momentarily sidetracked by the memory of the night she'd met the diminutive warrior. Sophie had been drunk off her ass and boasted she was ex-Shadow, which Faith had scoffed at until Sophie challenged her to a fight out behind the bar and proceeded to kick Faith's ass up and down the alley. Faith had asked her for pointers, and they'd met periodically to spar, just for fun, but she'd never really known anything about Sophie beyond that, and Sophie had never mentioned the Shadow again.

Had she really had an ulterior motive? Or was Hart being, as usual, a paranoid shit-stirrer? If someone had hired the Shadow, why would they want to help Miranda become Queen? What other motive could they have, given that Sophie had had plenty of chances to kill Miranda when she was human, but had been, more or less, her friend? Had Sophie gone off mission when Miranda won her over to the Signet cause?

There was no way to know now. A search of Sophie's old studio had turned up absolutely no personal effects whatsoever, only a cache of weapons that were clean of any kind of fingerprints, even Miranda's.

Faith came back to reality in a rush as a loud clattering sound startled her. She looked up to see that Miranda was once again disarmed and David was standing over her, sword pointed at her throat. To his credit, at least he wasn't stepping on her neck.

"Goddamn it!" Miranda snarled. She tried to escape first to one side, then the other, but David was too fast for her and kept her pinned.

He was calm as always—Faith was sure it infuriated Miranda, because it infuriated most people. "Eventually you're going to have to learn to listen to me," David told her. "Sometimes life is unfair, beloved. If there were a war between our territories, Hart would hire hunters, send assassins by the dozen, and rally other Signets against us. If you want to do something for those girls, you're going to have to think of a better idea than charging in there to liberate them like some avenging man-smiting angel."

They glared at each other for a long moment, and Faith wasn't sure whether they were going to start fighting again or jump each other and have sex on the training room floor. She was pretty sure both had happened at least once.

"So you don't care at all what happens to them," Miranda accused. "You'll be fine with him taking them back to New York and using them as toys until they die."

Finally an edge of anger crept into David's voice. "I never said I was fine with it. But I have considered the consequences, which apparently you have chosen to ignore. In this case the price of their lives doesn't weigh more than all of those that would be lost in a war. They don't outweigh the thought of Hart having you killed, or worse, in revenge. This is how it is, Miranda. The decisions we make aren't pretty, but we have to consider the Shadow World as a whole, not just individual lives."

Miranda slapped his sword away, and he stepped back to allow her to stand. She ignored his proffered hand up. "Individual lives are what make up our world," she said. "If we're not willing to step in and help when someone is suffering, then why are we even here? To maintain some bullshit social order that in the end means nothing without justice and compassion? I tell myself you're not as heartless as you act, but sometimes I wonder if I'm wrong."

If anyone else had tried to bait the Prime, Faith would have run for cover. David, however, simply took a deep breath, retrieved both swords, and handed Miranda hers. He took his own and wiped the blade down, then sheathed it.

He addressed Faith. "I'll be in my workroom for the remainder of the evening."

Without looking at or speaking to Miranda, he walked away.

Miranda's anger seemed to deflate once he was gone, and she shook her head and went over to a bench to examine her sword.

Faith sat down next to her. Miranda still had no idea that Sophie's motives were in question. As far as she knew, the warrior had been her teacher and friend and had died helping her. Miranda treated Sophie's sword with reverence, even though it wasn't the ideal weapon for her—she needed something balanced a little differently, and a little shorter. They'd tried her out on other blades, including some from Sophie's collection, but so far nothing had been perfect enough to persuade Miranda to give up the one she had.

Miranda obviously didn't want to talk, and that was fine, although Faith knew in a few minutes she'd probably change her mind and get angry all over again.

Before Faith could offer any sort of conciliatory advice, however, her com chimed.

"Star-three here," Faith said.

*"This is Elite Sixty-two, door guard at the guest suites. I have a situation here that needs your urgent attention."*

Miranda sat forward, listening keenly, though the guard probably had no idea she was there.

"Go ahead, Elite Sixty-two," Faith said.

*"I have a woman here from Prime Hart's . . . entourage . . . asking to see the Queen."*

Faith and Miranda exchanged a look of shock, and Faith raised an eyebrow at her; Miranda nodded once.

"Request forwarded," Faith replied. "Stand by for further orders."

Miranda lifted her wrist and said, "Elite Sixty-two."

*"This is Elite Sixty-two, my Lady."*

"Bring the woman to the first-floor audience room. Keep her under heavy guard. I'll be waiting."

*"As you will it, my Lady."*

Miranda hit the door running with Faith one step behind her.


The audience chamber was one of the most pretentious things in the Haven, but under certain circumstances it was extremely useful. It was about the size of the other meeting rooms and studies where the Pair conducted receptions and business with the visiting Primes, but it was not set up to create comfort and camaraderie; it was a royal chamber whose entire design was meant to intimidate visitors and remind them who was in control.

Primes were occasionally called upon to settle disputes among the more powerful vampires of their territory, known as the Court—those who weren't warriors, but who were allies of the Signet, were considered noblemen and assisted the Signet in various ways. In return they were protected from gangs, hunters, and human interference in their affairs; smarter Primes like David kept up good relations with human institutions as well, particularly state and local governments, so if someone from the Court had, say, an issue with zoning laws or trade regulations, the Prime could use his influence—and occasionally his cash—to smooth things over. David had lent Elite to some of the higher-ranking vampires to help train their own personal security forces or run investigations into various forms of unrest, especially in other cities in the South where he couldn't be a constant presence as he was in Austin.

Some of the Court were entrepreneurs, and some came from old money. David's Court was made up of a combination of the two, weighted toward the former, as most of his friends were involved somehow in security, technology, or finance.

Vampires learned quickly that they could easily outlast their own money, and living in poverty wasn't exactly a fun way to pass the centuries, so those who were remotely intelligent found ways to save and invest. That was part of how David had become so wealthy even before taking the Signet. He knew a good thing when he saw one and had invested in little-known start-up companies like Apple and Intel. He still had a large sum in the market, but most of it was socked away in accounts all over the world, and he could live on the interest alone for another five centuries. Miranda was entitled to half of the Signet account, but she had her own separate account for her musical earnings as well, and with David's shrewd advice it had already grown by leaps and bounds.

Miranda and Faith made it to the audience room in less than a minute, and the Queen took her chair, to the right of the Prime's at the far end of the room facing the doors. Aside from those two chairs the only other furniture was long benches lining the sides of the room, so that whoever came before the Pair had to stand. Their seats were elevated, as they would be in any throne room.

She really hated the place, but it seemed appropriate for the situation; there was no way to know what this woman wanted, whose side she might be on, or what her true intentions might be. David had said Hart had brought his "girls" here to taunt the Pair, and if he knew they would oppose his perversions, he might have sent her as bait. David might not think much of Miranda's diplomatic abilities, but she wasn't a complete idiot.

They waited a few minutes, long enough that Miranda started to wonder if the whole thing was Hart's idea of a joke, but then there was a chime, and Faith had a brief conversation on her com.

"They're here," Faith said. "It took a minute because they had to find someone who speaks Italian—the girl's English is rudimentary at best."

"Bring them in," Miranda replied.

Faith nodded and strode over to the double doors. Miranda took a minute to compose herself—too bad she hadn't had a chance to shower beforehand, so she wouldn't be such a sweaty mess—and sat up straight and tall in her chair, one ankle crossed over the other, her hands folded. Her Signet was plain to see, as was her sword, and she quickly reached up and yanked the elastic from her hair so it fell loose down her back. A ponytail wasn't nearly as impressive.

Faith held the door open as Elite 62 and three other guards escorted a pitifully thin figure into the room. She was leaning on Elite 62, who treated her with surprising tenderness, helping her walk the long expanse to the dais, steadying her when she stumbled. The other three guards followed at a respectful distance, as if the woman were an honored guest and not a potential enemy.

Miranda saw Faith's mouth set in a grim line at the sight of the woman, and as she got closer, it was clear why. The girl couldn't be more than seventeen physically, perhaps even younger; she was so skeletally thin that it was hard to tell. Her skin, once olive and probably beautiful, was ashen, her eyes sunken in with dark circles beneath them. Her dark hair was waist-length, but lank, dull. She was dressed in a gauzy thing that barely covered her wreck of a body. Miranda saw the shadows of bruises on her breasts and legs, and she had a fading black eye that, on a vampire, should have healed in thirty seconds.

Miranda gripped the arms of her chair until her fingers went numb.

One of the Elite, 29 if Miranda remembered correctly, stepped forward and offered herself as translator; Miranda nodded to her. Elite 29 went to the woman and touched her shoulder lightly, gesturing for her to speak.

The girl's voice was tremulous but held the faintest hint that it might once have been very different. "My name is Cora," she said through Elite 29. "The Master brought me here to your Haven."

"Welcome, Cora," Miranda said. "I am Miranda Grey-Solomon, Ninth Queen of the Southern United States. How can I be of service to you?"

Cora looked like she was sure Miranda, or possibly one of the Elite, was going to strike her down at any second for what she intended to say. "I . . . I need your help, Lady Queen. I want to leave my Master's house, where he keeps me as a slave to his lusts. If I do not get away from him, I will die like all the others do. I want . . ."

She looked around helplessly, waving her pencil-thin arm weakly as if to take in the Elite, the Queen, and everything around her. "I want to be free of him."

Miranda took a deep breath. "Come here, child."

The Elite helped Cora approach the dais, close enough that Miranda could lean forward and look directly into her eyes. "Are you here of your own free will?"

Cora was taken aback by the question. Apparently the thought had never occurred to her, but slowly, she nodded. "Yes."

"Be still a moment, please."

Miranda extended her empathic power toward Cora, who seemed not to feel the intrusion at all; she wasn't shielded, but as weak as she was she probably had no need for psychic protection. If she had any gifts, they were buried under years of hunger, fear, and shame . . . but something was there, some barely shining potential struggling to be released. Miranda held the girl's mind and heart in her palm, looking her over, trying not to be harsh in her touch. She knew how it felt to have one violation piled on top of a mountain of others. There was no need for that.

Miranda clamped down on the immediate reaction of her body, which was to charge into the guest suites and rip Hart's dick off and feed it to him. Right now she had to think of Cora . . . who had risked her life and everything she knew to crawl toward something better. That simple courage sparked something fierce and protective in Miranda.

She would not allow Hart to hurt Cora again. If David didn't understand, he would just have to, as Kat would say, put on his big-girl panties and deal with it.

"Very well, Cora." Miranda stood and walked down from the dais to stand eye to eye with her. The girl shrank back, but Miranda caught and held her gaze. "If it is your will to leave Prime Hart's . . . employ, then as Queen of this territory, I offer you asylum here at our Haven until such time as you are safe and strong again, after which you may choose your own fate. As a refugee you bear the same concomitant rights and responsibilities under the law as any other vampire under the mantle of our authority. Do you accept?"

Cora was shaking hard, tears running down her face, and her relief was like rain coming to the desert. "Yes. I do."

Miranda nodded. "Then welcome to our Haven, Cora. Let's see what we can do for you."

The Queen looked over at Faith. "I want her in one of the suites nearest our wing, with twenty-four-hour guard as long as she's here. She's not to go anywhere without a bodyguard and is to be restricted to the gardens and common areas for now. Have the Elite medic look her over, then see to it that she has as much blood as she needs, and for God's sake, find her some clothes."

Faith bowed. There was satisfaction in her face. "As you will it, my Lady."

Cora was still crying, swaying back and forth, but she looked up and met Miranda's eyes. *"La ringrazio,"* she whispered. *"Grazie mille."*

Miranda smiled. *"Prego."*

Just then, the doors opened and David walked in, his expression grave; when Cora saw his Signet and realized who he was, she all but melted into Miranda's side, trying to hide from him.

The other Elite parted to let him pass and he came up to them, silent for a moment as he stared hard at Miranda.

She stared right back. "Go ahead," she said. "Look Cora in the face and tell her she has to go back to him."

David shook his head in exasperation, but when he turned to Cora, his expression softened, and he spoke in a low voice, in perfect Italian that, Miranda had to admit, made her insides shiver a little.

"Welcome to our Haven, young miss," he said—the Elite translator leaned closer to Miranda and told her so. "I am Prime David Solomon, and I would like to assure you that you are safe here for as long as you need sanctuary. Please allow the guards to escort you to your room."

She stammered a question, and he smiled. "No, you will not have to share it with anyone. You'll have a bed of your own and your own bath as well. Once you've fed properly, you'll feel much better."

He gestured to the guards, and Elite 62 bowed politely to Cora, then took her arm and slowly led her away.

Then he faced Miranda. "She asked for asylum?"

"Yes," she replied. "Completely of her own volition. I don't know what motivated her to do it, but I looked into her as deeply as I could, and she's clean. Innocent. And broken."

David's eyes followed the girl and the guards out the door. "Well, she's safe now."

"What about Hart declaring war?"

The Prime crossed his arms, giving her an unreadable look. "I told you. Going in and taking the harem would be a declaration. She came to you. That's different. Cora is a refugee. Under the law we can take her in and Hart has no recourse against her or us. Any action he takes against us therefore becomes an act of war and he'll have the full Council to deal with."

"What about the other girls?"

"Unless they ask for asylum as well, things are exactly as I said before. But depending on how he reacts when he finds out about Cora, he might tip his hand and give us the opportunity to take the rest—we'll just have to see how—"

*"Where is she?"*

David's com chimed a second after the voice roared in the hallway, and one of the Elite said, *"Sire . . . incoming."*

Prime James Hart flung open the double doors of the audience room, scattering the Elite who were still in attendance as he shoved his way past them toward the dais. "I demand an explanation for this!" he thundered. His eyes were pure silver, practically glowing, and his teeth pressed downward, though not quite enough to impair his speech as he yelled, "You will return the girl this instant!"

Miranda wasn't afraid of Hart, but the sheer strength of his rage almost made her take a step back. She stood her ground at David's side, and the Prime crossed his arms and regarded Hart coolly.

One of these days she was going to figure out how to do that.

"Be very careful, Lord Prime," David told Hart. "You are not in your home territory and there are now four crossbows pointed at your back."

Miranda kept her eyes on Hart, but she heard the creak of wood from the corners of the room, where four Elite had appeared and were now awaiting the order to shoot.

"This is an outrage," Hart ground out, towering over David, who merely looked up at him with a completely neutral expression. Hart was a tall man, imposing, used to intimidating people, but he couldn't intimidate David. It simply wasn't possible. "Give her back."

"No."

"This is an act of—"

"Say it, Hart," David hissed, eyes narrowing, their blue going silver at the edges. "Say the word and I'll have you shot before you take another breath. Start a war between us right now and it will be finished right now."

Hart snarled, "You had no right to steal what rightfully belongs to me."

"I stole nothing. Cora came to my Queen and asked for asylum. She has exposed your cruelty and your participation in illegal slavery—and we'll see what the Council has to say now that we have evidence to back up the rumors."

Hart turned on Miranda. "You did this, then. I should have known. You stupid little whore—no woman takes what's mine. I'll teach you—"

Hart raised his arm to backhand her, and Miranda felt David start toward them, but finally, Miranda's rage and hatred toward this sick excuse for a man had an outlet, and she let it fly, drawing up her power and *pushing*—

Hart flew backward, thrown hard across the room, and the sound of a body hitting the far wall and the crunch of breaking bones caused the Elite to freeze where they stood, staring with huge eyes at their Queen . . .

. . . their Queen, whose palm was outstretched toward where Hart had been standing.

She was breathing hard, but her body sang with pleasure and satisfaction, and she knew she was smiling.

David crossed the room to stand over Hart, and she heard him say very quietly, "You have exactly one hour to leave my Haven. If you stay one moment longer, you will die. You are to leave the other three women here. Now, go."

He turned his back on Hart and returned to where Miranda stood; the armed Elite converged upon Hart and waited while he got to his feet, one arm sticking out at an unnatural angle, and limped away with the four crossbows still trained on him.

Miranda lowered her hand, grounding herself, letting the excess power drain out of her. When she looked up at David he was staring at her, and to her amazement, he looked completely dumbfounded.

"That was you," he said.

She nodded. "Yeah. I know; I shouldn't have lost my temper."

"No, Miranda—it was *you*. You threw him."

"So?"

"With your *brain*."

She frowned for a minute before she understood what he was saying. "Oh."

"How did you do that?"

Miranda's heart was pounding. "I . . . I don't know. Is that . . . not normal?"

"No . . . it's beyond not normal. Pairs share power, but they don't share talents. That's not possible. How could you suddenly be telekinetic?"

David had all the answers. The thought that there was something that baffled him this much, and obviously worried him, worried her even more. "I don't know. But I didn't know I was prescient, either, until that thing with Kat yesterday."

"Every Queen has that talent to some degree. It usually doesn't fully develop until after she takes her Signet." Seeing her distress, and moreover feeling it, David took a deep breath, then came over and put his arms around her. "It's all right, beloved. I'm sorry I overreacted—there must be an explanation. I'll see what I can find out. Maybe it is normal; I've never heard of gift transfer, but I've never had a Queen, either."

She leaned into his shoulder, suddenly exhausted by the whole evening, wanting nothing more than to climb into bed with him and shut the world away. "And you're not angry at me over Cora?"

"No. You did the right thing. I'm proud of you."

"Good," she said. "I was afraid I was going to have to kick your ass."

He sighed. "You don't really think I'm a heartless bastard, do you?"

She chuckled in spite of herself. "I think you know a lot more than I do about all of this, and we're going to butt heads a lot until I figure it all out. But if you can be patient with me, I'll be patient with you, and it will all work out."

"I hope so," he said, holding her tightly. "I hope so."


A little over an hour later Faith followed the frantic call of Elite 18 to the guest suites. One of the servants had gone into the rooms that Hart had abandoned to start what would no doubt be an arduous cleanup, and her scream had brought the guards running.

Faith stood in the doorway, gripping the frame with one hand, the other on her sword hilt.

Hart had destroyed his own room, dumping books from shelves and knocking over furniture. He had thrown anything breakable he could get his hands on onto the wall, and there were bits of broken glass and ceramic all over the wood floor. Nothing appeared to be missing, just smashed and torn.

Faith, however, was in the doorway to the smaller bedroom, which reeked of sex and blood. The only thing in the room that had been broken was a single wooden chair. Three of the legs had been snapped off.

Each leg now protruded from the chest of a naked woman.

Hart had stripped them, murdered them, and then thrown them into a pile, their long bony limbs splayed out on the floor of the bedroom.

Faith had seen a great many dead bodies in her life, mostly from violence without warning. So many faces had been marked with horror and fear at the moment of death. Here, on the other hand, she saw girls whose dying expressions had been utter indifference to fate, and one was even smiling.

Elite 18 was kneeling by the bodies and pointed to one of their bare stomachs, where it looked like Hart had slashed her with a knife. "Look," he said.

Faith came closer and squinted. The slashes weren't random. They were letters.

"Clean it off," she said. Elite 18 nodded and grabbed a discarded pillowcase, wiping gently at the dead girl's midsection; a servant brought a cup of water, and they scrubbed at the dried blood until the letters were visible.

Faith's chest tightened as she read it.

*SOON, BITCH.*

"All right," Faith said quietly. "That's enough. Let's take care of these poor girls."

She ordered them separated, cleaned, shrouded, and burned, and everything in both rooms stripped and replaced from the handful of bedrooms toward the back of the Haven that hadn't been used in decades.

Then she shook her head with heavyhearted resignation and went to call the Pair.

Before she could even say "Star-one," however, she heard footsteps behind her and a shakily drawn breath.

Faith turned to the Queen. "My Lady—"

Miranda darted into the bathroom without speaking, and Faith heard her retching.

Several of the sturdier-stomached servants had converged on the bodies and were gently coaxing the girls apart, laying them out on plastic sheeting. Esther, who normally saw to the Pair's wing, had arrived with cleaning supplies and grim determination and was overseeing the whole operation; the little woman had been on staff longer than Faith had been in Texas, and, having worked for Auren, surely she had seen worse.

By the time Miranda emerged from the bathroom, her composure regained though she was still pale and a little green, David had arrived, and he drew the Queen into his arms and held her, silently, while the bodies were tended to.

"We should never have left him alone with them," Miranda said softly. "We should have had guards on the suite as soon as he walked out . . . why didn't we send guards?"

"It's my fault," David said, sounding as disturbed as Faith had ever heard him. "I was so rattled by you throwing him that I didn't think . . . I just didn't think."

Faith could see the anger in David's silver eyes, and the shock and guilt in Miranda's, and after a few minutes, Miranda visibly steeled herself and stepped away from him to kneel next to the girls.

She gestured to one of the servants, who handed her a wet washcloth, and joined in on the nearest victim, helping to draw the bloody stake from her chest and then swab her cold skin clean.

Faith sighed and looked over at David, who through his carefully lidded rage was obviously unsurprised by the violence of Hart's reaction . . . sickened, yes, but not surprised. The Prime took a deep breath, then turned to Elite 18, who couldn't seem to bear looking at the girls but had devoted herself to righting the pieces of furniture that weren't hopelessly damaged. David touched her shoulder and said something to her quietly.

Elite 18, clearly relieved, nodded, bowed, and disappeared.

David took over for the warrior, examining a chair and then moving it to the side of the room where the usable items were being stacked.

Faith nodded to herself and joined the others on the floor, where she lent her hands to help Esther wrap the first girl in a clean white sheet.

They all worked in silence until there was motion at the door, and Elite 18 said in a low voice, "I've brought her, Sire."

Faith looked at David, who inclined his head toward the door; she rose and followed him into the hallway.

Elite 18 had in her company the refugee woman, Cora, who looked positively petrified at being led back to Hart's suite. Seeing her fear, David and Faith both placed themselves between her and the door so she couldn't see inside.

David spoke to Cora in Italian, but Faith knew what he was asking. He wanted to know the names of the other women.

Cora stammered a little, but answered him. He thanked her, then told her, gently, what had happened.

Cora didn't seem to react at first. She looked over Faith's shoulder at the doorway, then down at the floor, and said something; her voice was wooden, but her eyes were full of tears.

"Of course," David said in English. Then to Elite 18: "You can take her back to her room now. Make sure she's comfortable and has fed before you leave her. Then see to the pyre, please."

"As you will it, Sire."

After she left, Faith raised an eyebrow at David. "She didn't seem too upset."

He crossed his arms. "The women in the harem don't interact much. The black girl's name is Naomi, the blonde is Marie, and the Chinese girl is Mei. Cora wasn't sure about the last one—Mei was new and no one else spoke her language."

"At least we know what to call them now . . . they won't have to be burned without identities, such as they are."

"True."

They returned to the room, and David joined Faith and the Queen next to the bodies. He lightly touched each of the girls' heads in turn and told everyone their names.

Miranda was helping Esther wrap Mei, whose skin had been carved with Hart's scathing, vicious message to her, in the sheet that would be her burial shroud. "I'm sorry, Mei," the Queen whispered as she covered the dead girl's face. "I wish we had helped you sooner. This is the best we can do for you now . . . be at peace."

David knew better than to think he'd be able to sleep that morning.

After he was sure that Miranda was out, he carefully untangled himself from her arms and legs and put clothes on, then left their suite for his workroom.

He was not happy. He was grateful that Hart was gone, but the whole situation had left him fighting mad, and the downside was that Hart wasn't there to punch in the face. Now he was left to figure out what steps to take next in the wake of Hart's dramatic exit.

The Council had to be informed, of course. He would notify all his allies that he and Hart had officially severed all relations, and the news would be all over the world inside an hour. Though Hart had friends, nobody really *liked* him; those who sided with him shared his beliefs but would be more than happy to throw him under the bus if it served their interests.

David sank into his chair, leaning forward to put his head in his hands for a moment; he had a mighty headache but he wasn't about to wake Miranda up to heal it. She was going to have trouble sleeping today as it was.

Despite the horror of Hart's aftermath, one question kept returning to David's mind:

How had Miranda done it?

David had felt her drawing on their combined strength, but that happened all the time. That was what their connection was for, to make them more powerful as a whole. But he had never heard of anything like one member of a Pair inheriting the psychic abilities of the other. He hadn't developed empathy . . . not yet, anyway, thank God.

It frustrated him how little was known about the history of the Signets, and how little the others seemed to care. He had proposed a research project more than once and been sneered at. As long as they had power and money, it made no difference to them where it came from. It wasn't as if they could do anything with the knowledge anyway.

Fools. Old, blind fools with their heads planted firmly up their asses and their hands planted firmly in their pocketbooks. Now here David was, with a burning question he had no way to answer.

It was possible that Deven might know—he was one of the oldest Primes in the Council and had been all over the world before settling in California to rule over his territory. He'd never shown any interest in Signet lore, but that didn't mean he had no knowledge of it.

It was, however, the middle of the day, and a quick look at his computer told David that the Prime was not online. It was the pinnacle of bad manners to wake a Prime during daylight. His questions and vague nameless fears would just have to wait until sunset.

To distract himself he decided to try to crack open Hart's little toy. He retrieved it from the locked cabinet where he'd stashed it, as well as a number of tools, a scanning module he'd built, a vise, and a handheld laser-cutting torch.

He placed the earpiece in the vise and hooked up the scanner to his computer, then spent a while running preliminary tests to see if he could learn anything from the piece without breaking into it. There wasn't much to learn; it didn't put out any sort of signal, and even if it had, that signal wouldn't have made it past the Haven without being hopelessly scrambled. Whatever network it had been connected to, it was dead now.

David paused here and there to type up a few quick notes. *Casing appears to be a similar titanium-aluminum alloy to the fourth-generation wrist coms. Seamless except for a single hole approx. 1 mm in diameter. No obvious signs of manufacturer, not recognizable as belonging to any well-known designers in the communications industry. Possible DOD origin?*

Unlikely. The Defense Department could scarcely make a move without his knowing it.

He changed the scanner's setup to tell him more about the internal makeup of the piece so at least he'd know how thick the shell was and could calibrate the cutting laser appropriately.

It was unusually thin, barely an eggshell over an interior tightly packed with wiring and what looked like a single tiny chip.

Before he tried opening the thing, he had the scanner take surface images and put all the technical scans into a folder, then moved his laptop away from the table in case of any accidents. He turned the vise and raised it slightly, then switched on the laser, a compact handheld model he'd won in a poker game from the head of research and development at one of the other defense contractors. It was a thing of beauty, precise and lightweight, and could cut through anything at any thickness without damaging whatever was inside.

He could only imagine the mischief it would cause if the outside world got hold of it, which was why, like all his toys, it was locked in this room.

David calibrated the beam and got to work.

Given how small the thing was, it didn't take long to neatly bisect the casing. He set the torch aside and pulled on a pair of gloves to make sure he didn't damage the components or get anything toxic on his skin. He unscrewed the vise and transferred the piece to a tray sized to fit under the microscope.

With a pair of long tweezers and a probe, he peeled one side back from the other, gingerly exposing the perfect twist of wires within. He slid the probe into the wires and teased it apart, exposing the chip like a pearl inside an oyster.

The explosion sent Miranda screaming out of sleep.

# Five

"Mother *fuck*!"

Miranda had known David for a little over a year, and she had never heard him curse quite so much.

Faith slapped his hand. "Lie still," she said. "Do you want this out or not?"

Elite 12, who was known to his peers simply as Mo, was the official medic for the entire Haven; for the most part a vampire's healing abilities made short work of any injuries, but if something was embedded in a limb, something was torn off, or the victim was weakened to the point that his or her abilities were compromised, Mo took care of things, even sewing on a few fingers now and then until a warrior's natural defenses kicked back in. Infection and the presence of foreign substances slowed the process down, too, so in cases of serious wounds, antiseptics and hygiene were as important to vampires as they were to humans. It was even possible to poison a vampire given the right ingredients, though it couldn't kill one, and Mo had been called upon more than once to administer antidotes to painful and debilitating toxins.

Mo leaned over the Prime, who was laid out on his worktable with a shard of metal buried in his left eye.

"You know, Sire," Mo said, his cheerful Iranian accent unusually stern, "I have said many times that you must wear eye protection when you play with sharp things."

"Yes, and I've said many times you can stuff it where

Allah don't shine," David said irritably. "Son of a bitch! What are you using, a fucking jackhammer?"

Miranda snorted.

Mo was unperturbed. "Sire, if you do not stay still, I may do more damage to your eye or perhaps the nerves around it. It would be rather painful and I think perhaps your Queen would kill us both."

She had sprinted into the workroom to find David on the floor bleeding from several small wounds where Hart's mystery earpiece had shattered and flown everywhere. Nothing else in the room appeared to be damaged, although David had urgently commanded her to hit the override on the fire alarm so that the smoke—scant though it was— wouldn't trip the system.

Mo had already removed shrapnel from David's face, neck, and left arm, all of which had closed and healed as soon as the bits were taken out. If they had been wood splinters, it would have taken twice as long, if not longer. Apparently a titanium-aluminum alloy was no big deal unless it was stuck in your cornea.

Miranda couldn't watch. She'd nearly been sick when she saw his blood; the thought of seeing a scalpel in her husband's eye made her queasy. She had already sent up a dozen thank-yous to whatever god watched over vampires who were too pigheaded to wear safety glasses.

It amused her that, even three and a half centuries old and so far removed from human notions of masculinity, David was as much a drama queen about pain as every man she'd ever met.

"Stop being a baby," Faith admonished the Prime. "You're lucky that thing didn't blow your head off."

David grunted but lay still, letting Mo hold his eyelid open so he could dig in and retrieve the shard. Even Faith looked a little nauseated at the sight and pointedly turned her gaze up toward the ceiling.

"It wasn't meant to kill anyone," David muttered, trying not to move his jaw too much and disturb Mo's arm. "From what little I saw it was basically just a nanotransmitter."

"Could you make something like it?" Faith asked.

The Prime made a noise that might have been a sardonic laugh, but it ended up being a pained growl as Mo pulled his hand back, revealing a centimeter-long arrowhead of silver metal held in his tweezers. Unfortunately Miranda looked just in time to see a scarlet tear of blood oozing from the corner of David's eye. She turned away, groaning, nauseated, determined not to be sick a second time in twenty-four hours.

"All right, Sire, go ahead," Mo told him.

David clamped his eyes shut and in a few seconds opened them again, blinked, and sat up. "Good work, Mo. Thank you."

The medic shrugged. "All in a day's—and I do mean day, Sire, it's ten in the morning—work."

David looked chagrined as he wiped the blood away. "Sorry to get you out of bed. You're dismissed."

Mo smiled, gathered his supplies, and left. "Let me know if you notice any other stray poking things poking you."

David blinked a few more times, focusing his gaze on Miranda, and smiled at her. "I'm fine," he insisted. "It wasn't a disaster."

She glared at him, unwilling to concede the point. "It could have been. Hart could have easily made that thing as a bomb and conveniently let you have it knowing you couldn't resist taking it apart."

"It wasn't a bomb," he said, which wasn't in the least bit reassuring. "It was a pressure-sensitive trigger designed to destroy the tech if someone got it open. It wasn't intended to do any real harm to the person unless they happened to be staring right into it at the time. Hart is a technophobe—and as much of a psychopath as he is, I honestly believe him that this came from somewhere else. And in answer to your question"— he turned to Faith—"of course I could make something like it. What little data I got suggested it's not nearly as complex as the coms. It was a lovely little thing, though. Beautifully crafted. I wish I could have studied it more."

"You're hopeless," Miranda said. "I'm going back to bed."

She pushed herself out of the chair and left the workroom, pausing to let the guards know everything was all right and commend them on their quick response. They looked as frightened as she had been. It still surprised her how loyal they were to him—and now, her—and how invested they were in the Pair's welfare. It was unsettling to know that her fate governed the lives of so many people . . . Faith had said so to her a dozen times, but it had yet to fully sink in.

Miranda knew better than to think she could really sleep until David joined her and she could run her hands over his body to convince herself he was really okay. But she also knew his fastidious nature and knew he would clean up the workroom before coming to bed. There was no point in even trying to rest until then.

She picked up her guitar from where she'd left it earlier, leaning next to her chair by the fireplace. Then she sat down cross-legged on the sofa with her guitar and picked at it mindlessly for a few minutes, letting whatever needed to be played arise.

Esther had been in, kind soul, and added another log to the fire at some point; the woman was a born nurturer and no doubt had been at a loss as to how to help David after the accident, so she did what she could do: She made the room comfortable. She'd straightened up the room, built up the fire, and hung a bundle of some kind of herb from the mantel, probably one of her Mexican folk charms. Esther knew all kinds of arcane things for protection from the Evil Eye, to bring money, to lure in a lover . . . she had trained with a *curandera* when she was human and would have been one herself if she hadn't been brought across. Miranda loved everything about her, especially the way she still called Miranda *reinita*, "little Queen."

The Queen closed her eyes and started humming, then let music and voice both evolve into an actual song, one she'd covered onstage a dozen times.

*Like you're trying to fight gravity on a planet that insists*
*that love is like falling and falling is like this . . .*

When she finished the song, she looked up at the Prime, who was watching and listening while he leaned against the bedpost, smiling softly as if nothing in the world existed but her. He had taken off his shirt, and the firelight bathed his bare skin in flickering gold.

Was it stranger that the Elite cared so much about him or that she did?

"Come to bed, beloved," he said.

She set her guitar aside and rose, holding his gaze until she was close enough to fold herself gratefully into his embrace.


Faith went into the city with David, Miranda, and her bodyguards Thursday night, but they split up as soon as they reached Austin. Miranda, Jake, and Lali disembarked and headed toward the Bat Cave studio, where Miranda would have her first recording session; Faith and David stayed in the car, bound for a high-rise in the heart of downtown Austin, with everyone set to rendezvous in front of the Bat Cave at three A.M.

David was understandably tense. Word had gone out about the drama with Hart, and now he was waiting to see how the other Signets reacted. He anticipated that twelve total would side with him without any argument, and seven with Hart; that left six wild cards who could be swayed either way. Some would be easy enough, like Tanaka, who always maintained his neutrality but considered David one of his oldest friends and, given the evidence presented by Cora, would throw in his lot with David. He required only good reasons and good evidence before making a move, which was understandable, given that he was the parliamentary leader of the Council and was expected to stay as fair as possible.

In the end, however, Hart would make the next move. If he never spoke of the incident again and never returned to Texas, there might not be a fight. If assassins started showing up in Austin, it would be obvious to whom they belonged. If Hart was smart, and Faith doubted he was, he would let the matter drop and keep his distance from now on.

But Hart had been bested by a woman, and that would rankle him to the point of madness. He hated women pathologically, with religious fervor that rivaled the Blackthorn gang's hatred of gays. It was Miranda's act of defiance that would drive any plans he had for revenge. His bloody message left on the corpse of an innocent woman had made the point quite succinctly.

David was quiet on the drive. He brooded far less now that Miranda had come into his life, but he was still prone to long periods of stewing, and Faith could guess at least a dozen of the subjects that might be on his mind tonight.

"Is it Hart, the Council, the attack on the Queen, her sudden bout of telekinesis, what to do with your new houseguest, your Queen's security tonight, the Red Shadow's involvement with Hart, its involvement with Sophie, or the exploding hearing aid that's got you all knotted up?" she asked.

David leaned back in his seat and groaned. "It wasn't any of those things until you brought them up. Thank you, Second."

"Then what were you mulling over?"

"Signet history. Why we threw away our own past. How much there is out there to learn and what it could do for us. Imagine if there are powers we don't even know we can access—things even more miraculous than Misting. Pairs can combine their power and boost one or the other's abilities, but I've never heard of a case where one took on the other's abilities and used them without any training or prior talent. What if we can all do that?"

Faith smiled. "Then Jonathan could borrow Deven's fighting ability and Deven wouldn't constantly bitch about what a horrible warrior he Paired with."

"There has to be a way to find out more. Archives somewhere. Journals. Something. I can't believe that nobody in our entire history has agreed with me on this. We can't all have been that stupid."

Harlan pulled up to the front entrance of the building, and Faith and David got out; the Prime leaned in to tell Harlan something, probably a reminder of their rendezvous plans, then straightened, adjusting his coat. It was another cold night; since the hard freeze the night of Hart's arrival, the weather had been insanely frigid with the constant threat of ice on bridges.

They took the concrete steps up to the glass front of the building, where a security guard met them and asked for ID.

David smiled and opened the neck of his coat, revealing the Signet.

The guard nodded and unlocked the door.

Near the elevators, a gray-haired man in a white lab coat was waiting for them. Their steps echoed in the empty atrium, only a few lights on at this hour.

"Sire, Faith," the man said. "A pleasure to see you again."

"Doctor Novotny." David shook his hand and the doctor turned to lead them to the elevator. "You said you have made progress."

Faith watched the human as they took the elevator up to the twelfth floor; he was reasonably comfortable in their presence, but he still seemed a bit twitchy once the doors slid shut and he was trapped in the small chamber with two vampires. Novotny was hardly psychic, but a human in a coma would have been able to sense something strange about David. Usually it wasn't anything they would be able to pinpoint, but it was instinct for mortals to edge away, to keep one eye on the door. If there had been ten people in the elevator, by the time they got to their floor, it would have been Faith and the Prime in one corner and all ten humans clustered on the other side. Those who knew what they were, or were gifted enough to know what they were sensing, tended to be much more relaxed around them.

Novotny's research lab took up the entire twelfth floor and was accessible only by a special elevator code. The company, Hunter Development, was one of several that David worked with when he needed something done he couldn't design, fabricate, or investigate himself. Naturally he owned about 80 percent of it.

The doctor led them to a locked room that scanned his

retinas, fingerprints, and voice before allowing them access. Inside were two long tables and a variety of machines whose purpose Faith could only guess.

"So you say the thing exploded?" Novotny was asking with interest.

David smiled. So did Faith, to herself, at the idea that David had associates as geeky as he was. "I've brought you what was left." He retrieved a flat metal case about the size of a pack of cigarettes from his coat and handed it to the doctor. "There's not much, but if you get anything off it, let me know. All of my preliminary findings are on the drive inside."

"Excellent, excellent. It sounds like pretty standard stuff, but you never know. Now, over here . . ."

Opening a small door in the far wall—also encoded—Novotny retrieved another case, this one larger, and laid it on the steel table in front of them. "We ran it through the full battery of parameters."

Novotny opened the case to reveal a sharpened wood cylinder inside a plastic evidence bag, resting in a nest of gray foam. It didn't look much different from when Faith had taken it from the crime scene, except that Miranda's blood had been cleaned off and a few splinters seemed to have been picked out of it for testing.

The scientist went on, "It was easy enough to identify it as *Betula pendula*, silver birch, found widely in Europe. This particular specimen can be traced all the way to the Lapland region of Finland."

"Finland," David repeated. "That's different. Can you tell if it was made there, or imported to the States first?"

"There are traces of low-grade steel in the grooves left by the carving implement, and that steel is well over a century old—it predates the Bessemer process. Our conclusion, based on contaminant elements in the steel, is that whatever was used to carve the stake was also made in Finland. Based on traces of soil in the grooves, I can say with confidence that the stake was carved there as well."

"What about the person who carved it?"

"There I'm afraid the data is inconclusive. I can tell you

that he or she was right-handed based on the carving strokes, and there was no extractable DNA except that of the Queen. The blood soaked into the wood enough that it caused interference. As you know, we've made considerable progress analyzing vampire blood on its own, but in the presence of so many other variables, it made in-depth analysis impossible."

It was a strange quirk of vampire biology that as soon as their blood was exposed to air, it began to break down very quickly. To the naked eye it still looked like blood, but on a microscopic level it essentially died, the cells dissolving as if in an acid. When ultraviolet light touched it, it actually began to smoke. That made it very difficult to study, and Dr. Novotny's people were some of the few who had had any success. Thanks to their work, David had been able to develop the DNA scanners inside the coms, primarily using skin cells.

On the bright side it meant that human authorities couldn't positively isolate vampire blood at a crime scene or learn anything about it in a standard forensics lab. On the downside, it meant the stake probably wasn't going to tell them anything useful about the woman who had attacked the Queen.

David looked disappointed but not entirely surprised. "So we're possibly dealing with a Finnish woman, although the stake may not have been hers to begin with, and possibly a vampire because it's so old, though we don't know that for sure either."

"She moved way too fast to be human," Faith pointed out.

"Have you made any progress on the sensor failure?" David asked.

Novotny shook his head. "No more than you have, Sire. We have no idea why this assassin didn't register on the network. She was perfectly average in height and weight, based on the Queen's description. Psychic shields wouldn't block the sensors—they read purely physical traits. Somehow she found a way to confuse the signal, like a stealth bomber. I'm guessing some sort of scrambling device."

"Which gives her more than passing familiarity with

the system," Faith observed uneasily. "How many people outside the Haven know how it works?"

"I want another check run on Elite and staff," David said to Faith. "This time concentrate on hires since the war. Look into their prior associations, employers, friends. Find any connection you can to Finland—it's worth a try. Flag anyone who was separated from their patrol unit or otherwise unaccounted for at any time, for any reason. Pull them in for questioning."

"I thought you monitored all your staff and Elite," Novotny said. "If one of them is passing on information, when and how would they go about it?"

"Last time it was through the mail," Faith responded.

"Security is tight," David added, "but no system is perfect. I learned that the hard way."

"In reality all someone would have to do is leave a note somewhere that's picked up by someone else," said Faith, discouraged. "We've gotten a lot more detailed in our security screenings on hire, and we track everywhere they go through the coms, but there are always holes."

"Frankly I'm more concerned with motive at the moment," David said, crossing his arms. "It's highly unlikely a gang would have organized so quickly in Austin after the war; aside from the sensor network, we have operatives on the streets of every city in the territory listening for unrest or organization. There hasn't been a single group formed since the battle at the Haven. They're still far too nervous, and they're waiting to see just how strong Miranda and I are before they try anything. To me that suggests we're dealing with a vendetta."

Faith nodded. "I was thinking the same thing. Also, Sire . . . I've been considering the exact sequence of events, and I had an observation. The assassin posed as a reporter, which means she knew enough about Miranda to worm her way in to see her. Given how young and new to the Signet Miranda is, word of her two careers hasn't had time to spread very far. As a musician she's well-known locally, but not much beyond Texas. Then there are the questions she asked—she fished for information about the Haven's location. If we were looking at someone in cahoots with one of our people, why wouldn't they already know where the Haven is?"

David leaned back against the table, chin lowered, a typical listening-and-mulling-over posture for him. "Go on."

"One more thing. The woman told Miranda she was stupid, which suggests a certain arrogance on the assassin's part. That's not typical of gang hit men. They generally don't banter, and when dealing with a Signet they don't risk wasting time with insults. Either you take out a Signet on the first shot or you die yourself. Again, I think we've got someone here who has a personal reason to kill Miranda."

Novotny considered that as he closed the case and returned the stake to its cabinet in the wall. "Is your Queen the sort of woman who makes enemies?"

David laughed. "She's getting better at it."

Miranda had already decided to like her new bodyguards, especially Lali, a petite woman originally from India who, underneath her Elite uniform, wore a T-shirt emblazoned with *Om Shanti, Bitches!* Lali had a biting wit that seemed out of place with her quiet, melodic voice, and by the end of her first shift with the Queen the two were chatting like old friends.

Jake was more stoic, more a stickler for professional demeanor, but he exuded calm confidence and competence, and though he looked like a Marine Corps rookie he moved like some kind of exotic jungle cat. He was from Laredo originally, son of an honest-to-God Texas cowboy, which took Miranda forever to get out of him. By the night she went into the studio, Jake seemed to have warmed to her, and even cracked a joke or two. He wordlessly picked up her guitar from the car's trunk and carried it for her, and though she might have protested anyone else doing the same, Jake was simply being courteous, not implying she couldn't handle it herself.

Miranda was ready for the recording experience to be a bit grueling, but she was still amazed at how exhausted it left her. Grizzly Behr, the owner and sound engineer, was a cheerful fellow with a big beer gut, a big beard, and a big accent, and he laughed sympathetically at the way she wilted as the hours went on.

"It sucks a goat's balls, but it's worth it," he told her from the far side of the glass, where he and the producer were going back over the third take of the song they were working on. It had taken an hour to get everything set up, another for Grizzly and the producer to record some preliminary tracks to adjust the headphones and mikes, and two more to actually record the song, listen to it, go back and fix the second verse where her voice wobbled, listen to it again, record the harmony, listen again . . . Miranda was starting to hate the damn song, though Lali, in the corner of the control room keeping an eye on things, gave her a thumbs-up more than once after hearing what they'd captured.

At least they were starting with an acoustic song that didn't require any other instruments. There were eight more songs to go, and they were far more complicated. They were going to have to get a Bösendorfer in the studio for several of them, which Grizzly assured her was going to be child's play. He had a larger studio room where orchestral groups had recorded, and it was big enough for a grand piano. That would be Saturday's session, however. Tonight was simple . . . comparatively speaking.

Finally at about two A.M. Grizzly called a halt to things. She wanted to kiss him.

"Good job," he said, shaking her hand when she joined them in the control room. "And thank you for not being a bitchy prima donna. We get a lot of those."

She grinned. "Funny—I thought I got a little bitchy there for a while."

"Nah. Just wait until we do 'Bleed.' That one should be fun."

Miranda gave an exaggerated groan. "God have mercy. Have you found a violinist yet?"

"Actually I was just talking to your friend here, and she says she plays."

Miranda looked at Lali. "You do?"

The Elite smiled. "I do indeed, ma'am."

"Congratulations," Miranda said. "You're my new favorite person."

By the time they were packed up and ready to go, it was twenty till three. Miranda was grateful for the freezing cold air outside; she was sweaty and sleepy and the chill perked her up a little.

Harlan was already parked out in front of the studio, along with the second Haven car for Lali and Jake. Jake, who had been on front door duty, stowed her guitar in the Town Car's trunk. While it was open Miranda fetched a bottle of water from the pack that was always there, in a small cooler that typically held an emergency supply of blood as well. She also took a moment to put on her coat and strap her sword in its place on her hip. She'd been reluctant to take the blade inside the studio in case someone noticed it and raised awkward questions.

"I'll get you the demo CD for the songs where we need a violin," Miranda told Lali. "If you're on board, I'll pay you whatever the going hourly studio rate is plus a bonus."

Lali looked thrilled and was about to reply, but Miranda held up a hand to shush her, lowering her water bottle and staring hard into the night.

What had she heard?

She concentrated, extending her senses around the parking lot and the intersection adjacent to the studio, sweeping the area for anomalies as she tried to hear the noise again. Her hearing could catch sounds half a mile away, and if she focused her energy on a particular location, she could pick up conversation at more than twice that distance.

It came again, this time clear as a bell: a woman screaming.

Miranda was off and running before either of the guards could react.

Adrenaline surged through her body, and she let her

muscles take over for her brain, carrying her faster than even an Olympic sprinter. The streets were nearly empty at this hour, the sounds of traffic distant in this neighborhood tucked away off Lamar Boulevard. She made it to Lamar in seconds, then across, snaking between cars whose drivers could barely see her as she closed in on a spot that burned in her mind with fear and violence.

A quarter mile later Miranda skidded to a halt, drawing her sword, her mind and senses both spinning in a circle as they tried to take in the scene before her.

A woman in a business suit was on the ground, sobbing, the contents of her purse strewn around her. Her hair had been ripped loose from its clip, and her lip was bleeding where she'd been hit. Her clothes were in disarray and she had lost one of her pumps.

The Queen's gaze lifted from the woman, and her heart seemed to thud onto the scene as her feet had moments ago, lumbering to a stop in her chest.

In the watery glare of the streetlight a figure stood over the struggling form of a man. The human, a thirty-something white male with eyes huge and rolling in panic, scrabbled uselessly at the sidewalk, trying to escape the black leather boot placed squarely on his neck.

"Step away from the human," Miranda commanded, letting her powers flare around her. That alone should have warned the standing figure away, and the sight of a woman holding a sword ought to have at least surprised him.

He merely looked at her, chin tilted slightly to the left, as if translating her words into a foreign language.

Staring back at him, Miranda felt a slow quake of unease in her stomach . . . unease and recognition.

He looked like little more than a teenager, but the shadows in his blue-lavender eyes spoke of great age, of a creature older than she could even imagine now that she, too, was immortal. The way he held himself was regal and proud, as one born to the crown.

It was something of a contrast with his wardrobe. He wore black leather: a coat down to his knees, pants, and boots nearly as tall as the coat was long, covered in buckles and rivets. Several pounds of silver jewelry adorned his neck, hands, and face; his eyebrow, nose, and ear were all pierced, the eyebrow three times. His fingernails were painted black, and black perfectly outlined his large, long-lashed eyes. Spiky dark hair over a high-cheekboned, ivory face gave him the look of a punk angel, just as likely to be Lucifer as Gabriel.

He was absolutely beautiful, both ethereal and sensual . . . and so powerful Miranda had to steel herself not to take a step back.

"I am the Queen of this territory," she said, pushing iron into her voice and energy into her aura. Her Signet brightened with her words. "You will do as I say."

Vampires and humans both had quailed before that tone of her voice. A few had bolted. Several had cried.

He simply looked at her a moment longer, then lifted one hand and opened one side of his coat.

The streetlamp caught the gleaming edge of a sword concealed inside, as well as at least three other knives and what might have been a throwing star.

That, however, wasn't what sent Miranda's pulse sky-rocketing.

At his throat, nestled in among the chains and a heavy silver ankh, was an amulet set with a huge emerald.

The stone was glowing.

Slowly, deliberately, Miranda lowered her sword.

Slowly, deliberately, he closed his coat.

"All right," she said. "Who the hell are you?"

Ignoring the question, he smiled. She noticed the pointed canines. "At last . . . the flame of the South."

He had a gentle voice that still carried to her easily. Something about it, and about the smile, offered up a realization that she didn't especially want, and she nodded, the pieces falling into place.

"My Lord," she said.

He bowed slightly. "My Lady."

The Prime of California had arrived.

# Six

"My Lady! Are you all right?"

Lali came thundering around the corner, ready to fling herself into peril on her Queen's behalf, and nearly ran smack into Miranda. A few beats behind her, David and Faith appeared, both coming to an abrupt halt on either side of the Queen, both staring at their . . . visitor.

"Holy crap," she heard Faith mutter.

Completely oblivious to the injured woman or the still-struggling man, David broke out into a grin and walked forward, laughing. "Sire," the Prime said, "it's good to see you again."

"It's good to be seen."

David held out his hand, but the other Prime reached up, pulled David's head down, and kissed him on the mouth.

Miranda felt her mouth drop open as David returned the kiss . . . for several seconds.

When they pulled back, smiling at each other far more intimately than she would have believed possible, the visitor said, "There's my boy."

David turned back to Miranda, who was gaping at the entire tableau and feeling rather like she'd stepped through the Looking Glass. "It's all right, beloved," he told her. "Allow me to present Prime Deven O'Donnell of the Western United States and its adjacent territories. Lord Prime, this is Miranda Grey-Solomon, Queen of the Southern United States."

Prime and Queen bowed to each other, and then Miranda said, a bit tersely, "Would you care to explain what's going on here, my Lord Prime?"

Deven looked down at the human under his foot with open disdain and gestured toward the woman. "An attempted robbery, near as I could tell. I found this thing attempting bodily harm toward the young woman, and I intervened."

"Lali, see to the human," Miranda ordered. Behind her Lali dove to the woman's side and began reassuring her, checking her for injuries; the human was bawling, confused and still terrified, but didn't look badly hurt. "Faith, call it in. Inform APD that we have a mugger in custody, and—"

She glanced back at Deven in time to see him bring his foot down hard, and with a horrible crack, the assailant's neck snapped beneath his boot. The man twitched twice and then lay still, eyes still staring.

"For Christ's sake, Dev," David said, wincing. "Was that really necessary?"

Deven looked down at the corpse, then back up at them, and asked politely, "Oh, I'm sorry . . . did you need that?"

"This is a no-kill territory." Miranda stepped forward.

Deven walked over the body and came up to her; they were almost exactly the same height, but he gave off the aura of someone twice as tall and twice as broad. There was a dare in his voice. "Execute me."

Then he moved over to David. "Jonathan is waiting at the car a block east," he said. "Shall we follow you?"

David looked a tiny bit bewildered by the way his Queen and the Prime were staring daggers at each other, but he said, "Yes, good idea."

Deven gave him a genuine smile, bowed, and walked away.

Free of the Prime's presence, Miranda felt her stomach unclench, and she took a deep breath.

There was a moment of silence before Faith said, "Okay . . . er . . . APD is on its way, with an ambulance for our victim here. Lali has altered her memory to delete us and insert a struggle with the assailant that ended in him breaking his neck as he tried to climb the fire escape nearby. We're good to go—Lali, stay here until the police arrive and make sure she gets to the hospital, then head back with Jake . . . where's Jake?"

Everyone looked around. Jake was nowhere to be seen. "He must have stayed with the car," Lali said.

Prime, Queen, and Second started back toward the Bat Cave, and David went ahead a bit so he could call the Haven and get a guest suite ready for the Littlest Magnificent Bastard and his Consort.

Out of earshot, Miranda said, "So . . . that's Deven."

Faith grinned. "That's him."

"He's . . . quite a bit to take in."

"That is the popular opinion, yes." Faith looked at her keenly. "What's wrong?"

"Besides yet another Prime coming into my town and waving his dick around? Nothing."

Faith laughed. "I promise, he's nothing like Hart. Underneath the swagger is a very kind soul."

"Right."

The Second raised an eyebrow. "What else?"

"Nothing, just . . . are they always like that? Him and David?"

"What do you mean?"

Miranda made a helpless gesture. "With the . . . kissing."

Faith, perplexed, shrugged. "I suppose so. Why?"

"It's just strange seeing David acting affectionately toward anyone besides me. Is he like that with all his friends? He just shook hands with Tanaka."

Faith's mouth formed an O of surprise. "You . . . didn't know?"

"Know what? Am I missing something?"

By now they had arrived at the parking lot where Harlan

and both cars were waiting; to Miranda's surprise, Jake was nowhere to be seen. David was talking with Harlan, and as they approached, the Prime came to them, his expression serious.

"Harlan says Jake took off after you and Lali. I tried to raise him on the coms and there's nothing."

"Oh, shit," Miranda said. "Faith—"

"I'm on it," Faith interrupted, already barking out orders into her com to get a search team to the area immediately. There should be a patrol unit nearby that could be diverted; Jake being off mission was one thing, but not answering his com . . .

David had just pulled out his phone when it sent up a network alarm. "We've lost his signal," the Prime said. "That's not good."

"You're not even getting life signs?" Miranda asked, peering around his arm at the tiny map of their current location.

"No," David replied. "He just disappeared. Faith, get the team to Lake Street and Paredes. He dropped off network at the eastern corner. It's about a block that way." He gestured toward the right. "It looks like he started to follow you but then got distracted. He may have seen or heard something, or been ambushed."

He turned to Miranda. "We should head back and let Faith handle this."

Miranda agreed reluctantly and joined him in the car. Faith came over to shut the door, ducked her head in, and said, "I've got Unit Five coming in to search for him—ETA three minutes. I'm heading to Lake and Paredes now. I'll com you as soon as I have news." Her expression briefly switched from all business to all mischief: "Enjoy your ride home."

"Do you think he's okay?" Miranda asked once the door was shut. David merely looked at her, and she shook her head, heart sinking. "I don't think so either."

Neither spoke again until they were on the highway, and Miranda wrestled with the other question on her mind for quite a while before she was ready to say it: "So . . . about Deven."

David smiled. "He just likes to make an entrance. The exterior's a little spiky, but inside he's really a good friend."

"Is that all?" she asked.

"What do you mean?"

She took a deep breath. "I mean, were you ever more than friends?"

David blinked, mouth opening slightly, as though he had expected any question but that one and had no idea how to respond. Then he said hesitantly, "I thought Faith told you."

"Told me what?"

Now he looked actively sheepish. "That Deven and I were lovers."

She knew she must look like a stranded fish, but she couldn't help it. "When?"

"When I was in California. We both served in Arrabicci's Elite, as co-Seconds. We got together about ten years before the assassination. Then Deven took the Signet and we stayed together until Jonathan came along."

"Ten *years*?" She put her hand on her forehead, unable to think of anything else to do. "And it never occurred to you to bring it up?"

"As I said, I thought you knew. I didn't realize it would be such a problem."

"It's not, it's . . . God, I don't know."

Now he looked amused, and it annoyed her. "Would it be easier to take if he were a woman?"

"Honestly, I have no idea. Although since I had no idea you were bi, it does kind of force my perceptions to realign a little, and I wasn't expecting that."

"Oh, I wouldn't say bi, exactly. If you add up all the people I've slept with in three hundred fifty years, men account for less than two percent."

"Except that you weren't with anyone else for a full decade, were you?"

"Well, no."

"So you can see why this throws me just a bit?" Miranda's

thoughts and emotions were falling over themselves, and she didn't like it. She wasn't going to be some jealous wife who couldn't stand being around her husband's ex when that ex was his best friend; it was a long time ago, and besides, he'd had plenty of women in his time, including a wife. Why was this any different?

"I understand that you're upset," he told her, touching her face. "I wish I'd realized you didn't know. We could have talked about it before they got here. I'm sorry to have dropped it on you like this."

"It's fine," she insisted. "I mean, it's not fine, as in I'm a little freaked-out, but not because . . . I mean . . . it's just . . . weird. I learn something about you every day, and I love that, but considering how significant this one is, maybe you could have *mentioned* it at some point?"

David was thoughtful for a minute, but then he said, "There are a lot of things you still don't know about my past, beloved. I have about three hundred twenty-five years' worth of history on you."

"I know," she said. "I think about that a lot."

He met her eyes. "Then ask," he told her gently. "Whatever you want to know, just ask. I don't ever want you to think I'm keeping secrets. There are some things I don't like to talk about, true, but if you want to know, you deserve to. We're going to be with each other a long time, and that means we have to be honest. No hiding."

"Thank you." She leaned over and kissed his nose, smiling a little. "I take it since you never talk about that part of your past, and you're not together anymore, it's not an entirely happy story."

His eyes flicked away from hers just long enough for her to know she was right.

"It didn't end well," he said. "At least, not for me."

"Wait . . . you mean he dumped you?"

David's smile was touched with regret, and it made her heart hurt, realizing how much pain was underneath the words as he said, "Unceremoniously and resoundingly."

"But . . . why?" Even before the question was out, though,

she knew. "Because of Jonathan. That's why you left California. It wasn't about getting your doctorate as much as it was about getting away from Deven."

"Yes."

"Were you in love?"

Again, the smile, but it faded quickly. "Very much so. But everyone knows that a Prime is destined only to be with his Consort. Everyone in the Court thought that the Signet would choose me, but it didn't, and within six months, it chose someone else that Deven had known for all of ten minutes. The two of them fell for each other instantly, as if they'd been struck by lightning, and I . . . I ceased to exist."

"That little bastard!"

He made an indefinite move of his head: half a shake, half a nod. "He was as confused by it as I was, I think. I pretended everything was all right between us and that I understood, but of course I was a wreck. Jonathan was the one who realized I was lying, but by the time Deven grasped how badly he'd hurt me, I had fled California, and I never went back."

There was old, old grief in his voice, and she took his hands and kissed them, almost regretting bringing the subject up at all. "I'm so sorry."

"It took years to repair our friendship," David went on, staring down at their joined hands, stroking her palm with his thumb. "As soon as Jonathan had the vision that I would take the South, I began to understand why Deven and I had never Paired, and that helped. I had my own path to take and I couldn't do it with him. Not to mention," he said, smiling again, this time without such sadness, "I had you to look forward to."

"But it still hurt," Miranda said, moving closer to him. "You still had your heart broken."

He put his arms around her and said with a sigh, "Yes. Worse than I think I ever had in my life . . . except for when I thought you were dead."

She leaned back enough to look him in the eye. "And I'm supposed to like this guy?"

David chuckled. "I hope you do . . . although I imagine it will take the two of you a while to get there. Dev is hard to know at the best of times. I think you'll find Jonathan much easier to get along with. He's more open, friendlier. But please, Miranda . . . give Deven a chance to win you over. For my sake."

"I'll try. But I'm going to have a hard time not kicking him in the balls for hurting you."

His smile broadened. "If you want to kick him in the balls, you have my blessing. God knows I wanted to for a long time."

"Can I ask you one more thing?"

"Anything, beloved."

"How the hell does he put on all that eyeliner without a mirror?"

David laughed, but before he could reply, his com chimed. He sobered, sighed resignedly, and said into it, "Star-one."

*"Sire, it's Faith. I have news about Jake."*

Prime and Queen looked at each other. Faith sounded unusually subdued. "Go ahead," he told the Second.

*"He's gone, Sire. Someone took him—without his com."*

"How is that possible? They can't come off."

*"They can if the hand comes off, too."*

David closed his eyes. "You found his hand."

*"Yes. It had been severed at the wrist and left in the middle of the sidewalk. There's a lot of blood. The team had a forensics kit so they were able to determine it was Jake's. But there's no other evidence we can see. We're trying to track them, but so far there's just nothing to go on. No footprints, no fingerprints, nothing on the sensors. No body. He could still be alive."*

"God," Miranda whispered, resting her head on the cool glass of the car's window. "Poor Jake. And poor Lali . . . they were friends."

"Keep looking," David said. "I'll run a search and review activity in the area. Return to the Haven before dawn and give me a full report."

*"As you will it. Star-three, out."*

"He might be alive," Miranda muttered, holding back tears of both sorrow and anger. "Why would someone kill him and just leave his hand?"

"I don't know. If they wanted him for information, it stands to reason they'd remove the com so we couldn't find him . . . but even for a vampire that's a serious wound."

"Would he bleed to death?"

"It depends." David unconsciously rubbed his own wrist. "It would be easy enough to reattach the hand; almost any vampire could do that in a few minutes, though it would take several hours to get all the feeling back. Without the hand . . . if it were me, I could stop the bleeding and force the wound to close, assuming I was conscious, in about twenty seconds. But if he had other injuries, or had been knocked out, or was hung upside down so gravity was working against him . . ."

"That's enough," Miranda said, covering her face with her hands. "I get it."

"We don't know for sure," David told her. "Let's not assume the worst until Faith reports back."

Even as he said it, though, Miranda knew what he was thinking, and she knew, in her gut, he was right. Jake might have survived the amputation, but they wouldn't find him alive.

"Poor Jake," Miranda repeated, wiping at her eyes. "I liked him."

David drew her head to his shoulder again and they spent the rest of the trip home in silence . . . but in her heart Miranda knew that whoever was behind this wouldn't stop with one murder . . .

This was only the beginning.

David was right about one thing: Jonathan was nothing like his Prime. In fact, Miranda adored the Consort the moment they met.

"Jonathan Burke," he said, taking Miranda's hand and

kissing it gallantly. "I'm so excited to finally meet the woman who got David's head out of his Mac."

Miranda smiled. "Once in a while, at least."

"Good God, David, you didn't tell us how beautiful she is," Jonathan added as he looked Miranda up and down with obvious appreciation that was neither lecherous nor invasive. "You're not nearly good enough for her."

Now Miranda laughed, as did David. "You're absolutely right," David replied. "But I was hoping she wouldn't figure that out for a few decades at least."

After the formal introductions they retired to the same study where David had taken Hart, although the Pair were given a suite of rooms closer to the Signet wing, in recognition of their relationship with the South.

Miranda walked alongside Jonathan, who was a good six inches taller than David and therefore almost a foot taller than both Miranda and Deven. He was built like a football player, broad-shouldered with formidable muscles, but he carried himself the way all Signet bearers did, with uncanny grace and comfort in his own skin. It would have been easy for him to be a lunkheaded lumbering giant, but he was good-natured and refreshingly open, with a cheerful British accent and sparkling hazel eyes under his unruly blond hair. He wasn't as stereotypically hot as many of the vampires she'd met, either; he was handsome, but in a rugged way, someone you wouldn't want to meet in a dark alley but would want on your side in a bar fight.

He was dressed in a suit and tie in a gorgeous dark purple, and Miranda had to return his compliment: "You're pretty damned impressive looking yourself, my Lord."

Jonathan paused and did a runway-esque turn in the hallway. "Thank you, my Lady. I'd like to take credit for this, but I have the fashion sense of a blind Amish ditch-digger. Deven dresses me on special occasions; otherwise I'm strictly a jeans-and-tees sort of fellow."

Deven glanced back over his shoulder at Jonathan, and the smile he gave his Consort was fond, even gentle. "You're just lazy," he said.

"I am, indeed, darling. But I also know when to let an expert take over."

They entered the study and took up two love seats, one Pair in each. The servants had already brought a bottle of whiskey, which Deven picked up and read, then smiled at David.

"You're learning," Deven said. "Macallan Fine and Rare Collection, forty years old. Not bad at all."

David snorted softly. "That's to keep you from complaining about my trailer park taste."

"Jack Daniel's is worse than trailer park," Deven said. "It's a date with your sister at the family reunion."

"You, my love, are a snob," Jonathan told his Prime with a smile. "I've seen you drunk on just about everything from Château Lafite to bathtub gin."

The men all drank whiskey, which Miranda hated; she poured a glass of Cabernet and sipped it, admiring the way the firelight caught the wine's jewel tones and made it look like blood-colored stained glass.

"I understand you had something of a row with Hart," Deven said. "Well done."

"That was Miranda's doing," David replied, taking her hand. "It's been a long time coming, but Cora, one of Hart's women, was the catalyst and Miranda the spark. After he murdered the other girls, any hope of amity between us was done for. The next Council gathering should be interesting."

"You've opened a bloody hornets' nest," Deven said, a bit sternly. "It's not wise to cross someone as unstable as Hart. This will come back to haunt you, I promise."

Miranda said coldly, "I'll gladly take that chance if it means saving Cora from that animal."

Deven looked at her over the rim of his glass. "That's because you're too young to know any better."

Her temper flared. "And would you have let him take her, Lord Prime? Knowing what she was going through and how she was going to die?"

Deven was unaffected by the edge in her voice. "In our

position we must consider the common good and not go courting wars because of our pet causes."

She knew her eyes were going silver, but she didn't care. "Perhaps you should consider the common good and not go courting wars to compensate for a cold heart or a small—"

"Miranda," David began, but Miranda held up a hand, and he fell silent. Meanwhile Jonathan was watching the whole exchange with a slight smile, glancing back and forth between the Queen and his Prime as though it were a highly entertaining tennis match.

Deven tilted his head again, set down his glass, and said, "Any fight between us, my Lady, will be short and unpleasant."

"Just like you," Miranda bit back.

Silence.

Then Deven laughed.

Miranda didn't, but she felt the tension in the air dispel and sat back with her wineglass.

"I like her," Deven told David. "She's bright and fearless, just like they say. Give her fifty years and she'll be a force of nature."

David gave Deven a look that made Miranda feel a lot better. "She's a force of nature right now, and I think you'd best keep that in mind, as well as the fact that regardless of our past relationship, I don't take kindly to anyone baiting my Queen."

Whatever words David had given her in the car, Miranda could sense now that things between him and Deven were far from resolved. There was anger there, steeped in the pain of betrayal.

"Jonathan," Miranda said, "how would you like a tour of our Haven while our Primes discuss whatever business they need to discuss? I'd love a chance to show you our home and get to know you better."

She pointedly ignored Deven as she spoke.

Jonathan grinned. "That would be lovely, my Lady. Shall we?"

He offered his arm, and Miranda smiled and took it,

leading the Consort out of the study and taking no little delight in closing the door firmly behind them.

"London?" Miranda asked.

Jonathan grinned, loosening his tie. "Good catch, my Lady. I was born and raised in Southwark, served the Queen for a good many years, then made my way across the Atlantic and, eventually, to the West, like so many settlers before me."

"How did you two meet?"

Jonathan clearly found that funny and chuckled as he flipped the caps off two of the beers from the six-pack they'd fetched on their way. He handed her a bottle and kept one for himself, and they clinked them together before taking a drink. "It was like something out of a bad romance novel," he said, leaning back against the chimney. "It was 1952—a big group of the Elite, and the Prime, were having an after-hours drink in a bar downtown, and I went to try to get a job with them. I was new in town; I figured I'd be on patrol duty for a few years and work my way up. I met David and Faith, who took me to meet the Prime, and the minute we shook hands, bam! His Signet lit up like Christmas. Five seconds later an assassin tried to take him down with a crossbow. I pushed Dev out of the way, took the hit, and woke up in his bed."

"You didn't know each other at all?"

"No. I didn't even know his name. But I knew I belonged with him." Jonathan smiled out over the roof at the woods surrounding the Haven. "Strange, really. I'd been with a hundred men over the years and they were all more like me—brawny and a bit on the brash side. Then here was this fragile-looking boy with his tattoos and scars, and I completely lost my mind."

"Scars?"

The Consort nodded. "Many. Inside and out."

"How old is Deven?"

"We don't know exactly, because there's no record of

his birth, but it was sometime in the early 1300s, in Ireland."

"He's seven hundred years old? Jesus!"

"One of the oldest living vampires on earth."

"And is he a dick to everyone, or am I just special?"

Another smile, another swig of his Shiner Bock. "Isn't it obvious, my Lady? He's jealous."

"Jealous? Why?"

They had gone to one of Miranda's favorite spots in the Haven, or rather, atop the Haven: a rooftop nook near the Signet suite that offered a sheltered place to watch the night go by. When she needed a minute alone she often sneaked off to the roof, and she was aware that David did the same thing, sometimes to this exact spot. It was quiet and the view was spectacular. From here she could see the pasture, where Isis and Osiris were currently grazing in slow circles, and the gardens she and David had walked through when she first came to live at the Haven.

Jonathan, whose long legs were dangling from the eaves, said, "They never really got any closure on their relationship," he said. "David ran away—rightly so—and Deven did his best to atone for being such a fool, but until a few months ago they hadn't even been in the same room. They put aside their feelings in order to keep their friendship, but it was never truly finished between them. And as long as David was on his own, things could stay that way. Now, you're here, and like it or not that chapter has closed for them. They're going to have to work it out somehow."

"Does that mean they still love each other?"

"Oh, undoubtedly." He saw Miranda's face and added quickly, "But you needn't worry."

"Are you kidding?"

"Listen to me, Miranda, and remember this, because it will save you a lot of heartache as the years go by." Jonathan sat forward, holding her gaze, his usually cheerful expression gone grave. "You are his soul mate. You are bound unto death and possibly longer than that. No one, and I mean this literally, *no one* can usurp your position in his life or heart. He will love you until the sun burns to dust. But that doesn't mean neither of you will ever love anyone else or want someone else. Forever is a long time, and even mortal relationships evolve—so must ours, if we are to survive."

Miranda sighed and picked at the label of her beer. "So you share Deven with other people?"

"Dev? Oh, hell no. He's not interested in extracurricular ass. He shares me."

"Seriously?" Miranda gave him an incredulous look. "I would think he'd be the one shagging every guy that moves."

Jonathan's smile returned, but she could feel something lurking beneath it that was all too familiar. "I won't go into the details of his past—that's for him to reveal. But I will say that when he and David first coupled, it had been over a hundred years since his last lover."

"Whoa. Really?"

"Yes. And our relationship isn't what you'd call passionate. Every Pair comes together to complete each other, and in our case, what he needed wasn't someone to have sex with, it was someone to love who would place no demands on him, just be a comfort and a companion who would never abandon him. We agreed early on that our sex life would be somewhat sporadic, and that if I felt the need for more, I was free to seek it out. It's a perfect arrangement for us." He laughed again at the look on her face. "As I said, forever is a long time. The 'in love' stage of a relationship is fleeting. What you need are partnership and companionship, a deeper and more abiding love that transcends the physical. Sometimes that's romantic and sexy, sometimes not. But over time you and David will find what works for you."

"No offense, Jonathan, but I find that kind of depressing."

He grinned. "No offense taken. I realize it sounds strange, especially since you probably spent your whole human life within the bounds of traditional human relationships. But we're not human . . . and the way we love isn't traditional. It can't be, when eternity is a factor. Not to mention, Dev . . . well, as I said, he has scars. And really, if he had it to do over again, he probably would have stayed out of Signet politics entirely and joined one of the Orders."

"Orders of . . ."

"Vampire monks," Jonathan explained. "Religious orders of immortals. There are several scattered around the world. Deven has connections with one of them, the Order of Eleusis—they're mystical metalworkers connected with the Eleusinian Mysteries of ancient Greece, and it's rumored they first forged the Signets themselves. Get Deven to show you his sword sometime; it was made by the Order, and it has their symbol, a waning crescent moon above the Greek symbol of infinity, worked into the blade's design."

Miranda had no idea what to think of that—it sounded so outlandish and unbelievable to think there were actual religions for vampires, although any race that had existed so long was bound to have its true believers. She wondered if David had looked into it, given how wildly curious he was about the origin of the Signet system. She'd have to mention it later.

"So, about Deven . . . what do I do when he gives me attitude?"

"Give it right back. Show him you've got balls and you're not going to back down, and he'll respect you. As soon as he feels like you're a match for David, he'll back off."

She raised an eyebrow at him. "Why are you so free with the advice? Why don't you give me the same grief he does?"

Jonathan snorted. "In case you haven't noticed, we're not the same person. I'm a Consort, which means I read people very well, so I knew you were fantastic from the get-go. Deven tends to reserve judgment. But the worst thing you can do is let him intimidate you."

"I hate to say this, and I hope it doesn't upset you, but right now I don't really care about his respect so much as I care about my foot planted on his ass."

The Consort broke into a loud and contagious laugh that had her laughing, too. "All right," he said. "You kick his ass, Miranda. He's earned it."

They clinked their bottles again and leaned back against the bricks to finish their beer as the cold night kept turning overhead.


Neither of them spoke for a while, but finally just to break the silence David observed, "You cut your hair off."

Deven lowered his glass. "Yes."

"How's being a roadie for the Cure working out for you?"

Deven shot him the finger, and they grinned at each other. "You're looking well," Deven noted. "Much better than last time I saw you." Crossing one knee over the other, he added, "Of course, now you have your lovely firebrand to keep you warm."

David's eyes narrowed. "Are you jealous, Deven?"

For once, Deven lowered his gaze first. "The Council is all atwitter about your break with the Northeast. I haven't heard much, but so far the gossip has been in your favor. Considering everyone hates Hart, it's not surprising, but still, the fallout is going to be interesting."

David didn't point out the change in subject. Deven had, without saying a word, answered the question. "I'm not going to lose sleep over Hart. Miranda's actions may have been rash, but they were right."

Deven smiled. "At long last you have a mate who shares your idealism. I hope that she doesn't become as cynical as I am once she's outlived her humanity."

"You're more human than you like to admit."

"There's no need to be insulting, David." Dev sipped his drink and added, "She has no reason to be threatened by me."

"Oh? After you show up and practically piss on me, when I hadn't even told her about us yet—"

"You hadn't *told* her?" Deven sounded genuinely incredulous, a rarity for him. "We were together ten years, I was your first and only long-term male lover, and you didn't tell her? What the hell have you two been talking about for the last three months, then? Horses and circuit boards?"

David had to admit that Deven was right, and saying that he'd expected Faith to have related the story to Miranda wasn't entirely honest . . . he had thought that, true, but knowing Miranda, if she *had* known, she would have wanted to talk about it with him as soon as she heard the story.

"I feel like a bit of an idiot about it," David said a little irritably. "I think part of me wanted to play it off like one of my many disastrous love affairs instead of what it really was."

Deven's eyes locked on his. "And what was it, David?"

David stared at him . . . God, he'd forgotten how good it felt to fall into those eyes, and how dangerous it was, for they went on forever and there was no way out. "It was a tragedy," David replied softly. "Perhaps the greatest tragedy of my life."

"Worse than Elizabeth?"

"Yes."

"Worse than Anna?"

David shut his eyes against the memory, stacking the pain of that loss against the pain of losing Deven . . . "Yes. You put me back together after Anna, but would you care to guess who put me back together after you?"

Deven sighed. "No one did. You were alone."

"Exactly. All those years on my own, living with your ghost, knowing you were happy with your new Consort and I had suddenly become useless to you, and you really wonder why I didn't want to tell Miranda about it?"

Deven looked like he wanted to say something, but paused, then told David, "You don't need to protect her from me. She's a strong, capable woman who can fend for herself."

"I know that."

"But she is young and needs to learn to pick her battles.

She could have found a less combative way to help that girl, and you could have had time to find out what Hart was really doing here."

"I did, actually, or at least part of it. He's having a little assassination problem—he claims the Red Shadow is behind the deaths of several of his Elite."

Deven's brows knitted in surprise. "Based on what?"

"He found something—a silver earpiece. I tried to analyze it but it had a self-destruct mechanism and nearly put my eye out last night. Hart claims it's Shadow technology, but he has only hunches and hearsay to back it up. He also thought I had something to do with it because of my predilection for gadgetry and because Miranda learned to fight from a vampire claiming to have been a former member of the Shadow."

Deven looked even more dubious. "They don't have former members, do they? I thought joining the Shadow was a lifelong commitment."

"Faith said she met Sophie in a bar, and they hit it off and got drunk together. In the course of the night Sophie told her she was ex-Shadow."

"I find that unlikely," said Deven. "The girl may have been a hell of a warrior, but if you were the Alpha, how would you react knowing one of your employees was spilling her guts in public?"

"There is that. I'm guessing that the Alpha would have killed her—but Sophie died in the battle here, months after she told Faith who she was."

"Not terribly efficient for an organization that's supposed to be untraceable," Deven pointed out.

"How much do you know about them, then?"

The Prime circled his glass around in his hand, the ice clinking. "I've heard all the usual rumors. All that can really be verified is that they're a network of operatives who hire out to human clients for insane amounts of money. They answer to a single individual called the Alpha. They always work alone, and I've heard none of them even know each other. Code names, that kind of thing, all very cloak-

and-dagger. I can't imagine why they would start picking off Hart's Elite, unless a human has a grudge against him and hired them, which I admit isn't impossible."

"Do you think that an earpiece like that is something they'd use?"

"If the stories are true and they're all solo, with whom would they be communicating?"

"The Alpha?"

"Maybe. But it seems like it would be more efficient to use phones or, perhaps, something like your coms. An earpiece is too easily lost."

"That's what I thought. Plus, they're supposed to be the ultra-Elite; one of them just dropping evidence like that is pretty sloppy."

"And completely out of line with their MO," Deven added. "As I understand it, most of their work is totally covert, but sometimes people hire them not just to kill someone but to send a message. In that case they always leave something behind, a calling card of sorts."

"Which is?"

Deven knocked back the rest of his whiskey and reached for the bottle. "The victim's left hand."

David dropped his glass.

# Seven

For the first time in her memory, Cora was alone.

She sprawled on her back on the huge soft bed that was miraculously all hers—not only did she not have to share it, she could sleep there as much as she wanted, roll around and disrupt the covers, even jump up and down if she liked. It had thick blankets and velvety sheets that kept her warm all day long, and it was about the most wondrous thing she had ever seen.

She could sleep all day without the fear that sweaty hands would seize her and drag her across the room. She didn't have to listen to the other girls wheezing and whimpering. There was no screaming, no cursing, only the sound of the fire crackling.

Wonders were hardly scarce here, though. She had an entire room to herself! There was a guard outside, but he didn't bother her except to knock on the door and bring her blood.

All the blood she wanted!

She drank so much the first time, just because she could, that she was sick to her stomach, but after that she took things slowly and carefully and managed to keep down more and more each time she fed. She kept the leftovers in a small refrigerator in the room, and warmed them in the microwave as the servants had shown her, but if she had wanted, she could have requested a brand-new bag every day. Every day! Just for her!

Even that next night she felt stronger. Her limbs no longer shook. She wasn't freezing all the time. Her skin felt less stretched over her bones.

She spent hours in the large bathtub, just soaking and splashing like a child, or standing under the scalding hot shower spray and scrubbing herself over and over with lavender-scented soap. Then she dressed herself in the nondescript but comfortable clothes the Elite had brought her: black cotton pants and a short-sleeved shirt which were apparently standard issue for sleeping and working out at the Haven. She had never worn pants before, but she loved them. She had plush socks on her feet and a hairbrush all her own.

It was an unbelievable amount of luxury for a woman who had spent so many years sharing a room with eight other women.

Those few people she had encountered so far seemed taken aback by her naïve appreciation for such commonalities, but for her they weren't common.

She had not yet seen the Queen again, which was fine by her; in person, the Queen had been terrifying, though she had swept in like an avenging angel—or goddess—and taken Cora in like her own fledgling. The Prime, too, had been frightening, but he had given her a reassuring smile and spoken to her in her own language, a courtesy she would never have expected for a nothing like her.

Cora had been spared a last meeting with the Master, but she knew he was gone, just as she had known there would be consequences even before she found out what had happened to the other girls. He might come back for her, or kill her. He might simply abandon her and find another slave. But for now, at least, she was at peace.

Finally she began to get a little bored, or at least a little interested in what lay beyond her door. She didn't want to interact with anyone if she could help it, but she was curious about this huge place that was, for the moment, her home.

She poked her head out and saw that her guard had gone; it was shift change, so another would be along in a few minutes. She knew they would be unhappy if she wandered too far afield. But surely it wouldn't hurt just to walk down the hall and back again? She wasn't strong enough to get much farther than that anyway.

Cora took the hooded jacket that had been given to her and put it on to keep the late autumn chill off her skinny arms. She had no shoes, but she didn't intend to go outside, and the floors here were so immaculate she could have eaten off them. Certainly the Haven she had lived in was never this clean. Here there was no dust, no underlying reek of unwashed bodies and sex. She smelled furniture polish, fireplace smoke, and candle wax.

She still had to move slowly. Years of starvation and abuse had left her weaker than a newborn barn cat, and sometimes her legs simply gave out beneath her and she toppled to the floor, bruised and embarrassed.

The hallway turned out not to be terribly interesting. It was lined with closed doors, but she spent some time looking at the artwork and decorative objects as she made her way along the corridor. She peeked into a few open doors, finding a few unused bedrooms, a chamber full of antique weapons, and a study of some sort.

Finally she took a left-hand turn down a hallway that had far more light than hers. She realized what it was: windows.

Almost giddy with excitement, Cora made her way toward them, and her breath caught when she looked out. She hadn't seen the outside world in so long . . . she had had glimpses when the van carrying her and the other three girls arrived here, but before that, it had been years. There were no windows in the harem room. The Master hated natural light, even from the moon, and didn't want to give them any ideas about escape or suicide, not that they could have if they had been so inclined.

She stared out, hand to her mouth.

It was so beautiful.

The hallway was on the second floor, looking out over a garden labyrinth and beyond it, a forest. The stars were burning in their diamond finery, and by the half-moon's light she could see deer picking at the outermost shrubs. The garden was full of night-blooming flowers, and though she didn't know their names, some were familiar, whispering to her of a long-lost life lived on grassy hillsides, punctuated with youthful laughter and the sound of cows lowing in the distance.

Cora stood there staring at the world, her mind whirling, her heart so full it hurt, for a long time. She watched owls swoop down from the trees to snatch small creatures from the grass. She watched a buck with gleaming silver antlers make his regal way along the edge of the wood. She watched the stars turn, and she wept with silent joy.

She was so absorbed in witnessing the night that she didn't hear footsteps, but she felt someone move up beside her.

She shrank back, turning, ready to run—or try to run, whatever her body would let her do.

"Don't be afraid," he said softly. "I won't hurt you."

Now, instead of staring at the window, she stared at him.

He was a young-looking, slender vampire, stranger than anything she had ever seen at the Master's Haven. He had an angelic face run through in several places with silver rings, and his hair was dark; he wore a short-sleeved shirt that showed tattoos covering both of his arms from wrist to shoulder. On one side was an angel with a sword; on the other, a winged demon holding a dove.

She saw the amulet around his neck, this one glowing faintly emerald green, and she swallowed hard around her fear, dropping painfully to her knees.

"Forgive me, Sire," she whispered.

"For what?" he asked curiously.

"I did not avert my eyes."

He made a disgusted noise and muttered something about a dickless bastard, then gently lifted her chin with his hand so their eyes met. "Never avert your eyes to anyone, Cora," he told her. He spoke nearly flawless Italian save for the lingering traces of some lilting accent. "Now, get up."

She obeyed, wiping her eyes.

He joined her at the window, looking out as she had. "This place is magnificent," he said, maintaining his distance but speaking to her casually. "I wish my own Haven had a tenth of its beauty."

Cora swallowed again and asked, haltingly, "Where do you live, my Lord?"

"California. I think you'd like it; our home reminds me a lot of Italy."

"How . . . how did you know my name?"

He smiled. "I heard all about you from Prime Solomon and his Queen. Your room is down the hall from ours."

"Your Queen is here with you?"

"My Consort," he corrected. "His name is Jonathan."

"Oh . . ." She suddenly knew who he was; she had heard the Master ranting about him, his deviant ways, his perversions . . . he had made him out to be some kind of twisted monster, not . . . like this. "You are Prime Deven."

"I am. It's a pleasure to meet you, Cora."

He took her hand and kissed it lightly, and she blushed. It was the most courtesy a man had ever shown her. She had been so afraid of the Prime of the South, but this Deven was different; she knew by instinct that he had no interest in doing the things to her that Hart had done, no interest in touching any woman out of rage or lust. It was comforting.

"My Master hates you," she said.

Deven chuckled. "I know. It gives me such pride, as does knowing I could tear his limbs off with one hand. He likes to think he's strong, but if he were half as powerful as he claims to be, he would have laid me low long ago. He knows he can't. And, Cora . . . he isn't your master now. You are a free woman, your own master."

Cora digested this for a moment, but it left her feeling

shaky in her stomach, panicky. "What am I to do?" she whispered.

"Nothing, for now," he told her. There was such caring in his eyes, which in the darkness glittered like amethysts. "For now, concentrate on becoming strong and healthy. The Pair will let you stay as long as you want to, no questions asked. You're safe under their care."

"Why is everyone here so kind to me?" she blurted, then felt her cheeks growing even more scarlet. "I'm no one. I don't matter to anybody."

Deven put his hand on her face, and she felt warmth and strength flowing into her body that helped her stand a little straighter and get her tears under control.

Standing there with his palm touching her skin, she felt something . . . something stirred in her, and an image flashed in her mind's eye: She saw a young man with deep violet eyes and auburn hair, standing at the edge of a wood with one hand on the trunk of a tree, smiling at her . . . no, not at her . . . at Deven. The image was gone as soon as it came, and she had no idea how to interpret it, or if it was in any way real.

"You matter," he said, startling her out of her mental tumble. "I assure you, you do. As to why . . . well, I can tell you that the Prime and Queen are both good people, very protective of those who cannot protect themselves. At heart that is why the Signets exist, but most of us have forgotten that. And, Cora . . . I don't have the level of sight that my Consort has, but I know one thing: You have work to do in this world. I know it."

She was shaken by what she had seen—and all the more by his words—but she had a feeling, deep in her belly, that she shouldn't speak of it. Not yet. "You do?"

He smiled again. "Yes, I do. Now . . . will you be able to find your room again, when you're ready to rest? It's just around this corner, five doors down on the right. And if you go another two doors and cross the hall, you'll find us. We'll be here a few days, so if you need anything, you need only come ask."

Sniffling, she nodded. "Thank you, Sire."

He stepped back and bowed. "Good night, young one."

Cora wiped her eyes one last time on the sleeve of her jacket, then turned back to the window, where she stayed until her legs could barely hold her up, then made her slow way back to her room, smiling.

"Wait, wait . . . you're telling me David had a boyfriend?"

Miranda nodded. "More like a husband, really. And he's a total jackass."

"Wow." Kat leaned back in her chair, watching Miranda wriggle into the black vinyl corset top, shaking her head in disbelief. "That's crazy. I mean, yeah, he's a little swishy, but—"

"You think David's swishy?" Miranda asked, pausing, a bit out of breath from trying to get the damn thing zipped. "I never noticed that."

"It's nothing in particular, just a . . . quality."

"Well, I had no idea. The whole thing completely caught me by surprise." Miranda pulled the top into place, then leaned over to wiggle her breasts into it properly. "Is it wrong that I feel weird about it?"

Kat made a face. "Mira, of *course* you feel weird. Think about it: In relationships we form concepts of people based on their behavior and what we know about their histories. Those concepts can be accurate or not, and they can be healthy or not, but regardless, if something shakes them, it shakes us, too. You knew David one way, and it turns out that way wasn't entirely on target, so now you have to adjust. Given how close you are, that makes it even harder."

Miranda faced her friend. "Well?"

Kat frowned, eyeing the outfit. "I liked the first one better—the red lace brings out your eyes, makes the green more intense."

Miranda wished for a moment that she could see herself; instead she was in a dressing room with a curtain pulled over the mirror and Kat there to critique her. She'd never really liked shopping, and she liked shopping for stage clothes even less. Luckily she trusted Kat's judgment. "You're right. Let me try the other one with these pants—if I can get the pants zipped. Jesus, Goth girls are skinny. At least I've got an ass."

"And a killer rack," Kat commented. "Especially in that getup."

Miranda ran her hands down over her torso to smooth the shirt, which wasn't a real corset; she couldn't wear a real one onstage and sing the way she did. There were also limits to the cleavage she could manage with a guitar hanging over her middle.

"I'll bet that there are much more disturbing things in David's past than a jerk boyfriend." Kat returned to the subject, handing her back the first top. "He's three hundred fifty years old, after all. And he probably didn't get where he is by being nice."

"No, he didn't." Miranda hadn't told Kat much about David's past, not even how he had gotten his Signet; she wasn't sure if Kat was ready for that. "He's been through a lot and done a lot."

"Well, if you can deal with all of that, you can deal with a little swish. It's not like it's a bad thing. Bi is the new hotness, you know."

Miranda rolled her eyes. "Only if it's two women in a porno movie for straight guys."

"And as for the ex being a jackass—if David still likes him, and his hubby is a great guy like you said and loves him, he must not be all bad. Maybe you should try to find some common ground. Besides David, I mean, because that could get weird."

Miranda smiled at her. "How did you get so damn wise?"

Kat snorted. "Wise would be if I hadn't gotten knocked up."

The Queen sat down on the changing room's bench, abandoning her quest for a moment. She'd been avoiding the subject for most of the evening because she knew Kat was tired of thinking about it every moment of every day, but now that Kat had brought it up, Miranda asked what she'd been wanting to since meeting Kat outside the shop: "What did Drew say?"

Kat shrugged. "He's overjoyed. He wants to get married."

Miranda could hear the ambivalence, and moreover she could feel it. "And you?"

"I don't know. I'm done panicking, so that's progress. And I'm glad I didn't go through with the abortion before Drew got back. But I still don't know what I'm going to do."

Miranda didn't say anything, though the desire to make Kat promise to keep the baby was so strong she had to bite her lip against the words. It must be part of her prescient gift, if it could be called a gift. She knew, she just *knew*, that Kat would have the baby, and that it would be a girl, and somehow . . . somehow that little girl would grow up to be very important to a lot of people. But she wasn't about to put pressure on Kat.

"I love kids," Kat went on. "But I've seen so many who were so screwed up, and seen how the world is so hard for them . . . how can I have a kid?"

Miranda took a deep breath, stood, and changed into the red-trimmed top, saying as casually as she could, "Maybe you're exactly the kind of person who *should* have kids, then. Someone who's been there and seen the best and worst of people. Someone educated, with common sense. You could give a kid a great home, with or without Drew."

"But am I ready for this?"

Miranda leaned over and did the boob shake again, settling into the outfit and testing it out to see if she could breathe. So far so good. "Is anyone?"

Kat leaned the chair back on two legs, sighing heavily. "Distract me, okay? Tell me more about your big gay husband." Miranda threw a hair scrunchie at her. Kat laughed, setting the chair back down. "Oh, come on. Is the guy at least hot?"

"Disgustingly," Miranda replied. "He's all Goth and leather."

"And he's really old and powerful?"

"Over seven hundred years old, and yeah. Apparently most regular vampires only live to about five hundred at the outside, so he's like a little fanged Yoda."

Kat gave her a playful grin. "Have you had any fantasies yet?"

"About what?"

"About the two of them getting it on."

"God, Kat! No!"

Kat laughed. "Which means yes. Admit it, Mira, it's a turn-on! Just picture them in bed—"

"Kat!" Miranda groaned, looking for something else to throw.

"Who do you think would be on top?" Kat pondered eagerly.

"Quit it!" Miranda tried to sound outraged, but she was laughing too hard, and said, "Okay, I'll give you this, seeing them kiss was kind of . . . sexy."

"They kissed? Was there tongue?"

This time Miranda threw a balled-up shirt at her. "Not that I saw. Now tell me what you think, so I can either buy this thing or get the hell out of here."

Kat looked her over again, then flashed her a thumbs-up. "Perfect. I dare anybody to be a jackass to you in that outfit."

"Thank God. I've had enough of this shopping crap for one night. Let me put my real clothes back on and we'll go for ice cream."

A few minutes later Miranda was mercifully back in her jeans, although she was wearing a lace-up black top with belled sleeves and her favorite big black boots. She'd spent long enough slobbing around in threadbare T-shirts back when she was crazy; comfort still came first, but she knew she looked good in slightly more . . . vampire-appropriate clothing.

She took the new outfit up to the counter, where the bored girl with the pierced upper lip and six pounds of white foundation looked up from her copy of *Catcher in the Rye*. "Can I help you?"

"Yes," Miranda said. "Do you have the pants in a size ten? These are a little snug."

The girl didn't roll her eyes, but Miranda knew she was doing it in her mind. Her tone was both bored and dismissive as she said, "Did you see any on the rack?"

Miranda's temper flared, and she looked into the girl's eyes and said, power and immortality both clear in her voice, "Go check in the back, please."

The girl went pale under her Urban Decay and stammered for a second before saying, "Yes, of course. Hold on just a sec."

Miranda shook her head and glanced at Kat, who was looking at her appraisingly. "You didn't even have to vamp-mojo her."

Miranda smiled. "How do you know?"

"I remember that tone of voice from the time I took you to the ER and you almost flattened that nurse. You were standing there in your panties and you might as well have had a crown on your head."

The clerk returned with a pair of pants guaranteed to fit the Queen, who handed over her Visa wordlessly.

"Aren't you going to check the price?" Kat asked.

Miranda shrugged. "I'm not worried about it. I have to wear this in front of an audience, so I don't mind spending more."

"Oh, right, I forgot, you're Miss Gotbucks von Rich-Ass now."

Miranda signed the charge slip and said, laughing, "That's Queen Gotbucks von Rich-Ass, thank you very much. Now come on—there's a double-scoop Mexican vanilla hot fudge sundae out there with my name on it."


David wasn't the kind of man to procrastinate, and he certainly wasn't one to avoid facing his problems—at least, not anymore. Once upon a time he had run as far and fast from Deven as he could, and only when there were several thousand miles between them could he breathe again.

He'd thought that all those miles and all those years had done what apologies could not. He'd thought that the past was past, and now that they both had Consorts and were presumably happy and settled in their reigns, it would be just like it had once been, when he had been Deven's student in the training ring and they had been friends outside it.

Denial, denial, denial.

Now here he was, in his bedroom pondering the sword in his hand—a sword that Deven himself had given David after he took the Southern Signet—growing progressively later and later for their appointment in the training room, and David Solomon, Prime of the Southern United States, was scared out of his mind.

It was all coming back now. The flash of Deven's smile, the softness of his mouth, the way he moved like a dancer and an assassin in one . . . the cold fire in his wide eyes that belied the molten passionate core of him, a core that had only ever laid itself open for one man . . . and that man was not Jonathan.

For ten years David and Deven had been inseparable. From the night they first fell into David's bed, stripping off each other's Elite uniforms and pressing needy, sharp canines into each other's flesh, they had been bound by blood and sex so tightly that neither of them knew their boundaries anymore.

Finally Prime Arrabicci had gotten wind of what was going on in his Elite and called the Second and his lieutenant into the Prime's office.

"I've heard some disturbing rumors regarding the two of you," Arrabicci had said tiredly, and David had known exactly who had been in here first, ranting and raving about the perverts in their midst. "Lieutenant Torvald has informed me that the two of you have been conducting some sort of horrible sexual relationship."

David and Deven had stood side by side in front of their Prime, and Deven had said, "Sir, Lieutenant Torvald is, as always, mistaken. David and I are not conducting some horrible sexual relationship. We are in fact conducting a fucking fantastic sexual relationship."

Arrabicci had groaned and put his head in his hands. "Do you two see the position you've put me in here? Aside from any concerns about the two of you doing . . . whatever you do, the fact is we have rules about senior Elite consorting with their juniors. I could have you both thrown out of here on your asses."

"But you won't, Sire," David had pointed out. "You've said yourself we have the best record in the Elite. To toss us out just because we sleep together—off duty, Sire—would be strategically unwise."

"Rules are rules, Lieutenant. Therefore I have no choice but to promote you."

David had paused, frowned. "I'm sorry, Sire?"

"You are hereby promoted to co-captain and will serve at Deven's side. You aren't to be granted any privileges or pay raises before a six-month probationary period, just to make it clear that I'm not rewarding deviant behavior—I want everyone to see you've earned your place at the top, David. And as for your . . . relationship . . ."

David had braced himself.

But all the Prime had said was, "Obviously it's affecting your fighting abilities in a positive and useful manner. You've both gone from the best damn warriors in my Elite to the best damn warriors I've ever seen. So whatever you two are doing to each other in bed, keep doing it . . . just don't let me hear about it."

"As you will it, Sire," they had both said together.

Then they had left the office and walked with utmost dignity back to Deven's quarters, where they proceeded to shag each other senseless for the entire rest of the night and the following day.

Deven had needed someone to bring him out of his darkness. David had needed someone who wouldn't die on him. At first it had been an ideal friendship, two very different lone wolves in search of a pack . . . but soon . . . a look began to linger; a touch seemed to happen of its own accord; and was there a softness in Deven's eyes when speaking of him? Neither had been looking for a lover, yet they had tripped and fallen headfirst in love like a pair of hormone-ridden teenagers.

They had spent ten years fighting gangs and making love. Their desire for each other thrived on combat. A victory in the streets meant they would be half naked and going at it in the car on the ride home. Their blood boiled and they tore into each other rabidly. David's entire world contracted to whichever bed they were in, the exquisite pleasure-pain of who was sucking or stroking whom, the sweetness of Deven's blood on his tongue.

And now, when things were so very different, his traitorous heart wanted to travel back in time, back before either of them knew the burden of a Signet, back when he had believed they had a future together.

*No. It's over with. You're friends now. Nothing more.*

It was understandable that seeing Dev again would cause old feelings, and old hurts, to bubble to the surface. The last time they'd seen each other, David had been lost in his grief for Miranda, so there was no time for any of that, only time for Deven to help bring him out of it, set him back on his feet, and leave him ready to go back to work. This time there were no such emotional distractions. Now, the Pair were here, and he was about to go to sparring practice as they had a thousand times, and either they would start airing some things out or their friendship was ultimately doomed.

Logical, yes . . . and about as appealing as a fireplace-poker lobotomy.

The bedroom door opened and Miranda walked in laden with several shopping bags and the expression of a woman who had just been victorious in an epic battle.

"Thank God that's over," she said breathlessly, dropping her plunder on her chair by the fireplace. "I'm set for a few months provided I don't acquire too much more muscle."

She came over and kissed him on the forehead. "Aren't

you supposed to be in the training room beating up our houseguest? Whoa . . . what's wrong, baby? You look like you've seen a ghost."

She knelt in front of him. He leaned his forehead against hers. "In a way, I have," he managed. "I don't suppose you would come with me?"

She looked into his eyes, and he didn't bother trying to hide his feelings. It would be pointless.

Miranda laid her hands on the blade he was holding, projecting calm support, though if he were her he would be a bit perturbed at finding his husband in such a twist over an ex. "Tell me what you're afraid of."

David tried to find words. "I don't want to upset you."

"All the more reason why you should," she said. "If there's something you think you can't tell me, it must be important. No secrets, remember? Although . . . I can guess."

"Can you?"

"Of course. I'm not blind, David."

He rested his head on her shoulder. "What should I do? Force a confrontation? Go on pretending nothing's wrong?"

"I don't think that would work," Miranda told him. "It's just going to keep getting in the way—and if you want to stay friends you're going to have to get it all out in the open and just deal with it head-on."

"I hope you're not worried that I'll . . ."

"I trust you, David. I know you wouldn't do anything to jeopardize our relationship. Besides, I can sense . . . it was really intense between you, but intensity has a way of burning to ash in the real world."

"I don't know," he murmured, tracing her upper lip with his thumb. "I think things with you and me get pretty intense sometimes."

She smiled, and her tongue flicked out to touch his skin, sending electricity between them. "True, but I have a few distinct advantages over Deven."

"What are those, beloved?"

"One: I have a vagina, which statistically you prefer.

Two: I'm prettier. Three: I'm not a total asshole." She stood, pulling him along with her. "Now, come on. No hiding, remember? You go and cross swords—and I mean that in a martial arts sense, thank you—and try to get some of this angst out of your system. I'm going to take a shower, and then Jonathan has asked to hear me play."

"Are you sure you won't come with me?" He tried not to sound plaintive.

"I'm sure. You're the Prime of the Southern United States, baby. You strike terror into the souls of lawbreakers and tremors into the thighs of your Queen. There's nothing in your heart that you need to fear."

He smiled at her, kissed her, then said, "I am the luckiest bastard on this earth to have found you."

Miranda nodded. "I know."

Then she handed him his sword and ushered him out the door.

Gossip traveled with vampiric speed in the Haven, and by the time David reached the training room a sizable crowd of off-duty Elite, including Faith, had gathered to watch him go up against the Prime of the West.

Deven was already there, punctual as always, and David wished that Miranda had come—not because of his dread of the whole thing, but because she would have loved to see Deven out of his rock star apparel. Dev wore the same sort of black workout clothes as anyone else who practiced in the training ring; even without all the leather, though, he was still an impressive sight, as the shirt he wore revealed the full-sleeve tattoos he'd had as long as David had known him.

"You're late," Deven observed mildly.

"Prime's prerogative," David answered, shucking his coat and shifting his sword from its concealed sheath to one at his belt. Underneath the coat he, too, was dressed to fight. He gestured at Deven's tattoos. "Did you get the angel touched up?"

Deven glanced down at his right arm. "The color was

fading in places. Ironically the other side hasn't changed at all."

David smiled. "I don't find that particularly ironic, Sire."

Dev flashed him a blinding grin. "Ready to have your ass whipped?"

"Not in front of all these people," David fired back with an arched eyebrow. It was easy, so easy, to slip back into the mildly flirtatious banter that had been a hallmark of their early years. It even felt good—but sex had complicated everything. It always did.

"You realize of course that you can't possibly beat me," Deven said, drawing his sword. The blade caught the light perfectly, and Deven raised it, then bowed, something he'd learned during his time in Japan when, legend had it, he'd studied with the samurai.

"You may be surprised," David said, echoing the salute.

They circled slowly around each other for a moment . . . and then dove in.

David had no intention of losing easily, even though Deven was right—the Prime of the West had a number of advantages in this fight, even aside from his age and experience. Deven had two psychic talents, neither of which were terribly common: He had been born with healing ability, which differed from what Pairs shared in that he could use it on anyone, even humans; and he had a strange combination of telepathy and low-grade prescience that, coupled with his strength and agility, enabled him to anticipate an opponent's moves. He had taught the technique to a few people, including David, but without the psychic gift itself there was a limit to how much one could learn.

David was not prescient—Miranda was, as Queen, but her talent was still new and undeveloped. If she were ever able to harness it, she might learn to power-dance the way Deven could. David, however, had to make do with his inhuman speed and grace.

The sound of sword against sword was sharp and rhythmic, the two Primes spinning around each other like twin stars, the training room's simulated moonlight catching the steel with every slice through the air. With his Elite watching, David refused to embarrass himself; he threw everything into the match, letting his awareness of the room slip . . . then his awareness of himself.

Power flowed through him, liquid silver flame like the blade. He drank it in and poured it into his body. He could feel himself starting to tire, but he reached for more energy along the connection to Miranda.

Deven was clearly surprised at how much he had improved since they'd last fought, but he didn't miss a strike, moving so fast he would be practically invisible to a human and a blur even to the gathered Elite. David had been his apprentice for years and knew his style as well as anyone could.

The room disappeared. David felt something in himself fly open, and he blinked. Suddenly, his vision seemed to double, but the two images were different—in one, Deven was in front of him, and in the other he was a scant inch to the right . . .

David realized what he was seeing just in time to counter the move and, when Deven swung his sword around toward David's throat, David was no longer there.

The Prime's shock was obvious, but it didn't distract him long. Gradually they fell into a perfect rhythm, each knowing the other's actions a split second in advance, neither able to gain the advantage. It was as if they were fighting with themselves.

At exactly the same moment, they both spun away from each other and stopped.

Prime and Prime, both wide-eyed and breathing hard, stared at each other.

They continued to stare at each other as the crowd burst into applause.

# Eight

The worst part about unplanned pregnancy was that until she made up her mind what to do, Kat couldn't even get wasted and forget about it.

She couldn't think about anything else. Sitting at her desk, wrangling funding for the new family shelter, she pictured herself as one of the battered women escaping domestic hell with a baby in tow. Talking to a teenage runaway—a pregnant one, of course—about her options, she was weighing those same options herself. Giving a talk on birth control to inner-city kids, passing out condoms and info sheets on local clinics that provided low-cost contraceptives, she felt like an utter hypocrite. Here she was, with enough money and education to know where babies came from and keep them from happening, and she was no better off than the girls whose eyes were filled with fear of parents, peers, and the wrath of God.

Kat glanced up at the clock, then shut down her computer and put her head in her hands. She wasn't being fair. She was way better off than those girls—she had a stable home, a caring boyfriend, and the money to either keep or abort. She wasn't hamstrung by supposedly celibate male clergy claiming to understand a young woman's problems.

She was lucky.

If she decided to keep the baby, it wouldn't be because of

religious guilt or cultural pressure; it would be because she wanted to raise a child, to be a mother.

*Mother.* She had thought that *Queen* was the most intimidating noun she'd ever come up against. Drew could be a great father, and would, if she'd give him the chance . . . but could she be a mother?

Drew seemed to think so. He already had stars in his eyes over the idea of them as a little family. Drew played five instruments and painted in his spare time; he was a music teacher and fabulous with kids. They were both bilingual and college educated. Kat had studied child psychology and development during her undergrad. They both had a lot to offer a child . . . even Miranda, who had the maternal instinct of a doorknob, had made noises that she thought having the baby was the right thing to do.

Kat's inner rebellious teenager balked at the feeling that it had been decided for her, but she had to admit that bit by bit the idea was scaring her less and less.

She ran her hand over her head; it was getting stubbly and needed another pass with the razor. She'd have to do that tonight when she got home. Five o'clock shadow on your head was kind of ridiculous looking.

Kat was the last one to leave the office most nights. Sometimes she was stuck doing paperwork, and sometimes the clients who came to see her could make it only after regular office hours. She didn't mind. She'd known when she left college that the reality of social work was gritty and thankless.

But today she had helped a fifteen-year-old decide to put her baby up for adoption and move into the shelter while her boyfriend was in jail. They'd lined up classes for her to get her GED and go to trade school after the birth. The girl had cried and hugged her, thanking her in two languages; the hardest thing was always that feeling of drowning, without anyone to help. Kat's job was to throw the rope out and pull kids to the boat. Then she got to watch the best part: the drowning victim, armed with resources and with advocates on her side, saving herself.

Gritty, thankless, and worth every minute.

She switched off the lights and locked the office, then headed to her car, keys in her hand. East Austin at night could be hazardous for a lone woman, even if that woman was bald and tattooed and carried a gun. Austin was a relatively safe city—it beat the hell out of Houston, Dallas, and El Paso—but bad things still happened. She was up to her eyeballs in the aftermath of those things every day.

Unbidden, the thought of Miranda arose. Yes, bad things had happened to Miranda . . . and Kat hadn't even known until months later. She still ached thinking about Miranda dealing with it all by herself, out there in the middle of nowhere surrounded by all those . . . people. It was a miracle she had come through it with any semblance of sanity, which Kat grudgingly admitted was at least partly David's doing.

Damn it, she was starting to like him. She really didn't want to.

She looked around as she walked, staying alert, but also wondering: Were any vampires nearby? The whole city was teeming with them, apparently, which was part of why Austin was safer than other Texas cities . . . ironic. There were fewer unexplained murders because the vampires here weren't allowed to kill people. The Elite were under orders to intervene in human crime when they saw it, too, and although David had Elite outposts in all the cities and towns of his territory that had vampire populations of a certain density, it was safest to live in a Haven city, both for vampires themselves and for their human prey.

Not every Signet was so kindly disposed toward humans, though. Miranda had made that clear talking about that douchebag Hart and David's ex-boyfriend—boyfriend!—Deven.

They could be watching her right now.

Suddenly nervous, Kat picked up her pace. Her car was a block from the building; parking was at a premium down here, and always an adventure.

It was a cold, clear night, and a few brave stars even peeked through the urban haze overhead. The temperature had dropped early this year, which was fine by most people who lived in Austin. Texas was pure hell in the summer and dreary in the winter, but spring and fall were gorgeous, with sunny days and brilliant blue skies . . .

. . . blue skies that her best friend could never see again . . .

Kat sighed as she walked. Her breath came out in a cloud. She had to stop worrying about Mira; she could take care of herself, obviously. Still, it was such a violent transition into such a violent world. Kat couldn't imagine dealing with it. It was hard enough to deal with one step removed.

She snorted to herself. She would much rather think about vampires than being pregnant. Awesome.

As she reached her car, she saw a shadow move across the lot and frowned, staring at it hard. It could have been anything, anyone; it was far enough away not to be a threat.

Right?

Kat unlocked the car and cast an anxious glance around her, her heart suddenly in her throat. Some instinct she couldn't name made her slide her hand into the flap of her purse and close around the grip of her gun.

Was something over there? Had she imagined it?

The hair on the back of her neck stood up, and she broke out in gooseflesh. She should have worn a hat and scarf, this weather was bad for her scalp . . .

Were those footsteps?

Kat took a quick look in her backseat, then all but scrambled into the car and locked it, panting.

There . . .

She stared into the darkness, her eyes picking out the silhouette of a figure in the alley beyond the parking lot. It looked like a woman . . . a woman who was watching her.

Kat's stomach churned with acid as she got a feeling . . . barely restrained menace, even hatred, aimed at her, an oily black desire to drain the life from her, leave her bleeding on the street . . .

Kat jammed her key in the ignition and started the car, at the same time groping for her cell phone—should she call 911, or Drew, or Miranda? Was it a vampire or a mugger? Could the cops do anything if it was a vampire?

But when she looked up, the woman was gone.

Relieved, somewhat, Kat threw the car into reverse and pulled out of her spot, not caring one bit that she squealed her tires around the corner as she floored the gas pedal and headed home.

Miranda did not react well.

"I want her under surveillance twenty-four/seven, and under guard from dusk till dawn. Why the hell isn't the sensor network catching this bitch?"

Kat, who was curled up on her couch drinking a cup of chamomile tea, shook her head. "I don't want to be watched all the time, Mira."

"Too damn bad," the Queen snapped. "If she's after you, it's because you know me, and I'm not going to get you killed."

"Miranda," David said evenly, "Kat's safe for now. That's what matters."

Miranda shot him a distinctly uncalm look. "But what about tomorrow night? And after that?"

"No surveillance," Kat said firmly. "I'm serious."

Kat had to hand it to David; the Prime had listened to Kat's story without interrupting and was considering it from all sides without reacting emotionally. He practically oozed confidence and security, and he neither coddled nor silenced Miranda but tried to calm her down without discounting her fears. He was either a born leader or a master manipulator; the two weren't mutually exclusive.

It was weird having him in her house, though. It reminded Kat of the night he had shown up on Miranda's doorstep while Kat and Drew were there and swept into the room like Death popping in for a game of chess.

As if summoned by the memory, there was the sound of a key turning in the front door lock, and while Miranda spun toward the entrance with her hand already seeking beneath her coat for a weapon, David reached out and touched his Queen's arm, shaking his head.

Drew burst into the house in a flurry of coat and brief-case and clarinet case, all of which he dropped by the door so he could be at Kat's side in a heartbeat. "Are you okay?"

Kat smiled and took his hand. "I'm fine, honey, I told you I was."

It wasn't until she glanced up at Miranda that Drew seemed to realize they had company. He looked up at the Pair and went just a little pale before taking a breath and saying, "All right, what are we going to do to make sure this doesn't happen again?"

David regarded Drew much the same way he had the first time they'd met, as if he were some sort of curious creature in a zoo, but when Drew didn't avert his eyes, the Prime gave a measured nod. "You will do nothing," David said firmly. "There's no need to risk your own life."

"Bullshit," Drew countered, and Kat felt a little tug at her heartstrings at the way he refused to be cowed by a being who could quite obviously snap him in half like a twig.

David raised an eyebrow, and Drew just glared at him. Kat found herself smiling.

"Here's the thing, Drew," David said. "It's entirely likely that whoever was watching Kat was, in fact, one of our kind. If that's the case, there's nothing you can do to pro-tect Kat. Even the weakest vampire could tear you apart before you could draw a gun . . . assuming you're armed, like Kat, and have impeccable aim. Even then, bullets can-not kill a vampire. They only piss us off."

"So how do we kill a vampire? Wooden stakes?"

Miranda snorted quietly. "Drew . . . you don't. Unless you have specialized weaponry or arm muscles like a wrestler, you wouldn't be able to get a stake through the sternum into the heart. You're not a vampire hunter. Giving you weapons you can't use would be stupid. It's better to concentrate on staying alert and keeping in contact with us until this all blows over. You have to use the resources you have—like your brain. You can watch and listen and remain aware of your surroundings at all times. Leave the killing to us."

Drew took a deep breath, weighing his protective instinct with what Kat knew was the truth. David and Miranda were both right; if they were dealing with vampires, vampires were their best shot at staying alive. "Okay. What can *you* do, then?"

David returned his attention to Kat. "During the day you're typically surrounded by people, yes?"

Kat nodded. "Even on weekends. The office itself has security and cameras, but the parking lots don't."

He said, reasonably, "We can't be absolutely sure yet that we're looking at a vampire, but regardless, it's unlikely you'll be attacked during daylight in a public place, so there's no real need for daytime surveillance. I would like to put a night guard on you, however, until we figure out whom exactly we're dealing with. Just one, at a distance, strictly non-interfering."

Kat started to protest that it sounded like surveillance to her, but for some reason she didn't want to disagree with David. He seemed like he'd be hard to argue with. "Okay. But it's only temporary."

"Absolutely." David reached into his coat pocket. "May I have a look at your phone, please?"

Nonplussed, Kat handed it to him. He had pulled out his own, and he fiddled with the settings on hers for a second before taking a thin cable and connecting it to both phones.

"What are you doing?" Kat asked.

David ignored her, absorbed in his work. Meanwhile Miranda was pacing up and down the living room, making Kat faintly seasick, and Drew was squeezing her hand so tightly she was starting to lose feeling.

She looked at him. "Honey, you're cutting off my circulation."

Sheepish, he let go, nervously wiping his hands on his jeans. "Sorry. I just don't like feeling so helpless."

"It was probably nothing," Kat ventured, but she didn't believe it and neither did they.

"Whoever it was didn't show up on our network," David said without looking up. "That means it was either a human, which is easily dealt with, or the assassin who came after Miranda . . . and that's a much thornier issue. We can't track her and we don't know why, but she's already made an attempt on Miranda's life."

"Seriously, though, why me?" Kat asked. "I get that I'm connected to Mira, but if this chick has already been after her, why come after me? I'm not standing between them. I'm not a threat."

Now David looked at her. "Do you really want to hear my theory? I doubt it will make you feel better."

Kat pursed her lips. "Don't sugarcoat it, Count. Just tell me."

"I would guess that this isn't about killing Miranda . . . or, not *just* about that. There may be a personal feud involved. Someone who wants to hurt Miranda, not just kill her. The best way to do that is to start with her friends, particularly the human ones who are weak and vulnerable."

David saw their faces, gave a one-shouldered shrug, and unclipped the cable from the two phones. "As I said, it's just a theory."

He handed Kat her phone back. "Your signal is now coded onto our network," he told her. "Keep the phone on you at all times, and we'll be able to find you anywhere in the city at a second's notice. More important: I've set up a panic button. Hit star-one and it will trigger an alarm; a patrol unit will be sent to your location immediately and you'll get a call from me within thirty seconds to check on your safety."

"Wow," Drew said, sounding reluctantly impressed. "You did all of that in less than two minutes?"

David smiled. "Didn't Miranda tell you? I'm a genius."

"You didn't tell her the whole truth," Miranda pointed out as they left Kat's house and walked up the street to where the car was waiting.

"She doesn't need to know the whole truth." David looked at her sharply. "She already knows way more than she should about us."

"But her life is in danger."

"Irrelevant." He put his hands in his coat pockets as he walked, and added, "The whole truth isn't always the best truth."

"What about Jake?" she asked. "We still haven't found his body. I find it hard to believe that it's not connected—what are the chances of someone kidnapping my bodyguard right after someone tries to kill me, and then someone else making fang-eyes at my best friend?"

"Remote," he admitted. "I'm almost certain the same person or people are behind it . . . and, if what Deven said holds true, it may in fact be connected to the Red Shadow, and possibly even to Hart. But we don't *know*, Miranda. We have no real evidence to bind it all together yet. And the more Kat and Drew know, the more danger they're in."

Just then, his phone rang. Miranda stopped, her first worry that it was Kat's panic button, but David didn't look concerned; he merely said, "Yes?"

Miranda could hear the murmur of a male voice.

"Chief Brady, it's good to hear from you," David said. "To what do I owe this honor?"

She watched his face go from neutral to ever so slightly confused, then angry, then back to neutral again. Her heart sank.

"We'll be right there," he said, and hung up.

"What is it?" she asked, but David was already speaking into his com.

"Star-three."

*"Yes, Sire?"* Faith piped up.

"We have an Alpha Seven at 4109 North Grafton, apartment 28. The Queen and I are en route; send a team."

*"As you will it, Sire."*

Alpha Seven . . . a human murdered by a vampire. She hadn't heard that code since the war . . . but usually APD contacted Faith for suspected Shadow World crime, and for the chief himself to call . . . it had to be serious. "What's going on?" she demanded.

David met her eyes. "Denise."

The sun was well up, the Haven was silent, and Miranda was still sitting in her chair staring into the fire.

David had tried to ease her guilt and coax her into bed, but she refused; she just needed time to sit with what she was feeling. He had nodded, kissed her cheek, and let her be.

Denise MacNeil had been missing for about twenty-four hours; she hadn't shown up at the office, and by midafternoon her secretary was worried. Calls had gone out and Denise's landlady had finally agreed to check on her. The door was locked from the inside. The police had to break it down.

Dried blood was splattered all over the immaculate kitchen counters, soaked into the living room carpet and the sofa. Assuming it all came from Denise, it added up to fatal blood loss.

There had been a struggle: lamps knocked over, several things broken. The stereo was still playing, the same three CDs repeating over and over. There was a glass of wine undisturbed on the side table and a folder of redlined contracts still lying open on the couch.

All that remained of Denise was her left hand.

The police had called David because they knew Denise was Miranda's agent and there might be a connection. So far the police had no leads.

The Haven had one.

The Elite team had taken samples from the scene, and they would be sent to Dr. Novotny for further testing. It was still too soon for the results on Jake, but Miranda hoped fervently there would be something, any clue, no matter how tiny, to link the two to the assassin who had called herself Stacey. That woman was the only possible suspect they had.

Miranda sat by the fire until almost nine in the morning, her heart heavy. First Jake, now Denise . . . was Kat next? It looked like she was already staked out as a possible target. Yes, she was under guard, but Miranda had been under Haven guard once, too, and Ariana Blackthorn had killed her in the middle of the city and dumped her body in the lake. Were they going to find Kat's left hand next? And whose after that?

Leaving the hand, Deven had said, was the Red Shadow's way of leaving a message. But if it was the Shadow, for whom were they working? Who could possibly hate Miranda enough to go to this much trouble?

It could be a remnant of the Blackthorn . . . or it could be Hart . . . but the Shadow didn't work for vampires, and they commanded huge sums for their services. Hart could pull it off, but none of the Blackthorn or their cronies had been very wealthy. Then again, what human would want to hurt her this way? She barely knew any other humans *before* she had come to the Haven; who would be after her now? It made no sense.

Too restless and anxious to sit still anymore, she got up off the chair and left the suite.

She glanced over at the bed to see David deep in slumber, and she smiled in spite of herself. He was sleeping in the same position they tended to end up in, except that his arm was stretched over an empty expanse of blankets when it should have been around her body. For the first couple of weeks she'd had trouble sleeping with anyone so close to her, but she had already come to depend on his presence at her back.

Emergency tunnels connected the main house to the other buildings, so if she really wanted to, she could go work out; she could also go to the library, or pound her stress into the piano or her guitar strings. None of those options sounded appealing, for once, but there was something that did.

There was a study right between their wing and the guest wing, where David and Tanaka had held informal

chats; it wasn't her favorite room, being far more mascu-
line in décor than she preferred, but she happened to know
it had the most well-stocked liquor cabinet in the Haven as
well as a fridge that hopefully still housed some of David's
ice cream stash.

She nodded to the hallway guard as she passed, then
opened the study door.

To her dismay she found she wasn't alone.

"Oh, it's you," she said.

Prime Deven sat with his feet up on a dark leather chair,
one hand around a half-empty bottle of whiskey. He looked
about as thrilled to see her as she was to see him.

He said something in what she guessed was Gaelic.

"Come again?"

With a slightly lazy smile, he translated, "The flame
enters and casts all the world 'round her into shade."

"Are you drunk?"

He shrugged. "I'm Irish," he said. "I've spent most of
the last millennium drunk."

"You have an accent when you're drunk," she observed.

"I have an accent all the time," he replied. "It hides its
head in shame when I'm sober."

Miranda had to smile at that, as well as at the marked
contrast in his appearance and demeanor to all their
other meetings. He was dressed casually in old jeans and a
T-shirt advertising the Vatican gift shop; barefoot, his
hair damp from a recent washing and therefore not glamor-
ously spiked, without any makeup on, he looked . . . almost
normal.

She found she was fascinated by the tattoos, though,
and tried not to stare as she entered the room, closed the
door, and headed over to the cabinet to fetch a bottle of her
own, this one of rum. She also grabbed a bottle of Coke
and a glass of ice.

"Are you religious?" she asked as she set her wares on the
coffee table and flopped down on the couch opposite his.

Deven rolled his eyes. "I'm far too old to believe in fairy
tales."

She indicated his arms with the neck of the bottle. "What are those about, then?"

He laid one hand on his shoulder and absently ran his fingers along the line of the angel's wing. She noticed, looking more closely, that the feathers had been designed to run parallel to a series of long scars in his upper arm; the scars were almost invisible with the angel carved over them.

"It's a giant Catholic yin-yang," Deven replied, closing his eyes blearily. He seemed so tired; was it a function of being seven hundred years old, or something else? What kept one of the world's oldest vampires awake all morning?

Miranda poured rum halfway up her glass, then topped it off with a splash of Coke and took a long swallow, making a face at the taste. "And the scars? Are they from a giant Catholic lion attack?"

He took another hit off the whiskey but didn't seem affected by the bite of the alcohol. She suspected the bottle had been full when he started. "A whip," he answered. "You should see my back."

"Who whipped you?"

"The abbot."

"Why?"

He opened his eyes and fixed her with a stare. "He caught me in bed with one of the other novices."

Miranda wasn't sure how to respond to that. "So you were a monk?"

"Until the day I died." He drank again, then again, before saying, "I was the fourth son of a farmer in southern Ireland. I was a weak little thing, far too frail to work the fields. So when I was eleven years old my father sent me to my uncle, who ran a monastery. I was basically a tithe to bribe the Almighty for a better harvest."

"That must have been hard for you, to leave home so young," she said.

"On the contrary, that journey was the first time I ever remember looking forward to anything. I loved God. I was born to be a monk. I had no desire for a wife or family or land of my own. I longed only for silence around me and the light of God within. I spent hours in prayer, on my knees at my bedside. I hated the farm, my rough rowdy brothers, and the drudgery of our lives. I wanted to devote my life to Christ and to the written word—monks back then were some of the only scholars."

"But when you got there . . ."

"It didn't take long for my uncle to suspect there was something abnormal about me," Deven said. There was strangely little emotion in his words; even for something so long ago she would have expected a little anger, or sorrow, but it almost sounded as though he were telling someone else's story. "I know now that he started the monastery after being driven out of his old one for accusations of pedophilia. He was obsessed with purity and chastity, and to sublimate his own sexual urges he tried to beat mine out of me. He decided it was his mission to make me fit to stand before God. He forced me to pray for twelve to twenty hours at a time, on my knees, even after I had lost my voice; I was only allowed to eat every few days; I had to recite Leviticus while he tore open my back with the whip. Between broken bones, infection, and starvation I came close to dying more times than I can count . . . but I was so afraid of the damnation I faced that I dragged myself back to life every time."

"I'm sorry," Miranda said softly.

"I don't want your pity, Queen," he snapped. "Don't think that we have some common bond because men treated us both like trash."

"I don't think that," Miranda said, her own anger flashing at him. "We're nothing alike. What happened to me didn't turn me into a drunken prick who tries to get in his old boyfriend's pants after fucking him over. Trust me, I don't want to claim any common ground with you."

"If I wanted David, I'd take him," Deven informed her venomously.

"What the hell is wrong with you?" she demanded. "You

have a fantastic Consort who for some reason I can't figure out loves the hell out of you, and you're fixated on a married ex who doesn't want you anymore? Who are you trying to hurt—me? David? Or yourself?" Miranda sat up straight and leveled a look of loathing on the Prime. "You missed your chance, Deven," she snarled. "You blew it. It's over now. You drove him away, now he's with me, and I'm not going anywhere. So get the fuck over it."

The ire seemed to drain out of Deven as quickly as it had come.

Silence sat awkwardly, and drunkenly, between them while she finished her drink and poured another. The Prime didn't react to her outburst at all for a while.

Finally he said, "You can hate me all you want, but I'm not going anywhere either."

"Yeah, I know."

"I suppose for David's sake we should try to get along."

"Probably." Another pause. Then she asked, "What do you think is happening to David and me?"

"What makes you think I would know?"

Now it was her turn to roll her eyes. "Oh, come on. Even David thinks you know everything. You can't tell me that in all the years you've been around, you've never heard of psychic gifts being contagious."

"As a matter of fact, I haven't," he said.

"I picked up on his telekinesis, and he picked up on your fighting mojo. How could that happen?"

Deven leaned over the arm of the couch and felt around for a moment before coming up with a second bottle of whiskey, this one new. As he opened it, he corrected her. "He didn't get it from me; he got it from you."

"But I don't have it."

"You've got precog because you're a Queen," he said. "It's still untrained, and so is his. The telekinesis you got from him was already honed and focused—it took him years to learn how to direct it enough to throw a living thing. What I have isn't a single gift, it's a combination of three factors: prescience, telepathy, and technique. I taught him the third, he already had the second, and from you he got the first. His work was still a little sloppy around the edges, but once he got out of his own way, it was genuinely powerful."

"Why is it harder to throw living things?"

Deven shrugged. "They wiggle?"

"Sophie showed me how to do something similar to that," Miranda recalled. "I wonder where she learned it from."

"No idea. But the thing to remember is you've had precog your whole life—it's part of who you are. It just didn't start to actively manifest until you became Queen. It's practically unheard of for someone to just spontaneously develop a psychic talent without at least some latent ability . . . and even less heard of to start manifesting someone else's."

"Still, the central question isn't answered. How did it happen?"

"I would venture to guess that the answer is somewhere in our history. Legend has it that back in the ancient days, when the Signets were new, we had abilities we can only dream of, abilities we lost somewhere along the way. We are a mere echo of what we once were."

Miranda held her glass tightly. "But some of it is still possible."

"Most likely all of it is, if you know where to find it. As to that, I'm as clueless as anyone. I didn't become Prime for mystical powers . . . actually I didn't do it on purpose at all, so I was never all that interested in some grand destiny."

She crunched a half-melted piece of ice in her teeth. "Did you mean it when you said you don't believe in God anymore?"

He crossed his arms and leaned back. "I went to live in the house of God and spent six years tormented by his holy representative. I prayed and prayed for deliverance, and all I got were broken fingers and lye burns, because God didn't care to save a wretched little sodomite like me. I learned I was hellspawn because of the things I could do, and the only atonement was to let my uncle abuse my body in the name of Christ our Lord. After that I lived for seven centuries, Miranda, and spent much of that looking for some sign, anything, to bring back my faith. I tried. I traveled the world searching. And do you know what I saw?"

"What?" she asked softly, unsure how to deal with his sudden, complete honesty.

"I saw men raping women and children. I saw men killing each other in God's name. I saw greed and poverty and despair and murder of every conceivable kind. I learned that the loving Father I had yearned for wanted me to burn in hell because I fell in love with the wrong kind of person. I saw mass murder, terrorism, genocide, oppression, and repression, and all of it, all of it, was dedicated to a God who seemed neither to notice nor care. So you tell me, Miranda. What should I believe?"

Miranda had tears in her eyes. She couldn't help it, thinking of all that had been done to an innocent child, and all that seemed to still be happening to him, in his memory, seven hundred years later. She could feel, even through his words, the pain that it caused him to feel betrayed by the belief system that had been his reason for living, once upon a time. "But you don't have to be Catholic," she said. "You don't have to define God by what his fan clubs do."

Deven smiled, and again her heart hurt for him. "It's too late for me, Miranda. Some doors, once closed, can never be opened again."

"What . . . what things could you do, that the monks condemned you for?"

As if beaten down by the irony of it, Deven's voice was stony and dull. "I'm a healer," he said. "I've cured the plague. I've reattached limbs. I've brought mortals and immortals both back from the very edge of death."

"That sounds like the kind of gift God would love," she said.

"God, perhaps. At least I like to think so. Man? Never. To men, God is a weapon. A stick to beat the souls of others into submission. A blade to stab and bleed anyone with power of her own. If there is a God, he has abandoned us all to fear and eventual despair. But in the end, what does it matter to us? Nowhere is it written that heaven would open its doors to a vampire."

He met Miranda's eyes. "We're alone, Miranda. Our kind have no savior, no paradise to look forward to. Some of us do evil, so perhaps they'll go to hell, but for those of us who don't . . . we're no less damned. But perhaps our damnation is worse, for all I can see ahead is nothingness. No God, no devil, nothing. Just an eternity wandering the outer darkness."

"Wow," Miranda said. "I think you may be the most pessimistic person I've ever met."

"Thank you."

"But you're wrong," she told him. "We're not alone. We have each other. You have Jonathan, and I have David. Maybe the reason we have soul mates is to make the darkness easier to face . . . forever."

Deven gave her a slightly patronizing smile. "Oh, don't worry. You won't have to worry about it forever. Now that you have a Signet I give you, say, two hundred years."

With that, he pushed himself up off the couch and, taking the half-empty whiskey bottle with him, left her alone in the study with even more unpleasant thoughts than she'd come in with.

"I talked to Deven," Miranda said, falling into step beside David.

The Prime gave her a once-over. "I don't see any blood, so I assume it went well?"

"As well as can be expected."

They walked together along the main street of the Shadow District downtown, while all around them the usual hubbub of a Saturday night in the city flashed and bumped and laughed from the open doors of bars and clubs. The vampires of Austin were out in droves tonight, and though most avoided the Pair's gaze and simply bowed as they passed by, a few made eye contact and called greetings.

David paused here and there to visit with club owners or other businesspeople in the area and in some cases introduced her to people she hadn't had the chance to meet; even those who looked at her with some suspicion were friendly to her face, and she tried to be as gracious as possible to lure them into thinking her harmless. She preferred the element of surprise.

Clearly some of them had heard about Hart and kept their distance from her or spoke very vaguely about their business dealings, in case she should deem them immoral or illegal on a whim. Miranda found that hilarious but held her tongue.

Between visits she told David more about her conversation with the Prime. "I still can't say I like him . . . but I understand him a little better now. I just wish he weren't so fatalistic—especially about God."

David looked at her and said curiously, "I didn't realize you were religious."

"I'm not, really. I never really felt called to that kind of thing except for some experiments in college. But Deven is different. He needs that belief. If he could find it again, he might be able to finally heal—he's spent seven centuries as a miserable bastard because he lost his faith."

The Prime nodded. "I agree with you. But I don't think it's totally lost; I just think he's been unable to reconcile what he's seen with what he wants to believe about God. He's been alive a very long time, beloved. His perspective is broad, yes, but it's also deeply flawed."

"What did he mean when he said I had two hundred years?"

"The longest a Prime has held a Signet was three hundred twenty years—one hundred without a Queen, two hundred twenty with her."

"So the truth is, even though we're immortal because we're vampires, we'll still die because we're Signet bearers."

"Eventually, yes. An ordinary vampire could stay out of sight, live quietly. We can't do that. We'll always be in the public eye, always a target for someone who wants to take our place." David just shrugged and offered a smile. "But I have every intention of living at least that long, my darling. I hope that's all right with you. I'm determined to see the future of society no matter how it turns out."

"Why? What could be so great that you'd wait three centuries to see it?"

He looked over at her again, the uncharacteristically youthful earnestness on his face so adorable that she started to giggle. When he replied it was as if the answer should have been perfectly obvious. "Are you kidding? Vampires in space!"

Miranda's giggles redoubled, and she had to stop and kiss him. "I love you, you big geek."

After the events of the past week David had suggested it was a good time for the two of them to take a walk, making their presence known to the Shadow World, to remind everyone who was in charge. They had arranged to meet Deven and Jonathan at the Black Door, a popular hunting ground and dance club, to end the evening; the Pair would be on their way back to California the next night, their state visit officially concluded and considered a success from a diplomatic standpoint.

Personally, though, it didn't seem anything had concluded successfully. So far David and Deven hadn't had any sort of serious talk about their relationship, and Miranda still wanted to punch Deven in the face. She didn't feel at all satisfied with how things had gone, but there was no help for it; a Pair couldn't be away from home for long without chaos breaking out in their territory.

But, she reasoned, it wasn't like they were getting any older. At least now David had admitted there were things to resolve instead of pretending it was all fine and dandy between him and Deven. That was a start.

"I love this city," David was saying, looking up at the buildings that rose on either side of them. "Its energy, its people . . . I don't even mind the blistering summers. I'm proud of what I've accomplished here."

"You should be," she replied. "After what I've learned about the other Primes and what life is like in their territories—for humans and vampires alike—I can see what an amazing leader you are."

He smiled and put his arm around her as they walked. "And just think . . . soon the world will speak of you the same way, and our legacy together will be one of peace through strength. They'll see our tenure as the moment when the Shadow World began to evolve past its primitive history and become something greater."

"Hopefully my legacy will include a string of platinum albums," Miranda laughed. "If I can ever get this one finished." She grew serious for a minute and said, "You know . . . I've learned a lot the last three months, but I think the most important thing so far is how lucky I am."

He lifted her hand and kissed it. "You and I both."

Miranda had never been into dance clubs—she preferred the sort of place where there was live music and less techno—but she was quite fond of the Black Door. At first it had bothered her knowing what the place was for. The term "hunting ground" wasn't a euphemism; humans came to dance and drink, and vampires came to feed. Everything about the club drew mortals in: There was no cover charge, and drinks were deliberately priced below the Sixth Street average; the place was clean and spacious and had a huge dance floor surrounded by a second level of tables and booths. It had two bars, one above and one below, and the music was slightly quieter on the second level. It was one of the most popular clubs in Austin, found purely through word of mouth—no advertising, no website.

What the humans didn't know was that there was a separate entrance for vampires. A limited number were allowed in at a time, and security kept a close eye both on them and on humans leaving the club. A vampire who made any trouble was permanently barred from entry. If a human displayed any sign of injury beyond the usual fatigue and confusion of being bitten, he or she was immediately given a cab to a nearby clinic, which, of course, was also run by the Signet. Great care was taken to ensure that the mortal patrons had no reason to complain and every reason to tell their friends about the awesome place where they'd danced the night away.

It seemed so . . . manipulative and wrong, like a factory farm, and Miranda had refused to have any part of it until David had persuaded her to go one night and she had seen firsthand how it was all managed. In any other territory things might be very different, but this was the South. The Prime would not allow his human charges to be molested. Vampires needed to feed, and the Shadow World had to remain a secret. Austin had a dense vampire population, and somehow all those vampires had to be fed discreetly; if they were unsatisfied for long, they began to get angry at the authority that kept them from killing, and that was how gangs and rebellions were born.

They walked to the front of the human line; David used the front entrance so that everyone inside would know the Signet was in attendance. The doorman took one look at them, bowed, and unclipped the velvet rope to let them in.

The bass began to pound its way into her body as they crossed the threshold and walked down the short hallway that led into the club. She shot David a grin, and he kissed her hand one last time before releasing her. Miranda squared off her shoulders, drew her power around her like a cloak, bolstered her shields, and strode into the club with her Signet out where every vampire would see it and know her for their Queen.

The Black Door was packed. Only months ago the sheer weight of all those minds rubbing against hers would have sent Miranda to the ground screaming, but she was no longer human and no longer afraid. She nodded to the security staff as they passed; sometimes those who didn't make the Elite but still scored high in the tryouts were offered jobs at Signet-owned establishments, and a few made their way to the Haven after proving themselves here. She recognized a few faces.

Not far inside, Lali fell into step behind her, along with Aaron, one of the other two bodyguards. Miranda had offered Lali bereavement leave after Jake was declared dead, but Lali wouldn't have it. Jake, she had said, was devoted to his job, and she was going to honor that devotion by doing her own. Miranda had hugged her, thanked her, and let Faith put her back on the rotation. They were going to have to assign another guard so that they'd have even pairs; Faith said she would go back over the candidates who hadn't been picked and submit her recommendation by Monday.

As a matter of fact, Faith was here tonight; Miranda let her gaze meander from one end of the Door's vast space to the other, and she caught sight of Faith not far away, sipping a martini and talking with another Elite. Faith looked devastatingly gorgeous: For once she was out of uniform, in a short green dress with her hair out of its braids and pulled up on top of her head. Miranda wished, sometimes, that she could pull off the glamorous look Faith did without any apparent effort.

Then, of course, there was Deven.

Miranda wasn't looking for him, but she happened to glance over at her Prime and noticed he was staring off at something. She knew without asking what that something was and followed his gaze to the dance floor.

Sure enough, the Prime of the West was in the center of the crowd, surrounded by both men and women who seemed unable to take their eyes off him. He was currently pressed up against a petite blond woman . . . and a striking dark-haired boy of perhaps twenty. Deven was back to his usual wardrobe, this time a black jacket over a dark gray shirt, his Signet visible amid the rest of his jewelry, the allure around him as intense as it had been that night in the alley.

The look on David's face was unmistakable, and it filled Miranda's heart with shards of ice: *hunger*. In that moment he wanted more than anything in the world to be at Deven's side, or better yet, pinning him to the wall with deep, hard kisses.

"I'm going to get someone to drink," she said, not giving David time to protest as she tore herself from his side and made her way to the bar. She intended to get one of the mixed drinks that the Black Door specialized in—the kind with blood in it—but when she saw Jonathan at the bar, she decided she was more interested in getting blind drunk than anything else at the moment.

"My Lady," Jonathan said, raising his beer in salute. "Shiner?"

"I think I need something a little stronger," she replied, motioning to the bartender, who set aside the row of drinks he was making and came for her order instantly. She asked for a shot of Patrón.

Jonathan frowned. "Tequila," he said. "That doesn't bode well. What's wrong?"

She gestured out at the dance floor. "Something about my husband dancing with someone else makes me want to rip that someone's little pixie head off. Sorry, Jonathan. I guess I'm just not as evolved as you."

"Actually, he's not," Jonathan said, looking out at the floor. "He's looking for you."

Miranda turned to see that Deven was still by himself, though now one of the sexy mortals in his bevy of admirers had two tiny holes in his neck that were swiftly closing; meanwhile, David was standing next to Faith, but his deep blue eyes were scanning the crowd, and when his eyes met Miranda's, he broke out into a smile.

Her heart climbed back up from where it had sunk into her feet, and she smiled back, knocked back her shot, and left the empty glass on the bar.

Jonathan was chuckling to himself and shook his head. "Jealousy doesn't become you, Miranda. Especially when it's totally unfounded."

Bristling, Miranda walked away without answering, but if he'd been a telepath her reply would have been crystal clear: *Blindness isn't particularly attractive either.*

She might be young and new to her Signet, but she was well aware that she was one of the strongest empaths among her kind, and she knew quite well there was nothing unfounded about her jealousy, becoming or otherwise. But it seemed that a certain amount of denial was just a part of the Pair's relationship, and she wasn't going to disillusion Jonathan. She liked him too much. If he was content to go on pretending it really didn't bother him, well, so be it.

But she was still glad the Pair were getting the hell out of her territory.

When she came into view David held out his hands, and she took them, stepping up to him and then turning, slightly, to draw him out onto the floor. One of his hands slid down her back to her waist and the other up to her chin, and she put her lips up to his, claiming his mouth fiercely enough to banish, she hoped, all thought of anything . . . or anyone . . . else. She pulled him with her into the song that pounded all around them, her fingernails scratching lightly through his shirt, her teeth tugging gently on his lower lip.

Miranda remembered once, in a philosophy class, hearing about Plato's theory that humans once had had four arms, two heads, and four legs, but they had been split in half by the gods, and spent the rest of their lives seeking that sundered half with whom they fit so perfectly. At the time it had been a fanciful sort of story, ancient philosophy as written by Disney.

She believed it now.

She was exactly tall enough to rest her head on his shoulder, his arms reaching just right around her middle, hip locking into hip as if they had grown that way from the dark soil of some overgrown, night-blooming garden. She'd danced with him a dozen times and not once had there ever been any awkward bumping; he grabbed her hand and spun her away, then back, and she was laughing at the ridiculousness of such a ballroom move in the middle of a floor crowded with youngsters, but when she came back to him she fit just where she had been, and the electrical charge of that contact nearly tore a gasp from her throat.

One hand circling her waist, he tilted her back, and she bent almost double, her hair sweeping the floor. There were, of course, people watching; if anyone in this room knew vampires existed, they knew these two, and knew that the connection between them was stronger than the forces that held atoms together and kept the moon spinning around the earth.

She wanted desperately to drag him into a corner of the room and wrap herself around him, but as the song came to an end and his mouth found hers again, she barely had time to immerse herself in the delirium of the kiss before a familiar, and unwelcome, sound broke into the moment.

"Damn it," David hissed, pulling his lips away to look down at his phone.

His gaze jerked up to her. "It's Kat."

"Answer it!" Miranda felt cold dread falling as a stone into her belly.

As David said "Star-one," another noise shrilled out, this one a network alarm.

"Faith!" Miranda all but yelled into her com. "I need you!"

"Here," the Second said, appearing beside her almost instantly. "What's happening?"

"Coordinates," Miranda said to David, who was trying to call Kat back and getting no answer. He switched the screen to his view of the network sensor grid and drew a line with his finger over the screen, spinning the diagram around to match their location.

"Not far from here," David said. "Faith, get a team to East Seventh and Comal immediately."

Faith didn't even bother replying; she simply darted away, already issuing orders into her com, her stiletto heels hitting the floor with as much purpose as her usual combat boots. Meanwhile, Miranda had her phone out and was trying to get Kat, but it kept going right to voice mail.

Fear rose in her throat. "Kat . . . Kat . . . David, something's wrong, we have to find her . . ."

David pulled her off the dance floor, over to a clear space by the bar where Jonathan and Deven were drinking. Both Prime and Consort looked startled at David's grim expression and her rapidly spiraling panic.

David was still staring down at his phone. "Her signal dropped off here, but her call came half a block away, so we can assume she's being taken north—"

"There's no time for your dicking around," Deven snapped, and for once Miranda wanted to hug him. "You. Me. Mist. Now."

David looked up, shocked, but nodded.

About two seconds later, the Primes had vanished into thin air.

Miranda was still on the verge of a breakdown. "I have to get there . . . I can't run that fast. The car won't be here in time. Jonathan, what do I do? Kat's in trouble, she might be dying, oh, God—"

"You haven't learned to Mist?" Jonathan asked, amazed. "Well, then, we'll start right now. Grab my arm and hold tight—there's no time for finesse, so as soon as we land be prepared to skin your knees and vomit."

She didn't care about the consequences. All she could think of was getting to Kat. She seized Jonathan's proffered arm and felt a sickening lurch . . .

. . . and the club spun away into darkness.

# Nine

True to Jonathan's word, the second Miranda landed, her knees hit the concrete hard enough that she felt one of her kneecaps fracture, and she pitched forward and threw up all over the median grass.

Then she forced herself to her feet, fighting the waves of vertigo that kept battering her from all sides as well as the pain in her knee, and tried to make sense of the scene before her.

The first thing she saw was blood, and it nearly made her sick again, because she knew whose it was.

"Kat!" she cried, pushing herself forward from the street into the alley. "Where is she? Kat!"

Footsteps thundered up to Miranda's side, and Faith grabbed her arm and steadied her. "Miranda, listen to me—you can't help her now. Just stand back and everything will be fine."

"I can help her! Let me go!" The panic was so overwhelming that Miranda nearly shoved Faith away, but before she could summon the energy, she felt someone else grabbing her other arm—David.

"It's all right, beloved," he said. "Just hold on."

Miranda, however, was beside herself and couldn't be consoled. "Is she dead? Did they find her hand? I want to see her hand! David, please, I need to see . . ."

"Easy," David murmured. "Come with me . . . one step . . . and another . . . it's all right, just take it slow . . ."

He led her around the crowd of Elite—the patrol team that had come as soon as Kat's emergency signal went out, and the second team headed by Faith that was arriving as Miranda stumbled toward the scene.

The street corner was splattered with blood. A woman's form lay sprawled out on the concrete, blood oozing out around her, her car keys flung several feet away.

Kat was trying so hard not to scream. She was panting, half sobbing, every other breath almost a wail. Her bald head was dripping with blood, as was her arm . . . from the cleanly sliced stump where her hand had been severed. Someone had tied a strip of fabric as a tourniquet and it was already soaked.

Worst of all, there was a knife protruding obscenely from her abdomen.

"Kat, Kat . . ." Miranda was sobbing as Kat was sobbing, and the Queen fell down beside her friend, her best friend she couldn't protect with all the immortal power in the world. "Help is coming, Kat, I promise." She tried to reassure the human, doing anything she could, because it was why she was here . . . for all the good it did anyone.

*"Miranda."*

A sharp voice cut through her panic, and she looked over Kat's bleeding, broken body to see a pair of ice-cold lavender eyes fixed on hers.

"Pull yourself together, Queen," Deven commanded gently. "She doesn't need to see you like this."

Miranda took a deep, shaking breath and threw her energy into grounding, bolstering her shields, and calming herself enough that she could look at the situation realistically.

She knelt beside Kat's body, holding Kat's still-attached right hand, while the Elite tried to stop the bleeding from her left arm and the wound to her gut. A few inches from Kat's arm, the severed hand lay on a clean cloth, blood soaking into it.

Deven's voice grabbed Miranda again. "Listen to me.

You need to tell your people to step back and maintain their distance. The forensic team must start searching for evidence. There should be a trail—we caught the attacker by surprise and I wounded her. Tell them now."

Miranda jerked her head up and gave her orders, and the Elite scattered.

"Now. You have a connection to this woman, so I will need your help to help her. Do you understand me? Let yourself be open to me, as if I were David calling for your energy. I'll pull from both you and Jonathan. It will work faster this way. Open yourself, and stay grounded."

Miranda fell into a cross-legged position that mirrored Deven's, though he was on the side of Kat with the . . . hand . . .

"Focus!"

The snapped command made her look away from the gruesome sight and back down at Kat's anguished face. Kat was crying, shaking, and so pale . . . Miranda opened her shields as she'd been told, but she also spared a tendril of her power to reach softly around Kat's heart and soothe her fear, let her know that she was loved and taken care of, and now she was safe. She was safe, and loved . . . safe . . .

Kat stopped flailing against the hands that held her, and those hands lifted.

Miranda watched in rapt fascination as Deven closed his eyes and held his palms out over Kat's body, first over her belly. He reached down and carefully drew the knife out of her flesh, laying the weapon on a sheet of plastic that would be wrapped for evidence. Then he held both palms over the wound and became very still.

All around them, sound seemed suddenly muffled, a strange peace descending over the chaotic scene. Everyone came to a standstill and turned to stare as the light in Deven's Signet began to glow brighter and brighter . . . At first it seemed almost like a trick of the streetlamp, but soon it was too bright for that, becoming like an aura, or a halo . . .

Miranda felt a gentle tug at her shields, and she opened them wider to him, feeling him reach in and lift tiny sips of power at a time, feeding them into Kat's body as if she were a starving baby bird. Blended with his own energy, and his Consort's through their bond, Miranda's power added strength and love to the mix, and soon she felt the wound begin to close, all the rips and gouges mending themselves, until even the skin that covered the wound began to knit, first an angry red wound, then a dark jagged scar, then softening to pink, then fading to white.

Miranda felt her own energy start to wane just a little and reached sideways to her Prime, who opened himself willingly; now, all four of them were part of the web, each feeding power into Deven, which he fused with his own and directed with utmost care to where it was needed, cell by cell repaired to blossoming health.

But Deven still hadn't lifted his hands; his eyes were closed but his brow furrowed in concentration. He looked up at Kat and asked softly, "Shall I bring her back, Katerina?"

Kat, too, had been overcome with peace and was breathing in tandem with the Prime, who waited for her answer. She smiled and said hoarsely, "Yes."

Nodding, Deven closed his eyes again and went back to work; a second later Miranda felt something . . . something inside Kat fluttered, like a tiny hand waving hello.

Then he moved his attention up to her left arm, and this time picked up the poor severed hand and placed it against her wrist, holding his own hands over the joining, closing his eyes and breathing . . . in and out . . . in and out . . . for several minutes, while Miranda felt the ebb and flow of power through her, David, and Jonathan, then through Deven, and into Kat's arm.

Finally, Deven withdrew both energy and hands, and a gasp went up all around them as the Elite saw that Kat's wrist was whole again, without even a scratch.

Deven disengaged himself from the power matrix, and each of them did the same until their bonds were only for each other again. The connection among them was so infused with serenity, Miranda was reluctant to leave it, but she could feel everyone weakening. It was time to let go.

Miranda was crying, but she met Deven's eyes. He looked like he was about to lose consciousness. "Thank you," she whispered.

The smile he gave her was one she would always remember: It was one of pure peace, even bliss. Whatever his other gifts were, whatever creature he was, Deven had just done what he had been born to do. He was a healer. She would never doubt that again.

"David," Deven said, "catch her."

Just as Deven passed out and sagged sideways into Jonathan's arms, so did Miranda do the same, falling backward against her Prime, who held her tightly and picked her up to carry her home.

"Thank you, Mr. Behr. Let me know when would work for you and your staff to reschedule, and send me a bill for their time tonight as well—I know it's extremely inconvenient for you to have a no-show, especially when you go out of your way to set up for us late at night. Again, I apologize. Have a good evening."

David hung up with a sigh and stood at the foot of the bed, watching Miranda sleep; she and Deven had been the worst off, and so far neither had woken in almost twenty hours. Jonathan said that he had seen Dev heal so intensely only two or three times before, and it always wiped him out for a day or two; vampires simply weren't designed to burn energy that way. They were predators, not healers.

He wondered: Had Deven been born at a different time, with the abilities he had, would he have been a valued member of his tribe, perhaps a shaman or priest, instead of constantly coming under the scrutiny and abuse of men who thought their God couldn't possibly have shared such astonishing powers with another? Or would he have been burned at the stake the way Lizzie had been? God, it seemed, had a rather caustic sense of humor.

David checked his phone again: a text from Elite 43, the guard he'd already assigned to watch over Kat, who was presently with her at the Signet-run clinic, where she slept in recovery. The clinic specialized in vampire-related injuries and had several immortal staff members who could alter memories as well as manage the symptoms of an attack or overzealous feeding. Kat had none of those, but no normal hospital would understand what she had been through. It was best to keep her somewhere that the doctors knew what she knew and wouldn't refer her to the psych ward or try to involve the police.

The Prime had also ordered a guest suite at the Haven prepared for Kat. He doubted she would go along quietly, but he wasn't about to let her stay on her own after tonight.

Another message, this one from Faith's team on the scene: The blood trail had gotten them nowhere, vanishing midstride in the middle of the street, but they had collected samples that went immediately to Novotny, and hopefully the good doctor could discern something in the blood before it died. The weapon used to stab Kat had also been retrieved; an egregious error on the attacker's part, but then, she had been interrupted.

David and Deven had Misted within five feet of Kat's prone body and the vampire kneeling over her with a knife. Dev had been quicker on the draw and slammed a throwing stake into the woman's back; she screamed and bolted, not even looking back. The stake fell out as she ran, and it, too, had been cataloged as evidence and taken in for trace analysis.

Surely, *surely* something would be found. No criminal was brilliant enough to attack four people without leaving a single speck of evidence. She was clumsy enough to leave both the stake in Miranda's shoulder and the knife in Kat's stomach; she had to slip up somewhere. Red Shadow or not, nobody was that good.

He sat down beside Miranda and straightened the covers around her gingerly so as not to wake her. He'd never seen anyone twist sheets the way she did. He laid his hand on her forehead, pleased that her body temperature had dropped to normal; when he first put her to bed she'd had a fever. Her body hadn't known what to do with the wild fluctuation in her energy and had reacted as though it were ill until he woke her long enough to coax her into drinking some blood from their emergency store. She had done as he bade her, murmured something about it tasting old, and fallen back to sleep before the sentence was finished.

After a moment of watching, he sighed and stretched out alongside his Queen for a while, facing her, the slow rise and fall of her chest more comforting than he would ever have thought possible.

He touched her face, brushing his fingers along her lip, loving every inch of her and gripped, for a moment, with fear; someone was after her, and their reasons didn't matter. What mattered was that he would find whoever it was and hurt them until they begged for death . . . but lying there staring at her, he couldn't think of torture and violence . . . he could only think of how strange and wonderful it was to love her, to have her here, every day, to wake beside her when he had come so close to losing her.

He was grateful that the Signet bond ensured that, should she die, he would die within minutes. The thought of existing on this planet without her, as he had for so many years, was too horrible to contemplate.

There, he knew, was the difference between how he felt about her and how he had felt about Deven. Losing Dev had been heart-crushingly painful, yes, and there had been days he could barely get out of bed beneath the weight of his sorrow, but that night he had stood before the smoldering ruins of Miranda's apartment, desperate for any hope but deep down knowing there was none, had been the worst moment of his life.

The thought, though, brought images to his mind that he didn't want, and a longing that spread from his belly outward, that part of him that still yearned, whispering, wondering what it would be like, for just an hour . . . remembering another face on the pillow before him, another mouth catching his in the darkness, another back arching against his hands . . .

Suddenly he had to be out of the bed. Thinking about

Deven while lying with Miranda was flat-out blasphemous to them both. David got up, feeling imbalanced and uncomfortable in his skin. Thank God she was asleep.

He sat down at his desk and for a moment covered his eyes with his hands, wishing to God or any convenient higher power that he could stop feeling this way. He had thought that he loved Miranda with every inch of his heart, and that there couldn't possibly be room for anyone else. Yet some dark corner of his being had held on to what once was, all this time, and was slowly crawling through his veins, leaving behind an old fire and a new fear. He could tell himself it was purely physical, or just nostalgia . . . but he knew a lie when he heard one.

He tried checking his e-mail and messages, but there was nothing new. Still, there had to be something he could do in his workroom, and once he was out of the suite he could talk to Faith without waking Miranda.

Once in the hallway, though, he found that his feet refused to carry him to the workroom; they seemed to have an agenda all their own, and he was headed down the corridor before he realized where he was going.

*Damn it.*

He told himself it would be remiss not to check in on them; they were his guests, after all, and he needed to check on when they were planning to leave now that they would have to reschedule their flight. He could stop by, get a status report from Jonathan, and then go find Faith to go over whatever evidence they'd gathered from the scene. He could also put in a call to Novotny to check on the tests they were running on Jake's and Denise's hands. Pathological analysis took time, but there might be some preliminary results by now.

He arrived at the guest suite, where two California Elite were standing guard; it was traditional for visiting Pairs to bring a half dozen or so of their own warriors for personal security. The two guards bowed to him, and one opened the door for him.

David looked in, expecting to see Jonathan on the couch

while Deven slept nearby, but to his surprise he didn't see the Consort anywhere.

"Come in," said a tired voice.

The guard closed the suite door behind David, who walked slowly into the room, looking around curiously. "Hello?"

There was a faint movement and he realized that it was Deven who was on the sofa, curled up against the arm, under a blanket, nursing a glass of blood. The hearth was bright and warm, the rest of the room dark.

"Where's Jonathan?" David asked, a bit nervous without the Consort in earshot.

"Remember?" Deven said. "He said he asked if he could take Isis out tonight, and you agreed."

"Oh, right." He did remember; they'd been having a brief discussion about the attack and healing once everyone was safely back at the Haven, and Jonathan had said that they would probably remain in Austin until Monday just to be sure Deven was up for travel. Jonathan had expressed interest in the Friesians, and David had been more than happy to give him access to the stables whenever he liked. Jonathan was one of the few people David knew who shared his enthusiasm for the animals and one of the few he would trust with them.

He was also probably one of the only people whom Isis would allow near her without biting off a finger just for spite.

A bit wary of the situation, David lowered himself into the empty chair, asking, "How are you feeling? I thought you'd still be asleep."

Deven half shrugged. "You know how it goes."

"Nightmares?"

The Prime nodded without lifting his head from the blanket. He looked so young and vulnerable like that, it made David's heart ache. "Whenever I do something foolish with my power I have a hard time shielding myself from the dreams. Jonathan can help, but he was wide awake, so I told him I'd just nap here until he came back and not to worry."

"Is there anything I can get you?"

"No. Nothing."

There was a moment's silence, with the fire crackling and Deven breathing slowly and evenly, though he wasn't asleep. His eyes were partway open, staring at the flames.

"What you did for Kat was . . . nothing short of miraculous," David said quietly. "Thank you. And I know Miranda will thank you when she can."

"She did already." Dev's eyes opened a little wider, and he fixed David with his gaze, eyes nearly as violet as irises in this light. "David . . . there's something you must know about Miranda. Something important."

"What? What is it?"

The Prime carefully pushed himself more upright. "She's not like the others, David. She's not like Jonathan, nothing like any other Queen. What she's brought to you . . . nothing like your bond has been seen in the Council in over a thousand years. I wish I could explain it to you, but I don't know what it means, or even *how* it's different . . . but I can feel it. No Pair can expect to lead an ordinary life, but you . . . the two of you have something very important to do together."

"I thought Jonathan was the prescient one," David stammered, trying and failing to cover how rattled he was by Deven's words.

"You know I have it, too, in smaller measure. I never use it except to fight, but this time . . . trust me, my darling. It's not a matter of seeing the future. I *know* this. Whatever life you had planned, whatever peace you had hoped to attain, you'll never have it. Accept that now and you'll be much happier."

They stared at each other a long moment before Deven relaxed back into the cushions and said, "It makes it hurt less, somehow, knowing that you were meant for such a life."

David raised an eyebrow. "You were the one who—"

"I know." Deven cut him off, waving a hand. "I've heard it all before." He ran his hand back through his hair. "David . . ." A note of entreaty entered Deven's voice, as well as reluctance, even fear, to say what had to be said. "I've tried my best to make up for how I treated you. For years now I've done everything I could to earn back your trust. I've done things that . . ." He trailed off, eyes returning to the fire.

David frowned. "What have you done?"

Deven ignored the question. "I can't force you to forgive me. And if you never will . . . how can we remain friends at all? We've been dancing around this since I arrived . . . no, for years. Somehow we have to move on from here."

David, restless, got up from the chair and came over to straighten out the blanket around the Prime as he had earlier with Miranda. "To be honest, Deven, I don't know if we can. I thought I was past all of this, but I think I was just far away from it. From you. Maybe that's the best thing, for us to keep our distance."

Deven grabbed his arm, forcing him to stop looking for something else to think about. "Is that really what you want?"

Again their eyes held. David found he could barely breathe. "No."

"I should never have let you go," Deven said softly, lifting one hand and brushing a stray hair from David's eyes.

It felt like his spine was melting under the heat of that one light touch. David knelt in front of the couch, putting his head about level with Deven's. "What about Jonathan?"

"Jonathan would have understood. He's said so many times."

"He would have shared you with me?"

"Of course. He's always had his lovers. So could I, within the terms of our relationship."

David smiled wryly. "You're basing your regrets on the assumption that I would have been willing to share."

The smile was returned, this time ruefully. "We do a lot of insane things for love. I thought I was doing the right thing by breaking it off with you . . . but what kind of life could we have now if you had stayed?"

David's smile faded. "You would have all of your soul mate's heart and all of mine, and I would have, perhaps, half of yours. So things would be wonderful for you, which is what matters, isn't it?"

"Are you suggesting that I'm selfish, David?"

"No, Deven, I'm saying it. You're selfish. You would rather I were warming your bed with only half a soul than finding fulfillment in my own life—and I'm sure you were much happier before I met Miranda. And now you think, what, that you can walk back into my life and claim some piece of me for yourself after you left me in the gutter with a broken heart?"

"You're wrong," Deven snapped, anger sparking in his eyes as they went silver around the edges. "You have no idea how wrong you are. How can you think that of me after everything we've been through together? How can you think I don't want to see you happy?"

The Prime sat up, pulling away from David, then shoved the blanket aside and forced himself to his feet. "You should go," Deven said, voice going cold. "I need to pack."

But Deven wavered where he stood, dizziness catching up to him, and David caught him as his knees buckled, his heart pounding at the sudden feeling of Deven's slender body against his. Dev tried to push him away, but the effort was halfhearted at best and he was still weak. David held on to him, some desperate wild thing in his chest refusing to withdraw, and after a moment Deven gave up and leaned into his arms.

"I don't want to feel this way," Deven murmured into David's chest. "I want to forget we were ever in love and be content with friendship. But I don't think I can, David. I can keep my distance and I can honor your commitment, but I can't ever stop loving you."

David drew back to look at him. There was such anguish in his face, and David felt it just as keenly himself even if it didn't show. "I know," he said. "Neither can I."

Deven shook his head. "You should go. Go, now, before we do something that . . ."

He didn't have a chance to finish the sentence. David's mouth had already covered his.

# Ten

Kat woke to a world that had changed, and changed profoundly, without her permission.

She didn't want to open her eyes. There were nightmares in the dark, but she had no idea what being awake would prove or disprove about the night gone by, and better the devil she knew than the one she didn't . . . although . . . what was that beeping?

Curiosity got the better of her and she slit one eye open to get at least some idea of where she was. Could it be . . . just maybe . . . she was in her own bed, beneath the handmade quilt her grandmother had left unfinished when she died, the blue and purple one Kat had clumsily handstitched the last square onto? Was she in her cozy bedroom in the townhouse she had bought in a bid to feel grounded someplace, finally at home for the first time in her life, the furniture and DVDs testimony to the fact that she had chosen to call Austin her town after years of wandering around the planet?

The beep came again just as her eye opened enough to admit light, and her heart sank as confusion set in. No, this wasn't home. Home wasn't stark white and cold, and it certainly didn't have a bank of machines up by the headboard.

"Kat?"

She pried her eye open the rest of the way, then its partner, and turned her sight on the origin of the voice, a dark-haired young man whose brow was creased with worry.

"Hey," she croaked.

Drew let out a breath of relief and squeezed her hand almost too hard; she was aware, then, of something poking her, and a second later realized it was an IV.

"Am I in the hospital?" she asked, surprised at how weak her voice was. She sounded like she'd had the flu.

He made an indefinite gesture with his head. "Sort of. It's the Anna Hausmann Memorial Clinic down on Fifteenth."

"Never heard of it."

"Yeah, me neither. I got a call last night that you . . . that you were here. I think . . ." Drew looked around as if worried someone would overhear, then said quietly, "I think Miranda's people run it."

Kat blinked. Vampires had doctors? Why? She looked around the small, private room, which could have been in any hospital in Austin. It even had a window whose blinds were open, so at least the nurses had to be human.

On the wall, there was a dry-erase board that read, *Welcome to the Hausmann Clinic! Your nurse today is . . .* The space had been filled in by a different hand, with *Jackie.* At the top corner where the hospital logo would have been was a symbol like a family crest, with an S in the center. *Solomon.*

Kat shut her eyes tightly as flashes of memory began to intrude . . . not visual, but visceral, the memory of pain, of terror . . .

She choked back tears. "What happened to me?" she whispered.

Drew stood and leaned over her, putting his arms around her. He smelled like he always did: patchouli, books, and the faint musty scent of the music department classrooms at UT. He'd started a program there for underprivileged kids, teaching piano lessons for free after school. That, his regular class schedule, and all his other volunteer work took up so much time, combined with her crazy hours, that they hardly got to see each other these days. Most guys would have bailed on her by now, but he wanted to sign up for the long haul. He might just be as crazy as she was.

She sobbed, and he held her close, while the collective horror of the night sank in.

"I lost it," she gasped. "I lost the baby. But then I found her again. They saved me. I was so scared . . ."

Just like before when she'd been walking to her car. But this time, it wasn't her imagination or a random stranger. This time it was someone who wanted her dead.

She'd barely had a second to hit the panic button on her phone before someone slammed into her from behind, knocking her to the ground, wrestling her to her back. She had looked up into an inhuman face, and all she had seen were teeth . . . the flash of a knife . . . and then there was so much pain, her memory simply stopped. Her brain couldn't cope with reality and everything went gray and silent until . . .

She had heard a calm male voice beside her and looked up to see an angelic face—maybe it really was an angel; hell, if vampires were real, what else might be?—just before she heard Miranda, panicked, calling her name. Then there was . . .

*"Shall I bring her back, Katerina?"*

Then she woke up here.

She tried to tell Drew what had happened, or as much of it as she could make sense of. He looked like he wasn't sure whether to hold her or set something on fire. Drew wasn't an angry person; in fact he was one of the kindest, most compassionate people she had ever met. Knowing that she was the source of his anger made her heart shudder with guilt.

Not too long after she got herself back together, there was a knock, and the door swung open to reveal a tiny round woman with a clipboard and a digital thermometer. "Hi there," she said, her Texas accent pronounced and comforting. "I'm Jackie."

"Kat."

"Nice to meet you, sweetie. And you must be Drew." Jackie reached over and shook his hand, somehow without putting down her things, an impressive feat. "I'm just here to take Kat's vitals. Do you have any questions?"

"Yeah," Drew said, more forceful than Kat had ever heard him. "What the hell happened to her last night?"

Jackie got to work checking Kat's various monitors and making adjustments in things, saying, "The official word is that you were attacked by a vampire—I understand you're under Signet protection? Good, then I can be a little more candid. The woman who attacked you is suspected of several murders and an attack on the Queen."

"Several murders?" Drew demanded. "I thought she had just gone after Kat and Miranda. You mean she's been killing other people and they haven't caught her yet?"

"Drew," Kat said quietly, "calm down."

Jackie didn't look upset by Drew's outburst. She jotted Kat's temperature on her clipboard before replying, "I'm afraid she's still at large, but Prime Deven wounded her, and there was evidence at the scene that's being analyzed right now. Someone will be in shortly to ask you a few questions, Kat, about the attacker."

"Police?" Kat asked.

"Elite," Jackie answered. "Police aren't much good in this sort of situation."

"What kind of place is this?"

Jackie smiled. "The Hausmann was established by Prime Solomon to look after human victims of vampire feeding— even with the laws they have in place, sometimes unfortunate things happen. Our staff are trained to recognize and deal with specific conditions resulting from vampire-related injuries, including abortive transformations and various forms of anemia. We're not very big or very busy, but normal medical facilities often don't know how to treat this sort of thing or its emotional toll. We have . . . counselors for that."

The nurse spoke so matter-of-factly about her job that

Kat felt a creeping sense of surreality all around her. "Is . . . can you tell if the baby's okay?"

Jackie paused and looked at her. "It's tough to say, as early as it is. She's still got a good strong heartbeat and there's been no damage we could see in the scans. You'll want to follow up with your OB/GYN as soon as possible, but I would say, cautiously, it looks like she'll be fine."

"How do you know it's a she?" Drew asked.

Jackie looked thoughtful. "I don't, really," she replied. "It just came out. Would you prefer I not use a gender pronoun? It is, as I said, really early in the pregnancy."

"No, that's all right," Kat said. "I know it's a girl, too . . . and . . . I'm going to keep her. So it's okay."

She saw the shock on Drew's face but didn't say anything to him just yet. She was still getting used to the idea herself. Just saying it out loud was jarring enough.

"All right, then, I'll get out of your hair," Jackie said with a grin. "All your vitals are stable, and I'm pretty sure you'll be able to go home in the morning. I'll have dinner sent up to you within the hour."

"Thanks."

Kat saw quite plainly the question Drew was about to ask. "Let's . . . not talk about it right now, okay?" She reached up with her non-IV-laden hand and touched his face. "As soon as I get out of here and there's not somebody trying to kill me, we can start making plans."

Drew smiled, nodded, and said, "Whatever you want, babe, but you do realize that I'm moving in now even if I have to sleep on the front porch."

Kat couldn't help but smile back. "Fine by me," she said. "Saves me the trouble of housebreaking a Rottweiler."

They both laughed a little, though Kat still felt more like crying.

Jackie stuck her head back in the door. "You have another visitor," she said. "Do you feel up to a few questions now?"

Kat shrugged. Why not?

Drew started to say something—and Kat had her theories as to what—but the words died on his lips as a woman walked into the room.

She was petite, but muscular, and looked Japanese; her hair was a shining fall of ebony braided back from her face. She wore one of the black uniforms that Kat had seen on the Elite, including the silver wristband that they used to communicate.

She also had a sword.

"My name is Faith," she said, her smooth voice all business. "I am Second in Command of the Southern Elite. You must be Kat."

If Jackie's warmth had been reassuring, Faith's coolness was, too; clearly this was not a person to mess with. Where had she been, Kat wondered, when Kat was on her back with a knife in her gut?

"I have a few questions about your attacker," Faith said. "I won't keep you long; I know you need your rest."

"Fire away," Kat said, trying to sound hearty but mostly coming off as a bit pathetic. "Have a seat."

Faith declined, preferring to stand by the bed with her arms crossed, looking incredibly fucking scary. "What can you tell me about her appearance?"

Kat closed her eyes and swallowed, trying to concentrate. "She was blond," she said. "Short hair . . . really short, kind of severe. I didn't really focus on her eye color because it was dark and I was being stabbed and all."

"Understandable," Faith said. "Just give me whatever you can remember."

"She was wearing black like all of you. Her teeth were . . . out. I mean, they were all fangy and pointed. She was skinny . . . I don't know how tall, but she seemed about average height."

"Did she speak to you?"

Kat shook her head. "She just grunted. No, wait . . ." Kat thought hard, trying to fight her way through the fog around the memories. "There was one thing . . . something startled her, and she jumped up and ran. She made this noise like something hit her, and she said . . . I heard her say something, like the way you'd say 'Holy shit!' or 'Goddamn it.' "

"But it wasn't in English," Faith surmised. "What language was it?"

"I have no idea. It sounded like a cross between German and something out of Tolkien."

Something flickered in Faith's expression, but it was gone as quickly as it came. "One more thing, Kat . . . was she wearing any sort of technological gadget, like a Bluetooth earpiece or one of these?" Faith lifted her arm to show the metal band on her wrist.

"No. Not that I saw."

Faith nodded. "Thank you."

She started to leave, but Kat called her back with, "What happens now?"

Faith turned to her. "Meaning?"

"Well, obviously having one guard on me wasn't enough."

A raised eyebrow. "I was given to understand that you had refused additional guards."

"Something about having my hand chopped off made me rethink that."

Faith nodded. "I suppose it would. There's a room for you at the Haven, where you'll be under twenty-four-hour watch and safer than any other place on the planet. Your man would be welcome to join you. I would guess, however, that you don't want to give up your job and life for the duration of the investigation, in which case you go home, but we assign you a full Elite detail of bodyguards and digital surveillance. It's up to you, but either way you need to be watched much more closely until the situation has been dealt with."

Kat passed her hands over her face. The tube from her IV hit her lightly on the nose. "Can I think about it?"

"Of course. The staff wants to keep you until morning; you can notify us of your decision then. There are two guards outside your room."

"Thank you."

Faith bowed, then departed.

They sat without speaking for a minute, Kat fiddling with her IV, Drew pointedly not talking about the baby. Kat found that she was exhausted just from the two short exchanges, and though the last thing she wanted was to spend the night in a hospital bed, she got why they wanted her there. She felt like her entire body had been beaten with a bat.

She'd nearly died. Her hand had been cut off and then reattached . . . with magic. She'd been jumped in the dark and stabbed in the abdomen. Whoever had stabbed her might try again . . . and it was all because her best friend was a vampire.

She was pregnant. She hurt . . . God, she hurt . . .

And she couldn't even have any real painkillers. Somehow she didn't think Tylenol would do much good after all this . . . What she really wanted was a bottle of vodka and a plane ticket to anywhere else in the world but here.

Drew didn't ask why she was weeping again. He just held her and let her cry herself to sleep.

The spell went unbroken through long, soul-shaking kisses; through clothes and sheets thrown aside with reckless anticipation; through teeth piercing skin, nails clawing shoulders, the soft cry of joining together and the raggedly drawn breaths that rose and fell; through the world-shattering peak and subsequent tumble down, down . . .

. . . until, shaking and bruised, David lowered himself onto the mattress, and his heart battered its way through his rib cage, screaming the question into his mind: *My God, what have we done?*

Neither Prime could speak. For a long time the only sound was panting as David tried to slow his breath and still the cyclone of his thoughts, most of which were a single word: *No.*

He looked up, meeting eyes that were as dazed as his

own. He knew that whatever shame and shock he was feeling, for once Deven felt it just as strongly, if not more so, because he would never, ever have expected David to do . . . this. Deven's hands were still twisted in the pillows, holding on, perhaps, to the last precious seconds before reality drowned them both.

David tore his eyes away and sat up, feeling the air in the room cold on his bare, sweaty skin. He wasn't sure what was worse: lying there entwined with his transgressions or pulling himself away.

Strong, warm hands touched his shoulders, and he felt Dev lean against him and kiss the back of his neck. "It's all right," Deven whispered.

"No, it's not," David said back, barely able to summon words. "It's so very not all right."

"I mean . . . this isn't your fault. I accept the blame."

Tempting as the idea was, David couldn't let it happen. "No. I started it. I could have stopped at any moment, but . . ."

"You didn't, and neither did I." He ran his hands down over David's biceps, and for a moment, just a moment, David let himself forget what existed outside the room and almost relaxed into the embrace. They had shattered the world beyond the door, but if it would just stay closed a few more minutes . . .

It was Deven who broke the silence, sounding achingly young and sad when he asked softly, "How are we going to tell them?"

"Her," came a voice.

Both their heads snapped up at once.

Jonathan had entered the room without making a sound and shut the door behind him; he was standing just inside the threshold, watching them.

They were both frozen in place, unable to pull away from each other, as if it would have made a difference in what the Consort knew. But Jonathan didn't look shocked or angry; his expression was one of resignation.

"You knew this would happen," Deven said.

Jonathan smiled with an uncharacteristic edge of bitterness. "Of course I did."

"You didn't try to stop us."

The Consort tipped his head to one side, making a noise something like a laugh. "Who can stop the earth from quaking?"

"We could have," David said, carefully moving away from Deven and pulling the sheet up around himself, acutely ashamed, like Adam in the Garden. "No one forced us to do this—not fate, not anything. Either one of us could have said no."

Now Jonathan looked amused; he often did when David tried to argue with his assertions of destiny. "You're not helping your case any here."

"I'm not trying to." David couldn't look at Deven, and he couldn't meet Jonathan's eyes, but he spoke as certainly as he could, given the aftershocks in his mind. "I'm not asking for a pardon . . . if you're going to be angry at someone, let it be me. Don't take it out on Deven."

"I'm not angry."

"How can you not be?"

"I told you, I already knew. I knew before we even came here. There was a ghost between you that had to be exorcised." He fixed his Prime with a steady glare. "And you haven't violated the terms of our relationship by any means. What's fair is fair. I'm not really the one you need to worry about."

Deven didn't say anything. For the first time since the night they had met, Deven looked utterly lost . . . and David understood that when it came down to it, Deven would do whatever Jonathan asked, would abandon David again, would sever all ties with the South if Jonathan wanted him to . . . because in the end, David wasn't the one he was bound to. They could love each other until the stars burned out, but they weren't, and had never been, mated in soul. They would never live together, nor die together.

David closed his eyes against the denial that rose up rebellious in his heart, but it was the truth. This had been a stolen moment. He couldn't have Deven . . . not ever. He'd wanted closure, and in a way he had it . . . but there was no resolving this, not really.

And now things were so much worse.

"Well now," Jonathan said. "I smell like a barnyard, so I'm going to have a shower. Close the door behind you, please, David, on your way out—oh, and Deven, if it wouldn't be too much of a bother, change the fucking sheets before I come back."

The last sentence was hissed, with so much anger in it that both Primes were taken aback, but Jonathan didn't say anything else until he had reached the bathroom door.

He looked over at David. His voice was perfectly even again, perfectly factual. "Incidentally, you're not going to have to tell Miranda either. You haven't had time to learn this, but when you have a bond like ours, you can feel when your husband has an orgasm . . . no matter who it's with."

The Consort closed and locked the bathroom door.

"Oh, God . . ." David put his head in his hands. "Miranda. How am I going to face her?"

Deven almost said something sarcastic—David knew the look on his face—but at the last second the spark drained out of him and he said only, "Honestly."

"She'll never forgive me. Three months and I broke faith with her . . . there's nothing I can say to make this right."

Again, Deven sounded drained . . . no, defeated. All of his arrogance and self-possession were gone. "You made a mistake, David. She will forgive you."

David looked at him. "A mistake?"

He sighed. "Yes. A beautiful, terrible mistake that can never happen again. Now we'll go home to the West, and you'll go back to your Queen, and we'll all do the best we can to act as though it never happened. And we'll maintain good relations in Council, and talk on the phone when we need to, but we'll probably never be alone together again."

"Deven—"

"Go, David. Please. Just go."

There was nothing else David could say. He gathered his discarded clothes and put them on with numb hands, aware of Deven's eyes on him.

He left the room without looking back, afraid that if he did he would fall apart. He avoided the faces of the guards as well; they belonged to California, not him, so what they thought didn't matter, but once down the hall, approaching the nearest Elite post, he found that he couldn't make himself walk past them . . . and so, risking exhaustion to save face, he Misted, holding the image of his suite tightly in his mind and pulling it toward him, passing through space at a thought.

He reappeared just inside the door . . . where Miranda was waiting for him.

"Is this the part where I storm out and leave you?" she asked very, very calmly.

David was staring at her as if he expected her to do far worse than that; keeping an eye on her, he approached the fireplace and took his chair, each movement deliberate, the way he did when one of the horses got spooked and he didn't want to get kicked in the head.

"Seriously, you need to tell me," she went on. Her voice was so even she might have been discussing the weather. "I've never been cheated on before. I'm not sure what my job is here. Do I yell? Do I cry? Throw things? Kill you? Oh, wait . . . I can't do that."

He still didn't speak. She could feel the guilt, and the shame, radiating off him, poisonous. Worse, she could smell it . . . sweat, and sex, and *him*.

"I could kill you," she reasoned. "I'd only live for about two minutes, but they'd be a very satisfying two minutes."

Nothing.

"I hope it was worth it," she went on. The pitch of her voice rose just a tiny bit. She couldn't stop it. "It felt like it was pretty fantastic. I was lying in bed feeling almost well enough to get up and go to the music room, not thinking about my best friend who almost died because of me, and wham! Suddenly I was so turned on I couldn't stand it . . . but it wasn't me. Was it good, baby?" Her hands gripped the arms of her chair so hard they were white. "You smell like a good hard fuck. Is it better with a guy? You never did tell me. Do my breasts get in the way? I know I'm pretty good, but did you scream louder for him?"

He shrank back further into himself with her every word, staring at her, eyes wide and fearful. She was starting to sound slightly hysterical, but again, she couldn't seem to help it, and besides, she didn't care. She had been waiting for him for more than an hour, feeling vicarious waves of pleasure and pain, her own body responding traitorously even though there were no hands touching her, no tongue against her thigh. She tasted blood in her mouth— not David's, and not hers.

Bile rose in her throat, and she stood up. "Was it worth it? Tell me, David. *Was it?*"

He couldn't look at her. "No."

"Am I supposed to just sit around barefoot like a good little wife, keep the home fires burning, while you're out sucking off your boyfriend?"

He looked up at her. "It was a mistake," he said. "I didn't mean for it to happen."

"You didn't mean for it to happen? What does that even mean? You lay down on the ground and he tripped and fell on your dick?"

"Beloved, please . . ."

The quaint term of endearment had always made her smile, but now it brought a thunderous wave of rage through her body, and she hit him.

He didn't fall back, but his head snapped around, and when he faced her again blood oozed from the corner of his mouth.

Her vision went scarlet. She hit him again.

"Get up, you bastard!" she all but screamed. "If it's so fucking easy to hurt me, do it right! Get up!"

He stayed where he was, bleeding, and she punched him

again, and again, cursing him, each time her voice rising until she lost her hold on the English language and simply wailed, throwing her betrayal at him the only way she knew how.

She heard glass shattering; the force of her emotions was seeping into the room and causing things to fall off shelves. She didn't care. All she could do was scream until her voice gave out and she sobbed incoherently, collapsing on the floor, unable to hurt him badly enough, to make him bleed enough, to match the way she was bleeding.

He pushed himself off the chair and came to her, folding her into his arms; at first she tried to fight him off, but he wouldn't let her go, and at last they both wept, clinging to each other like children on a battlefield.

"I'm sorry," he whispered brokenly, over and over again.

"God, I wish I could hate you," she moaned, striking his shoulder with a halfhearted fist. "Why did you bring me into this life and then do this to me?"

Shaking, he reached up to his throat and pulled the Signet from it, pressing it into her hands. "Here," he said, face wet with tears. "Break it. Break it, Miranda."

She drew a tremulous breath, not comprehending. "Why?"

"Kill one of us and we both die. Break one stone and its wearer dies. It's the only way to sever the bond—otherwise you're trapped here with me forever."

She stared down at the amulet in her hand. "Just like that?"

"It's something everyone knows but no one has ever done. I don't know what would happen to you afterward. You might not survive long, but at least . . . at least you'd be free."

She was still crying, but she shook her head. "No." She lifted the stone and fastened it back around his neck. Her voice was barely a whisper. "You don't get off that easy, baby."

She left one hand on his Signet and moved the other hand to cover her own. "I'm not going to let you run away at the first test," she went on. "I'll stay with you . . . but you have to stay with me."

"Anything," he said. "I would do anything for you."

"Okay," she replied, touching her forehead to his. "The first thing you can do is take a shower."

"Yes . . ." He wiped his eyes, seeming bewildered by the display of emotion that had escaped his habitual walls, and got to his feet.

She felt so hollow inside, and still weak; she hadn't been ready for this. She tried to stand, too, and couldn't. David saw her struggling and reached down to lift her.

Miranda stood, hands on his arms. "Let me help you to bed," he said.

"Not yet. First, I'm going with you." She fixed a stony, but not angry, stare into his eyes. "I want to do it myself."

He didn't fully understand, but didn't argue, and helped her to the bathroom, then stepped back to see what she had been talking about.

She took a deep breath. "Turn the water on. Hot."

He obeyed.

Miranda nodded and came over to him, unbuttoning his shirt without touching his skin; she couldn't touch him, not yet. He let her without protest or comment.

Fighting her weariness, she unzipped his jeans, and finished stripping him slowly and clinically, taking each item of clothing and dropping it in the trash.

Then she removed her own, her tank top and yoga pants going into a pile on the floor. When they were both naked, she nudged him toward the shower.

The steam made her dizzy, but she was too intent on her task to give in to her body's desire to curl up and sleep. She pushed him into the water spray, for once not pausing to enjoy the sight of hot water cascading down over his body; instead, she took washcloth and soap and, with deliberate slowness, washed him from head to foot, scrubbing some places hard enough to leave the skin raw.

There had been a few bruises lingering on his flesh, but by the time she was finished they were gone, as was the faint black eye that she had given him. He stood perfectly still, moving only when instructed, until she was satisfied that nothing of Deven remained on his body, and every last inch of him was clean.

"Get out and dry off," she told him. "Then go to bed."

He had questions but didn't ask them. He only did what he was told.

She gave herself the same treatment, only robotically, her body numb to her own touch and the slickness of the soap. It was her favorite scent, but she couldn't smell it. As she washed, tears streamed from her eyes again, another surge of impotent anger and agony hitting her. She sagged back against the shower wall, washcloth still in her hand, and folded up on herself, sinking to her knees with the water hitting her in the head, dragging her hair into her face as she cried, and shook, until the wave had passed.

She took her time drying and putting on clean clothes. She returned to the bedroom, where he was waiting in bed, lying on his side facing her without making eye contact.

She considered sleeping on the couch, or making him do it, but something inside her started keening at the thought and she was too wrung out from tears to make herself face the morning in an empty bed. Wordlessly, she climbed in on her side, pulling the covers up around her. David waited for her to indicate it was okay to touch her, but she ignored him and rolled over to face the wall. Couch or no couch, she might as well have been across the ocean.

Neither of them slept.

Only Faith showed up the next night at midnight to officially bid the West farewell. She was surprised, and made deeply uneasy, by the way the Prime had ordered her to see them off, with no explanation; he didn't sound like himself at all, and it wasn't like him to command her without giving her reasons.

When she saw Deven and Jonathan, she knew exactly what was going on.

Deven emerged from the Haven first, by himself, which was also weird; he nodded to her without smiling and got in the car, not even saying good-bye. He looked normal, for Deven, in leather coat and studs, a bit more casual this time with fingerless gloves against the chill, his nails freshly painted. He was as stoic as always, but something was missing that she couldn't quite put her finger on . . . until Jonathan came outside.

He wasn't smiling either. In fact, he glanced in Deven's direction and the almost undetectable flicker in his eyes gave it away, as did the way he looked back at the Haven as if he'd rather be staked and quartered than ever set foot inside again.

"Jonathan," Faith said, unable to keep to protocol any longer, "are you all right?"

He paused and gave her a smile that was lacking in its usual good humor. "Not particularly, Faith. But don't worry about us. We'll make it, I promise." He lifted his eyes to the Haven again. "Worry about your own house instead."

"Oh, no," she said. "You don't mean . . ."

"They're going to need you more than ever," he replied. "Promise me, Faith, that you'll do what you can to help them work things out. They could come through this stronger than before . . . and then, perhaps everything won't have gone to waste."

"You know I will," she said. "I promise."

"Good. Time to go home now . . . I hope we'll see you again someday."

With that Jonathan got in the car, and one of their Elite shut the door.

She watched the car pull away, unsure what to feel, but pretty sure she wanted to go kick David in the balls, then find Miranda and hug her—to hell with protocol and professionalism. What must the Queen be going through, if what Faith suspected was true? Miranda wasn't as jaded as the rest of them yet. She couldn't have seen it coming like Faith had. Half the Elite had been taking bets, since that evening in the training room when the two Primes had fought each other into a trance, on how long it would take them to wind up in bed together. But Miranda . . . she was so young, and had been a vampire and Queen for only a few months . . . and, from what Faith remembered, she didn't have much of a history with love. Faith had to check on her.

She went back into the building, intent on heading for the Pair's wing to see if she could find Miranda without making it too obvious that she was looking, but one of the other Elite caught sight of her and hurried over to her side.

"Lali," Faith said. "You're off shift, aren't you? Why are you still in uniform?"

Lali was holding a familiar-looking metal case. "I've been waiting for you," she said. "The Prime sent me to town just after sunset to pick something up from Hunter Development. Doctor Novotny, the human researcher, had something for him—I mean, this. He said the results are inside on a thumb drive, and that I must deliver them only to you or the Pair, in person. But no one seems to know where the Prime is tonight, so I came to you."

"Thank you, Lali—I'll take it from here."

The bodyguard bowed and went her own way, no doubt to get out of uniform and relax with her violin.

Faith took the case with her to the Signet wing, but to her consternation neither Prime nor Queen were to be found in their suite, the music room, David's workroom, or any of their other usual haunts. She would have been alerted if they'd gone to town, so it stood to reason they were somewhere around the Haven, and given what was going on, chances were they weren't together.

"Star-one," she said into her com.

She was one of only a handful of Elite who had direct access to David's com; in some situations he granted temporary permission for one of the others to relay information to him, and of course he could listen in on anyone on the network whenever he wanted, but for the most part everything went through Faith. She, then, was one of the few who recognized the series of tones she heard as a message: The Prime was not talking to anyone, but she could basically leave him a voice mail, and he would listen to it when he felt like it. It was rare for him to use it, but she had heard it before.

"Sire," she said, "Elite Sixteen brought in the case that Doctor Novotny sent over. I'm leaving it in your workroom now. Star-three, out."

Faith also had clearance for the workroom, so she unlocked it and went inside, half expecting to find David there ignoring her previous knock.

He wasn't; the room was dark. She flipped on the lights and set the case down on the table, fully intending to leave it there without snooping; but technically she did have the authority to look inside, and the need to know what the hell was going on in their city overrode the fear of highly unlikely reprisals from the Prime.

She flipped the case open and found what she expected: two wooden stakes and a knife, along with a USB drive containing all of Hunter's test results.

Faith noted the contrast between the two stakes: They appeared to be made out of a similar sort of wood, which was unremarkable. Certain woods were favored by vampire hunters because they were harder and more durable. The assassin's stake from the attack on Miranda, however, was traditionally carved; the other, Deven's, was an exquisitely crafted piece of weaponry. It was about half the size of the traditional stake and had a steel hilt that was weighted for throwing. From seeing its ilk before, she knew that the wood was fitted onto a steel shaft. The wood could be removed and replaced if it splintered or dulled, and the shaft inside helped it fly straighter and penetrate farther. Deven's weapons collection was a thing of beauty and had been gathered from all over the globe, but he commissioned the throwing stakes from his own design even down to the elaborate carving on the hilt.

The knife, on the other hand, was not the centuries-old implement that Novotny said had carved the Finnish woman's stake. It was a fairly nondescript blade, of decent quality but no real artistry. It had been used to stab Kat in the abdomen, and though the blood had been cleaned off, Faith could still imagine it seething with deadly purpose. Whoever this woman was, she knew a lot about Miranda and her friends, even that Kat was pregnant. It was just the sort of thing the Red Shadow was supposed to be paid to know.

Faith took the USB drive over to the bank of computers and interactive screens that performed various arcane functions for the Prime and plugged it in. She was no technological wizard, but the files inside were in pretty basic format, and she knew the password to unlock them.

Most of what she saw made no sense whatsoever. The lab had tested for a vast array of trace elements and volatile compounds, many of which could have come from anywhere in the city. Luckily, for the sake of those who, unlike David, didn't get their jollies reading chromatograms, there was an overview of the results and a chart that compared the numbers for all three weapons at a glance.

It was there, nestled among polysyllabic chemical names and ratios, that she saw it.

Faith stared at the data, rereading it, then again; but the facts didn't change.

Still staring, she raised her arm and said into her com, "Star-one."

When the same tones alerted her to the voice mail, she said, "Security override, authorization Star-three." The override would push her through to the Prime's com no matter where he was or what he was doing, and it would boost her signal to a practically earsplitting level. David had threatened mayhem if she ever used it, but there were times when mayhem was the least of her worries.

A recorded female voice informed her that her identity and clearance were being confirmed; please wait.

*"Security override granted."*

Faith said, as clearly as possible, "Sire, this is Faith. I'm in the workroom with Novotny's results. You need to come down here right now." She looked over at the box with its trio of deadly weapons. "There's something here you need to see."

PART TWO

# Lilith's Blade

# Eleven

The squatty little man reminded David very strongly of a toad. His eyes were beady and small, his mouth a long line in a broad, flat face; he might hit David's shoulder if they stood back-to-back, but he was about three times as wide. He had long arms and his torso was heavily muscled from wielding hammers and other heavy implements for two hundred years.

David stared at him, and he stared right back, indifferent to his surroundings or his interrogator.

"So you're Volundr," David said.

A grunted affirmative.

"I imagine you're wondering why we brought you here."

Another grunt. The man's voice was deep and . . . well, croaky. "Got something to do with the stakes."

"Yes, it does. I have a few questions for you about these."

David gestured to his left, at the table where Faith had placed the stake that had been shot at Miranda and the one that Deven had thrown at the assassin.

A third grunt, betraying no surprise.

David glanced over at Faith, who stood in front of the door, arms crossed, listening impassively. It had taken three weeks to find this man and get him to Austin—three weeks and the cooperation of the West, who had extradited him from Washington state where he had dwelt in the forest in a dim little house and forge for centuries. David wasn't sure how the Pair had convinced Volundr to surrender quietly; he was clearly not the type to be easily intimidated.

David picked up the first stake. "This was fired from a miniaturized speargun at my Queen," he said. "It's been identified as silver birch from Lapland. The second one belonged to Prime Deven of the West. The Prime identifies you as the man who crafted the interior shaft and hilt, then carved the wood tips for him . . . out of silver birch. We've confirmed that these two stakes not only are the same kind of wood, they came from the same exact forest."

"Coincidence," Volundr said with a shrug.

"Right." David laid the stake back down in its foam casing. "A search of your property turned up about nine different kinds of wood in addition to all the metals you work with—most were just firewood, but two, the birch and a supply of coastal redwood, are known for their use in battle-ready stakes. Silver birch, however, isn't typical of the Pacific Northwest. Where did you get it?"

He shrugged again.

"Did a woman from Finland supply you with it when you made stakes for her?"

Nothing.

"Sir," David said, letting a little hardness enter his voice, "I feel I've been very patient up to this point. We are trying to catch a killer in my territory. I know you're not the killer because you're neither female nor athletic—I don't doubt your strength with the hammer, but you're hardly assassin material. The birch that we found on your property matches these two stakes exactly. You are without a doubt connected to all of this."

"What do you want, boy?" Volundr finally asked. "What do I have to tell you so you'll have your little toy soldiers take me home to my work?"

"I want a list of your clients."

Volundr looked at David in silence for a moment before he laughed out loud; it was a brash, unpleasant sound that nearly made David flinch. "If this girl is such a problem for *you*, maybe she threatened *me* and I'm too scared to talk."

David raised an eyebrow at him. "Oh, come on."

"Or maybe I don't know this girl," Volundr went on. "Maybe I bought the wood from the same dealer as her and you're wasting my time."

David exhaled slowly. He'd been expecting about as much. "You do understand that until I get a satisfactory answer you'll be held here."

A flicker of reaction. The smith didn't like being away from home; that much was clear. He probably hadn't traveled out of Washington as long as he'd been living there. He wasn't a psychically strong vampire, living as he did in the middle of nowhere away from a steady supply of human blood, but he was physically strong and his skills were in high demand. He was one of three weapons crafters that Deven trusted with his own designs, and Deven had not been at all pleased to bring Volundr in for questioning; he had agreed, however, as something of a peace offering.

Yet peace was not to be found . . . not here. David had let Faith arrange everything. David had spoken to Deven exactly twice since the Pair had returned to the West: once, when Faith's realization about the two stakes drove David to call Deven and essentially accuse him of collusion with the assassin; and again, when David called to apologize after Faith—and Miranda, who had maintained a remarkably level head about the whole thing—pointed out that Deven had no motive whatsoever to kill Miranda, as doing so would kill David, too . . . and, the truth was, if Deven wanted Miranda dead, she already would be.

Deven's acceptance of his apology had been icy and insincere, but out of hurt, not anger. David now had one more sin to add to the growing list of wrongs against those he professed to love.

He stared at the smith for a moment before saying, "All I want are names, Volundr. Give me a list of people who might be the woman I'm after, and you can go back to work."

"I have no loyalty to the South."

"What about the West? Surely the Prime's money has bought your loyalty over the years."

Volundr shook his head. "Little faggot invaded my house and turned me over to you. I don't owe him sh—"

The end of the sentence turned into another grunt as the smith flew backward, slammed into the far wall of the interrogation room, and landed on his ass on the stone floor.

The Prime waited until he'd struggled to his feet to say, "We can do this the easy way, Volundr, or the fun way. I'll be the first one to tell you I'd find a great deal of satisfaction in dislocating all of your joints one by one, or possibly peeling the skin from your back and pouring acid on your muscle tissue . . . but I respect you as a craftsman and I would hate to see one of the most talented of your trade treated in such an undignified manner."

Yet another shrug. "I'll heal. I got nothing to say to you, boy."

"I'm older than you," David snapped, losing just a tiny bit of his patience—he'd had precious little of it these past few weeks, and what was left was wearing perilously thin. "And my respect only goes so far. If you want this to hurt, it can hurt. You know very well what I'm capable of, Volundr— you're no stranger to the Signets. Give me what I want or I start with your fingers."

"I'm not afraid of that glowing rock round your neck," Volundr said, still disturbingly undisturbed about the prospect of bodily harm. "You think you're the biggest power in the world? You're hardly out of diapers. I know power a hundred times older than you . . . sleeping in the rocks of the earth."

David sighed. "You're not going to give me some poetic tripe about stones and steel and the might of your anvil, are you? That's just pathetically phallic."

"I'm not talking about my dick, boy. I'm talking about the Firstborn."

Whatever threat David had intended to deliver died on his lips, and he blinked in confusion at the smith, who looked smugly satisfied at his reaction.

"Firstborn," David repeated. "That's ridiculous. They're a myth."

"Oh, are they?"

"Volundr," David told him, smiling a little, "you're not going to distract me with fairy tales. I can see that you take me for a fool, but I'm afraid you're wrong . . . and you're wrong in thinking that you have nothing to say to me. An hour from now you're going to have a lot to say."

The Prime flicked his hand, and Volundr flew back against the wall again, this time pinned a foot off the ground by the force of David's power.

David looked at the man, trying to maintain his dispassion, but beneath it, dreading the next few hours. *Just talk. Don't make me do this.*

He moved close enough that he was only a foot away from Volundr and held the smith's eyes. "You are giving me no choice," he said quietly. "I will protect my Queen and my territory at all cost, and I know that you know the name of the assassin. Whatever she's offered you in return for your silence . . . it won't be worth what comes next."

Volundr was still calm. "I don't know who it is," he said.

"You're lying."

"I don't know who it is," he said again, this time with a faint touch of anger. "And I'm not giving up any names. People pay me to build things and keep them secret. No bratty little upstart with a Signet is gonna get me to break two hundred years of silence. I answer to people way more important to you. You won't dare wake them up."

David stepped back, nodding. "All right, Volundr. I understand your position. But there's one piece of advice I should probably have given you before we began."

Volundr sucked in a pained breath as the first of his fingers snapped backward.

David crossed his arms, and each word was punctuated with the dull sound of breaking bone as he said, "Never . . . ever . . . dare me."

A few days of unseasonable . . . or seasonable, as it turned out . . . warmth unfolded gently over the Haven, and finally

Cora felt strong enough, and brave enough, to go outside and see the world for herself.

She had heard the servants talking about this year's cold weather. Winter in Texas was apparently about as mild as that of Italy, but this year there had been ice already and there might even be snow before January at this rate. Mostly the servants seemed upset about the volume of firewood they were burning through.

They didn't talk much to Cora directly, but she was gradually picking up more of their language thanks to the computing machine in her room and its language discs. Mostly she listened, rather than speaking; she learned so much more that way . . . and not just about English.

Something had gone terribly wrong here in the last month. She knew that even before she caught snatches of conversation here and there that affirmed the tension she could practically taste in the air. She could feel the change even before she asked one of the door guards if Prime Deven was taking visitors, only to be informed that the Prime had departed the night before. The guard's tone suggested she not make further inquiries, but she caught something in the words, some . . . faint embarrassment, almost. She went over the conversation in her mind and decided that the man was not embarrassed about Deven himself, but about something that had happened to cause the Prime's premature exit from the Haven. Cora didn't know what to make of it.

So she went outside.

She asked the guards if it was all right, but these days they barely seemed to notice her comings and goings, and that was fine with her; she had explored the house pretty thoroughly, but what really interested her were the grounds and gardens, and one night during the warm spell she decided now was the time. She put on her newest discovery—blue jeans—her hooded sweatshirt, and the soft shoes the Elite had lent her, and left her room.

The closest exterior door she had found on her wanderings let her out in the back gardens near a wide trail that she guessed was for the horses. A fence ran alongside it, bordering a pasture.

She stayed with her back against the wall for a moment, getting used to the broad expanse of the night sky and the sheer openness of the world in front of her. Her heart was pounding with fear—it felt so exposed, so wrong—and she very nearly gave up and fled back to the safety of her room.

*No. I have lived my life afraid.*

Biting her lip, Cora pushed herself off the wall and took a few halting steps forward, then a few more. Neither the hand of God nor a lightning strike smote her where she stood. A few more steps and she reached the pasture fence, to which she clung for a moment, panting.

"Better," she murmured. "Perhaps there's hope for you yet, girl."

She heard a muted, thumping sort of noise growing nearer, along with the rustle of grass. When she lifted her head, she yelped and leapt backward.

An enormous black horse was standing on the other side of the fence, staring at her with a distinct look of amusement in its round, dark eyes.

It had been many years since Cora had seen a horse up close, but she'd been familiar with them once, and as soon as the shock of such a huge animal sneaking up on her wore off, she moved back to the fence, looking the animal over as it looked her over.

"You're lovely," she said to the horse with a quick look to discern that it was, in fact, a female. "A lovely lady."

The horse seemed to agree with Cora and dipped her head to rip up a mouthful of grass. It was strange that she should be out at night; could horses see in the dark, Cora wondered? There were lights along the trail, and enough were lit that to Cora's eyes it was nearly as bright as day, but she wondered how odd it must be for such animals to live according to a vampire's schedule.

Cora reached through the fence with one arm, gesturing for the horse to come to her; black ears flicked in response, and the horse's plate-sized hooves clomped toward the fence.

The horse inclined her head and gave Cora's hand an imperious sniff, then allowed Cora to scratch her between the eyes.

"It's a miracle," someone said wryly.

Cora jumped but managed not to cry out this time, and she twisted around to see the uniformed woman who had come up behind her and was now watching her with surprise in her almond-shaped eyes.

"Her name is Isis," Faith said. "She bites."

Cora looked back at the horse. "She is very proud."

Faith chuckled. "That's putting it mildly. Only a handful of people have ever gotten that close to her, and it's never her idea. She must like you."

Isis gave Faith a look of mild disdain and then ignored her, permitting Cora to continue petting her head and neck. "Were you looking for me?" Cora asked Faith. She had to speak slowly to keep the English organized in her head, but Faith didn't appear to have a problem understanding her.

"Yes. I know that with everything that's been going on you've gotten a bit lost in the shuffle, so I wanted to check on you and see if you need anything."

Cora frowned and decided to take the plunge. "What has happened?"

The Second came to lean against the fence. "I'm not at liberty to say," she replied, "but I can assure you that your safety is still guaranteed. You have nothing to worry about."

"I am not," Cora said, adding, "but I know everyone else here is worried about something. Is it my Mas . . . I mean, Prime Hart?"

Faith shook her head. "Right now he's the least of our problems. Let's just say there is a situation and we're working to contain it as quickly as we can."

"Does the situation have to do with Prime Deven?"

Faith's eyebrows lifted. "You're more observant than I thought."

Cora wasn't sure whether to consider that a compliment or an insult. She said nothing and merely went on stroking Isis.

"Have you given any thought to what you want to do next?" Faith asked.

"Yes," Cora said. "I have no idea."

The Second smiled. "There's no hurry, of course. I was just curious. I know after everything you've been through, the peace and quiet here must be heavenly, but I also know that eventually you're going to get bored."

Cora gave her a sad smile in return. "I have no education, no money, no family, and I barely even know how to turn on a computer. I do not think I will have many options."

Faith shrugged. "I'm sure if you want to go to school the Pair will be happy to help you. I can arrange a tutor for you if you'd like to speed up your English lessons or start learning other subjects. We can get you an American ID. Really, you just have to decide what you want."

Cora withdrew her hand from Isis and leaned back on the fence as Faith had, looking up at the black dome of the sky. "I have never been free to want anything," she said. "I'm not sure I know how."

Faith reached over and patted her on the shoulder. "You'll figure it out. There's time."

As Faith touched her, for the second time Cora felt the strange shivering she had with Prime Deven, and for a heartbeat's length she saw Faith in her mind's eye, standing at a window somewhere in the Haven, wiping impatiently at her eyes with one hand. Cora's eyes followed Faith's to the scene she was gazing at, but before she could see what had stirred the Second so, her vision cleared, and she heard Faith's voice: "I almost forgot to give you this."

Cora looked down at the bracelet Faith was fastening around her wrist, recognizing it as one of the devices the Elite all wore to talk to each other.

"This will let us know where you are in the Haven," Faith was saying. "We can already track you on the sensor network, but this way if there's a problem you can call for assistance. It's easy: Just speak into the com and say, 'Starthree,' and I'll answer. It doesn't have to be in English, either; the system recognizes about thirty languages."

"Thank you," Cora said.

"I have to go—I'm due in the city shortly. Are you sure there's nothing you need?"

"A purpose?"

Faith grinned. "You could always join the Elite."

Cora couldn't stop herself from laughing aloud. "I lack the grace to walk without tripping. I would slice off my own arm if given a sword."

Faith laughed, too, and said, "You know, I think I have an idea that might help you with that. I'll come back to see you tomorrow."

"Thank you," Cora said again. The Second gave her a slight bow and a brief smile and left her at the fence, where Isis was already nosing up to her for an ear scratching, giving her a commanding snort and tossing her head impatiently.

Cora sighed and carefully climbed up on the bottom rung of the fence so she could reach the horse better.

For tonight, at least, this was as close to a purpose as she was going to get.

*Baby I bleed*
*I bleed without you*
*Kiss me one more time*
*Then twist the knife*
*And walk away . . .*

Everyone in the studio was crying.

The rented Bösendorfer took up perhaps half the room, but its sound, and the sound of heartbreak, filled every inch of space, crawling into every nook and cranny like an oak's roots through concrete.

Miranda had decided, seemingly out of nowhere, to record

a bonus version of the album's title track. The first version was lushly produced and had a string quartet. This one was just her and the piano, stripped down and raw.

*You carved your name into my heart*
*You said we were forever*
*But everything falls*
*Everything falls apart . . .*

She didn't know if her empathic influence would translate through digital media, or if it was only something that worked in live performance, but if it did, no one who heard the song would be able to stop their tears; they would pause in whatever they were doing and find themselves reliving the worst possible breakups, betrayals, and disappointments of their histories. Chances were after hearing the track they would skip it every time they played the CD, preferring the first version of the song. She didn't especially care either way.

As they wrapped the session, she looked into the control room to see that Kat had arrived and was sitting on the stool that Lali usually occupied. Lali had been recording her part for one of the other tracks, so she was out at the car stowing her violin.

Kat looked tired. Pregnancy symptoms had hit her like a truck in the last two weeks, and she spent most of her mornings with her head in the toilet. Under the boyish half inch of hair that had grown since the attack, her face was drawn and looked a little clammy, but at least she seemed glad to be there.

Things were still a bit weird. Miranda hadn't pushed; she knew Kat was having a hard time with what had happened. So was Miranda . . . even worse than Kat, thanks to a heavy dose of guilt on her back knowing she was the reason the assassin had targeted her friend.

They were reasonably comfortable with each other again . . . as long as Drew wasn't around. Aside from the fact that he tended to stare at Miranda as if she were about to pop Kat's head like the tab on a Coke and slurp her dry, Miranda found it increasingly difficult to put up with how he doted on Kat. Every other word out of his mouth was *honey*, and he fussed over her like a child when he wasn't gazing at Kat like she'd hung the moon. There might have been a time when Miranda thought that sort of thing was cute, or at least tolerable.

Now was not that time.

In fact, Miranda wanted to smack the shit out of every couple she saw—the more affectionate they were, the more she wanted to strangle them. *What kind of moron are you?* she wanted to yell at them. *He's fucking your sister! She only cares about your money! He posted those pictures on the Internet! She's leaving as soon as she gets her birthday present!*

It was possible she was a little bitter.

"So," Kat said as they walked out of the studio into the frigid night, "how are . . . things?"

"The same. You?"

"Basically the same, but with even more barfing."

"How long does that last?" Miranda asked, motioning to Lali and Aaron to follow at a distance but stay unobtrusive.

"It depends on the person—it's supposed to be a first-trimester thing, but for some people it never stops."

"Sounds awesome."

"Oh yeah." Kat shifted her bag on her shoulder, and Miranda thought about offering to carry it but knew it would irritate Kat to be treated like an invalid—she already rolled her eyes behind Drew's back when he fluttered around her. "Look at me, I'm a breeder. Bun in the oven. In the family way. Up the duff. The rabbit died."

Miranda smiled, her eyes on the grimy sidewalk that was wet with yet another round of late-autumn rain. She was wearing gloves in addition to her coat; she had been taken aback by how deeply the cold affected her, thinking back to when it was weird to her that the Haven burned its fireplaces in August. It also made a lot more sense to her now that the vampire population of Texas was much higher than in, say, Canada, though she'd heard caribou blood was tasty.

"I noticed a lot of red eyes when I got there tonight," Kat was saying. "Were you mojo-ing them?"

"I guess. I'm curious to see if it comes through on the recording."

"I've been meaning to ask you something—what happens if your CD sells like hotcakes and you're famous? Can you tour? Won't people ask a lot of questions?"

"Who believes in vampires?" Miranda asked wryly. "I was thinking about it, too, and I figure, people who think anything about my weird behavior will sound like loonies in the press, and if I need to I can address them head on and make them sound even more loony. As for touring, well . . . I can be away from home for a few days at a time. I probably can't do anything international, though."

"His Highness can't police things without you?"

"It's not that. This thing, this connection between us . . . if we go too long without touching, it starts to make us crazy. Physical contact reinforces the balance of power. Apparently once we learn to manage it we can go a week, but right now I get twitchy after about three days."

Kat raised an eyebrow at her sideways. "So you're still touching, even though you're not sleeping in the same room?"

"We're spending time together. Just not like before. I just . . . I needed some space, Kat."

Kat held up her hands. "I know, sweetie. I'm not being judgmental. I just want to know you're okay."

Miranda wanted to stop and kick a rock, but there weren't any around. "I'm not okay. Not by a long shot. But we're doing the best we can. It's just going to take a while. It helps that he's so torn up about it—and that I can feel he's sincere. I'm not as angry knowing how bewildered and confused he is . . . The guilt feels nice, too."

Kat chuckled. "Bloodthirsty wench."

"Exactly."

"What I texted him last week still holds, just so you know."

Now Miranda's smile was genuine. "I appreciate that, Kat."

"What about . . . the other two? Have you heard anything from Jonathan?"

"No." Miranda's voice went flat when she said it, and Kat took the hint and changed the subject.

"So what do you want to do tonight? It's pretty early yet. Ice cream?"

What Miranda really wanted was blood . . . her thirst had escalated in the last three weeks, compensating for the sheer amount of energy she spent working out, sparring, performing onstage, and stalking the streets of Austin looking for a fight. Somehow, though, she didn't think hunting would be a good girls'-night-out activity.

"Movie?" she asked. "We could go to the Alamo Drafthouse, watch stuff blow up, drink Guinness milkshakes."

"You can have a Guinness shake," Kat pointed out. "I'm out of commission for the next seven months or so, remember? But a movie sounds good. We'll eat fries with a fuckton of *queso* and indulge in some testosterone poisoning. I've been wanting to see the new Johnny Depp. He gives me the tickle."

Miranda laughed. "Lucky you. I haven't had a tickle in weeks."

"Man, that sucks . . . having a guilt-ridden undead stud at your beck and call and not wanting to take advantage of him."

"All right," Miranda said, stopping. "I'm going to call Harlan and we'll bring up the movie schedule on the computer in the car. From this point in the evening, I declare a moratorium on relationship talk, baby talk, and vampire talk in general. Tonight we're going to just be two friends looking for some escapism."

"Sounds like a plan," Kat said.

Smiling, almost believing it would work, they shook on it.

*   *   *

The Winchester Bank building was one of the Prime's favorite vantage points from which to watch the city go by. It wasn't the tallest in Austin, or the flashiest, but it suited him sometimes with its stone gargoyles and half-crumbling architecture. There were nights when he felt like a young god, untouchable; on those nights he took to the tallest skyscrapers. On other nights he felt like a fading relic in a world that would be content to go on without him. Those were the nights when he sought refuge atop the Winchester.

Time seemed determined to slog ever onward whether he went with it or not. In fact, at the Haven it was as though time had crawled backward to an earlier, more sorrowful era . . . and if only it were a new beginning instead of falling apart.

David could feel Miranda on the streets below, walking with Kat; he could sense her but was too far away to hear anything specific unless Miranda wanted him to . . . and she never did, anymore. For weeks she had kept him almost entirely shut out of her mind, her body, and her life. He wanted to howl his loss and shame at the night above, to fling himself off the building if he thought for a moment that it might help him atone, but all he could do was tell himself, over and over, *She's still here. She stayed.*

She stayed, and though she avoided him for large parts of the night and slept by herself, she didn't torment them both with her absence longer than necessary; she came in to see him every morning, and they sat in their chairs by the fire and talked about what they'd been up to, had a drink, made a few jokes, and tried . . . just tried to keep going.

She spent more time in the city than he did, so she was usually the one who prowled the streets of the Shadow District to keep their presence at the forefront of everyone's minds. They were rarely seen together.

Meanwhile he was still enmeshed in the investigation. Coordinating investigations among the West, his Elite,

APD, Hunter Development, and the FBI forensics unit took a lot of time and diplomacy. Faith's discovery—that the stakes were carved of the exact same wood, thereby connecting the assassin to the West—had led them to Volundr, and though the smith had finally wheezed out four names in the midst of choking on his own blood, David wasn't confident that any of them would prove a viable lead.

Still, the Prime had been true to his word, and as soon as Volundr broke and gave up the names, David turned him over to the Elite, who had cleaned and fed him and were now arranging transport to return him to his home, along with what Faith considered an obscene amount of money . . . blood money, a penance that would do nothing to erase the sound of the smith's screams from David's memory . . . or the feeling that even as desperate as they were to find their killer, the ends may never justify the means.

The wind whipped past him, catching the hem of his coat, but he was far enough from the edge that it didn't hit him too hard. The dreary weather suited his mood.

His phone rang: a voice call rather than data. That first week he'd received a text from Kat that simply said, *Your balls + my gun, you rat bastard.* He hadn't been able to think of a clever reply.

He glanced down to see who it was and took a deep breath.

"Hello?"

"Are you alone?" Deven asked. His voice had two simultaneous effects on David: His stomach clenched with anxiety, but his heart quivered with something else entirely. It was maddening that as much as he wanted to stay away from Deven, the investigation kept forcing them back together.

"I wouldn't have picked up otherwise. What do you need?"

His brusque tone apparently surprised the Prime, who said uncertainly, "I wanted you to know I got the list you sent me and I'm bringing them all in for questioning."

"You could have told me that over e-mail."

"Fine," Deven snapped. "I was checking up on you. Excuse the hell out of me for caring."

"Well if you want to know, Deven, I'm lousy," David replied acidly. "I spent the evening torturing an old man. There's a murderer on the loose threatening my Elite and my Queen. She could strike again at any time and I have no idea how to find her or what her endgame is. Not to mention, my wife is barely speaking to me. Your Consort may have instantly forgiven you, but mine isn't so enlightened, or whatever you and Jonathan call your little arrangement."

"Don't throw all your shame on me, boy. As I recall, there were two of us in that bed, and moreover, you started it."

"I didn't notice you having any qualms."

"I'm not saying I did. I'm just saying, don't expect me to shoulder all the guilt here just because Jonathan is older and wiser."

"Are you trying to imply that—"

"David," Deven said firmly, brooking no refusal, "I'm not going to do this again."

David fell silent, as he always had when Deven— whether his friend, his teacher, his lover, his peer, or his employer—used that tone. He sagged back against the wall of the building. "You're right. I can't fight the world and you, too."

"You have to give her time, David," Deven said, going from angry to sympathetic with remarkable speed, which told David he hadn't really been angry in the first place, only reacting to David's foolish clinging to emotional drama. A simple fact of life that David had discovered in his three hundred fifty years was that in the end, problems weren't resolved with hysterics and screaming fits. They were solved in the night-by-night work of honesty and the glacially slow rebuilding of trust. Up until now he had lived that as a given; he just wasn't the kind of person who displayed emotion. But this whole thing had knocked him so far off center that he had no idea how to react to anything anymore. The mere idea that he'd considered throwing himself off the

Winchester like some kind of grief-stricken Gothic widow made him cringe.

"I know . . . I just hate that I've made her so unhappy. She deserves so much better. As a Prime, I can solve problems, put down insurrections, behead lawbreakers . . . as a husband, I'm useless."

A note of amusement entered Deven's voice. "Last time you were a husband you were still a teenager, and your wife couldn't even vote or pray aloud in church. Not even you can be instantly good at everything."

"What do I do?" David asked, barely able to hear himself over the rush of the wind.

"Give her what she needs," he replied. "Space, time, whatever. Let her come to you when she's ready to deal with you . . . but make sure she always knows you're there for her."

"There are days I wish she had killed me, Dev. What do I do with that feeling?"

A quiet chuckle. "You're not a coward, David. You don't run away from your pain."

"I did last time."

"This is different," Deven told him. "Last time you didn't do anything wrong . . . and perhaps you ran, but only because I drove you away. This time you can't put two time zones between you. You have to fight for Miranda . . . for her sake, for yours . . . and mine."

Dev couldn't see him making a skeptical face, but David was sure it came across in his voice. "What good does it do you if we work things out?"

"I have a vested interest in you and your Queen, dear one."

"Meaning?"

"If you split up, I owe my Second twenty dollars."

David rolled his eyes. "You're so full of shit."

"I'll let that comment slide right by. I have to go . . . the first of those suspects is here cooling her heels in the Elite training room, and I have to go terrify her into talking."

"All right. Let me know what you find out."

"I will. I l—" Deven stopped midword and corrected himself with, "I'll talk to you later."

David stared at the phone for a minute after he had hung up.

The worst thing—well, one of a hundred worst things in this situation—was that the dam had officially broken. He could no longer pretend, to himself or anyone else, that he didn't still have feelings for Deven that were, to his continued amazement, fully requited. And though he had always prided himself on self-control, he honestly didn't think he and Deven would ever be able to be in the same room without a chaperone. Miranda's trust in him had been shattered, yes, but he no longer trusted himself either.

Emotions simply didn't jump and claim him this way. He had fought long and hard to master his heart . . . yet from the moment Miranda had come into his life, that wall he had built brick by brick had begun to fracture, overgrown by tenacious flowering vines that, with each bloom, cracked him open more and more, and now he couldn't be certain of anything except that somehow, some way, he had to make things right with her.

It was lucky they were immortal. It might very well take eternity at this rate.

His com chimed, and Miranda said, *"We're going to a movie—go ahead and head home, I'll get a ride with Faith later."*

Her voice had exactly the same effect Deven's did . . . no, worse. "I'll go back with Faith," he said. "You keep the car. That way Harlan can take Kat home, too. I have some work to do here in town anyway."

*"All right."*

"Have fun," he said hopefully, but there was no reply. She was always more terse when she spoke to him in front of Kat; he wondered if the two of them were discussing his sins, Kat tearing him apart with her quick tongue . . . no. Kat wasn't a behind-the-back-bitching kind of woman. She was direct. She would listen to Miranda and commiserate but wouldn't go out of her way to vilify him.

He hadn't been kidding when he told Kat he liked her or that he appreciated her friendship with Miranda. Without Kat she had no one to talk to right now. Faith had been making overtures, but Miranda needed someone who wasn't directly involved, who had known her as long as Kat had.

He tapped the back of his head against the concrete wall. Enough wallowing for one night. He did have work to do.

He pulled his coat tightly around him, drew in his power, and then allowed the edges of his body to blur, forming the picture of where he wanted to go in his mind and *pulling*.

He solidified on the ground a block away; he could have Misted right at his destination, but he preferred to limit the distance unless it was an emergency. Misting was useful, kept one's tracks hidden, and tended to impress the hell out of people, but it took a lot of power. Before Miranda had come along he had rarely used it, but now that he had a Queen, he could draw on their combined power to restore himself afterward, so it was much less draining. Short trips were still best.

He'd been giving Miranda the basics of the theory behind Misting when they talked in the mornings, and he'd given her a meditation to do to prepare her for it, but it was very dangerous to undertake without a lot of practice and a lot of strength. Her first experience with it had been hard on her, even with Jonathan to guide her. David had heard of Primes accidentally scattering themselves all over the place, which wouldn't kill a vampire any more than a gunshot would, but it took days to drag themselves back together and the burnout factor was astronomical. Prime Al-Bahin was actually missing part of a finger from a botched Mist early in his tenure.

Most of the city's sensors were installed on exterior walls about four feet off the ground, but in areas where the vampire population was especially dense, he had added extra surveillance from above and below, and the device in question was at the top corner of a three-story building. He was going to have to stand on a foot-wide ledge to reach the thing.

Before he got down to business, however, he spoke into his com: "Star-three."

*"Yes, Sire?"*

"Faith, I'm going to need a ride home. Can you meet me at these coordinates when you're off patrol?"

*"Absolutely, Sire. I'll see you shortly."*

"Star-one, out."

David walked down the street without really paying much heed to the city teeming around him. He'd chosen a time and day when the district wouldn't be very busy, and the building he was headed for didn't house a club or bar. It was two stories of apartments over a set of offices, nothing glamorous enough to attract attention. He didn't relish the idea of having an audience, especially because most of the sensors went unnoticed by vampire passersby and he wanted to keep it that way.

He glanced around to make sure no one was watching, then Misted again, reappearing thirty feet aboveground perched nimbly on the ledge, letting his instincts take over to balance him. He was probably going to pay for the energy expenditure with a migraine later, but it was worth keeping his work out of sight. The last thing he needed was people sabotaging the sensors.

He reached up to unscrew the sensor from its housing with one hand and reached into his coat with the other, pulling out what amounted to an entirely new computer system for the device.

The sensor itself was about the size of a golf ball, convex like a store security mirror, with a hard black plastic casing. He swapped out its insides in a few seconds with deft hands, removing a small screwdriver from his coat and wiring the new unit into place, stowing the old one to strip for parts when he got home.

Then he accessed the device from his phone and ran the initial calibration routine. It would have to be fine-tuned from the Haven, but it came online without any glitches, which pleased him. He needed as few problems as possible if he was going to upgrade in a few days.

Compared to this system the original sensor network had been a clumsy, buggy mess thrown together out of necessity with little finesse. In July he had switched the entire network to something a bit more sophisticated, and teams in several other cities were installing systems for those areas. Within a year he'd have every major metropolitan area in the South wired and monitored like Austin was. That would make it much easier for the satellite Elite garrisons to keep things under control. Houston, New Orleans, and Atlanta were first.

His lieutenant in Louisiana, Elite 249, who simply called herself Laveau, had already dealt with quite a bit of grumbling over it. Vampires in New Orleans liked their city just as it was, mystery and mayhem intact. They were David's most opinionated constituents.

As Miranda had said, they could suck it up and deal.

He put away his tools, turning around on the ledge to face outward, reflecting that it would be extraordinarily embarrassing to fall off and break his neck on the street in front of half the vampires of Austin, although chances were he could . . .

Out of nowhere, he heard a whistle, then felt something thud lightly into his arm.

David looked down to see a small wooden projectile sticking out of his coat; the pain registered a second later.

He pressed himself back against the wall and swept the block with his senses, staring in the direction the hit had come from—east. He bent his will in that direction, seeking any sign of whoever had shot at him . . .

It all happened in a matter of seconds. The pain from the little stake, which was no bigger around than a chopstick, became searing, and he felt something hot snaking out from the dart into his bloodstream, dispersing through veins and capillaries in the space of perhaps two heartbeats. By the time he even understood what was happening, his senses had gone totally haywire and dizziness swept over him.

*Poison.*

He grabbed the projectile and yanked it out; sure enough, it was a steel dart with a wooden head, and it smelled strongly of chemicals and now, blood. The wound it left was already closing. Poison couldn't kill a vampire; the only reasons to use poison were either to cause pain during torture or to tranquilize the victim and transport him or her somewhere else . . .

. . . perhaps after cutting off the victim's left hand . . .

David dug his fingers into the bricks so hard his nails split, but he could feel himself swimming sideways; there was nothing he could do. He couldn't even get a thought organized in his mind, let alone coordinate his limbs to stay balanced. He fought hard to remember where he was, why it was so cold . . .

Suddenly a voice cut through the fog. *"Emergency rescue team to Block SD-Three, building Nineteen-A—authorization Star-two. Code Alpha One. I repeat: Code Alpha One."*

He had time to register the fear in Miranda's voice, just before the poison worked its way to his brain, and he felt blood vessels inside his head exploding.

It was excruciating even through the fog. He groaned and put his hands on his head, trying to block the light from his eyes, but the pain was coming from inside, and it got worse and worse . . . this must be a stroke, blood clots in the brain, they'd heal in minutes as long as . . .

"Sire! Holy shit!"

The voice was a hundred miles away, which translated to about thirty feet below him.

"Can anyone get up there?"

*Probably not . . . but I can certainly get down there.*

David didn't even consciously choose to roll over; his body just did it, almost thrashing, his whole being too focused on the pain in his skull to care about staying aloft.

The freezing wind rushed past him, and he waited to hit the pavement and hopefully break his head open to release the demons tormenting him, but instead four strong arms caught him and lowered him gently to the ground.

"Sire! Can you hear me?"

He grunted an affirmative, though Faith's voice was fading in and out. His face felt wet; he patted his skin with a shaking hand and looked blearily at his fingers. Blood. He was bleeding from his mouth, nose, and eyes.

Everything was burning . . . cracking . . . his insides were scorched. He could feel his strength sapping as his vampiric powers burned themselves to a crisp trying to stay ahead of the damage. More than anything, he wanted unconsciousness . . . oh, God, oblivion . . . anything to make it stop . . .

"Get that thing to Novotny—don't touch it with your bare hands! Help me get him into the car. I've got Mo on standby over at the Hausmann. Okay, one, two, three . . . lift . . ."

David felt them picking him up off the ground and carrying him over to the street; before his senses completely shut down he heard the car door slamming and Miranda's anxious voice asking from his wrist, *"Are you all right, baby? Come on, talk to me. David!"*

# Twelve

Miranda could tell that Kat wasn't very happy to be back at the Hausmann. The blonde hovered in the rear of the crowd as the Elite, Faith, and Miranda bore David's unresponsive body into the clinic, where Mo and the entire staff were waiting to care for their Prime.

Miranda turned to Kat breathlessly. "You don't have to stay," she said. "Harlan will take you home."

"Yeah," Kat said, her eyes wide with remembered fear. "I think that's a good idea."

Miranda ushered her back outside, told Harlan to take her wherever she wanted to go, and paused long enough to hug Kat. "Thank you for being here."

"Thanks for the night out. And tell the Count thanks for not getting shot until the movie was over."

Miranda waved at her quickly as the car pulled away, then ran back up the steps into the clinic, her heart lurching clumsily in her rib cage.

". . . poison," she heard Faith say as she burst back into the clinic. "The dart had something on it. If he hadn't called me for a ride, we wouldn't have been there to catch him, and whoever fired the shot could have dragged him off the street without anyone seeing."

Mo didn't normally work at the Hausmann, but this week as luck would have it he had been asked to come train a new mortal intern on vampire medicine and the needs and rights of the fed-on human. That intern was also standing back, looking bewildered and unsure of himself as the doctors moved the Prime onto an exam table and set about stripping off his coat and shirt to see the wound.

"All right," Mo said, taking control of the situation, "I need a pint of O negative infused with antitoxin serum. I'll start a line—Nurse, if you would get the monitors hooked up, please, and reset them to vampiric levels."

They looked relieved at having someone tell them what to do. Most of the staff were human. They had never had to deal with an injured Prime; probably none of them had ever even seen their employer in real life. Normally the direst situation Mo had to deal with was a severed thumb, but obviously he was well versed in his craft.

"I can heal him," Miranda said, her voice cracking. "Let me do it."

Mo saw the state she was in and came over to speak to her. "My Lady," he said calmly, "right now if you tried, you would drain yourself for nothing. This is not an injury that requires a bone set or a laceration healed. The only way to deal with poison is to force it through his system faster, and your mutual healing ability cannot do that. Just as with a stake, the invading body must be removed before healing can begin. We use the antitoxin kit for that, but *antitoxin* is a misnomer; it is more of a toxin accelerator. It changes the toxin's half-life so that it metabolizes much more quickly. Once it is out of his system, then you come in and heal the damage the antitoxins will cause."

"Like chemotherapy," she supplied lamely. "Kill the cancer and hope nothing else dies with it."

"Essentially. Now, you must prepare yourself, my Lady . . . some of the substances in the kit may make things worse for a short while. It will not kill him, of course, but it will hurt. It might be best if you left the room for this."

Miranda shook her head and struggled to her feet. "No," she said stubbornly. "I want to be here. I can't leave him alone."

Mo knew better than to contradict a Queen, so he went

back to his work. David's vital signs were erratic; a vampire's pulse and blood pressure were low compared to a human's, but his had dropped almost to nothing. The only thing that reassured her that he wasn't dying was that she could still feel him, his warm presence in her mind where it belonged, and though it was weakened it showed no sign of letting go.

But he was in pain. His brain was bleeding . . . if they didn't get the poison out of his body soon, the damage might take weeks to heal, and the brain was such a delicate organ, what if . . . she imagined him losing some part of his vast intellect, even temporarily, and helpless tears flooded her eyes. Aside from the horror of it, it would leave the South vulnerable if anyone found out the Prime was mentally compromised.

She half stumbled to the bedside and pulled up a chair, sinking into it and reaching for the hand that they hadn't run the IV into. On the other side, Jackie, one of the nurses, was setting up the bag of blood mixed with a half-dozen specially treated virulent substances, both natural and human created. Mo informed Miranda matter-of-factly that it included tetrodotoxin, botulinum, and dioxin, which were all known to affect vampires strongly. Botulinum was the most agonizing; it passed through fairly quickly but caused such excruciating pain that the victim often snapped his spine spasming before he could metabolize it. The other toxins weren't as painful but would take about an hour total to break down.

Miranda's eyes, blurred with tears, were locked on her husband's ashen face and the blood that had marred its flawless features. "Give me something to clean the blood off," she said quietly, but she knew everyone heard her. Someone pressed a damp cloth into her hand.

At the touch of the fabric, David's eyes fluttered open and she could feel him trying to focus on her.

"It's okay," she said. "I'm here . . . and you're going to be all right."

He couldn't answer. His eyes rolled back, and he was no

longer aware of her presence. She kept at her work, concentrating on wiping the blood away so she wouldn't lose her sanity. She tried to project comforting energy, but she was so scared she had started to go numb.

Gentle but strong hands took her shoulders and guided her back into her chair.

"Easy," Faith said. "You've got to ground, Miranda, and reinforce your shields. You're freaking out the mortals."

Miranda looked up and saw that the human staff members, every one, had huge frightened eyes, and some were shaking from the carryover of her fear.

"They can't do their jobs like that," Faith pointed out. "Pull it back in."

Miranda nodded. She forced herself to let go of David's hand for a minute and breathe deeply, seeking the place of silence and stillness she had fought so hard to create inside herself. With each breath she intensified her shields until she was so strongly walled off from the others that she could barely feel the air on her skin.

The staff's relief was obvious. They sighed, blinked, and did a little deep breathing of their own—chances were they had no idea where their sudden anxiety had come from.

On the other side of the bed, Mo hooked up the IV and switched it on.

Miranda watched the infused blood traveling through the tube into David's wrist. She could hardly breathe as she waited for it to take effect.

When it did, everyone knew.

The Prime's body stiffened, and he gasped. He squeezed Miranda's hand so hard it nearly broke her fingers. A soft sound of surprise and pain escaped his lips, and sweat broke out all over his body; then, like magic, it seemed to pass, and he breathed out.

She almost believed for a moment that it had been that easy.

A minute later, he cried out again, and spasms began to rock through him so powerfully she heard something in his body snap.

Wave after wave of seizures hit him, and Miranda could feel the pain, even through her shields: great hands crushing his skull, needles jabbing, claws ripping out his insides. The light in his Signet was fading in and out, as if it had a short in its wires.

Miranda heard screaming. She didn't understand at first where it was coming from, as no one else seemed to notice it, but then she knew: It was inside his mind, and inside hers.

One of the nurses made a mewling noise, and Miranda's head jerked up in time to see what might be the oddest thing she'd seen so far in her life: Lightweight objects all over the room were floating. A syringe, a pen, several medical tools whose purpose Miranda couldn't divine, and even the intern's necktie were suspended a few inches in midair.

"Oxygen mask, please," Mo said, totally calm. Miranda didn't know if he'd seen this before, but if he was worried it didn't show. He fitted the mask onto David's face and flipped a switch in the wall. David's breathing deepened somewhat and it seemed to calm him a little; a few seconds later there was an assortment of clattering noises as all the levitating items fell back down.

The screaming in Miranda's head went on and on, silent but deafening, and she clung to his hand, afraid to get any closer. His skin had a sick, yellowish pallor now, and another spasm arched his back. Finally Miranda couldn't take it anymore. She buried her head in her free arm and shut her eyes tight.

She heard Mo saying something about liver damage and jaundice. The nurses were talking, too, reading out numbers to each other and asking the intern for various things. But all Miranda really knew was the screaming, with its answering echo in her heart, and it felt like it went on forever.

Then, finally, something indefinable began to ease. The spasms became less frequent and less hard. His pulse began to even out.

Miranda raised her eyes hesitantly and saw that the color of his skin was returning to something like normal.

He was still even paler than a vampire was supposed to be, but the yellow tinge was gone. She could hear him breathing more deeply.

"All right," Mo said. "We are on the downhill run. Nurse Jackie, administer a liter of lactated Ringer's solution, please." To Miranda's questioning look, he replied, "To restore the electrolytes. The poison will be out of his system soon, but it's left his body chemistry in a state of chaos. Anything we can do to bring order will help him recover much more quickly and help your energy repair the cellular damage. The less power you use, the more he'll have available."

She nodded. When she spoke she sounded as if she'd been screaming for hours, though she hadn't made a sound aloud. "Can I do it now?"

Mo checked the monitors, then said, "By all means."

Miranda lurched to her feet and put both her hands on David's chest. He was cold . . . much too cold, though his skin was damp with sweat. It barely felt like there was any life left in him. She had never really worked with their Signet-born healing abilities herself; David had used them on her, but she hadn't needed to try them on him. She had thought he was indestructible.

She reached into herself and found the bond between them, then started to push as much power into him as she could—but then she remembered the way Deven had healed Kat, slowly and gently, and tried to do the same, controlling the flow of energy so that it moved into the Prime gradually as a stream instead of a roaring tsunami. She allowed her awareness to sync up more with his, pushing aside the barriers she'd kept between them for the last three weeks so she could see if it was working.

It was. She could feel damaged organs and tissues regenerating, scarred veins smoothing out, and, most important, the blood that had erupted in his skull being reabsorbed, returning to balance. Mo had been right—doing this before the poison was out would have been futile, because every time she healed him the poison would just undo her efforts until it had run its course. There was no way to know yet how long that would have taken, but she knew it would have been much longer than an hour.

When she felt that a tentative equilibrium had been reached, she withdrew, not wanting to overwhelm his system with too much energy.

To her relief he looked a hundred times better. Mo removed the oxygen mask. "I would say we have succeeded," the medic said, satisfied. "We have blood samples for basic toxicology—the Hausmann has the equipment for a narrow range of tests, so we can run them before the samples die. I already sent a courier with additional samples to Hunter Development; perhaps they can get something from them if they hurry."

"So we don't know what it was," Faith said. She was standing nearby with her arms crossed, her face lined with worry.

"Not yet. Once he is awake I will ask him about his symptoms, and that will tell us much about the culprit."

"I think the odds are pretty good we're dealing with our assassin," Faith added. "But I don't really understand why suddenly she'd be using poison."

Miranda was staring at David's drawn, exhausted face. "To hurt me," she said. "She couldn't just kill him without killing me, too, but she could hurt him."

"Going after a Prime is pretty ballsy," Faith observed. "And stupid. She's going to regret it."

Miranda gave a choked half laugh. "Not if we never catch her."

It was midafternoon when David woke, more exhausted than he could remember feeling in a century but otherwise comfortable. The absence of pain was such a stark contrast to the hour before he had passed out that he was confused for a minute, feeling out along his body without recognizing the sensations of warmth, softness, and relaxation.

There was something nearby that gave off a lot of heat and was also making a rhythmic sound, like a drum . . . it was comforting, and he lay there listening to it for a long time before he tried opening his eyes.

The first thing he saw was red hair.

"Hey," she said softly.

She looked about as tired as he felt, and he sensed she hadn't slept at all. She was stretched out beside him in the bed, propped up on one elbow, watching him wake.

She was in bed. Their bed. Next to him.

His heart did a cartwheel.

"Hey," he answered back. His voice was like sandpaper in his throat. "How long was I out?"

"It's Tuesday afternoon."

He would have expressed shock, but he could barely move. "So, most of a day. You . . . haven't been here the whole time, have you?"

Miranda shrugged. "Most of it. I did the patrol meetings and stuff at dawn but then I came back here." She reached over and straightened out the comforter. "Can I get you anything?"

"No . . . you're enough."

A smile, tentative but genuine. She left her hand on his chest, right over his heart, and said, "You scared the hell out of me."

"I'm sorry."

"I'm not," she said. "I mean, I'm sorry you were hurt, but I'm not sorry that we're here now."

"Does that mean I'm forgiven?"

"I don't know. We can't just flip a switch and have everything back the way it was, but . . . I moved my things back in here this morning. I want to be with you, for better or for worse."

He started to say something but heard his phone ring, and Miranda twisted backward to pick it up off the night-stand. She saw who it was and paused for a minute before biting her lip and handing it to him.

"Go on," she said. "I'm sure he's been worried about you."

David shut his eyes, not wanting to deal with this right

now when everything felt so good, but he hit talk anyway. "Hello?"

The anxiety in Deven's voice made him sound young. "Are you all right?"

"I'll live."

"God, David, I . . . I'm so sorry. Jonathan knew something was going to happen, but he didn't know when or where. I should have called you anyway, just so you'd be on your guard."

David sighed. "It wasn't your fault."

Deven took a deep breath. "I can't stay on. I just wanted to hear your voice—Jonathan's been saying you would be fine, but I had to hear it for myself."

"Really, Deven, I'm all right. I'm weak, and I feel like I could drink an entire volleyball team, but I'm all right."

"Let me know when you figure out what that shit was."

"Okay. Good-bye."

David didn't wait for a farewell; talking took too much effort. He handed the phone back to Miranda. "Put that thing on silent," he said.

She arched an eyebrow at him. "Did you really just say that? Maybe that stuff did eat your brain."

"I just want an hour of peace."

With a smile, she turned off the ringer and put the phone back on the nightstand, then returned her attention to him. "Let me get you some blood," she said. "I had a fresh batch brought in—you haven't fed since the intern at the clinic. Don't worry," she added, knowing how he'd feel about feeding on his employees, "I asked for volunteers and offered a hefty bonus in return. The boy was happy to help, and it was much easier than going out and finding someone."

"Wait," he said as she started to get up. "Stay here for a moment."

She met his eyes, then nodded and lay back down, scooting closer and, after a second's hesitation, putting her arm around him.

Being free of poison had been nothing compared to the relief of that touch.

She burrowed her face into his shoulder, and he inhaled the scent of her hair; they settled in together as they had a hundred times before, and he felt her sigh against his skin.

"I deserved this," he said. "That's all I could think while I was lying there . . . for what I did to you, and what I did to that horrible old man . . ."

"Oh, David," she sighed. "You can't torture yourself . . . sorry . . . for what you have to do as Prime. I don't like it . . . and I know you don't either . . . but think of what will happen if this assassin succeeds and we die. There will be anarchy in the South and a lot of people will be killed. You told me yourself, a long time ago, that sometimes being Prime means doing what no one else should have to . . . that you can't always afford the moral high road."

He looked at her face. "You didn't always feel that way."

She smiled sadly. "You didn't always get this upset over these things." She ran her hand back through his hair and added, "I think we've changed each other, you and I."

"I know you've changed me."

Miranda was silent for a moment, but then said simply, "I missed you."

"I missed you, too."

"I don't know if . . ." She trailed off, searching for words, but he intuited her meaning.

"I understand," he replied. "I've never asked you for anything you weren't ready to give."

"I know." She smiled again. "That's one of the things I love about you . . . you philandering bastard."

He couldn't help but laugh, and she laughed a little, too, hugging him, and then kissing his neck. It was the first time she'd kissed him in three weeks.

"I just wish you hadn't fucked up so badly, so I could go on thinking you were the perfect man," she added, sighing again.

He snorted softly. "I could tell you a thousand stories that prove I'm anything but perfect."

"Truthfully, I already knew you weren't. You listen to rap."

"I listen to everything." He grinned. "Miss 'three songs by Britney Spears on my iPod that I don't think anyone knows about—' "

"Hey, no snooping!"

"I didn't. That night I came home and you were singing in the shower with the stereo going, I looked at the playlist because I couldn't believe what I was hearing."

"If you have such exalted taste, how did you know it was Britney?"

They were both laughing, and it felt so incredibly good, but it was tiring, and he quieted out of necessity. "I love you," he said.

She took a deep breath. "I love you, too."

He could feel that she meant it. He had never been in danger of losing her love, only her faith in him. He couldn't say how or when he would earn it back, but he would. He would find a way. They were a Pair. So much in the world was uncertain . . . but that much, he knew with every bone in his body now, was unbreakable. Somehow he would restore her trust and they would find a way to live with what he'd done . . . for her sake, so she could have the happiness she deserved.

"Go to sleep," she whispered to him.

He closed his eyes. "Sing to me."

He could hear her smiling. "All right."

And, as she sang softly into his ear, and he began to drift off into sleep, he couldn't help but think that being poisoned might be the best thing that had ever happened to him.

*You're in my blood like holy wine*
*You taste so bitter and so sweet . . .*

Running the South on her own was exhausting, but there was satisfaction in knowing that she could handle it, at least for a couple of days.

In the evening at sunset she met with Faith for a briefing on the night's upcoming patrols, and then just at dawn, when the shutters of the Haven had closed and the teams had all returned from the city, she met with them to go over the night's events. Sometimes David simply took a summary report from Faith, but with the assassin on the loose Miranda wanted to hear everything herself.

And though she didn't have anything like David's technological genius, she knew how to monitor the sensor network, routing it through her phone to alert her to problems. He had shown her how to run the routine on the main server that compiled all the night's data into a single report and saved it for later reference. Technically she didn't need to look it over, because the system was programmed to contact the administrator if anything weird happened, but she gave it a once-over anyway. There were always two Elite monitoring it from the office where the property's security cameras were based, but they could only watch, not interpret, and David had them observing the network mostly as a backup in case on some off chance he or the alert system missed something.

Tuesday night she had to mediate a dispute between two members of the Court. Both were nightclub owners and one suspected the other of using mind control to steal patrons. The second owner claimed the humans were migrating to her club because she had started serving food—in fact the *Austin Chronicle* had voted her tapas the best in the city. As petty and ridiculous as the whole thing seemed, if the issue wasn't officially settled it could lead to violence, intimidation, and the risk of exposure. Miranda made both owners submit to a psychic evaluation, looked into their hearts, and found something interesting: The second owner had not been coercing her patrons, but the first one *had* been, in retaliation for a perceived threat to his business. He'd been sending his employees over to the second club to "advertise" for his own place, meaning to compel a few humans here and there to come back.

The Queen was within her rights to shut him down completely, but she knew from watching David deal with similar situations that a popular vampire establishment disappearing would raise a lot of questions, and besides, she wanted people to feel that the South was a solid place to do business. She slapped him with the maximum fine demarcated for the circumstances and ordered him to pay restitution to the other owner, then informed him that there would be Elite watching both establishments for any further misbehavior.

Surprisingly, the first owner wasn't terribly angry about the loss of income—he was more satisfied that his rival hadn't been stealing his customers. Both left the Haven feeling that the results were fair, and Miranda was pleased.

She'd been half afraid since the incident with Prime Hart that she had no political savvy at all and was going to have to stay out of administrative and judicial affairs, which she hated to do because it was what all the other Queens did. But it gave her a shot of confidence knowing that she *could* learn and that she just needed experience and patience. She didn't have much of either, but she was working on it. Her empathy gave her an advantage in this kind of mediation, and the more she learned to use it the better she would be at all of this . . . she would never have believed a year ago that she would think of her gift as anything but a curse, but now she found herself wanting to push it further, see where its edges were, experiment . . .

She had to laugh at herself. Yes . . . David had influenced her, all right.

She persuaded David to take it easy Tuesday night, although he was totally recovered by the time he woke up and fed. She knew he agreed just to make her happy, but she didn't care. She wanted to be sure he was back to 100 percent before hitting the Austin streets again.

Seeing him hurt had shaken her badly. His being hit in the eye with earpiece shrapnel had been minor, but it had freaked her out; this was the real thing. The assassin hadn't been trying to kill him, but she had wanted him down, and if Mo hadn't used the antitoxin kit on him he would have been left in a coma. The preliminary analysis on the dart was that it was a synthetic toxin that targeted blood vessels in the brain; nervous system injuries were tricky and delicate to heal, and something that extreme would have taken even a Prime a week or better to recover from. A lesser vampire could have been out of commission for more than a month. It would have killed a human in minutes.

Maybe it hadn't been life-or-death, but feeling his pain and knowing that even the most powerful vampire in the Southern United States could be hurt so badly terrified her beyond rational sense. She wanted to lock the doors, tie him to the bed, and do anything she could to protect him, and therefore herself, from going through that again. Part of her was still so angry at him, yet part of her—a bigger, deeper part that she couldn't deny—just wanted her husband back and was willing to throw aside everything just to make sure he was safe.

It was so aggravating. She wasn't ready to stop being upset. She had thought she wanted to hurt him for what he had done to her, but then she realized that was the last thing in the world she could stand to see, and now she was left with a pile of conflicting feelings and the nagging knowledge that she was going to forgive him, even though part of her never wanted to. It offended her knowing that something as cliché as having a soul mate could override her perfectly justified outrage.

Things with Kat were still awkward. Though Faith had made it clear she was happy to listen, Miranda hated to put the Second in the middle of her and David's relationship troubles. Faith had been David's friend first, and Miranda could sense she felt conflicted about the situation already. Miranda didn't know what else to do . . . so, in a fit of desperation for someone to talk to, she finally called Jonathan, and they were on the phone for more than an hour.

"How in hell are you doing it?" she asked.

She could tell he was smiling. "For starters, you can't compare your coping skills to mine or anybody else's. Everyone deals with life's steaming shit piles in a different way."

"So you're just . . . okay with the fact that he cheated on you?"

Jonathan chuckled. "There you go again. You forget: We don't have cheating, because we decided at the beginning that there were going to be other men in our lives. Of course . . ." He paused, then clarified, "I don't deny I was angry. It shocked me how angry I was, because I thought I was all right with the idea of his taking a lover at some point. It was so hypocritical of me, not to mention totally out of character. But then once we were back home, on familiar ground, I was able to think about it rationally, and I realized the problem was that this wasn't just some blowjob at the zoo."

"The zoo?"

"Don't ask. The point is, I'm not emotionally attached to any of the people I step out with. It's just sex and we both know it. But whether you or I like it or not, David and Deven love each other, and it's not going away. We can either accept that and deal with it, or we can wallow in our misery for all eternity. I'm accepting it for two reasons. One, because I love Deven and don't want to lose what we have. Two, because he's a recovering Catholic and you wouldn't *believe* the guilty mess he's been, both for damaging your marriage and for making me upset. He's spent too much of his life hating himself. I can't bear to make it worse . . . which goes back to reason number one. I love him. And one way or another, we're going to work all of this out, as are you."

Miranda sighed, picking at a loose thread in the throw she'd draped around herself when she flopped on the couch with her phone. "How old do I have to get before I'm as well adjusted as you?"

"It's a matter of priority. I just know that I want to stay with the love of my life . . . above and beyond the fact that I can't leave. Technically we could live separately and only see each other every few days when the need gets overwhelming, but it would be an awful existence."

"Yeah. I tried that. It sucked."

"My advice is just this: Do what feels right whether it's 'appropriate' or not. Emotions have no manners. They don't care about what people in relationships are 'supposed' to do. You're not Mr. and Mrs. Solomon living in the Austin suburbs, after all."

Miranda smiled. "Really, this whole thing is more like a cross between the British monarchy and *Dawson's Creek*."

"Perhaps. In fact, definitely. But after sixty years I can say in all honesty that it's worth it. Trust me, Miranda. It's worth it."

After they hung up she sat staring at the fireplace for a while, digesting everything he'd said. She felt a lot better just having talked to someone; there had been such a weight on her back, and she hadn't felt comfortable unburdening herself to Kat, or Faith, or anyone. There were some things that only another Consort would understand.

A moment later the suite door opened and David returned from an evening spent in the stables. He looked disheveled but content, and smelled like sweat and horse.

They smiled at each other. "How are you feeling?" she asked.

"Right as rain," he replied. "Except I have some news that might not be entirely welcome."

"Oh, God, what now? Did you hear back from the West about those clients of Volundr's? Were they all dead ends?"

David shook his head. "Not yet. They're still questioning them. This is something else."

"Go on."

He put his phone on its charging dock and his wallet on the desk in preparation for taking a shower—he knew she wouldn't let him sit on the couch if he smelled like Osiris. "Another state visit."

Miranda let her head fall back on the couch. "You've got to be kidding. Can't we put it off?"

"Only if we want the Council to start gossiping. The others will want to know why we're stalling, then they'll speculate on what's going on in our territory . . . they love nothing more than blood in the water. Besides, it would be a breach of protocol."

"Fuck protocol."

"I feel the same way, to be honest. But we have to present a strong front."

"I know, I know. So who is it this time? Someone I'll have to throw at a wall, or someone else you've slept with?"

He looked away when she said that, but said, "Neither. It's Eastern Europe—Prime Janousek. He's an ally and a friend, but nothing more."

She almost felt bad for needling him . . . almost. "No Queen?"

"No. He's been in power for eighty-seven years, so it's a bit unusual that he's still solitary. And a bit sad, because he's a good man and a solid member of the Council. No real enemies, no drama. He's a competent ruler and a decent warrior. I think you'll like him."

She nodded. "That doesn't sound too bad. When's he getting here?"

"Next Monday. He'll only be here for three days. It should be painless."

"Let's not tempt fate by saying that."

"Good point." He pulled his sweater off over his head, then the T-shirt underneath. "At any rate, the visits should slow down after he leaves. There are five or six others who will want to come in the next few months, then after that it will probably stop until a full year has gone by."

"Good," Miranda said. "I've had enough Magnificent Bastards for a while. That will make seven, right?"

David ticked them off on his fingers. "Japan, the Plains region of the U.S., the Middle East, Western Europe, the Northeastern U.S., and the Western U.S., plus Eastern Europe. Seven."

"And Kelley will probably show up sometime in the middle, right?"

"Most likely. He's not leaving Chicago until he absolutely has to—the gang war there has been going on for years, and his Court is teeming with strife. I don't really hold it against him, although he is a bit of an ass. He's not nearly as bad as Hart, but he's been responsible for a lot of the corruption in that city."

"This Janousek's territory includes Finland, doesn't it?"

"Yes. That's another reason I didn't try to put him off. There's a chance he may be able to help us."

As he spoke he got the rest of his clothes off, and she rested her chin on the back of the couch so she could watch; another downside of sleeping in the mistress suite was not getting to see him naked. Her mind, heart, and body all had differing opinions on how best to proceed with their relationship.

He saw her watching and smiled. "Would you like me to flex something for you?"

She giggled. "Just turn around and go take a shower."

A few weeks ago that would have been her cue to take off her own clothes and either ambush him in the shower or be waiting in the bed when he came out. Now, though . . . she turned back toward the fire, biting her lip, torn once again. Her body was quite adamant that she should make up for those three weeks of sleeping alone, but . . . all she had to do was close her eyes and think about sex, and that feeling came over her again . . . that night, feeling him with Deven across the Haven, the sensations and satisfaction that had been devoted to her suddenly given to someone else. Could she even lie there with him without thinking about it? Was she doomed to share a bed with Deven forever?

She imagined herself in Jonathan's shoes, finding most of his sexual enjoyment outside the Haven—perhaps it worked for them, but she couldn't imagine being happy in that kind of arrangement, knowing that David was out shagging who knew who every night . . . or on the other side of it, being bound to someone she loved so much who just . . . didn't want her that way. If she held herself apart from David for now, it wasn't because she didn't want him, it was because she wasn't ready to be that intimate again after such an egregious breach of trust . . . or was she? Was she just punishing herself now?

One thing was for sure: Sitting and stewing about it wasn't helping.

She tossed the blanket aside and left the couch, going over to turn off the lights so the fireplace was the only source of illumination in the room. It was about half an hour before dawn, and she could smell daybreak in the air. The Haven's shutters had closed thirty minutes earlier—they always closed at least an hour before any trace of sunlight entered the sky. The room was warm and dark with a hint of steam coming from beneath the bathroom door; she could hear the water being switched off as she turned back the comforter and sheets and drew the curtains around the bed so that it was mostly closed off, cavelike, its own little world.

Miranda took off the yoga pants and tank top she usually slept in and climbed in beneath the covers, considering for a moment before pushing the comforter down to the foot of the bed and letting the sheet fall over her as she lay on her side, waiting.

A few minutes later David pulled back the curtain; he had on his bathrobe and his hair was damp. When he saw her he froze.

They stared at each other for a long time; she knew he wanted to ask questions but was afraid to, lest she change her mind about being there. Still, he didn't move from where he was standing until she deliberately reached over and patted the bed.

The Prime took a deep breath and nodded, then took off his robe and slid in next to her, the flickering firelight making him look even more uncertain than she knew he was. They held each other's eyes for a long time, neither sure what to do to break the silence.

Miranda understood that he was leaving it up to her. Somehow knowing that made up her mind.

She leaned forward and kissed him very softly on the lips, a light touch, almost virginal. She could feel how much he wanted to simply seize her body and reclaim the ground he had lost, but he held himself back, letting her do what she was comfortable with. So close to perfect, even with his flaws—there was no way in heaven or hell she could ever have hated him, no matter what he did.

She kissed him again, this time more firmly, pausing to run her tongue along his lower lip and then nuzzle the line of his jaw until she reached his ear. She nibbled his earlobe a moment, eliciting a shiver and a sigh, then let her tongue snake out to touch just behind and below his ear, pressing in. He groaned.

She took his shoulders and turned him onto his back, then cast the sheet off her body and let him look at her as she rose up on her knees and tossed her hair back out of the way.

She stretched out over him, propping herself up on her elbows to look down into his face. He smiled and sighed at the touch of her skin, eyes drifting shut.

"These are the first of my terms," she said. "The rest will be communicated to you as I think of them."

His eyes flicked open, but he was still smiling. "Go on."

"Tonight's is this: If I'm going to sleep in this bed with you, I don't want to have any unpleasant thoughts or nagging fears keeping me awake. Therefore your task is to make sure I sleep soundly."

She leaned down and began reacquainting her mouth with his skin; he tasted like clean water, wine, and almond-scented soap. She loved the skin of his throat, especially; she could feel the pulse strong beneath it, harder right now than at rest, and it was sensitive to her nails scratching lightly over it or her teeth finding purchase in the flesh just where neck joined shoulder, leaving a dark purple bruise that faded immediately.

He drew a ragged breath and started to speak, but she wasn't finished. She laid her hand over his mouth.

"It will be very taxing for you," she informed him, shifting her hips down slightly to circle against his; she felt how painfully he wanted her, and smiled, continuing. "You'll have to work long hours and lose sleep of your own. And there will be mornings that I don't want you to lay a hand on me—somehow you'll have to find ways to tire me out regardless. It will be quite a challenge."

She caught and held his eyes. They were glazed with desire, and she knew that at this particular moment articulate speech would not be his strong suit. "Do you accept these terms, my Lord Prime?" she asked, reaching down between them to catch and stroke him until he was panting, tiny sounds of pleasure edged all around with pain escaping him with each breath.

He took a deep breath. "I accept, my Lady."

"Good. You can start at once."

"Thank you," he breathed, and clamped his mouth on hers.

She closed her eyes and let her lips part, allowing his tongue to thrust deep into her mouth, and she sucked on it hard, stealing the breath from his lungs. He grabbed her hips and flipped her onto her back without breaking the kiss, his own hand echoing the motion hers had taken on his body moments ago, but this time pressing in, and in, until she moaned and her back arched off the mattress.

His fingers did a ballet between her thighs, and she pressed her hips up to his palm, whimpering. Meanwhile he lifted his mouth from hers to take a slow, wandering path down over her breasts and belly, tracing spirals of kisses and bites, keeping it almost maddeningly leisurely considering what he was doing to her with his clever left hand. His right, he used to push himself down the bed as he continued his explorations until he had reoriented himself alongside her and, with one swift swap of positions, replaced his fingers with his tongue.

The noises that came from her were strange and unfamiliar, drawn out of her all the way down from her belly, almost animalistic. She writhed above him on the pillows, her hands clawing the sheets to keep herself from twisting into a knot, sweat glistening over her skin.

He lifted his head and looked at her, and she managed to catch her breath long enough to ask, "Why did you stop?"

He gave her a devilish grin. "I was simply wondering, my Lady, if I would be more likely to put you to sleep with two orgasms or three."

Miranda moaned and dropped her head to the pillow. "Three, goddamn it. Three!"

"As you will it." He lowered his head again and pressed harder, at the same time slipping fingers back in, faster.

Not thirty seconds later her entire body seemed to explode from the inside out, and she wailed like a banshee while her muscles contracted and her limbs shook.

Before she had even started to come down, however, he grabbed her hips and turned her over onto her stomach. She knew exactly what he had planned, and so she was ready for him, planting her knees and lifting her hips to let him enter her hard, then drive her forward onto her shoulders, her hands crawling up the mattress, seeking some sort of stability and finding only pillows.

He covered her powerfully on all fours, his chest pushing into her back, and he leaned down and bit her throat and sucked, timing each swallow with the rhythm of their bodies so that the pleasure-pain of being drawn from was boosted exponentially, so much joining, contact inside her body, her blood in his mouth, the smell of her on his breath, both of them sliding against each other on sweat-slicked skin.

Knowing exactly how it would affect her, he changed the angle of his hips and pressed forward, driving in so hard that she screamed, but not out of pain. She threw her own pelvis back to meet him each time, wanting him deeper, wanting him to disappear inside her so they shared a skin. It didn't seem like too much to ask.

Again, the explosion, and again, the earthquake. She bucked underneath him like a wild animal until the wave passed. Then she collapsed gracelessly face first into the sheets.

He let her be for a moment, her body going through the tremors and miniature spasms, tears gathering in her eyes that she wiped away with unsteady hands.

She turned over on her back, saw the self-satisfied look on his face, reached up and slapped the back of his head lightly. "That's two," she panted. "Or are you tired out already?" She pushed her hair out of her eyes and added, "I know at your age the stamina starts to go."

David gave her a narrow-eyed look of feigned irritation. "It would serve you right if I did stop."

She raised him a lazy smile. "And then what would you do with *that*?" she asked pointedly.

"Hmm . . . touché."

He stretched out next to her and, still not in a hurry, kissed her lips, eyelids, and nose. "You are so beautiful," he murmured, running his hand down over her arm, then around to her back to draw her against him. She wrapped one leg around him, gasping as they slid back in together.

Miranda opened her mind to him, and through their bond they were able to touch and connect to each other completely, one consciousness melting into the other the same way they wound around each other in the sheets, moving in a slow undulation, mingled breath the only sound in the room besides the crackling fire.

*Yes . . . this.* It was so easy to forget what they really were, with flesh and bone and space in the way, but beneath it all, in a place where pain and sorrow could never reach, they were one, a single soul that had chosen, for whatever reason, to spend this incarnation walking the earth in two bodies. Here in this place there was no separation, no names . . . but there was joy in duality sometimes, a beauty in moving from separation into unity then back again, the intensity building from a reverent give-and-take to something wild.

This time the tectonic shift hit them both. They clung to each other, breathing in tandem, drenched in each other's sweat, tasting each other's blood.

There was no need to say she loved him—right now words would only force a limit on reality when the truth was simply there soaking into every cell. He laid his head on her shoulder, and she threaded her fingers through his damp hair, her other hand tracing the lines of ink on his back she had already memorized.

Finally, knowing that she wouldn't be comfortable with him asleep on top of her, he shifted off, landing with a grunt to her right.

She looked over at him, grinned, and said, "Three."

# Thirteen

"What do you know about the Firstborn?"

Faith peered quizzically down at David. "It's an old vampire legend," she said, handing him the wrench he indicated with his free hand. She had to speak a little loudly to be heard over the bump of the garage's stereo bass. "Everybody's sire tells it—if you go back far enough in our history, you find references to the vampires who weren't sired, but born. Usually people say they're spawn of Lucifer or Hades or some other dark god. They're like the bogeyman. Behave, or the Firstborn will get you. But it's a myth, like you told Volundr . . . right?"

"As far as I know," David replied, sliding back under the car. "I just thought it was odd that he brought it up, of all the things he could have said."

"He was playing on the fact that vampire history is your pet cause," Faith reasoned. "I'm sure he'd heard that you've poked around for information over the years. A man like him hears everything, even living in the armpit of nowhere."

"I suppose." Faith heard clunking noises, and a moment later the Prime emerged again, handing her the wrench. "Hand me the seven-sixteenths ratchet wrench, please."

"Only if you'll turn the stereo down."

David sighed. "Philistine."

"Sire . . . I hate to tell you this, but you're awfully white to be listening to Tupac."

David rolled his eyes, then made a twisting motion with his hand, and the volume of the music dropped to a more reasonable level. "Unless all you listen to are bamboo flutes, Second, you can fuck right off."

Faith stared down at the row of shiny tools on the cart. "Which one's a ratchet again?"

"The one that—never mind."

Faith watched as one of the tools rose off the cart and flew over to the Prime's outstretched hand. She had long ago lost the ability to be shocked or mystified by his talent; now she merely said, "Why didn't you just do that to begin with?"

He shrugged. "You were standing right there."

"And why aren't you having a mechanic do this?"

David made a dismissive noise. "These cars are loaded with proprietary technology, Faith. I'm not letting anyone get their grubby hands on it unless they're vetted by security. Right now there's nobody in the Elite qualified to do it—let's put that on the list for the next batch of recruits, come to think of it. Someone with automotive repair experience as well as computer programming skills who I can train to do routine maintenance. Familiarity with solar power systems would be a plus."

"Yes, that's a combination you often find in warriors," Faith remarked wryly.

"Which is exactly why I'm doing this myself. Now, did you have an update for me?"

"Yes and no. Two of the four names on Volundr's list have alibis for all four attacks. One, Deven is still trying to track down for questioning."

"And the fourth?"

"Dead," Faith told him. "Cut down in a gang skirmish in Seattle two years ago."

"Damn," David muttered; he started to push himself back under the car but paused and said, "We're really screwing the pooch on this one, aren't we?"

Faith laughed loudly enough to startle one of the servants, who, nearby, was waxing one of the other cars. "Where on earth did you hear that phrase?" she asked.

"From Miranda. Where else?"

Faith wanted to ask how things were with the Queen, but she had learned to tread lightly there in the past month. She accompanied the Prime on his various forays into the city and on whatever mission he gave her, and tried to be as useful as possible, remembering what Jonathan had said. But neither of the Pair seemed inclined to open up to her. David simply wasn't the sharing type, but Miranda had become strangely quiet lately, which wasn't like her. Faith knew she'd talked to Jonathan a few times but wasn't spending as much time with Kat as before, and she seemed . . . a bit lost. The Pair were sleeping together again and working hard to put what had happened behind them, but still . . . there was something new and sad in the Queen's eyes, as if the first veil of illusion had been lifted and she found herself a tiny bit further from her mortal life than before.

Faith didn't envy her the next few years. That was the hardest part about becoming a vampire; in a lot of ways it just seemed like a new and different lifestyle, but if you had any ties left to humanity they were eventually severed one by one, either by time's incessant decay or by the hard reality that though the human world and the Shadow World might exist within the same cities, in truth they were a thousand miles apart.

Speak of the devil: The side door of the garage opened and Miranda's red head poked in. "David?"

The Prime responded to the sound of her voice like Pavlov's dog, and Faith heard him drop his wrench on the concrete as he rolled out from under the car and sat up.

Miranda gave him an appreciative look; he was dirty and sweaty, had engine grease smeared on his face, and wore a snug, ratty T-shirt bearing the slogan *Han Shot First*. Even Faith, who tried very hard not to look at her boss that way, had to admire the sight. The biceps alone were worth staring at.

He smiled at Miranda. "Yes, my Lady?"

She smiled back. For a second it almost seemed to Faith as if nothing had ever gone wrong. "We got a call from

Signet Air," the Queen said. "Janousek's flight landed in Newark thirty minutes ago. He's staying there for the morning. He'll arrive in Austin tomorrow evening at five fifty and be here at the Haven by eight."

"Good, thank you," the Prime replied. He looked up at Faith. "Is everything ready?"

"Yes, Sire. I've got the usual detail to meet the plane, and his suite is prepared. We're not anticipating any problems with this one."

"That's exactly why we need to be ready for problems. The last thing we need is this assassin going after Janousek on his way from the airport."

David returned his gaze to Miranda. "What do you have planned for the rest of the evening? Are you going into town?"

"Not tonight. Grizzly and the producers are mixing this week—they're going to call me when they have something for me to listen to. I've got a gig Wednesday but until then I kept things clear for Janousek's visit. Tonight I've got yoga."

"When did you take up yoga?" the Prime asked.

"Tonight, possibly. Lali has been giving Cora classes, and she asked if I wanted to join in." Miranda raised an eyebrow and smiled. "I'm sure you wouldn't object to my being more flexible."

"And on that note," Faith said, "I'm leaving."

"Are you on duty all night?" Miranda asked, stopping the Second. "You could come along—Lali says that it's a perfect complementary practice to all our fight training."

"No, thank you," Faith replied with a grin. "I tried it once and ended up with my legs stuck behind my head. Lali actually had to come undo me. How about you, Sire?"

David was laughing, probably at the mental image Faith had given him. "That's quite all right. I have two more cars to work on and then a conference call with Lieutenants Craig, Laveau, and Nguyen at eleven. After that it's back into the network upgrade. Oh—and I owe Novotny a call. He wants to run some additional tests on the hands."

"What kind of tests?" Miranda wanted to know.

"He finally got a full analysis back on the poison and wants to see if the assassin also used it on Jake and Denise."

"Do you think she did?" Faith asked.

"Yes and no," David said, reaching under the car for his discarded wrench and returning it to the cart. "If she'd poisoned Denise, there wouldn't have been nearly so much blood at the crime scene—Denise put up a hell of a fight for a human, and that toxin would have killed her before she could even struggle. But she might have poisoned Jake to bring him down before cutting off his hand. That's Novotny's theory, anyway. But he wanted to run the list of parameters by me first."

Miranda leaned her hip against the car, one hand trailing over its glossy finish. "I hate that we're stuck waiting for this bitch to make the next move, David. Something has to give."

"I know, beloved. I'm hoping that decreasing the network's cycle time from five seconds to three will give us something."

"What about the raw sensor data?" she asked. "How far back does it go?"

"Ninety days," he replied. "Why?"

"What if you compared the readings at the time of each attack and looked for blips?"

"You said there were no blips," Faith pointed out.

David nodded. "There weren't on the network itself. But when something moves past a sensor, it records an array of information. The network is calibrated to collect more than two dozen parameters, but only the important ones— height, weight, temperature, and speed—are analyzed, and then the system displays only combinations of readings that indicate a vampire's presence. If something corresponds to, say, a toddler or a German shepherd, it doesn't show up on the grid. But all the raw data is dumped every ten minutes into the backup server. There's a vast amount of data, so it overwrites every ninety days, otherwise we wouldn't have nearly enough drive space to store it all. Most of it is just noise."

Faith nodded. "Based on observations from you, Prime Deven, and Kat, our killer is totally average for a vampire, although she is damned fast."

Miranda said, "Something about her keeps her from showing on the grid. But the sensors might have picked up something else, something nonvampiric."

"Maybe she's a werewolf," Faith said, grinning at the dirty looks they both shot her. "Kidding."

"I did a search on the raw data right after Jake went missing and got nothing," David mused, "but once I get the upgrade done, the enhanced sensitivity and processing speed may produce something. I'll try it again. It certainly can't hurt at this point."

"I can't believe that with all the technology we have and all the brain power working on the problem, we can't find a single damn thing," said Faith irritably. "Who the hell is this woman? What could she have that makes her harder to find than the Blackthorn?"

"It could be magic," Miranda said.

David laughed. "Of course. She's a magical werewolf. Why didn't I see it before?"

"Don't laugh," Miranda admonished him. "You don't know how everything in this world works."

"Beloved, there's no such thing as magic."

She gave him a look that Faith almost laughed at. Few people ever seemed to think that David was capable of saying something stupid.

Miranda pointed wordlessly at her Signet.

The Prime considered that for a second. "I don't think it's magic. I think there's some technology to it that we simply don't understand yet. That's what magic is, in the end."

Again, Miranda gave him that look. "So you think that a glowing ruby that has the power to pick out your soul mate has a tiny little hamster on a wheel inside it? What about our psychic abilities, or Misting, or the fact that if one half of a Pair dies, the other does, too? What is that if it's not magic?"

He shrugged. "Physics is a mysterious thing, but it's not mystical."

Miranda shot Faith an amused glance, then said to her husband, "Whatever you say, dear." She leaned down and kissed the top of his head, earning a sweet smile. "I'm off to learn the Badass-asana."

After she had gone, David asked Faith, "Was she mocking me just now?"

Faith grinned. "I think it was more a case of humoring you than mocking you."

The Prime didn't seem bothered by that; in fact, quite the opposite. He looked relieved. "That's a good sign . . . isn't it?"

Faith stood out of the way while he rolled the tool cart and the flat thing he'd been lying on—a creeper, she thought it was called—over to the next car on the row. There were eight vehicles in the garage right now as a nasty autumn storm was supposed to move in sometime after two that morning. Faith's little red hybrid was at the far end, parked next to Miranda's Prius. There were two vans present of the three that shuttled patrol teams to and from the city; those, she guessed, were the ones David needed to work on next. The Town Car that Harlan drove was the Prime's ride of choice, but there was also a limo, a Rolls, and a Bentley, the three of which were rarely used as David hadn't converted them to solar yet. The two vans were gas/electric hybrids.

It had never really occurred to Faith before coming to serve the South that vampires should have an interest in the environment, but David had wisely decided that immortality would be far less pleasant on a burned-out husk of a planet, so one of the first things he had done upon taking the Signet was to put the entire Haven complex on solar power. Aside from the ecological impact, it helped keep the Haven concealed; they were completely off the city power grid, a self-contained village of vampires out in the Hill Country. If they could have grown their own blood, David would probably have the place running like the world's weirdest hippie commune.

"I think so," Faith responded, not sure what Miranda's

comment was a sign of, exactly, but wanting to be sup-
portive.

David moved on to the first of the two black vans, settling
himself on the creeper again. Faith did as Miranda had done,
leaning on the side of the van watching wrenches float from
the cart to the Prime, who dragged a plastic tub underneath
the van and set to unscrewing something—the oil filter?
Faith cheerfully admitted she didn't know a thing about cars.

"You shouldn't be so hard on yourself," Faith heard herself say before she could stop.

He rolled back out and looked at her. "Yes, I should.
What I did was indefensible."

"But you didn't hide it from her; you stepped up and
accepted the consequences. Believe me, a lot of men
wouldn't. You could have blamed it on Deven—there'd be
no love lost there. But you took responsibility and you're
doing everything you can to make it right. There's only so
much good that hair shirt is going to do you, Sire, before
you just have to stop castigating yourself and move on."

He frowned. "Are you saying that it's . . . no big deal?"

"No. You fucked up big-time."

"Good. As long as we're on the same page."

"I'm just saying that if the woman you love doesn't hate
you for what you did, then you shouldn't either."

He half smiled. "I'll take that under advisement, Second."

Faith rolled her eyes and started to leave the garage, but
David said, "Thank you, Faith," and she turned back to
him one more time.

"I appreciate that you've stood by me," he went on. "By
both of us. I'm sure you were angry at me for a while, too,
but it didn't interfere with our working relationship, and for
that I'm grateful."

Faith nodded, bowed. "Just don't do it again," she told
the Prime, "or I'll have to castrate you with a seven-
sixteenths ratchet wrench."

The Prime looked at the tool in his hand and laughed,

arching an eyebrow. "Seven-sixteenths wouldn't be nearly big enough."

Faith snorted. "Too much information, Sire. I'll take my leave now unless you need anything else."

"Nothing further. Dismissed."

He disappeared back underneath the van, and Faith left him to it, heading out to an advanced combat training session with several of the newer Elite.

Outside, she looked up at the lowering black sky where thick storm clouds hung amid the expectant, electric feel of an oncoming torrent. The wind had kicked up and was whirling leaves all over the gardens. Faith could smell the rain and the lightning and hoped the servants had all the windows shut; they'd been opening some of the ground-floor panes at night to let the fresh, crisp air in between cold fronts, to keep the Haven from feeling stuffy with so many fireplaces going.

A chill crawled over her skin. The weather had been building toward this storm for days . . . and as the first few drops began to fall, she hurried from the garage to the training building, hoping to avoid the worst of the rain.


Cora was more than one hundred years old and had spent all but eighteen of them trying very hard to divorce herself from her body, teaching herself to run away inside her mind so that she was distant, safe from Hart's perversions. The thought that she might one day want to reclaim her violated flesh and learn to live in it, or perhaps even enjoy physical sensation or, God forbid, sensuality had always been depressingly laughable.

Yet here she was, spending hours with her secondhand Elite workout clothes soaked in sweat, learning to twist and bend her body into dozens of unaccustomed shapes, pushing herself until her muscles shook and she was so exhausted she could barely stand while a tiny brown woman with a musical accent guided her from one pose into another.

Lalita called it Hatha yoga. It was an ancient art that

helped to train the body and the mind together, and Faith had prescribed it for Cora to help strengthen her muscles and bring health back into her pitiful body. Cora was too weak and clumsy for more conventional workouts, and too frightened to learn fighting skills, but Faith assured her there was nothing violent about yoga and that Lalita was a gentle and compassionate teacher.

Lalita's voice danced through the syllables of the sacred language of her homeland—the names of the poses and the words of chants far older than anything in the Haven. Cora liked the sound of it, and of Lalita's accented English.

Cora might not be an intelligent woman, but she learned the yoga poses quickly. Her body seemed to have its own memory, and a very good one. Only a few sessions in she could fumble her way through a Sun Salutation without prompting.

It was strange to be good at something that allowed her to keep her clothes on.

Cora usually arrived first, as Lalita had a full duty roster and had to come to the studio once her bodyguard shift was done. They had their sessions in a small room in one of the outbuildings, and Lalita had turned the utilitarian space into a soothing, quiet studio that smelled faintly of incense. Cora didn't mind being alone there; there was only one door, so she felt as safe there as she did in her bedroom. She usually spent those first few minutes in seated meditation as Lalita had taught her.

She had fought Lalita tooth and nail over meditation, claiming she didn't want to know the inner workings of her own mind, because there was nothing there except the grimy leavings of Hart's lusts. But she had seen a glimmer . . . just a glimmer . . . of something beyond that, something about her that was not broken, and could not ever be broken. She didn't know what to call it, but she wanted to learn more about it.

Once she had slept in a dirty nest of pillows, but now she sat on them with her spine straight, seeking the silence within herself.

Lalita, who had arrived silently and let her continue her meditations uninterrupted, sat down before her, mirroring her posture, and said, "Perhaps you are starting to see that there is much more to you than you thought."

One day, Cora hoped to be as graceful as Lalita. For now she would settle for being able to support her own body weight on her bird-thin legs.

"We have another student joining us tonight," Lalita said.

Cora tried to hide her dismay. "Oh?"

"Yes—but don't worry, she's a beginner like you were a few weeks ago."

Cora nodded. It wouldn't have occurred to her to object. These people, kind though they were, were still in control here, and if Lalita wanted more students she would have them. Besides, she had mentioned that she was pushing Faith to assign more of the Elite to her classes, claiming that they would be better warriors if they could find a calm center from which to fight. The new student might even be Faith herself, come to see what all the fuss was about.

At least it was a woman. Cora didn't think she could bear sharing this with a man. She knew from what Lalita had told her about India that yoga was invented mostly by men of the early Hindu traditions, and that every school of yoga and every teacher had his own style. Lalita's was peaceful and flowing, feminine, emphasizing balance and flexibility rather than brutal technical perfection. She had learned in two schools, Hatha and Kripalu, and combined the two to form something that she felt was appropriate for vampires, drawing on their enhanced sensory perception and the inherent strength of their bodies. Strength training wasn't usually an issue for Elite warriors, so Lalita focused on yoga's other benefits, especially on harmonizing body and mind.

It was an utterly alien philosophy for Cora, who had been taught—and had clung to the idea—that the body was meaningless and would fall to dust. That had made it easier to let Hart do what he liked with her. But Lalita had created her own spiritual tradition, combining the movements of yoga, meditation, and chanting, with devotion to a goddess named Green Tara who apparently came from the Tibetan Buddhist mythos. There was a statue of that deity in the corner of the studio, sitting on a low table with the incense burner and candles.

Cora found herself staring at the Tara often, thinking that she reminded Cora of the Virgin, a gentle mother who was still willing to step down from her throne to right the wrongs of the world.

After that Cora threw her fears to the wind and did whatever Lalita suggested. The most amazing thing about the teacher was that if Cora had reasons why something made her uncomfortable, Lalita would listen to her, suggest alternatives, and they would talk about it. There was no yelling, no force, no demands that she obey. Cora didn't know how to assert herself, so her tendency was to let things slide, but finally Lalita called her on it:

"You were strong enough to leave the Prime," Lalita reminded her as she went to the bench to remove her on-duty gear. "Don't forget that, Cora. You were taught that you were weak and undeserving, but you know that's not true. You, and you alone, walked out of that room to find something better. You had that strength. You still have it. All you need to do is believe in it and learn to draw on it."

The Elite had an array of items they carried: Each had a standard-issue sword, a wooden stake, a knife in one boot, a belt pouch whose contents Cora didn't know, and a device that she wasn't sure about.

Cora pulled her knees up to her chin and watched Lalita prepare for their session; curious, she asked, "Is that a telephone?"

Lalita looked down at the device and laughed. "Among other things. Our intra-Elite communication goes through the wrist coms, but this phone also shows us maps of the city, and some of us get to see parts of the sensor network. I can check the duty roster for the coming week and know when others are on or off shift, as well as accessing weather reports and other information."

"All of that in that tiny box?"

She grinned and nodded. "Remarkable, isn't it? When I was a young girl, no one could have dreamed of this sort of thing. Even radio was a fantasy back then. To get a message to someone took days of travel and now it takes seconds."

She handed Cora the phone, and Cora examined it gingerly, afraid to touch anything. The computer in her room was larger and looked less fragile, but it still confounded her for the most part. When she touched the phone's screen, it lit up, displaying a photograph of several cats playing on a rug; one was biting the other on the neck. Cora smiled.

Just then there was a knock at the studio door. Cora handed the phone back to Lalita, who took it and rose gracefully, unfolding herself like Green Tara from her lotus position.

"Come in, my Lady," she called.

Cora's heart clenched at the words . . . and did so again when the door opened and Queen Miranda entered the studio.

"Hello, Cora," the Queen said, smiling. "I hope you don't mind my joining you."

Cora swallowed. She tried to speak, but nothing would come out of her mouth. It was the first time she had seen the Queen since she had been granted asylum, and in the intervening days she had forgotten how frightening the woman was . . . she seemed to fill the entire studio with her presence and power, and even dressed in similar clothes to Cora with her abundant hair pulled back, being anywhere near her made Cora's pulse fly into chaos, fear destroying her meditative calm.

The Queen came over and knelt in front of her, concerned. "Are you all right?" She laid her hand on Cora's forehead, and her eyebrows shot up. "Good Lord, Cora . . . you have to learn to shield."

Lalita looked chagrined. "It never occurred to me that she would need to," she admitted. "Most of us have some telepathic ability, but hardly anyone here needs more than basic grounding and centering."

"What . . . what do I have?" Cora asked haltingly.

Miranda was staring at her hard, her hand still on Cora's forehead. "I'm not sure," the Queen replied. "Identifying gifts isn't something I'm good at, and it seems like most of your talent is still . . . asleep. Here . . . this will help you for now."

Cora felt . . . something . . . move through her, and it was as if someone had pulled a curtain down between her and the Queen; one second Cora was on the verge of panic, and the next she was simply sitting cross-legged in front of a woman with a messy red ponytail.

"I've put a shield around you," the Queen explained. "It's temporary, but it will keep me from freaking you out while we're here. I'll talk to Faith about having someone teach you to do it yourself. I would, but I'm not really experienced enough at it to show you the technique, and I have a feeling that you'd do better with a female teacher than with David."

The idea of having the Prime—even as kind as he seemed to be—so close to her, touching her energy, was so awful that she couldn't hide her reaction.

Miranda smiled. "I thought as much. But we'll find someone. It's something you absolutely must learn before you leave the Haven—our gifted Elite shield themselves, so you're safe here, but you've got enough ability just from what I can see that going out in the world without protection would drive you mad. Trust me, I know."

"I should add," Lalita said, "that the practices we are learning here in yoga can make such things worse for the gifted—if you have any abilities, meddling about with your chakras can intensify them, which is probably why Cora reacted so strongly. Fair warning, my Lady. I know you are very strongly shielded, but for your own sake, be careful."

Cora was surprised that Miranda deferred immediately to Lalita on the subject; she wouldn't have expected a Queen to listen to anyone. "I'll try to stay mindful," Miranda said.

"Excellent. Let's begin, shall we?" Lalita moved to the front of the studio, where her mat was already unfurled on the ground.

Cora had brought her own mat; there were several standing in the corner that anyone could use, but Lalita had given her one outright so that she could practice in her room if she wanted. Cora liked the slightly sticky purple foam, which had a paisley pattern in pink outlined along one end. She and the Queen stood up, and Cora rolled her mat out while Miranda sought one of the extras and did the same.

Cora hated to admit it, but she felt a tiny bit of satisfaction as the session got underway, because while she was strong and agile, the Queen was no yoga prodigy; her alignment was dreadful, and even with her considerable physical prowess she lost her balance at one point and actually toppled over, giggling.

"Why don't you try that one again?" Lalita suggested.

Miranda sobered and stood back up, and Lalita led her back into the pose; the Queen concentrated on her work, which was a relief, as Cora had feared she wouldn't take what they were doing seriously, especially not the first time. But Miranda was completely respectful of Lalita's knowledge and even paused to watch Cora during the Sun Salutation to get a different view of the flow of postures. Cora tried not to acknowledge her stare, but found herself blushing anyway.

"I'm sorry," the Queen said. "I don't mean to make you uncomfortable. But you really are a natural at this, Cora. You look like you were born to it."

Cora blushed even more fiercely. "Thank you, my Lady."

Lalita was smiling warmly at her. "I've taught yoga off and on for twenty years, and Cora is the quickest learner I've had so far. Just in the last few weeks she's gained so much poise and grace—I'm very proud of her."

Seeing how uncomfortable Cora was at being stared at, Lalita changed the subject. "All right, then, let us continue."

After they moved through the entire series of asanas and spent several minutes lying in Corpse Pose, Lalita began a guided meditation for chakra clearing; in her tradition the body had seven primary energy centers, each corresponding to a different aspect of a person's being, and those centers needed to stay healthy in order for the whole person to thrive. She led them through the meditation slowly, in deference to the Queen, and Cora visualized her energy moving up through her body, starting in the root chakra at the base of the spine and ending in the crown of the head. The energy opened each chakra, cleaned out any psychic debris, and left that aspect of the self running more smoothly. Cora wasn't sure how much of Lalita's spirituality she believed in, but when she did the meditation she could certainly feel something, and when it was done she always felt different, better.

When they reached the third-eye chakra, which was supposed to govern one's inner sight, Cora heard a gasp.

She opened one eye partway and saw that something odd was happening to the Queen.

Miranda was white as a sheet, and her breathing was shallow. She sat cross-legged as Cora and Lalita did, but her hands were clenched on her knees and her forehead was creased in what looked like pain.

"My Lady?" Cora asked in a whisper.

Lalita's eyes popped open and she, too, looked worried. "Are you . . ."

Before she could finish the question, the Queen's hands flew up to her forehead, covering her already-closed eyes. She moaned and doubled over. "No . . ."

Suddenly things all over the room began to shake.

Lalita put her hands on the Queen's shoulders and tried to rouse her, but the Queen didn't seem to hear; she was lost somewhere, and to Cora's dismay the shield she was holding up around Cora began to tremble and dissolve and Cora could feel the Queen's power again, this time surging dangerously. Hot, thick fear seized Cora's heart, and she pushed herself away, all but crawling backward to put as much space between herself and the Queen as she could.

Things began to topple over. Mats fell, the fabric hangings Lalita had draped around the room sagged and then slipped from the walls . . . the very ground felt like it was shaking.

Lalita cried out in alarm, and Cora followed her wide eyes to see that the ceiling fan overhead was coming loose from its wiring.

The Queen screamed.

The fan tore from the ceiling and fell.

Cora flung herself forward, trying to push Lalita out of the way, and the two women tumbled backward in the chaos—

—which stopped as quickly as it had started.

Cora, sprawled out over Lalita on the floor, craned her head back to see what had happened, and it was her turn to gasp.

Standing in the center of the room, one hand held up toward the fan that had frozen in midair, the other touching Miranda's forehead, was the Prime.

The Queen's eyes rolled back in her head and she fell sideways onto her mat, unconscious.

The Prime's eyes and hand followed the ceiling fan and it floated over to the corner, where it landed in a heap. He turned, looking around the room, and in seconds everything had righted itself, the scattered pieces of Lalita's altar returning to their places, the tapestries back on the walls.

He didn't ask if Cora and Lalita were all right, but she supposed it was unnecessary. Aside from shock they were both fine, not even a scratch on either. He bent and lifted the Queen into his arms, then gave them a quick nod of acknowledgment and strode out of the studio.

Cora and Lalita were left staring at each other.

*Blood . . . so much blood . . .*

*Someone was dying. She could hear Kat screaming— not in pain, but in panic, in horror, her heart—not her body—rent into tatters. Miranda tried to help her . . . she couldn't move . . . she was an outsider here, trapped behind a glass wall where all she could do was listen and watch, pounding her fists on an invisible barrier. She tried to scream but her voice died on the wind. She could only watch scattered images of the nightmare unfolding before her, powerless.*

*So much blood . . .*

*"I'm done for, Miranda. You have to save yourself."*

*Who was speaking? She strained to identify the voice but she couldn't reach it, couldn't . . .*

*She could hear something dripping . . . dripping . . . water, onto a bare floor . . . dripping . . . blood, dripping . . . dripping . . .*

*Bars. Her hands closed around cold steel bars.*

*"Please tell me this was all a nightmare, Miranda."*

*"Hello, darling." A man's voice, scornful.*

*She heard something shatter, saw shards of crystal catching moonlight as they fell . . .*

*"Miranda, NO!"*

*She could hear the screaming, she could smell the blood and taste it rusty and hot in the back of her throat, but she couldn't stop any of it.*

*"Please . . . you have to save him . . . you have to . . . promise me . . . you're the only one strong enough to do it. Promise me . . ."*

*"How dare you come into our house—"*

*Red light . . . red light . . . red . . . four, five, six . . . seven . . . eight . . . glowing red in a circle, one by one flashing, their light falling into sync . . .*

*"Hello, darling." A woman's voice, scornful.*

*Agony . . . searing, her soul being ripped in half, her screams tearing the silence of the night as she fell . . . and watched herself fall . . . only it wasn't her . . .*

*Warmth intruded. She felt herself being pulled back from the glass wall, gentle hands drawing her down, out, back into her body.*

*She strained to hear the last few words as she began to wake . . . it was almost as if someone were whispering into her ear.*

*Firstborn . . .*

*Eleusis . . .*

*Alpha* . . .
*Lydia* . . .
*Trinity* . . .

"Miranda."

That last voice, she recognized. She reached toward it, yearning for solid ground, for the waking world, and felt hands taking hers and drawing her down, down . . .

She was sobbing as she woke, relief and fear overcoming her, and she fled into David's arms, shaking.

"It's all right, beloved. I'm here. I've got you. You're safe now."

She was absolutely incoherent for a while but gradually got a toehold of control back, dragging herself toward calm one lurching inch at a time. She could feel a shield around her, probably as much to protect the rest of the Haven from her as to protect her from it. But the feeling—of being contained and held, safe, surrounded by such warm and loving energy—was grounding, and it helped her wrestle her powers back into her own grasp.

Once she was calm David lowered the shield around her, though she could still feel him around her, physically and otherwise. She breathed in the warmth of his body and let out a long, shaky breath.

"What did you see?" he asked her softly.

Miranda shut her eyes tightly and buried her face in his shoulder. "Death," she whispered. "I saw death."

"Whose?"

"I don't know," she said, barely holding back more tears. "It was all jumbled together—there were words, and sounds, and images, and smells . . . it was like I was watching five TV shows at once. It didn't make any sense."

He stroked her hair and murmured to her while she shook, but despite the possibility of dire circumstances rolling toward them he sounded concerned about her, but not about the future. "That's how it started for Jonathan," he said. "Dreams, mostly, so twisted around themselves that he couldn't interpret anything. It took time for him to learn how to see one thing at a time. You should talk to him—he can probably help you."

"You're not worried about what I saw?"

He shrugged. "Not really. Remember how it was with your empathy? All you could hear were the pain and suffering because they were the loudest. Now that you know how to control it, you feel things differently. It's the same with precognition. Death and misery are the most vivid because they play into your own fears. But that doesn't mean everything in the future is full of peril."

She shook her head, marveling at how calm he was about it. If he had seen . . . if he had heard . . . the screams, the blood . . . She shuddered and returned her head to his shoulder, covering her eyes. "It was awful."

"Do you want to tell me about it?"

"No . . . not yet. But . . . I do have one question, maybe you know . . . who's Lydia?"

David went very still. "Lydia?"

"Yes . . . there were words, like someone was whispering to me at the end. The only actual name in it was Lydia."

She looked at him. His eyes were wide.

"You know a Lydia?" Miranda asked.

David took a deep breath. "I've known one."

"Who was she?"

His grip on her arms tightened as if she were a teddy bear and he were afraid of the storm outside. "She was my sire."

# Fourteen

"There's really not much to tell," David said, handing Miranda the Coke he'd climbed out of bed to fetch her from the bar fridge. She was sitting up wrapped in the sheets, listening to him keenly, but practically inhaled the soda—that was another thing David remembered Deven remarking upon when Jonathan was new to the gift; after he had a vision he guzzled caffeine, and it kept him from getting a nasty third-eye migraine.

Sitting cross-legged on the bed in front of her, he went on, "When the Witchfinder came to our town, it didn't take long for Lizzie and me to be hauled in front of the court. She was a strong woman who spoke her mind, and I . . . well, there had been rumors about me since I was a child. You don't just start making things float without people noticing. My mother knew if I was ever found out I'd be hanged as a Witch, so she made me keep it secret, but there was still gossip."

Miranda stared at him over the Coke can. "So they threw you both in jail."

"Yes."

"Why did the Witchfinder come to town in the first place?"

"There were unexplained deaths all over the county. Bodies were found drained of blood in the woods and the fields."

Her eyebrows shot up. "Oh shit."

"Oh shit is right. Half a dozen people were killed—and then the burnings started."

"Wait . . . I thought you said Witches were hanged in that era."

"The most common method was hanging followed by a public burning of the corpse. It was nearly unheard of for someone to be burned alive in England. The panic that swept through places like Germany didn't grip our country; for the most part the judicial system kept things civilized, requiring evidence, a trial. But this Witchfinder preferred a more . . . flamboyant, if you'll forgive the pun, method of execution. He wanted the whole village to turn on each other out of fear. He was paid by the head, after all. The more Witches he found, the richer he became."

"Nobody suspected his motives? Not anyone?"

"Of course they did. But to speak up would have been an instant confession of collusion with the devil. I remember . . ." He flipped the tab on his own can, this one a Dr Pepper; he'd lived in the South for years before discovering an affection for the regional beverage of choice. "Lizzie was afraid—she knew that what had happened in other places would in ours. She'd heard about the burnings in Germany. She wanted to take Thomas and move away. But back then you couldn't just pick up and leave your home like that. My entire livelihood was there, and it wasn't terribly portable."

She grinned. "One of these days I want to see you bang a hammer on an anvil. It's got to be sexy as hell."

He smiled back. "It was the closest thing to engineering they had back then."

"So, you were put in jail . . ." Her smile disappeared. "Were you tortured?"

Now shame gripped him at the memory, and he lowered his eyes. "No. We were threatened with it, and a couple of victims who refused to confess were tortured, but again, it was the Witchfinder's method, not the town's. Still . . . hearing the screams . . . I was terrified. I confessed."

She looked genuinely surprised. "What about Lizzie?"

He had to smile at that. "She went to the stake raging, shrieking like a banshee that God would judge the town for its crimes and that her conscience was clear. I'm thankful she never knew that I took the coward's way out or she might never have forgiven me. But they didn't torture the women; they simply executed them, five in all over the course of a week. I begged the judge to leave me alive until Lizzie's brother arrived to take Thomas away and I knew he was safe. The judge was an old friend of my father's, so he managed to put the Witchfinder off for a day—because I had confessed I was promised a hanging before my burning. But then that night . . . a woman came to the jail."

"Lydia?"

"Lydia. I had never seen her before, but she knew my name and knew everything about me. She killed the guard, opened the cell, and attacked me."

He closed his eyes, trying to concentrate on the details. It had been so long ago, and the transformation had a way of scattering memories on the wind; that night and the week that followed were a blur of pain and fear and blood, faded by time. "She was pale," he said. "Her hair was golden, her eyes blue . . . exotic for our drab part of the country. So was the fact that she was fastidiously clean. I knew she had to be wealthy by her clothes and the way she moved. And just being near her . . . she was so powerful. She felt to me the way I imagine I feel to mortals now. She drained me near to death, and I woke in the forest just in time for her to force her blood into my mouth."

"Did she tell you who she was? What she wanted?"

"No. Only her name, and that I had to stay out of the sun. Then she vanished."

Miranda was staring at him, mouth open. "She just left you alone in the woods, not even knowing what you were?"

"I woke just before dawn and dragged myself to a cave I remembered from my childhood. I spent the next few days . . . well, you know."

Miranda nodded slowly, remembering. "God."

"When it was over I had to figure things out on my own. I nearly roasted in the sun and spent days recovering. I ate just about every small animal in the county trying to assuage my thirst, but in the end . . . there was only one thing to do."

He had slipped through the forest that night, lithe and deadly even in his fledgling power, only two things on his mind: blood and vengeance.

He started with the Witchfinder.

"By the time I left the town I had killed every man who had a hand in Lizzie's death. I stole their money and clothes, and I broke back into our house long enough to gather a few things. Then I stole a horse and put the town at my back. I made my way to London, where I could disappear into the city. After several months I finally found others of our kind."

"I don't understand," Miranda said. "Why would she bring you across and then disappear like that? I'm assuming she had been in the area long enough to kill those six people and find out all about you. And why you?"

"I have no idea, beloved. I tried to find her, for a while, but no one had ever heard of her. It was probably a fake name, after all. But for some reason, out of all the crappy little villages in England, she chose ours, and out of all the psychic smiths in the world, she chose me."

A blast of thunder rattled the windows, but with the shutters locked down there was no corresponding flash. A thought seemed to occur to Miranda, and she actually grinned. "Your original surname was Smith, wasn't it?"

He smiled at her. "Did you see anything else that involved Lydia?"

"I don't know. I don't think so. It was just a name. It doesn't feel connected to anything else. I wonder if that means she's going to appear at some point. I hope not. I think we have all the drama we need."

"From your lips to God's ears," David said, and they clinked their cans together. But even as he said the words, David thought about what Deven had said . . . that there was something about Miranda, and their bond, that would ensure that their life together was never peaceful . . . and even if he had been unconvinced of Deven's sincerity, he knew, beyond a shadow of a doubt, that *drama* was the understatement of the century for whatever they had ahead of them.

After the theatrics of Prime Hart's visit and the angst of Prime Deven's, Miranda braced herself for some kind of bullshit surrounding Janousek's arrival. She was ready for him to be an ass, or a sexist pig, or at the very least cold-hearted and arrogant.

She wasn't ready for him to be . . . nice.

"Prime Jacob Janousek, at your service," he said, bowing.

Her first thought was that he looked like a young hippie Jesus. He had brown hair falling down past his shoulders, and a neatly trimmed beard; his eyes were a warm brown, intelligent and kind, and held hers without the slightest bit of artifice or disdain. He looked to have been in his mid-twenties when he came across; David had mentioned that he was actually in his mid-220s. Aside from his Signet, which was set with amber, he wore a plain gold cross on a chain, but no other jewelry that Miranda could see.

Another thing he didn't have, which surprised her, was a noticeable accent. When she mentioned it, he laughed and said, "I'm no more Eastern European than your Prime is Southern American, my Lady. My ancestors are from the area now known as Slovakia, but in fact I was born in France and lived most of my life here in America. I moved to Prague because of my friendship with the former Prime, and when he died the Signet chose me. Rest assured, however, I've been there long enough that all of my other languages are accentless as well."

"How many do you speak?" she asked as they all settled in the study for the usual drill of drinks and conversation.

"Seventeen fluently," he replied. "I can fumble my way

through another half dozen and find beer and a lavatory in another three."

Miranda looked over at David. "That's more than you speak."

David smiled. "I've lived in the U.S. for a long time. The only two languages I've found necessary to get by here in Texas are American English and Spanish. The rest are just for fun."

The conversation was friendly and tension-free. Miranda didn't even know how to react to a Prime who was simply himself and had no hidden agenda for visiting; he had come because he liked David and wanted to further solidify their alliance, and that was it.

"How is Isis?" Janousek asked.

Miranda had forgotten until that moment that the Frie-sian had been a gift from the Prime of Eastern Europe; a bribe, David had said. Judging from the enthusiasm with which the two Primes talked about the horses, Miranda thought *bribe* was the wrong word, though it might have been accurate at the time.

". . . just foaled," Janousek was saying. "An absolutely gorgeous male—I'm hoping he'll be as bright as his sire, just like Isis was . . . but perhaps a bit less willful."

"Why don't we go out to the stables," David said. "We're due another round of storms tomorrow, so this might be the only chance while you're here to take her out, if you like. Miranda has business in the city tonight anyway."

Seeing the glint in the men's eyes, she chuckled. "You two go ahead," she told David as all three of them rose simultaneously. "It was lovely to meet you, Lord Prime. I'm quite pleased to have you as our ally."

Janousek bowed to her again. "Likewise, my Lady. I congratulate you both on winning the Pair lottery."

Miranda left the meeting feeling completely different than she had at any of the previous Magnificent Bastard arrivals; even Tanaka, who had been perfectly well man-nered and given no hint that he disliked Miranda, hadn't put her at ease, perhaps because he was so much older and more traditional than Janousek; and his Queen Mameha, though a fascinating person and blindingly intelligent, had been, Miranda freely admitted, intimidating as hell.

She met Lali and Aaron outside by the car. "How did it go?" Lali asked.

"Amazingly smoothly," she replied, slipping into the car with her bodyguards and motioning to Harlan to drive on. "I think I may finally have met a Prime I don't want to punch in the head."

"It was bound to happen sooner or later," Lali said, her ringing laugh filling the car. "Try not to be too disappointed."

"I wish I could be of more help," Jacob said regretfully. "As soon as you asked, I did what digging I could, but you didn't give me much to go on as far as your suspect goes."

"I know." David led the way back to the stables, the two Primes leading the Friesians on a slow walk after their outing; Isis and Osiris were in high spirits, which was more than David could say for himself. He'd known that asking Janousek for information about the assassin was a long shot, but still, he'd held out some hope. "You're right, of course. It's not as if you know every vampire who ever came from Finland."

"There aren't a lot," Jacob admitted. "Finland's population is pretty sparse. My territory, as you know, isn't the hotbed of vampire activity that yours is. There are practically no vampires north of Latvia, and aside from Prague, Krakow, and Riga, I just don't have that much density. And you know how contentious my borders are."

"I do. I suppose you should be glad that Demetriou has Romania—you don't have to deal with all the Dracula wannabes."

Janousek's territory was small compared to Western Europe's or the Black Sea's; historically the East had been dealt a lot of in-between countries, and the Prime of the Black Sea, who had ruled for longer than almost any other

Prime and was known for his insatiable—and somewhat archaic—greed for land, was a constant threat at Janousek's borders. Janousek had managed to bring a tentative peace, but at the last Council Demetriou had made yet another play for Croatia and Hungary. Janousek's good reputation in the Council had helped him keep his hold. Janousek's western border at Austria/the Czech Republic/Poland had been peaceful his entire tenure, but the eastern border was another story entirely.

David knew that part of the reason Jacob was anxious to keep him as an ally was that David's influence in the Council would help him hold his territory together; David didn't hold it against him. If he were Janousek, he'd want David's friendship, too. And if Jacob had been less than a good man with the interests of his people at heart, David would have been happy to leave him to Demetriou's wolves . . . well, that wasn't entirely true. Janousek would have to have been a cock on the order of Prime Hart to make David side with Demetriou.

Jacob chuckled. "Demetriou would go after Russia if it weren't for the fact that Dzhamgerchinov scares the devil out of him. Frankly he scares the devil out of me, too."

"I think I'm more frightened by how easily you pronounce his name."

Another laugh. "Nonsense. Everyone knows you're not afraid of anything or anyone."

They took the horses into the stable and got them groomed and fed for the night, letting the topic of conversation steer itself back to horses; finally, with the night waning, they headed back to the Haven itself.

"I understand you had a row with Hart," Janousek said as they walked. "Congratulations."

"What did you hear?"

He shrugged. "Just that you rescued one of his harem girls, he slaughtered three more in your Haven, your Queen threw him into a wall, and he slunk home with his tail between his legs. He's bitching to anyone who will listen, which isn't anyone really, so I would imagine he's got a good case of festering anger up there in New York—if I were you, I wouldn't let him out of my sight."

"I don't intend to. I would like to know who's been killing his Elite, though, if for no other reason than to send them a thank-you card."

"I heard it was the Red Shadow."

"Not unless they've changed their tactics pretty radically in the last few months. I am afraid they're behind what's going on here, though. I don't suppose you know any more about them than the rest of us do?"

Jacob gave him a sidelong look, pausing, before he said, "There is one thing. I doubt it will be of much help to you."

"I'm desperate, Jacob. Give me whatever you have."

He nodded. "I was Prime Horak's Second, as you know. I'm almost a hundred percent certain that back in the 1920s he was acquainted with the Alpha."

"How?"

"Horak never came out and said anything, but Elite are paid to be observant, after all. One night a messenger brought a note to Horak, and the next night one of Horak's human enemies turned up missing except for his left hand. All Horak would tell me was that a friend owed him a 'recruiting bonus.' "

"Recruiting bonus . . . so Horak found someone for the Alpha to hire as an agent, and the Alpha had someone killed for Horak as a reward," David surmised. "Do you remember anything about the note?"

"Horak threw it into the fireplace, but I was mad with curiosity, so I fished out what was left."

David stared at him. "What did it say?"

Janousek smiled and reached into his coat pocket. "You'll have to figure that out for yourself," he said, and handed David a small plastic bag. "I have no idea why I kept it all this time—Prime's instinct, I suppose. That and I admit I'm a bit of a pack rat. I had forgotten all about it until you asked for my help when we spoke last week. I had it stashed away in the archives with everything else from Horak's tenure. It took me hours to find it."

David took the scorched scrap of yellowed paper, so old it was crumbling. "My God."

He turned it over, trying to discern what was written on it. On one side all he could see was a number, 4.19, and the faded remains of a single word; on the other, it looked like there had been some kind of symbol.

"It's probably meaningless. But you're the mad scientist of the Council, so if anyone can make something of it, you can."

"Jacob, I could kiss you," David said.

A grin. "I appreciate the gesture, Lord Prime, but you're really not my type."

"This may be the first solid link we've had to the Alpha, or to the Shadow at all. I'll have it analyzed immediately. Thank you, Jacob."

"I hope it helps."

They had reached the main building, and the guards opened the doors for them.

"Now then," Janousek said, "I was wondering, Lord Prime—does your Haven have a chapel?"

David was too distracted by the paper in his hand to be surprised by the question. "Yes—it's in the South Wing. I can take you there now if you like."

"I would appreciate that."

David led the way down the hall. "I doubt ours is as nice as yours," he told Janousek.

"Nice is relative," Jacob replied. "But it's not stained glass and stone that matter, it's what's inside—what you can't see—that counts."

"This way." David showed him down a long corridor in the South Wing to a pair of double doors with a stained-glass inset flickering with candlelight.

David knew that some of the Elite used the chapel for weekly services; he'd been in the room only once or twice, but he remembered it being a fairly simple space with a peaceful atmosphere, pretty but not pretentious. It had been built without any specific iconography, like a military chapel, so that practitioners of multiple faiths could use it.

The far end of the room was oriented east, so even the four or five Muslim Elite he employed found it useful.

He didn't expect anyone to be inside now, but an Elite stood at the door; he recognized her as Elite 29, who had been assigned as Cora's main bodyguard because she was fluent in Italian. Cora had no idea how closely she was being watched; David had instructed the guards to keep their distance and let her come and go mostly as she pleased, but he had learned the hard way when Miranda had first come to the Haven that even with a com on her wrist, she could be vulnerable.

"Sire," the Elite said with a bow. "I hope this isn't a problem—there were no scheduled services and Miss Cora likes to come here."

"No problem at all," David told her. "Prime Janousek wanted to pay a visit."

He turned to the Prime. "The woman we offered asylum from Hart, Cora, is in there now; she's a bit shy of strangers, especially men."

Janousek nodded, understanding. "I'll wait out here, then, until she's done. I would hate to frighten her in the middle of her prayers."

"If you don't mind, then, I'll take my leave for the morning—I need to meet Faith and get this to my lab."

"I don't mind at all. I plan to spend an hour with God and then retire for the day. We'll speak again at sunset, of course."

"Thank you, Jacob."

David started to walk away, but the chapel door opened and Cora emerged.

She saw them and made a faint yelping sound, moving to duck back into the chapel.

"It's all right, Cora," David said quickly in Italian. "I was just leaving, and our guest wanted to use the chapel when you were finished. There's no hurry."

Cora swallowed hard and nodded. He noticed she looked a hundred times better than when she'd come to the Haven; he'd barely looked at her when he had raced into the yoga studio to answer the call of Miranda's distress, but she did look healthier, and even as frightened as she obviously was, she made eye contact with him.

Or at least, she did for a second. Her attention was pulled from him to Prime Janousek, who David realized was staring at her, wide-eyed.

She stared right back.

Suddenly David remembered where he had seen that thunderstruck expression before.

Sure enough, as Janousek opened his mouth to attempt to speak, the amber stone of his Signet flared once, twice . . . and began to flash.


Cora didn't understand why this man was looking at her as if she were some kind of ghost, but she knew one thing: As soon as she saw him, she was irresistibly drawn to him . . . and the only thing she could think to do was run.

The two men didn't chase her, not that it mattered; this was the Prime's house, and she had no right to run away, even if there was anyplace she could go that he couldn't follow. But still, she ran, as hard and fast as she could, until she had gained the safety of her room, flung herself backward against the door, and burst into tears.

Her mind and heart were spinning so fast she could barely breathe. The man's kind eyes were burned into her skull, inviting . . . something . . . some part of her that she hadn't even known existed rising up and reaching out . . .

She panicked, her breath coming in hoarse gasps, her only identifiable desire to hide. She ended up curled in a ball on the far side of the bed, wishing she could shrink into nothing.

What was happening? Who was he? What did he want with her? And why did she want to . . . what did she want?

She had been praying, feeling peaceful and at rest, almost . . . dared she say it . . . happy. Her guard had shown her the chapel a few days ago, and she had loved its simplicity: stone walls, a few stained-glass panels with electric lights behind them that cast a soft glow over the movable pews. The panels were images of the countryside where the Haven stood, nighttime images in blue and purple. A cabinet on one wall contained the trappings of several religions, and her guard had shown her where to find a painted resin statue of the Virgin to place on the altar, along with a cloth and some candles. The only rule was that she had to put things away when she was done.

Now her peace was shattered, and she prayed again, mumbling into her crossed arms, asking God to help her . . . whatever this was . . . *please, make it go away. Make him go away.*

God didn't seem to be listening, however. There was a soft knock at the door.

She couldn't speak, not even when a voice called, "Cora?"

She buried her head in her arms, hoping he would leave, but a moment later she heard the door open and footsteps approaching her.

"Cora," he said gently in her language, "you don't have to be afraid."

She lifted her head. "Who are you?"

He had settled cross-legged a few feet away from her, leaving plenty of room but close enough that he didn't have to raise his voice to be heard. "My name is Jacob," he said. "I am the Prime of Eastern Europe."

She stared at the Signet around his neck. It was still flashing, but not as brightly, now that it had their attention. "I don't understand what this means."

He nodded. "I had a feeling you didn't."

They looked at each other in silence for a moment, and she was struck by the overwhelming feeling that she knew him, though she had never seen him before tonight. Her fear, as habitual a response as it was, was fighting with a strange, new curiosity, wondering how she recognized the way his nose crinkled when he smiled.

"Do you know what Signets are for?" he asked her. She knew a little, but she couldn't make herself speak, and she shook her head mutely. "They are a badge of office to show the world who the strongest vampires are, but they choose their bearers themselves. It's magic as old as the world—there are even some vague references from biblical times. When a Signet finds its Prime, it flashes and continues to glow . . . and then when that Prime finds his Queen, it flashes again."

She hadn't thought it possible to be any more stunned than she already was, but now the shock was so complete she could barely breathe. Her vision swam, and she felt herself sagging sideways.

The Prime reached out for her and caught her with a light touch, reaching up with one hand to grab a pillow from the bed and ease it under her head while he lowered her the rest of the way to the floor and sat down beside her. It didn't occur to her for several seconds that she should have shrunk away from him; but as soon as she was lying down, he retreated again, still keeping his distance.

Tears spilled from her eyes, and she asked tremulously, "Does this mean I have to . . . lie with you?"

He looked positively aghast at the notion. "No," he said. "Absolutely not. I would never force you to do anything you didn't want to do, Cora. Someday, I hope, but not until you desire me in return. Especially not after everything you've been through."

"But I have to go with you," she said.

He sighed, pulling his knees to his chest and resting his chin on them. "I don't fully understand what intelligence guides these things, but I do know it's never been wrong."

Cora thought of Miranda. "I don't think I can be a Queen," she said, wiping her eyes. "I'm not that strong."

"You don't have to be like Queen Miranda. Not every Queen has an active role in government. And you are strong, Cora . . . I can feel it. You don't even realize how strong you are. You have the potential to be very powerful, and that's what seems to matter to the Signets—not where you begin, but who you can become."

He reached into the pocket of his coat and took out a

small velvet drawstring bag. She watched, entranced, as he opened it and withdrew another amulet like his, this one slightly smaller . . . and its stone was flashing, too.

"I've been carrying this with me for eighty-seven years," Jacob said quietly. "And every night without fail I've prayed to God that I would find the Queen I was destined for. I was starting to lose hope . . . I've been alone so long . . . but I think we can add this to the list of 'mysterious ways.'"

He held the Signet out to her. "Take it," he said. "It's yours. If you want time to think, I'll leave you alone until my state visit is over in two days."

She knew that giving her time was pointless. The Signet had spoken; all illusion of choice in the matter was just that. But still . . . he had offered her time, as if it were really something she had to decide, and she couldn't help but be touched at such a sign of respect. And she believed him when he said he wouldn't force her into his bed, or into anything . . . she believed him.

"I . . . I don't know if I can love you," she whispered.

"That's all right, Cora. We have time. We can get to know each other at whatever pace you need. Whatever you want, if I can find a way to give it to you, I promise you I will . . . but you don't owe me anything. All I ask is that you give me a chance."

Tentatively, she smiled through her tears and lifted her hand, letting her trembling fingers close around the Signet he held out to her.

Electricity crackled through her. She could feel warmth spreading up through her hand, along her arm and shoulder, into her entire body—suddenly it was as if something new had taken up residence in her skin, and she could feel the low murmur of a presence in her mind.

*Oh . . . oh my.*

She found she didn't want to withdraw her hand, and once again they stared at each other . . . but this time they were both smiling.

# Fifteen

"And just like that, she's a Queen? Just like you?"

"No, not just like me. Cora's going to need time to heal and figure herself out before she decides what kind of Queen she wants to be. She might be the type who stays out of the spotlight and just stands by her man."

"Yuck," Kat said.

Miranda shrugged. "I guess it's meant to be. Cora's okay with it, which is what matters. I wouldn't have let her leave if I thought he was going to treat her badly. But if I were going to pick a man for Cora, I think Janousek is exactly the type I'd choose—he's gentle, quiet, and clearly smitten. It's the damnedest thing I've ever seen."

"It still gets me that you guys just accept the idea that those things know what they're talking about. I think I'd trust a Magic 8 Ball first."

Miranda wanted to say that there was no way Kat could understand—she had no frame of reference whatsoever for how it felt to be bound the way Pairs were. But she knew that there were things going on in Kat's life that Miranda couldn't understand, either, and there was no way to really convey any of it to each other. There seemed to be a slowly growing list of things that would always hold them apart now . . . and they were still essentially the same age. How much worse would it be when Kat was forty and Miranda still twenty-seven?

She forced herself to put the thought out of her mind as

the waitress brought their drinks: hibiscus mint tea for Kat, a Shiner for Miranda. Right now, at least, things were fine . . . sort of. Kat was still under guard, there was still a killer on the loose . . . but she wanted to enjoy the simplicity of just hanging out with someone . . . while she could.

She tried to focus on Kat, to memorize all the things she loved about her best friend: her fuzzy head, her nose ring, the way she gestured when she was excited, the way her eyes lit up when she was talking about her job and the satisfaction it brought her to help people . . . how brave she was, not just for keeping the baby, but for staying friends with Miranda even after nearly dying because of her.

"Earth to Mira," Kat said. "You're zoning out again. And staring at me."

"Sorry," Miranda replied. "I'm . . ." She trailed off, not sure what to say, but as usual, Kat knew what was on her mind.

"You're feeling overwhelmed?"

"Yeah."

Kat smiled tiredly. "I can relate." She stirred a packet of raw sugar into her iced tea, looking thoughtful, then asked, "Have you found out anything new about that Finnish bitch?"

Miranda spun the cap from her bottle around on the table with her finger. "Maybe. David's going to the lab tonight— Novotny did some scans for him and wanted him to come see the results. David seems to think it'll be great news, but I'm not sure how."

"Maybe you should try using bait," Kat mused. "You could put me out somewhere and try to get her to come out—"

"Are you crazy?" Miranda interrupted. "No way."

"Come on, Miranda, I'm tired of waiting around to be stabbed," Kat said angrily. "I can't keep living like this."

"I'm not putting you at risk, Kat. If anything happened to you . . . no. Absolutely not."

Wisely, or perhaps because she was too tired to argue, Kat let the matter drop. Meanwhile their order arrived, and Kat dug into her black bean nachos. Miranda had ordered a brownie à la mode, and she picked at it, not really tasting it.

They didn't talk much while they ate—Kat was clearly starving and barely paused to take a breath until her entire platter of nachos was gone, and Miranda had a thousand things on her mind—but they'd known each other long enough that the occasional silence wasn't a huge deal.

Miranda's mind wandered as she scooped up tiny spoonfuls of ice cream. Janousek and Cora had left at sunset; Cora was still bewildered by the whole thing but was going along easily enough with the sudden change in her status. She also didn't seem afraid of Jacob, who was solicitous of her well-being but gave her plenty of space. Miranda could sense that he was eager to get Cora to Prague and show her her new home. The Eastern Haven was smaller than the Southern United States Haven, and Jacob had fewer constituents, so they would have a comparatively quiet life, at least until their own Magnificent Bastard Parade got underway. Cora wasn't exactly eager to fly across the ocean with a man she barely knew, but she wasn't afraid. Considering the life she had escaped from, that was a very good sign.

Miranda could sense something in Cora that had been hidden before by her weakness and fear. She wasn't sure what to call it besides *potential*, but Miranda's worry that Cora would never recover from what had happened faded somewhat once she had felt it. Cora had said herself, when Miranda spoke to her briefly before they left, that she was ready to look for a place for herself, and she had always known that place was not Austin. In Austin she could have a good, safe home, but not the life that she knew she was meant for. God, she had said, had led her to Miranda, and now to Jacob, and she was determined to follow.

At the very least, David would be able to count Janousek as an ally pretty much for the rest of his tenure. Janousek had given him what might turn out to be vital evidence, and David had, more or less, introduced Janousek to his Queen. Jacob had been all smiles when they departed, with David and Miranda's assurances that the South would be one of the first territories to pay a state visit as soon as Jacob declared the Haven open for the parade to begin.

"Are you going to finish that?" Kat asked.

Miranda looked down at her swiftly melting mound of ice cream and brownie. "I don't think so. Go ahead." She slid the bowl over to Kat, who grinned and picked up the spoon.

"So, I know this is a weird question, but, do you still pee?"

Miranda snorted, almost inhaling her beer, which caused Kat to laugh, too. "Yes," Miranda answered. "Much more if I drink other things besides the usual."

"Same deal if you eat real food?"

Miranda nodded. "Our digestive systems aren't really built for solids, but in small quantities it's okay. Stuff like ice cream that melts into a liquid is a lot easier."

"So no more breakfast tacos," Kat said, sounding a little sad. "That would suck."

"Not really. I don't want food anymore, for the most part. A lot of us have a sweet tooth, but I don't remember the biological reason for it—something to do with our body chemistry and glucose. Other things, though, I just don't really miss. The main reason any of us eat regular food is to pass as human."

Kat paused with the spoon partway to her mouth and said, "You know . . . I know that a lot of people would envy you for the whole immortality thing, but I don't think I do. I'm not sure I would want to outlive . . . everything."

"I haven't had much time to think about it, to be honest. Faith said that the reality of it doesn't really hit home until you've outlived a typical human life span."

"Speaking of life spans, doesn't it bother you that he's got three-hundred-something years on you and you don't know all that much about him—who he loved, where he lived, how he spent all of those years?"

"Sometimes. But really, do you know that much about Drew? You've only been together about as long as David and I have. You probably don't know every detail of his past yet—imagine if he had ten times more stories to tell."

Kat thought about it, then nodded. "Fair point."

It was rare for Kat to show any interest in the details of life as a vampire. Miranda didn't volunteer anything she didn't ask about; she knew that Kat was trying hard not to think of Miranda as some kind of monster who drank blood, and Miranda was grateful for that. As much as she'd objected to David's neglecting to tell Kat everything that was going on, the Queen was finally starting to agree that Kat already had enough to deal with, and there were some things she just didn't need to know.

A lot of things.

A few bites later Kat set down the spoon, suddenly looking a little green around the gills. "Ugh."

"You okay?" Miranda asked. "Do you need something fizzy?"

"No, I just . . . excuse me."

Kat darted away from the table, headed for the restrooms, and Miranda kept an eye on her until she'd rounded the corner, then nodded to Lali, who was stationed at a booth nearby, to watch the door and make sure no one approached Kat while she was down the hall alone. Miranda caught the waitress's eye and asked for the check; she had a feeling that Kat wouldn't be up for much else after dinner.

Sure enough, when Kat returned she looked pasty and nauseated. "Sorry," Kat said. "I don't know where that came from. I've been doing a lot better this week, but apparently the baby doesn't like nachos."

"Would you like me to take you home?" Miranda asked.

Kat looked torn. They'd both been excited about the new local band they were going to see, but clearly Kat wasn't feeling up to standing for two hours in a crowded bar surrounded by drunk people.

"It's okay," Miranda told her. "Really, Kat—Nice Marmot will have another gig. Maybe we can find somewhere to see them that has actual chairs."

Finally, Kat nodded. Her eyes were bright with tears. "If you're sure you don't mind . . . I think I need to lie down."

"Come on, then, Harlan will get us there."

Miranda kept a steadying hand on Kat's shoulder as they left the café; Lali, who had been able to hear their conversation, was already out front, and the car pulled around as soon as they'd gotten to the curb.

"I don't think I'd like the vamp thing, but the service sure rocks," Kat said.

Miranda grinned and waited until Kat was in the car to go around and get in herself. "Rank hath its privileges."

Sitting beside Kat as the car eased out onto South Lamar, Miranda watched her friend lean back with her eyes closed, her hands resting protectively on her belly, something Kat had taken to doing in the last couple of weeks that Miranda doubted she was even aware of. "Let me know if we need to pull over."

Kat opened one eye. "Don't worry, I'm not going to puke in your Lincoln."

"I'm worried about you, not the car."

She shook her head. "I think I'm okay, I just . . . I have this sick feeling, like I'm scared to death of something, but I don't know why."

Miranda frowned. "It's coming from your belly?"

"Yeah. It's like somebody spooked the little critter."

Before Kat even had the sentence out, dread seized Miranda's heart. She said into her com, "Elite One Nineteen."

*"Yes, my Lady?"*

"I'd like a security status update from your position."

*"Everything's quiet, my Lady. No one's gone near the house since you left."*

"Thank you. Star-two, out."

Kat was looking at her, eyes narrowed with concern. "What's wrong?"

"Do me a favor and call Drew, would you?"

"Why?"

Miranda couldn't explain it, except that if Kat's baby was giving her bad vibes, something was giving Miranda a full-blown anxiety attack that she was hiding by sheer force of will. Her heart had begun to pound, and she felt adrenaline beginning to surge through her veins. *Shit. Something's wrong. Something's wrong.*

"Please, Kat, just call him."

Kat shrugged and took out her phone. "It's ringing."

"Where's he at tonight?"

"The school," Kat said, still listening to the phone ring. "Weird . . . he always picks up by the third ring."

Miranda called to Harlan, "Take us to 228 East Chicon, as fast as you can." Then she said into her com, "All available patrol teams to 228 East Chicon."

"Miranda, what the hell is going on?" Kat demanded. "So he didn't answer, so what? He might not have his phone on him."

"Okay, Kat," Miranda told her, keeping her voice very calm despite the alarms going off in her head and her heart, "I'm going to go first and make sure everything's okay. You stay in the car until I come get you."

"Um . . . okay . . . but—"

Miranda didn't wait for her to ask. "Harlan, pull over." As the car rolled to a stop, the Queen shut her eyes and concentrated, forming the image of the school where Drew worked as firmly in her mind as she could. She'd never done this on her own before, but there was no time to lose . . . she knew it was in her power, if she could just . . .

She pulled hard on the image, doing as David had shown her and relaxing her hold on her body in a certain way that made everything feel blurry and strange.

She heard Kat gasp . . .

. . . and next thing she knew she was tumbling onto the sidewalk outside the school, forcing herself not to be sick as she scrambled to her feet and drew her sword.


David and Faith both sat in front of the screen while Novotny pulled up the scanned images of the scrap of paper Janousek had left.

"I apologize for the delay in getting this finished," the doctor said. "We had a hell of a time with it. The paper's so damaged by age and improper preservation it's a miracle there was any ink left at all."

David nodded. "I understand. I wasn't even sure you'd be able to do it."

Novotny chuckled. "Of course we could. It just required some creativity on our part. But that's why you pay us so well, Sire."

"True."

"Now, then." He tapped his touch pad and the image of the paper appeared, exactly as it had been when David brought it in, but laid over a grid of red light. "Here you see both sides in their original state. Upon first glance there are three things visible: the number 4.19, part of a word, and on the other side, a symbol of some kind. We broke the image down into individual pixels, as you see here, and then had the computer match areas of equal pigmentation, rendering each in its own shade."

The first side of the paper, with the number on it, was magnified as Novotny spoke, demonstrating what he was talking about. "We concentrated on the darkest areas and ran them through several filters to sharpen the image."

Rows of pixels changed color, moving from the top of the image to the bottom, and the writing became clearer. It was handwritten, and the number 4.19 was much clearer; beneath it, David could just barely make out a word. "Scarlet," he said.

"Yes. We ran the number 4.19 through our database trying to match it to known organizations, codes, and significant dates, but got nothing. I would assume that *scarlet* refers to the Red Shadow."

"What about the other side?"

"That was a lot harder, but we did the same to it, and came up with this."

Novotny spun the image around and flipped it, showing what amounted to half of a symbol on the screen.

David sat forward, his mouth falling open.

Beside him, Faith asked, "Is that what I think it is?"

"Show me the other side again," David commanded.

Novotny shrugged and complied.

"Oh, God."

Faith stared at the Prime. "What?"

David put his hand over his mouth, his heart frozen in his chest. It was a moment before he could speak. "I know that handwriting."

Just then, his phone tolled out a network alarm, as both his and Faith's coms burst to life and her phone began to ring.


Miranda let her instincts guide her around the side of the building to an unlit entrance that had obviously been jimmied open. Her mind still swimming from the Mist, she slid in the door, all her senses going into predator mode. Her vision morphed into blues and purples in the darkness, showing her details no mortal could see from tiny cracks in the plaster to the footprints of mice on the tile.

It was ten o'clock at night, and the building should have been empty. It was a small charter school that specialized in fine arts and languages, and Drew taught music both during the day and for free in the evenings to underprivileged kids. There were only three classrooms and a few offices. She'd been there twice before when she was still human.

She listened intently, extending her energy along the hallway to look for life signs. She might be wrong . . . Drew might already have left . . .

She heard a scream.

Miranda broke into a run, following the tortured sound to the last classroom branching off the hallway. There was faint light coming from the door; she remembered that the classrooms had windows along one wall.

She burst into the room snarling.

Desks had been shoved in all directions; in the center of the chaos a figure crouched over another, and the smell of blood hit Miranda's nostrils with the force of a gale wind.

The figure turned and rose, and Miranda heard the sound of a sword being drawn.

"You," Miranda hissed.

The assassin smiled nastily but didn't speak. It was, without doubt, the same woman who had shot Miranda—even without her wig or the librarian glasses, Miranda knew her face.

Behind the woman, a phone began to ring—Miranda's eyes darted to the cell phone on the floor, then to Drew's outstretched hand, and the blood flowing from the wrist that the woman had only partially managed to slice before being interrupted. From the amount of blood he had to have other wounds, and Miranda could tell he'd been beaten—he had tried to put up a fight, but against a vampire with a sword, there was no chance. She saw Drew's agonized face, felt him about to scream again.

Miranda spared a thread of power to take hold of Drew's mind and calm him, to let him know it would be all right, that help was coming—but she didn't have time to speak before the assassin took advantage of her distraction and dove in for the attack.

The Queen threw herself into the fight, dodging the woman's sword by a scant half inch and spinning around to counter the stroke.

Miranda knew from the beginning that she was outmatched, but she didn't care. All she had to do was keep the woman here until the others arrived, and the building would be surrounded with Elite. David would be there any moment, too, and although Miranda might not be able to take the woman down, he sure as hell could.

They fought from one end of the classroom to the other, the assassin shoving desks at her, Miranda jumping over them and meeting her sword slash for slash.

She could feel Drew weakening. She urged him to take his jacket off and press the fabric against his wrist—he was too far in shock to think of it on his own, but under her influence he did as she commanded, holding the jacket with a shaking hand. Miranda could hear someone speaking . . . the phone? Yes, it was Kat's voice—Drew must have answered it.

The woman made for the door, and Miranda flung herself toward it, reaching out with her mind to try to grab the nearest desk and pull it in the way; she saw it scoot a few inches, but that was all the concentration she could manage in the middle of a fight, and she ran for the doorway on the woman's heels.

The shadows inside the door frame seemed to shift and coalesce.

The Prime walked into the room, sword already drawn, and the woman changed course at the last second to avoid slamming into him; she skidded on the concrete floor and nearly lost her footing but got control back in time to parry the Prime's attack and double back toward Miranda.

For a few seconds the woman was caught between Prime and Queen, but Faith's voice erupted from the coms: *"Incoming!"*

David grabbed Miranda's arm and hauled her to the floor. They both dropped flat just in time with the sounds of shattering glass from the wall of windows, the click and whistle of a half-dozen crossbows, and the singing of wood through the air.

Miranda craned her neck to see two of the stakes hit the woman—one in her shoulder, one in her chest to the left of her heart. She flew backward, her sword clattering to the ground, the light catching off something shiny at her neck that also fell as she stumbled.

Miranda was sure she would fall, but by some twisted miracle, the woman stayed on her feet, blood streaming down her torso. She looked over and met Miranda's eyes.

"Give my regards to the Alpha," she hissed.

Then she ran forward, throwing herself into the glass wall and tackling one of the Elite who had fired at her. The two hit the ground hard, but the woman used the Elite's body as a springboard and sprinted past the others, who were immediately after her.

*"Tracking!"* Faith said. *"We've got her on the network, Sire! Four units in pursuit."*

Miranda pushed herself up to her hands and knees and got across the floor to Drew. She was about to com out for an ambulance, but she could already hear sirens in the distance; Faith, or David, must have called already.

"Drew," Miranda said. "Drew, can you hear me?"

She knelt next to him, tears already coming to her eyes. There was so much blood. Miranda quickly cataloged the visible injuries: hand severed, stab wounds in his stomach and shoulder . . . there was at least one penetrating wound to his lower back, maybe his kidney, but she didn't want to risk turning him over.

David joined her. His face had that blank expressionless look that Miranda recognized, and her heart sank.

"Keep pressure on the wound," he said quietly.

Their eyes met over Drew's battered body. Miranda knew what he was thinking. There was too much blood, and they had no healer. He'd been lying there bleeding for nearly ten minutes and it would take an ambulance another two to reach them.

"Miranda . . ." Drew whispered raggedly. "Give . . . give me the phone . . . please."

Miranda grabbed the cell and said into it, "Kat? Kat, honey, are you still there?"

Kat practically screamed, *"What's happening? Miranda, where is he?"*

"Here." Miranda choked on a sob, lowering the phone to Drew's face.

"Hey, baby," he said, coughing. His breath came in shallow gasps.

Miranda could hear Kat talking to him, could hear her crying.

"It's okay," Drew said. "Kat . . . just listen to me."

Miranda could hear the paramedics coming down the hall.

"I love you," Drew told Kat. "Very much. The baby, too. I think . . . you're going to make a great mom. I love you."

Softly, Miranda heard Kat say the same to him.

"Thanks," Drew managed weakly, looking up at Miranda. "Take care of her, okay?"

Miranda nodded. "I promise."

"Good . . . that's good . . ." His fingers barely returned the pressure of Miranda's, then slowly relaxed . . .

. . . and it was over.

The paramedics and two additional units of Elite entered the classroom to find the Queen weeping into the Prime's arms, as both knelt in a broad pool of blood, and a woman sobbed quietly over the phone that lay on the floor.

Miranda stared dumbly at the printout David had given her, trying to understand what she was seeing. Her worn-out, bewildered mind simply refused to accept it.

"What do we do?" she asked.

"I don't know," the Prime replied. He looked as exhausted and heartsick as she felt. "I honestly don't know."

Outside the car windows' heavy tint, the countryside scrolled by. Miranda wanted nothing more than to fall asleep and not wake up until the world made sense again. She was completely drained, both from the fight with the assassin and from her first real Mist—it was remarkable she hadn't ended up scattered across Austin. Between that and the weight of sorrow and guilt from Drew's death, she was perilously close to losing it.

It was only an hour before sunrise, and Harlan was breaking several traffic laws to get them home before it began to get light out. Dealing with the police had taken a lot longer than Miranda expected—the first responders had not been the people the Haven normally dealt with, and they wanted to take a lot of pictures and ask a lot of questions that were unnecessary and tedious. Finally David had simply called the chief of police and cut through all the red tape.

Kat had been taken to the Hausmann for observation in case the trauma had affected the baby, but so far all she'd done was sit and stare off into space, barely rousing enough to answer when the paramedics asked her for details that she hadn't been able to give. She had, as Miranda had asked, stayed in the car until the Queen came to her and led her over to the gurney to provide a positive ID on Drew's body. She had nodded at the police and then gone essentially unresponsive.

Miranda had directed the Elite to make sure Kat was

brought to the Haven as soon as the doctors deemed her fit, probably the next evening.

Finally, the Pair had headed home. They had changed into the spare set of clothes that they kept in the trunk, so at least Miranda didn't have to spend the whole drive back to the Haven soaked in Drew's blood, but she could still smell it, though she'd washed her hands and face and everything she could in the school's restroom.

"This is how it goes, isn't it?" Miranda said softly, staring out the car window. "One by one we lose everyone we knew."

David looked at her, and she could tell he wanted to be reassuring but couldn't lie to her. "That's what we are, beloved. We stand outside time and watch it slowly consume everything. My son died, his children died, their children died . . . the line continues, spread throughout the gene pool, but everything that made me human has long since faded."

She half smiled. "You're still more human than most of the men I've ever known."

"Thank you."

"I don't know if I can do this," she said.

"You can. You are Queen, Miranda. The strength you need is part of who you are."

"Sophie told me once that this life was a gift, and that I had to think long and hard about whether I was worthy, because there was no giving it back."

She looked down at the sword that lay across her lap, and the one lying on the floorboard wrapped in fabric—the assassin's blade. "I wasn't fast enough to kill her," Miranda lamented. "I wish I could have. I wish I had seen her bleed to death instead of Drew."

"So do I."

"What did Faith say?"

David sighed. "They lost her trail. She dropped off the network again about two miles into the pursuit, then detoured and disappeared into the city. After that it was so close to dawn I had to call them back. By dusk whatever trail is left will be cold."

"But she showed up on the sensors for a few minutes . . . why?"

"I think this has something to do with it." He held up the thing that had fallen from the woman's neck: a silver disk on a chain with some kind of script carved into it. "Whatever it is, I think it disrupts the network signal. After she dropped it, we could track her, but somehow she got her hands on another one, or had a spare she activated. I sent images of it to Novotny, and I'm going to run the symbols through my database before I hand it over to him."

"Why bother?" she asked. "We already know who's behind it, David."

He met her eyes. "We might be wrong."

The car slowed, then stopped, and a moment later the door opened. Lali stood by while they disembarked, then shut the doors and went ahead of them into the Haven with Aaron to clock off duty for the night.

"I thought you said you were sure," Miranda said, falling into step beside David as they walked down the hall to their suite.

David's face and voice both were bleak. "I'm sure. God help us, but I'm sure. The symbol, the handwriting . . . I've seen both a thousand times."

As David nodded to their door guards and opened the door into their suite, Miranda looked down at the page still in her hand, an image of the back side of Janousek's scrap of paper, which had been digitally restored by Novotny's people. She had never seen the symbol before, but she had heard of it:

A waning crescent moon and the Greek symbol of infinity.

David froze midstride and made a feline hissing noise. "Son of a bitch."

Miranda nearly ran into him but stopped in time to look over his shoulder into their suite.

There, sitting calmly in one of the chairs by the fire, sipping a glass of whiskey, was the Alpha.

"Hello, darling," Deven said.

# Sixteen

Miranda stayed behind David as he edged slowly into the room, his eyes riveted on Deven, his hand on the hilt of his sword.

"I see by your faces you've found me out," Deven said calmly over the rim of his glass. "May I ask how?"

Wordlessly Miranda held up the scan.

Deven made an exasperated noise. "Goddamn Horak. If I'd known that woman was going to cause all of this, I never would have taken his recommendation." He gestured at the other chairs. "Care to sit?"

"You bastard," Miranda said. "How dare you come into our house—"

Deven rolled his eyes. "Yes, yes, I know. How dare I, murdering monster I am, traitor, et cetera, et cetera. Now, both of you sit down."

Neither of the Pair budged. "I should kill you right here and now," David told him.

Deven sighed, looking down into his glass, and when he looked up there was something dark and menacing in his eyes that Miranda had never seen before. "Try," he replied. "But then you'll never have the answers you want, will you?"

"He came alone," Miranda observed. "No Elite, no Jonathan."

"Jonathan isn't a part of this," Deven said. "Well, he is,

because I am, but I didn't want him involved. So if you kill me, you'll be killing him, too, and he's as close to innocent as any of us are. I doubt you want that on your conscience. So, sit."

"I don't want to hear anything you have to say," David told him coldly. "Our alliance is terminated—consider yourself at—"

"Don't say it," Deven interrupted, eyes flashing. "Don't even think it. You don't want to declare war on me, David. You couldn't win. Don't give me that look, either; you have your technological toys and your psychic parlor tricks, but I have my own ace up my sleeve . . . dozens of aces, all over the world, ready to kill at my command—anyone, anywhere, any time."

"It was you all along," David said, and Miranda could feel the sickness in his heart. "You were the Alpha. You set the assassin on Miranda."

Deven's eyes were unyielding, like steel. "I am the Alpha. I have always been the Alpha. Each and every Shadow was trained by my own hand. I recruited them from every Elite, every mercenary guild, every class of warriors in six hundred years of history. And I would have done the same with you, darling, except I learned a long time ago not to sleep with my agents."

"What about Sophie?" Miranda asked, stepping forward. "Was she really one of yours?"

His eyes flicked toward her. "Sophia Castellano worked for me for almost one hundred years. She was one of my most talented agents, one of only four to earn the rank of Scarlet."

"Then why did she teach me if all you wanted was to kill me?" the Queen demanded.

"Why would I want to kill you, Miranda? What purpose would that serve?"

"Then what do you want?"

Deven took a long, slow breath, and said, "Marja Ovaska."

"Who?" David asked.

"Marja Ovaska is the woman who is after Miranda. She, and she alone, wants you dead, my Lady. I didn't set her on you. She has been out of the Shadow for two years."

"But no one leaves the Shadow," David said. "You said so yourself."

"No one ever had. I've trained hundreds of agents, and in all that time there has only been one way out—the sword. They die on mission or they die by my blade, but they never leave. It's a lifetime contract. Or it always was."

He set his glass down and crossed his arms, looking toward the fireplace; David and Miranda both kept their eyes on him, though he didn't seem at all concerned about it. And why should he be? He had gotten into the Haven, into their suite, completely undetected by the Elite, the servants, and the surveillance network.

"I have in the Shadow's entire history released exactly two agents alive," Deven said, his voice tempered with something Miranda realized was regret. "One was Marja Ovaska. The other was her lover . . . Sophia Castellano."

"So Sophie wasn't working for you?"

"Yes, she was."

"But you said—"

"Let him talk," David said quietly.

"Agents of the Shadow do not mingle," Deven went on. "They never see each other's faces. If they speak, it's over the phone. They all have code names. But once in a while a client needs more than one agent to get the job done. Agents 3.17 Scarlet and 4.19 Scarlet—Sophie and Marja—met on assignment, by accident, and as often happens in such tragedies they fell in love, in direct defiance of protocol and knowing that I would kill them both when I found out. I had them brought to me for execution."

Miranda knew what he was going to say next; she could feel it. "You couldn't do it."

"No, damn it. I should have. But for once in my life I allowed their sad little story to get to me. I had let myself grow attached to Sophie, fool that I am, and so I gave them a choice. They could die right then at my feet or they could each fulfill one last mission and then disappear. If I ever heard from either of them again, in any context, both of their lives were forfeit. They were to go underground and stay gone forever."

"And you believed they would?" Miranda asked.

"Of course I did. My agents are trained to go into certain death without hesitation. There's only one thing they are taught to fear: me."

"But Sophie didn't," David concluded. "She broke her end of the deal by telling Faith she was ex-Shadow."

Again, Deven rolled his eyes. "Please. Sophie was no fool. And she was no drunk. She was stone cold sober when she met Faith."

"Then why . . ."

"Why do you think?" Deven snapped. "Put it together, Prime. My Consort has the strongest precognitive gift in the Council. He knew you were going to take the South. Don't you think he knew you would eventually find a Queen?"

"I don't understand," David said.

But Miranda did. "You assigned her to me," she said softly. "Sophie's last work for you was to train me. War was coming . . . Jonathan saw it. And he knew that I had to be ready. If it weren't for Sophie—for you—I wouldn't be here."

Deven met her eyes, and his gaze finally seemed to lose some of its hardness. "Her job was to make sure you were strong enough and had the skills you needed to help put you in the right place at the right time to become Queen. As soon as that happened she could vanish."

"But she died in the battle . . ."

"She should never have been there. She was under orders not to go anywhere near the Haven itself, but to train you, then show you the way home and get the hell out." The Prime held her eyes. "She believed in you enough to go off mission . . . and then she died before she and Marja could be free."

"What was Marja's last mission?" Miranda asked, holding back tears.

"Irrelevant. But if Sophie had done as I told her and left you to fight your own way into the Haven that night, Ovaska would never have been heard from again."

Finally, Miranda sat down, head in her hands. "Sophie died . . . and now Marja wants me dead . . . to avenge her lover."

David asked, "How long have you known?"

Miranda looked up to see Deven shrug. "Not as long as I should have. I suspected Marja might be involved as soon as you mentioned a connection to Finland, but I wasn't sure until I hauled in Volundr, interrogated him myself, and then sent him to you."

"You let me torture Volundr even though you knew who we were looking for?"

Deven made an impatient noise. "I didn't think you'd have to torture the old toad. I paid him a ridiculous sum to tell you the truth—both Ovaska's identity and what he knew about her location—but apparently his loyalties have shifted. Your people took him back to California and he vanished—along with an entire order of blades I had already paid for, incidentally. You've cost me a fuckton of money."

Miranda was shaking her head, not sure whether to laugh at the absurdity of it all or scream herself sick. "All those people . . . Jake, Denise, Drew . . . they all died . . . Kat almost died . . . because I got Sophie killed."

"You did nothing of the kind," Deven contradicted her, though his tone wasn't attempting anything like comfort. "Sophie died in battle the way warriors have throughout history, and by her own choice. Ovaska wants someone to blame. She knows she can't kill me, but you are still vulnerable because you're young and rash and have human friends who are easily killed. She sized up your defenses in that first attack and planned out how to destroy you piece by piece. My agents are dangerous sociopaths who will do anything, kill anyone, torture or maim anybody if it means reaching the objective. Even Sophie was willing to paint a giant target on her head by telling Faith who she had worked for—she knew it was the only way Faith would believe that she had the skills necessary for your training."

"Oh, God," Miranda said, her memory suddenly intruding. She looked up at David helplessly. "The night of the battle, when we were watching you fight, she said she'd only ever seen one other vampire with your combat style. She was talking about Deven."

"That's right," Deven said. "The one who trained both David and Sophie."

David sat down beside Miranda, seeking her hand, but spoke to Deven. "What I don't understand here is *why*, Deven. Why would you intervene in Miranda's future? Why give Sophie that assignment?"

Deven sighed. "Miranda, if you wouldn't mind?"

Miranda wiped her eyes and said, "Because he loves you, David. And the only way to pay you back for how badly he treated you years ago was to make sure you found your own Consort . . . to make sure you were happy."

"You were never supposed to have any idea I was involved. I had hoped to hunt down Marja and have her eliminated before anything else happened," Deven said, and for a wonder he sounded sincere. "I am sorry for the loss of your friends."

"How exactly were you going to track her down from California?" David demanded coldly. "You don't have that kind of technology."

Deven smiled. "What do you think we did before computers? Good old-fashioned detective work. I happen to have many highly trained detectives at my disposal."

"You have an agent here in Austin?"

The smile turned wicked. "I have an agent in your house."

David blinked. "Bullshit."

Deven removed his cell phone from his coat pocket, giving Miranda a glimpse of the array of weaponry he wore. He touched the phone's screen several times, saying, "Before you ask—Hart's troubles have nothing to do with me. My people don't use earpieces; like I said, they're impractical. I would like to know who's harassing him, though. It tickles me."

A moment later there was a knock at the door. "Come in," David called without his eyes leaving Deven's face. Miranda could feel the tumble of anger, shock, and pain from her Prime, making her own confusion that much worse. She wanted to put her arms around him, but she was frozen in place, waiting for the other shoe to drop.

And drop it did.

Deven spoke again. "Allow me to introduce 5.23 Claret," he said.

The door opened.

"Oh my God," Miranda said. "Lali?"

The bodyguard bowed to the Pair, then again to Deven.

"Don't be angry at her," Deven said, gesturing for Lali to come stand beside his chair. "Everything about her, as your bodyguard, is true. She would die to defend you. She is in fact very fond of you. You seem to inspire that kind of devotion, my Lady."

"You've been working for me for ten years," David said to the Elite, completely thunderstruck by the revelation.

Lalita nodded. "Yes, Sire. But I have been working for the Alpha for two hundred. My loyalty to you is superseded only by my loyalty to him."

"There's no way you could have known," Deven told David. "Her history, her qualifications, all of it was authentic . . . just incomplete."

"How in hell do you communicate?"

Lali smiled. "Mostly via encoded pictures of cute animals."

"Now, then," Deven said, "enough chatter. Let's get to why I'm here."

"Not to tell us the truth?" David asked.

"Of course not. If I had been successful in taking out Ovaska myself, I would never have let on I was involved. In six centuries exactly three people besides the agents themselves have known who I was—Jonathan, and now you two."

"I could expose you," David said in a low voice, the anger making its way out past his defenses.

Deven sat forward, hands clasped, and glared into David's eyes. "Again . . . try it."

Miranda looked from one Prime to the other, took a deep breath, and asked, "How is Ovaska getting past our sensor network?"

Deven didn't avert his eyes from David's until David lowered his. "Magic," he replied. "Volundr made something for her. He wouldn't tell me how it worked, but he said he'd given her a set of seven amulets that would shield her from any form of detection except plain sight. The spell had a limited life span; each disc would last only a few days once activated."

David and Miranda exchanged a look. "She's used up most of them already," Miranda said, "unless she has another supplier."

"That is ridiculous," David responded. "Amulets, spells—there's no such thing."

Deven chuckled. "Darling, sometimes I think it's a good thing you're so pretty."

David looked like he was about to leap up and throttle Deven, but he didn't. "Tell us what you came to tell us, then, and get the hell out of my house."

Deven sat back, retrieving his whiskey. "You're angry."

"Damn right I am! I've known you almost a hundred years, and you never told me you were running the most notorious network of assassins in the world. You had a spy in my Haven all this time, and you've had your dirty little hands in every aspect of our lives. For all I know everything you're telling me now is a lie. You even broke into this house and got past my guards—"

"I Misted," Deven said simply. "This isn't exactly Hogwarts, you know. You might want to adjust your sensors in some way to account for the abilities of a Prime, although

I doubt you have to worry about anyone else sneaking in here solo."

Then he rose, taking out his phone. "As to why I'm here . . . I brought you this."

He held up the phone so the Pair could see the screen: a map with a single red dot in its center.

"This is where you'll find Marja Ovaska," Deven told them. "Thanks to Volundr's information and Lalita's excellent investigative work, I finally managed to pin down her location yesterday. I didn't want to trust this information to e-mail, so as soon as I could, I flew in. I want to be there when you find her. At sunset I'll take you there, and assuming she isn't on to us, you can kill her yourself."

"Why should we trust you?" David wanted to know.

"Trust me, don't trust me, whatever suits you. But if you don't act on this information, more people will die, up to and including both of you. Help me to help you, David. I made this mess. Help me clean it up."

"You're giving yourself too much credit," Miranda muttered. "Marja made her own choices."

"So did Sophie," Deven replied, "but you still feel guilty for her death."

Miranda nodded slowly, then said to David, "He's telling the truth."

David looked at her. "You're sure."

"I can feel it, David. Besides . . . he came here alone, and it's dawn. He knew he couldn't escape—there's nowhere to go until sunset. He put himself into our hands willingly."

Deven asked politely, "Would it make you feel better to cuff me and throw me in a cell?"

"I'd like to throw you out into the sunlight," David snapped. "But I trust Miranda's instincts. If she says you're telling the truth, I believe her."

Miranda listened silently, feeling numb from the mind outward, as David called in their door guards to escort Deven and Lali to a nearby guest suite and station as many warriors as they could spare at the entrance.

"Your weapons," David said flatly.

Deven looked at him for a long minute, then reached into his coat and began removing blades, handing them to the Elite who had come in to essentially arrest him. First his sword, then another shorter one, four knives of various lengths, two hilted throwing stakes, and a talon-shaped blade he wore in a slit near his heart that Miranda recognized—Sophie had had one just like it.

Lalita had only her Elite sword, a stake on her belt, and a single standard-issue folding knife. David let her keep her com for the time being, but Miranda knew he would put a network lock on it so her access would be limited.

"Is that all?" David asked.

Deven, completely unfazed at being disarmed, said, "Care to frisk me?"

Miranda knew better, and she assumed so did David, than to think that they had all of Deven's weapons, but David didn't push; in reality if Deven wanted to get out of the room he didn't need a sword. Even without Misting, he was still stronger and faster than any of them; he had spent the last seven centuries making himself into a weapon. Surrendering his toys to David was purely symbolic.

One of the Elite started to step toward Deven, but Deven fixed him with a look, and the guard fell back. Deven nodded to the guard to lead the way.

"Look to your Queen," Deven said to David as they left. "Get her some caffeine and blood before she passes out."

David pulled his eyes from the Prime to Miranda, who started to protest that she was fine, but she found she was simply too tired to speak. She shook her head silently, not sure what she was denying, exactly; but between one breath and the next David was pressing a bottle of Coke into her hand and calling Esther to bring her blood. It seemed like days ago she'd fed last . . . had it really been only a few hours since she and Kat had been at Kerbey Lane? Everything had changed so fast.

Almost as soon as Deven and Lali were led away, Faith came in, looking utterly confounded by the whole situation.

"What in the world is going on, Sire?" she asked. "I got an e-mail from Lali resigning her post, and now Deven's here in some kind of custody?"

David had his head in his hands, Deven's sword lying across his lap. "Sit down, Second," he said hollowly. "I have one hell of a briefing for you."

Just before sunset, the Prime and Queen dressed silently, each strapping on as many weapons as they could comfortably wear. Miranda pulled her hair back from her face in a tight ponytail and wore the same kind of clothing she had the night she and Sophie had joined in the battle at the Haven.

Miranda paused with her hands on her sword . . . Sophie's sword. It was the only blade she'd ever felt comfortable wearing, and it had been on her hip every time she went into the city since that first battle. She had used it to take the heads of the last few Blackthorn and had fought the assassin—Marja—with it. Miranda stared down at the shining steel, thinking back, wondering if there had been a moment when she might have detected an ulterior motive in Sophie's actions . . . but Sophie's act, however much of it had been an act, had been flawless.

David put his hand on hers. "She chose to fight with you when she could have run back to her lover and disappeared. In the end she cared enough about you to put her own life on the line. That means something, beloved."

Miranda looked him in the eyes. "So does what Deven did," she told him. "I know you're angry, but if you let this end your friendship you'll regret it forever."

David turned away, buckling his belt. "I'll think about that after we deal with Ovaska."

Miranda went to the mantel and lifted Deven's sword down from where David had left all of the Prime's confiscated weapons. She held it up to the firelight—Jonathan had been right, she could see the insignia of the Order of Eleusis, the same symbol that was on the note Deven had given Prime Horak, worked into the ornate carving that covered the blade. It was a beautiful sword, about the same size and weight as Sophie's, but a little shorter and built for a smaller hand.

There was, she noticed, some kind of writing on the other side near the hilt, but she was fairly certain it was in Gaelic. "Do you know what this means?" she asked.

David glanced at the script. "Probably its name. Deven names all of his swords."

"You don't read Gaelic?"

"No. I speak it, but I don't read it."

She offered it to him. "We need to give them their weapons back. We don't know what we're walking into tonight."

He pondered the blade, saying almost to himself, "I've never seen this one before . . . it must be new. His last one's name was Ghostlight." He turned back to Miranda and said, "We should make them both stay here. For all we know, this is all a plan he set up in collusion with Ovaska."

Miranda smiled slightly. "You do remember my saying that he was telling us the truth, right?"

"Someone as old as Deven could fool even your gift, Miranda."

"Not likely, baby. You're the one who told me that empathy is rare enough that it's hard to protect against and even harder to outwit. Besides, like I said when you first figured out those stakes came from the West, Deven has no motive to kill us. Even if you take his feelings for you out of the equation, you're his strongest ally in the Council, and without you the entire balance of power falls apart. I knew in my gut there was a reason that him being the Alpha didn't make sense to me—turns out it wasn't because he was the Alpha, but because the Alpha is not our enemy."

"I don't suppose your gut has anything to say about what we're doing tonight."

Miranda drew her awareness into her own mind for a moment to see if her fledgling precognitive gift was offering up any warnings, but mostly she just felt a vague sense of unease, probably the same thing she'd feel any time she was walking into a completely unknown situation to confront someone who wanted her dead. "No."

"We could send the Elite by themselves to check it out first," David reasoned.

"Do you really want to risk her getting away again? She was trained by a Prime—and not just any Prime. She could take down any of our Elite, even Faith. We don't know how long that amulet of hers is going to keep working, so we might not be able to track her if she escapes. I think we should stick to the plan."

David nodded; she knew he agreed with her, he was just reluctant, and understandably so, to risk more lives in the pursuit of Marja Ovaska just on Deven's word.

Miranda wanted to be angry with Deven, too, but for some reason she couldn't. She understood that David was having a hard time separating the truth from his perception of his former . . . sometimes . . . lover, but perhaps because she didn't claim to know Deven that well, or like him all that much, she was able to step back and see that as old as Deven was, it was naïve to think he *didn't* have secrets. Up until now there had been no reason for Deven's two worlds to collide, and she knew that he hadn't decided to reveal himself to them lightly. He didn't strike her as the kind of person who would overshare when there might be lives at stake. She got the feeling that, cold as he might act, he took responsibility for his agents' lives and counted their deaths against his own soul.

That didn't mean she didn't have the urge to slap the smug right off his face, but she might give him a pass if his information did bring an end to all of this.

"Ready?" David asked.

Miranda took a deep breath. "I think so."

"Are you sure you're up to this? I know last night wore you out—"

"I slept like the dead," she assured him gently, kissing his cheek. "And we'll feed when we get to town. I'll be fine."

He slid his arms around her, and they held on to each

other for a while, her head resting on his shoulder precisely where it was meant to.

"I just want this over with," he said.

Miranda sighed . . . a knot of knowledge was forming in her stomach, and she didn't want it, but she voiced it anyway. "It will be. One way or another this will be resolved by the time you and I come home."

David shut the weapons cabinet, and hand in hand they left the suite. Faith fell into step behind them as they took the hallway out of their wing. The Second didn't say anything—she, too, was troubled, though whether by the thought of going after Ovaska or the realization that Deven had a secret identity, Miranda couldn't say.

Four guards stood in a semicircle around the room where Deven and Lali were; it was the same room that Ariana Blackthorn had stayed in, but now it had a range of new security measures built into it, including a separate sensor system and audio surveillance. It was designed to house people who didn't know they were being watched. So far nothing out of the ordinary had happened; Lali had apparently slept most of the day, and Deven had called Jonathan on his cell phone, but that was it. David had recorded the conversation and said that Deven had let Jonathan know what they planned to do, reassured the Consort he was safe, and that was about it.

David nodded to the guards, and they moved aside, one of them unlocking the door and swinging it open.

Deven stepped out with Lali at his back. "Good evening, Lord Prime, my Lady," he said with measured deference. "Shall we?"

David looked at Miranda, who inclined her head toward Deven encouragingly.

David held out Deven's sword with both hands.

Deven met his eyes, then took it. As he buckled it on, David motioned for Faith and Aaron to bring forward the rest of Deven and Lali's weapons.

"Let's go," David said, and led the way out to where Harlan was waiting to take them into the city.

\* \* \*

Warmth and pleasure sang through Miranda's veins as she climbed back into the car with David sliding in beside her. She licked her lips reflexively, seeking any lingering trace of blood, and spared her husband a smile. His eyes were a ring of silver around dark pupil, still dilated from the hunt, and he leaned over and kissed her lightly.

Miranda resisted the urge to stick her tongue in David's mouth just to spite Deven . . . barely. Now wasn't the time to indulge in her passive-aggressive impulses, and truthfully she didn't want to make the tension between him and David any worse . . . but the idea was still appealing. Instead she took David's hand and squeezed it reassuringly.

Once they were moving again, Deven leaned forward so they could all see the screen of his phone. "Right here," he said. "It's an apartment in a small complex off Manor Road. The place looks appropriately seedy. It should be fairly easy to surround. I'd recommend a detail on the roof as well."

"Already on their way," David told him, switching to all-business mode. "I've got Faith in the van with two units set to rendezvous with us when we reach the block, and a third coming in armed for roof duty."

"Good. The layout is typical of cheap second-floor apartments. Stairs up to a concrete landing. One door with an adjacent window, two windows on the side, no other exits. Lalita's recon showed that half the building is empty, and this unit here on the first floor is a crack house. We probably don't have to worry about human interference."

David pulled up the sensor grid on his own phone. "There are no other vampires in the building and no signals of any kind coming in or out except for satellite television in the crack house. I'm still not picking her up, if she's there."

"She may not be," Deven admitted. "I know that's her home base, but there's no way to confirm she's actually there without a direct sighting. At the very least we should find some fun souvenirs."

"Are you sure she doesn't have anything else from

Volundr?" Miranda asked. "Other magical weapons like the amulets?"

"Not to my knowledge. Volundr was pretty forthcoming about the amulets, but he could easily have left something out. The way he talked about it, though, it sounded like crafting the amulets was a huge achievement for him. That kind of thing isn't easy to make, and it usually involves blood sacrifice at the very least. I doubt he was in the habit of selling that kind of favor—he just didn't have the psychic strength for that much magic. Either she paid him an outrageous sum for his help, or she was far more persuasive about her cause than I was about mine."

"Maybe he bought a shipment of fairy dust from Finland, too," David suggested.

Deven gave him a withering look. "If you don't have anything useful to share with the class, put your head down on your desk."

"How about you go to—"

"Boys," Miranda said tiredly, "can we save the cock-fight for later, please?"

"At any rate," Deven went on, glaring at David, "I don't believe she has anything else like that in her possession, but we can't rule anything out, so we have to proceed with caution."

"Two Primes, a Queen, a Second, a dozen Elite . . . surely we don't have anything to fear," Miranda pointed out. "She may be your prodigy, Lord Prime, but she's still only one woman."

"Oh, she's far more than one woman," Deven said with a grim smile. "I made sure of that. But between us I think we can take her—the worst that could happen is that she'll get away."

The car slowed to a halt, and Harlan said, "Sire, we're at the rendezvous location."

The night was bitterly cold, but at least it wasn't raining; Miranda felt the temperature distractedly, her body still running hot from feeding. She got out of the car and immediately swept the block with her senses, but all she could detect were Faith and the other Elite arriving on the scene and dispersing to await their orders.

The three Signets and Faith made their way toward the apartment building in silence, David in the lead, with Miranda at his right hand and Deven at his left. David scrutinized his phone as they walked, then motioned for them to stop just before they came into view of the building.

"Still no sign," David said quietly. "The Elite have the place surrounded and the rooftop team is in position. Faith, I want you on the side of the building to block any escape through the windows."

"Yes, Sire," Faith said, and melted into the shadows.

At the base of the stairs Deven held up his hand for them to wait. "I'll go in first," he said. "Wait for my signal."

"Why?" Miranda asked.

"I'm more likely to escape in one piece if it's a trap."

David shook his head. "If she's got any tech in there, it's not showing up."

Deven smiled grimly. "There are plenty of ways to booby-trap a place like this, and I know for a fact Ovaska knows most of them. I know what to look and listen for. Just stay back until I'm sure."

Miranda watched, heart pounding, as he took the stairs quickly without making so much as a footfall's sound. He pressed his back into the exterior wall beside the door, listening into the darkened apartment.

As he'd said, the place was a dump. It didn't look like anyone had lived there for years. There were lights on in the first-floor unit, but the target unit looked uninhabited; Miranda saw that one of the windows was boarded over, and the other had an air conditioner hanging out of it with a ribbon of torn duct tape fluttering in the air. A pile of old newspapers was stacked in front of the door, and one of the apartment numbers was hanging by a single nail.

Deven reached sideways to close his hand around the doorknob and gave it an experimental turn. He frowned; Miranda heard the knob turning freely. The door was unlocked.

With his other hand, Deven drew one of his stakes, clearly not trusting the situation any more than Miranda did.

Slowly, a tiny bit at a time, he opened the door, exposing a darkened entryway. Miranda listened hard, but she couldn't hear any movement inside. She glanced at David, who was watching Deven intently, the sensor grid up on his phone showing the positions of all the Elite.

In a motion almost too rapid for Miranda to see, Deven darted into the apartment. Miranda stared at the doorway for a long minute with her heart in her throat, waiting for the sounds of a struggle or at least conversation.

Finally Deven reappeared in the doorway and shook his head.

"Shit," David muttered. "She's not there." He addressed his com: "Suspect is not present. Hold your positions; I repeat, do not approach the building until it's cleared. Faith, give me a visual inspection of the building exterior."

The light in his phone blinked as Faith beamed in images from her camera; Miranda leaned over and looked, but there was nothing to see, just stills of the apartment's windows and the alley from different angles.

Miranda looked back up at the door, where Deven had again gone inside. "I'm going in," she said. "Are you coming?"

"Yes," David replied, standing still, eyes on the screen. "I'm right behind you. Let's have a look. Maybe we'll get something out of this wild-goose chase."

The stairs were rickety wood, and Miranda had no idea how Deven had managed to scale them without making any noise; she kept her steps light and still elicited a few creaks.

She peered carefully into the apartment. It smelled musty and damp . . . but not as if anyone lived there, human or otherwise. "Deven?"

"Hold on . . ."

Miranda watched the Prime move slowly around the room, looking for signs of something she couldn't see; he ran his hands along the windowsills, rapped carefully in several places on the drywall with his knuckles, then paused.

"Well," he said, "I think we've found the right place."

The Queen also looked around for any sign of habitation, but all her senses were telling her nobody had dwelled there in a long time. Even a vampire would leave behind some sense of her presence, and if Ovaska had stayed here for long, Miranda should have felt the echoes of her emotions, a vague sensory impression from buildup over time.

Miranda picked her way across the refuse-scattered floor and joined the Prime where he stood at a coffee table in front of a couch that had spewed half its stuffing all around. "Whoa."

The table was covered in papers: photographs of various locations around the Shadow District; images of Kat leaving work, taken from a distance; a map with the location of Drew's school highlighted in neon yellow as well as Mel's Bar, Denise's office building, and the Black Door.

"We should get the rest of the Elite in here to tear the place apart for more evidence," Miranda said, lifting her wrist. "Star-three—"

"Wait," Deven said shortly, grabbing her arm and pulling her com away from her mouth.

"What's wrong?"

Deven's head snapped up, and he looked around, something dawning on his face that left a burning chasm of fear in Miranda's stomach. "We have to get out of here."

"What—"

Deven's voice was urgent. "No agent of mine would leave evidence lying out in plain sight unless she knew we would see it. She knew we were coming. Go!"

He pushed her toward the door, just as David all but shouted from her wrist: *"Get out of there! A signal was just sent from the—"*

Miranda ran for the exit, and no sooner had her face hit the cold air than she was jerked back into something hard—Deven seized her by the shoulders and shoved them both forward, over the railing, twisting in midair to pull her against his chest.

The force of the explosion behind them threw them both through the air and into the street below.

Miranda felt her shoulder hit the ground and crack beneath her, a dull but fierce pain engulfing her as Deven landed on top of her, shielding her body from flying debris. The noise was deafening—Miranda was sure she screamed, but she could hear nothing but the thunder of the apartment's walls fragmenting and flying outward at lightning speed.

She felt pain throughout her body, both from her own wounds and from David's. Her shoulder was in agony, and something was stabbing her in the leg—no, David's leg.

"Fuck," she heard Deven grumble near her ear. "That was so stupid."

"David," she moaned. "*David!* He's hurt—get off me!"

"Calm down," Deven commanded harshly, not budging. "He's fine. You're still alive, aren't you? Hold still—we're pinned underneath something."

He shifted on top of her, and she became aware of a weight pressing down on her that wasn't him; he was, she realized, lighter than she had expected, probably lighter than her. She smelled scorched wood, so they were probably wedged under part of a wall. Beyond Deven's body she could hear chaos—Elite yelling, sirens wailing in the distance, Faith's voice giving orders. The odor of electrical fire and melted plastic and metal were thick in the air.

"*Miranda!*" David said from her com. "*Are you all right?*"

"I'm okay," she panted around the pain in her shoulder. "We're stuck under something. Where are you?"

David sounded breathless but otherwise okay, the panic leaving his voice once he heard hers. "*Near the stairs. I was halfway up when I saw the signal—I made it to the lee of the building and everything blew out over me, including you. I'm surrounded by debris and have a piece of rebar in my leg—stay where you are. Whatever you do, don't try to Mist if you're hurt. You won't be able to focus and you might scatter yourself.*"

She could feel his fear, for her and for Deven, and she probably would have been afraid, too, but she was so relieved that he was all right that there was no room for any other emotion.

"Can you move your legs apart?" Deven asked through gritted teeth.

Miranda obliged slowly and painfully. "Probably the first time you've ever asked a woman that," she said.

Deven snorted, then made a strained sound and pushed upward, one of his knees between hers using the ground as leverage. She felt the weight on them lifting, slowly at first, then angled hard off to the side.

Deven fell down next to her, breathing hard. "Stupid," he said again. "Should have known better . . . but I was sure we had her. The intel was good . . . 5.23 has never been wrong."

He forced himself up onto his knees, and Miranda saw that he was bloody and disheveled. As she started to push herself up, too, it felt like something in her shoulder tore, and she cried out. Deven put his hands on her and nudged her back down.

"Lie still," he said. "I'll fix your shoulder, but you have to give me a minute to catch my breath."

She nodded, trying to stay grounded and keep her breathing steady while Deven looked around them at the demolished scene. "We're all the way across the street," he commented, sounding impressed. "Whatever she used to blow the building had no smell, no vibration . . . I'd love to know what it was. It looks like the whole building went up . . . be glad you can't see it yet. There are . . . a lot of bodies. Humans . . . from the crack house. I don't see any Elite among them."

"Faith's okay," Miranda managed. "Have you . . ."

"Sire . . ."

The voice coming from Miranda's com was hoarse and faint, but she knew it. "Lali?" she asked. "Lali, where are you?"

A cough. "Sire . . . my Lord Alpha . . . I'm sorry. I failed you."

Deven leaned over toward Miranda, who held up her wrist. "No, Lalita."

*"I was sure of the intel . . . must have missed something . . . I failed you . . ."*

Miranda was astonished to see something shining in Deven's eyes. He replied to Lali in a language Miranda didn't understand, and Lali said something almost too quiet to hear. Then silence.

"David?" Miranda asked urgently. "Do you have Lali's signal?"

She heard him take a deep breath. *"She's gone, beloved."*

Miranda fought back tears as she asked Deven, "What did you tell her?"

The Prime looked away. "I told her I was proud of her."

"And she said good-bye," Miranda concluded, wiping her eyes with the hand of her uninjured arm.

Deven started to speak, then clapped one hand against the side of his neck. "What the hell . . ."

Miranda felt something small and hard hit her injured shoulder, and she whimpered, groping with her other hand and finding a thin cylinder of wood jutting out from her coat.

She looked up, alarmed, and saw Deven pull an identical object from his neck.

Then he gasped and fell forward, catching himself on his hands with a choked groan. She watched in horror as blood began to drip from his mouth and nose . . . he sucked in a hoarse breath, eyes clamping shut, raising both hands to his head.

It was only when the pain gripped Miranda's skull that the realization came to her . . . and by then it was too late . . . She was already losing consciousness, the pain engulfing her so completely that she couldn't even scream.

# Seventeen

*"Miranda!"*

David fought his way back to consciousness gasping, choking around the pain that racked his entire body as the antitoxin kit had its way with him.

"Sire, please . . . you must hold still."

Blinding light sent new flashes of agony through his head, but he opened his eyes anyway, struggling against the arms that held him down until he recognized the tense, pale faces hovering over his.

*Faith. Mo. Jackie.*

*Clinic.*

*Poison.*

*Miranda.*

"Where is she?" he demanded, his voice thin and raspy as if he'd been screaming—which, given the aftershocks still rolling through his body, was a distinct possibility. "Damn it, what happened?"

He tried to sit up again, and again they held him down. "Sire . . ." Faith's eyes were worried, but her voice was steady. "Tell me your name."

He shook his head. "Let me up."

"Not until I know you don't have brain damage. Name."

Rolling his eyes—which hurt like hell—he said, "David Solomon, Prime of the Southern United States. You're Faith, my Second in Command. This is the Anna Hausmann Memorial Clinic. Now tell me what the fuck happened!"

"We don't know," Faith replied as Mo moved over and fussed with a monitor. "We got you out of the debris and pulled you off the rebar, and you were in the middle of giving orders when someone darted you—Ovaska, I assume. You went down bleeding. She must have gotten all three of you within seconds of each other."

"All three . . . oh, God." David sought inside himself, trying to sense Miranda through the energy that linked them, but though he sensed she was alive, he had no sense of *where* she was or if she was hurt. He could always find her—he could be at her side in seconds, anywhere—but now something was blocking that knowledge, something that felt almost like . . .

"A shield," he murmured. "She's under some kind of shield . . . a powerful one. If she were at full strength, she might be able to break it, but if she was poisoned, too, she's weak."

"You can't find her," Faith said quietly, realizing what he meant. "Not psychically."

The fear was so thick in his mind he could barely think. "Did any of you see anything?"

Anguished, Faith shook her head. "I had just sent Aaron and two others to find them and bring them back when you were hit—by the time we realized you weren't the only one, they were gone."

"They . . . she got Deven, too?"

Faith nodded. "No trace of either of them at the scene. She moves fast."

Now David sat up slowly, and the others allowed him. He leaned his head in his hands, trying to force himself into some kind of mental clarity around the lingering pain from the poison, the antitoxins, and the underlying terror of being so far from his Queen, unable to sense her the way he should. In four months he had already grown to depend on their bond; it was a constant low hum in his mind and heart, like the white noise of a nearby but unseen ocean. That tide of energy sustained them both . . . with it blocked, and the two of them separated, it would be only a matter of days before they both went insane . . . if they even had that long.

"Faith," David said softly.

"Yes, Sire?"

He looked up into her eyes. "I don't know what to do."

A flash of fear—as uncharacteristic as his helplessness—crossed her face. Before she could speak again, one of the Elite standing guard at the door said, "Sire, you have a visitor."

Not really caring, David waved a hand, and the clinic door swung open.

A tall, broad figure ducked through the doorway, his dark gray trench coat swirling rather theatrically as a blast of cold wind accompanied him in from the streets. The light caught the glowing emerald at his throat.

Jonathan strode up to the gurney where David had been treated and crossed his arms, regarding the Prime gravely. "Now would be a really good time for one of your brilliant ideas," the Consort said.

"Thank God you're here," Faith told him, squeezing his arm. "We need all hands on deck."

Jonathan gave her a smile that was both genuine and distracted by his own worries. "They've been shielded from us," the Consort confirmed. "I can feel Deven . . . somewhere, but I can't tell where, or what shape he's in. Except . . . I know he's in pain. I felt it the minute he was poisoned." Jonathan moved to the side to let Mo come in to remove David's IV. "What will happen to them without the antitoxins?"

It was Mo who answered. "They will recover, but they will suffer first," he said. "Probably for much longer than the Prime has . . . although, Sire, I suspect this killer has adjusted her dosage, because it affected you for only about twenty minutes once we got the kit into your IV. Last time it took over an hour. I would venture to guess that they'll have two full hours of pain before the poison runs its course."

"That gives us two hours to find them," Jonathan said. "She won't kill them until then—otherwise she would have already. She wants them alert, so they'll know it's her."

"That first attack on me was a trial run," David realized. "I thought it was a self-contained attempt to knock me down so she could get to Miranda through me, and I was wrong. The first time she shot me was to see how the compound would affect a Signet—she just wanted to test it on me before the big show."

"All right," Jonathan said. "We need a plan. List the pertinents, please, Faith."

Faith glanced at David, who merely nodded; Jonathan could take charge if he felt up to it. David certainly didn't, not while he was still so foggy from the drugs. Jonathan and Deven had been Paired much longer than David and Miranda, and so they knew how to manage the separation better; Jonathan certainly seemed calm and rational for the moment.

"Last night we acted on Deven's intel and invaded the suspect's lair. Said lair was in fact wired to explode via a remote signal, which Prime David detected on the network just before it went off, giving him time to duck and cover. Queen Miranda and Prime Deven were thrown across the street underneath a segment of wall. We freed David from his entanglement and started to find the others, but Ovaska shot all three with toxin-loaded darts—seeing the Prime go down distracted the rest of us enough that she was able to make off with Miranda and Deven unseen."

"How did you get to Texas so fast?" David asked Jonathan.

The Consort gave him a *You really aren't that stupid, are you?* look. "I was here the whole time," he replied. "I checked into the Driskill while Deven came to the Haven to see you. I also brought twelve of my Elite—they're outside ready to assist."

"How many casualties were there from the explosion?" David asked Faith.

"Two Elite dead, five wounded; the wounded are all here at the Hausmann and have already healed, except Elite Seventy-three, who lost an arm."

"And the dead?"

Faith took a deep breath. "Aaron and Lali."

David looked over at Jonathan, who was clearly stricken by the news. "So you know all the agents, too?"

Jonathan shot David a warning look. "Mind how loudly you speak," he snapped. "And no, I don't know them all, but I did know Lalita."

"I'll talk about whatever I damn well please in my own territory," David returned coldly. "If it weren't for your Prime's lies and secrecy, we wouldn't be in this mess."

"That's beside the point—lives depend on our secrecy. Whatever regard you lack for us, have a care for them, and for Lalita, who died in the service of your Queen."

"And if both of you don't shut up and put this aside for now, Miranda and Deven are going to die," Faith interjected with surprising anger, given her usual reserve.

David and Jonathan both looked at her, then each other, and nodded. "You're right," Jonathan said. "Let's concentrate on finding them. David . . . David?"

The Prime blinked and refocused his gaze on Jonathan. "Sorry."

Jonathan nodded grimly. "You're already losing it. We don't have much time. If Miranda and Deven are shielded, we have to find a way to track Ovaska down."

David, hands on his temples, returned the nod and dragged himself mentally back into the room. "Faith, bring my laptop from the car. While I'm working, get all the Elite you can back to the scene and comb it for even a hair's worth of evidence. Put all available patrol units on the search for the Queen and Prime, but have them ready to divert at a moment's notice when we find them."

"As you will it, Sire," Faith said, and vanished.

David managed to wait until Mo had unclipped and unplugged the various machines and monitors from his body before climbing off the gurney and buttoning his shirt. "I need someplace quiet," he said.

Jackie, the head nurse, showed him to the administrative office, where Faith quickly brought his computer. He sat down at the desk and logged on to the sensor network and the Haven servers, though it took him a moment to remember his passwords, as there were twelve involved in just this part, each one different with at least twenty characters apiece. He had to pause once and shut his eyes, fighting against the panic of not knowing where she was, or how badly she might be hurt . . . she might be calling for him . . . she could be bleeding to death, or being tortured, her hand sliced off . . .

"David!" Jonathan's voice brought him back to reality, and he clapped his eyes back on the screen, where the master sensor grid was up and waiting for his commands. He brought up the Haven com network as well and overlaid the two.

"All right," David muttered. "Here we go. I'm going back through the data to analyze exactly what happened at the scene just before, during, and after the explosion. Here, look—the red dots are Elite, the blue dots are Miranda and I, and the white dot is Deven. There are no other vampires in the area. Deven and Miranda enter the apartment . . . and seventy-two seconds later a signal is sent from an outside location to the building."

The explosion showed on the network as a sudden relocation of every glowing dot—the Elite had either fallen, been blown forward, run, or died. Two of the dots flickered as their life signs faltered, then turned into Xs to indicate that the signal of the person wearing the com had ceased.

He clicked on each X, bringing up the designation of each. "That one's Lali," he said, pointing to the dot nearest Deven and the Queen. "She was running to help."

Deven and Miranda's signals were across the street from the apartment building; he watched, helpless, as the red dots all converged on his own, indicating that he'd just been shot with the poison dart. Seconds later, the other blue dot, and the white, disappeared, probably dragged by Marja, who still wasn't showing up. Her amulet must have still been working.

"Where did they go?" Jonathan asked. "Did she shield them, too?"

"She must have," David replied tersely. "Even if she loaded them into a car, they'd still show up on the network unless she had shields around them already. So whatever that amulet does, it must work on anyone she's touching as well as herself . . . and they conceal her from all indirect forms of detection, so it blocks the com signal, too. Faith, get a team to those coordinates, and see if there's a blood trail or any indication of where they went or how she transported them."

While Faith gave the order, he rewound the data again and scrutinized it a second time, then a third. "The answer isn't here," David said to himself. "We can't track her based just on what happened tonight. There has to be something . . ."

"Can you trace the signal that set off the bomb?"

David gave a frustrated sigh. "It was bounced from location to location and most likely originated from a pre-paid cell phone that was destroyed immediately afterward. I can narrow it down to within a one-block radius right now, but that doesn't tell us anything—we already know she was within a block of the explosion."

He put his head in his hands again, trying to think. "Miranda said we should go back through the raw sensor data. We can't track Ovaska herself—what if we could track the amulet?"

"There were seven of them," Jonathan pointed out.

"Yes, but they all have to work the same way. Before, when I tried to find anomalies in the network, I didn't know she had an amulet shielding her. I thought she might have some kind of scrambling device that would operate within known technological parameters and give off an electromagnetic field. This is something different."

"It's magic," said Jonathan. "How are you going to track magic?"

"Everything that people perceive as magic is just science in a party dress. Whatever energy they're sending out to block the sensors . . . it's still energy. It had to have affected the environment somehow, and those effects are traceable. If I can pinpoint those effects, I can recalibrate the network to search for them."

"That could take days," Jonathan said, dismayed. "They don't have days."

"Days," David said. "Right. Who am I, again? Give me twenty minutes."

His fingers flew over the keyboard, and he spared a second to dig in the laptop case and pull out the wireless mouse. He accessed the long-term data storage at the Haven and pulled up the readings for the night that Ovaska had killed Drew.

That night had been an anomaly in the attack history; she had momentarily lost her shield, then dropped off the network as soon as she activated another amulet. Somewhere, in that moment, was the answer. Whatever those amulets did, they had to disturb the energetic field of the city somehow. Everything gave off an energy signature, including humans and vampires. He dumped all of the raw data into a single file and ran search strings for commonalities between that night and tonight.

He compared the readings—air temperature, atmospheric pressure, even humidity, everything the sensors gathered, no matter how insignificant it seemed. The damn things had to be emitting some kind of signal or putting out some kind of field . . . even just a split-second blip each time . . .

"There," David said, pointing again. "At the exact moment that Ovaska activated the amulet outside the school, there was a temperature drop of one tenth of one degree and a twenty-pascal change in the atmospheric pressure where she was standing. If I compare the data from the night she attacked Miranda after her show . . . bringing up the temp and pressure of the entire room indexed in single square-foot sections, you can see a similar reading there . . . and watch it move . . . that's it. There's not an energy spike, there's an *absence*, like a single dead pixel on a screen. I just have to find the spot at tonight's scene where the temp and pressure are lower than the air surrounding it but she doesn't already show up as a vampire . . . then we can track her like a very localized weather front."

"She could have been anywhere—"

"No, not anywhere. She was within range to shoot all three of us within four seconds of each other, meaning she had to be somewhere *here*." He highlighted an area on the grid. "Given that the nearest building has no windows facing the street . . . she was either to one side of it or on the roof. With this type of dart, the gun she had to have used has a range of thirty feet, maximum. That building is three stories, but if she shot downward, the darts had to hit each of us at an angle, which they didn't. Mine was sticking straight out of my neck when I pulled it out. That means she was on the ground."

He focused the search on the area of the street where she could have reasonably been, given the wind's direction and speed and the locations of the three Signets at the time they were all shot.

A spot on the screen lit up and flashed with the temperature: 43.8 degrees, where at least the next five feet in every direction read 43.9. The air pressure showed a corresponding change.

He locked the search on those readings and ran a trace that would follow that same anomaly as it moved over the grid, allowing for a slight variation in temperature as Ovaska's body temp rose because of her physical exertion.

A few pixels at a time, agonizingly slowly, the computer began to draw a line across the screen, starting at the point where Ovaska must have been standing out of sight to fire the dart gun, closing on Miranda and Deven's location, then moving along the street as she dragged them both away from the scene.

He suspected that if he were to go back and run the data right next to Ovaska, he'd find corresponding tracks for Deven and Miranda, but there was no time for that . . . and he had what he needed.

The computer churned through immense amounts of data to provide the readings, and it was slow going, but the green line continued to snake its way through the streets of Austin . . . until it dead-ended deep in the warehouse district.

David looked up at Jonathan and Faith and gave them a feral smile. "Got her."


She woke shivering, her body wrung out and exhausted by pain, the smell of blood still filling her nostrils and a nauseating metallic taste in the back of her throat. Her head still ached dully, but the writhing agony had faded so that instead of wailing she wanted to curl up and whimper.

She could barely feel her fingers as she tried to move her hands, touching the ground beneath her, trying to learn anything she could about where she was.

Grimy concrete floor. Damp. Slowly, she extended her arm and kept feeling around until her hand hit something hard.

Bars.

She pried one eye open, groaning softly as light intruded and sent sparks through her head. Everything was blurry at first, but she blinked until her vision started to clear.

The only light came from a single incandescent bulb, leaving everything an otherworldly orange. She could make out the bars to her side, and turning her head a little she got a sense of the size of her prison: It was a cell about as big as a walk-in apartment closet.

She heard metal clank and tensed all over, waiting for a door to open or something to change, but nothing did. A moment later she heard a faint indrawn breath that hitched as if around a sudden stabbing pain.

She lifted her head. "Deven?"

Pale eyes still glazed with the aftereffects of the toxin met hers. "Aye."

"What are you doing up there?"

The Prime almost smiled. He had been chained by his wrists about a foot off the ground up against the back wall of a cell adjacent to hers. "You . . . don't remember?" he asked, panting slightly.

"No."

"You fought her," he replied, sounding about as well as she felt. "She was going to chain us both, but you woke up and started struggling like a wildcat. She couldn't hold you still enough, so she just dumped you on the floor and locked the cell. She was bleeding when she left."

Miranda heaved herself onto her side, wincing—her shoulder was still killing her and it felt like she'd been kicked in the kidneys. "Sounds pretty badass."

Deven chuckled weakly. "It was."

She ran her hands down over her body, patting herself for other injuries. "She took our weapons and phones . . . but I still have my hand, so I still have my com. Why?"

"Don't know. I didn't get a dramatic villain monologue out of her."

Miranda shut her eyes again, trying to concentrate. If she could summon enough strength, she could call for help—surely David would be able to sense her, even if they were really far away. She reached out with her senses . . .

. . . and found them blocked. She couldn't feel anything beyond the cell. That meant that David couldn't feel her either.

"Oh, God," she said. "I can't project. We're cut off."

"I know that."

"There's a room like this at the Haven . . . it's where I learned to shield myself. No matter what goes on inside, it can't get outside. Psychic signals, even cell phones and the coms . . . they won't be able to find us."

"It takes an incredible amount of power to create a shielded chamber," Deven noted, eyes wandering around the room. "Either she's got resources beyond a few amulets from Volundr or this place existed before she got here."

"What do we do?" she asked, starting to panic. "What do we do?"

"First . . . calm down. They might not be able to find us via the Signet bond, but there are other ways. You're married to a genius, remember?"

"He hasn't been able to find Ovaska so far. What if—"

"Things are different now. By kidnapping us, she changed her MO. That throws in more variables. They'll find us, Miranda. We just have to survive until they do."

"Can you Mist?"

Deven shook his head. "I'm way too scattered already."

"Why hasn't she killed us yet?"

Deven snorted quietly. "Clearly you've never been vengeful. Killing someone who can't see your face isn't nearly as satisfying . . . and killing us while we were in pain would have been merciful."

"So she could be here any minute to finish us off," Miranda concluded. "We have to be ready for her—I just need to get up—"

She didn't have a chance to finish the thought, much less formulate a plan. There was the sound of a metal bolt shooting home, and a door across from the cells swung open.

Marja Ovaska walked into the room, giving them both a nasty, self-satisfied smile. She was wearing a metal disc on a chain identical to the one she'd lost at Drew's school . . . and she was holding a hand-carved stake.

She stood in front of the cell doors for a minute, not speaking, just watching Miranda. She was, Miranda noticed, a strikingly beautiful woman with cropped blond hair and large blue eyes; Miranda pictured her standing next to Sophie's dark pixie looks, and the image made a wistful sort of sense. It also helped explain why Deven had developed a soft spot for the couple; physically they reminded Miranda of the Pair, with one small and dark, the other tall and blond.

Miranda started to speak, but Ovaska cut her off. "Don't bother," she said, and yes, she had an accent now that Miranda hadn't heard the night of Drew's death. "I don't care if you're sorry."

"Well, good," Deven said caustically. "Miranda may have sympathy for your sob story—poor you, your lover died, now you have to strike back. Cue the violins. I couldn't care less."

Ovaska looked at him with loathing . . . but also, Miranda sensed, with the slightest undercurrent of fear. Deven had been right . . . even though she had the power here, and even though she was no longer part of the Shadow, an agent was always an agent, and even chained to the wall at her mercy, the Alpha was still the Alpha.

"We both know this isn't about Miranda getting Sophie killed," Deven went on. "Sophie made her own choices—that's what's eating you alive. Because when it came down to it, she chose Miranda, and the Signets, over you."

"Shut up," Ovaska said softly.

"If you're going to kill us, kill us," the Prime told her. "If you stall, you'll be caught. I taught you better than that . . . unless . . ."

"Deven," Miranda interrupted, "don't taunt the crazy person with the stake!"

But Deven was staring at Ovaska hard, eyes narrowed. "She's not crazy. Are you, Marja? Did you really bring us here to kill us? This whole setup . . . the bomb, the cells, the poison . . . it's more than simple vengeance. I know you."

Now Ovaska smiled. "Do you think so?"

"You're not this sentimental. Sophie was the one who begged me not to kill you both. Even in love, even facing execution at my hands, you didn't betray a scrap of emotion. If all you wanted was revenge, you would have found a way to kill Miranda by now . . . you wouldn't have missed the first time."

"You said she was sizing me up," Miranda said. "And that killing the others was to hurt me."

Deven shook his head. "That may be true, but it's not

the whole story. The more complicated this whole thing became, the less sense it made. It's cliché, Marja. Scorned woman out for blood—bullshit. Volundr introduced you to someone, didn't he? Someone with a lot of money and a very particular purpose."

Still smiling, Ovaska took a key from her pocket and opened Deven's cell door. She walked up to him so that they were inches apart and said to him very calmly, "Now you're the one who's stalling."

She rested the point of the stake against Deven's cheek, then drew it slowly down his neck, over his chest. "What do you suppose would happen to the Red Shadow if I killed the Alpha?" she asked.

"Well," Deven replied, "given that I issued a kill order on you, even if you walk out of this building alive, you'll find out pretty quickly."

"I fooled you once," Marja told him. "You walked right into the trap I set for you. I evaded the Southern Elite for weeks. If I can do that, I can outfox your agents."

"Why did you set a trap, again?" Deven asked. "Why are we here?"

Miranda focused her will on her limbs, and slowly, very slowly, she got her hands underneath her to try and push herself up. She didn't know what she was going to do, but she wasn't going to lie there on the floor and wait for Ovaska to make a move. One way or another she was going to go down fighting.

Ovaska's head jerked toward her. "Don't try it," she snapped. "There's nowhere for you to go."

Deven seized her lapsed attention, pulled his knees up to his chest, and kicked Ovaska hard in the midsection. She staggered backward, hitting the bars with a loud clank, and flailed sideways to grab the bars and stay upright. The stake, knocked out of her hand, clattered to the floor inches from the wall of bars between the cells.

Miranda shoved herself up and dove for it, sticking her arm through the bars and getting her hand around the stake.

As she jerked backward Ovaska regained her footing, and pain exploded through Miranda's hand as Ovaska stomped on her fingers. Miranda cried out and dropped the stake, which Ovaska bent and retrieved. Miranda pulled her arm back just in time to avoid another stomp.

Miranda held her arm against her chest, the pain of her broken fingers nearly making her sick.

Ovaska glared down at her. "Bitch," she snarled.

She returned her attention to Deven, who didn't look particularly disappointed that the gamble hadn't worked. "Worth a try," he said.

Ovaska straightened her clothes, rotating her neck as if to work out a kink, then considered the stake in her hand and the Prime bound before her. "You're right," she said finally. "Yes, I wanted revenge. Killing all her little friends did make me feel better . . . although if one of them had talked, told me how to find the Haven, that would have made things much easier for me. Your people are nothing if not loyal. It's annoying. But it turns out there are greater powers out there than the Signets . . . and bigger paychecks than the Shadow."

Deven met her eyes. "Who are you working for, Marja?"

She smiled. "Not you."

She glanced over at Miranda. "The contract stipulates: one live Signet, physically intact, to be delivered tonight. As they say, I can kill two birds with one stone. I can destroy the woman who destroyed my life, and I can make myself obscenely rich and finally get out of the game. This is what I learned from you, Sire. Cold, calculating efficiency. This woman is important to my client, and to my desire for justice . . . and you . . ."

She ran her fingers down the shaft of the stake, pondering a moment longer, before she finished, "You, Sire, are expendable."

She smiled. Then she drove the stake into Deven's stomach.

# Eighteen

Deven held back his scream, just barely, but his head fell back and hit the wall, eliciting a strangled sound of pain that Miranda herself could feel throughout her body. Blood erupted from the wound, running in coppery dark rivers down over his legs, pooling on the floor.

Marja stepped back to avoid the blood and said, "There, now. That's the first problem dealt with. Now I just have to keep you quiet until my client arrives in an hour." She turned to Miranda. "Either you can stay where you are and not make trouble, and watch your friend bleed to death, or I can give you another shot of poison, and you can scream and writhe on the floor in your own blood while he bleeds to death. Up to you."

Miranda glared at her, wanting nothing more than to fling herself at the bars and tear them down to get her hands around Ovaska's throat, but she was still too injured and unfocused to Mist, and not strong enough to tear down walls.

Ovaska watched all those thoughts cross Miranda's face, her own expression deeply satisfied with Miranda's impotence. "Enjoy your last few moments together," Ovaska said to Miranda. "I'll be back soon."

She slammed the outer door shut and locked it.

Miranda's hand was still in agony, but she forced energy

into it to at least partially mend the broken fingers, and got up on her knees. "Deven!"

His head was hanging down, eyes closed, but she could hear him breathing, a shallow rattling in his chest. The blood was still flowing from his abdomen.

Miranda dragged herself to her feet and held on to the bars. "Can you heal it?" she asked.

Deven could barely focus on her enough to reply, but he said, "Can't . . . stake's still . . . in there. Can't pull it."

Miranda tried reaching through the bars, but he was chained at least two feet beyond her reach. Her heart was thundering around her rib cage as she tried to assess the situation for a solution: Deven's cell was still open, but hers was locked.

Miranda pushed herself over to the door of her cell and pulled on it as hard as she could, shaking it, trying to make it budge. If she could get it open, she could get into Deven's cell and pull the stake, and he could heal the wound before he bled to death . . . but she had to get the door open . . .

"Miranda . . ."

She stopped midshake and turned to Deven. "Just hold on," she said. "Just stop the bleeding as much as you can. I'll get that thing out of you, I just have to—"

"Miranda . . . I'm done for. Unless I can draw power from Jonathan, even if the stake comes out, I won't last long." He closed his eyes and leaned his head back against the wall. "You have to save yourself. Whatever that woman wants with you, it can't be good."

"Let me think," Miranda said. "I'll get us out of this."

"Miranda . . ."

"I'll think of something!" she said, and she turned to him, tears in her eyes. "I'm not going to let you die."

Deven smiled. "Why not?"

Miranda shook her head around her tears. "I'm not going to be the one who has to tell David you're dead. It would kill him to lose you. Jonathan, too. Literally."

Their eyes met, and to her astonishment Deven's were

shining, too. "I'm sorry," Deven said softly. "I'm sorry about David."

Miranda hung her head against the bars. "I forgive you," she whispered. "Thank you . . . for Sophie. She was . . ."

"She was a good friend," Deven finished, his own voice fading. "That's all you need to remember about her. She was your friend."

"I don't want you to die," she said, crying through the words. "Tell me what to do to save you."

"You're too weak from the poison to Mist," Deven said. "There's nothing else you can do."

Miranda watched Deven's blood falling, drop by drop, onto the cold floor, drop by drop his life draining out of his body, the light in his Signet beginning to dim.

"Jonathan," Deven whispered, his eyes slowly closing. "Oh, love . . . don't keep me waiting long . . ."

"No," Miranda whispered. "No . . ." She took a deep breath, planting her feet solidly on the ground and holding on to the bars hard.

She lifted her eyes from the blood trail to the stake jutting out of Deven's body, right through his solar plexus, making his breath labored, his healing ability unable to stay on top of the damage as it tore through his flesh over and over again each time he inhaled. If she could just get her arm far enough through the bars, she could get her hand . . . around it . . .

Miranda gasped.

She slid her hand through the bars again, extending her palm toward the stake, and drew up all the energy she could, trying to remember how she'd done it before . . . with Hart . . . she had acted without thinking, acted from emotion, from anger . . . and one thing Miranda knew how to do was manipulate emotion.

She reached down into herself and dragged out all the anger she could find: anger at Marja Ovaska for killing Drew, for attacking Kat, for poisoning David, for killing Jake and Denise . . . for bringing fear and violence to the streets of her city . . .

Miranda pushed that anger out along her arm, then focused her mind on the stake as if she were mentally wrapping her fingers around its hilt, feeling the wood grain against her fingers, the slickness of Deven's blood around the wood, as she grasped it, and with the force of her anger, *pulled*.

Deven cried out in pain as the stake flew out of his body, yanked so hard that it was flung back into Miranda's cell and hit the wall.

Breathing hard, barely able to stay conscious from the effort, Miranda held on to the bars. "Deven!"

He was icy white and not moving; she couldn't even hear him breathe. He hung limp in his chains . . . but the blood had stopped flowing.

"Deven? Are you still there?" she asked.

Several interminable seconds later, she heard, "Nice . . . work . . ."

Miranda slid down the bars onto her knees. She couldn't keep herself up anymore. "How long can you hold out?"

"Maybe . . . half an hour."

"Okay. That's a start." She turned and crawled over to the stake where it had landed on the floor. The point had been blunted when it hit the wall, but with enough force it could go through flesh. So they had a weapon; that was step one.

If she could get Ovaska into her cell, she could attack, and with the door open she could get out and call for help, find the keys to the shackles, and get them out of here. The only thing she could think to do was feign unconsciousness.

"How can we get her in here?"

Deven sighed. "Make a lot of noise."

Miranda nodded, leaning against the bars to rest for a moment. Exhaustion was dragging her down and she just wanted to sleep . . . no, she wanted to go home and fall asleep in her own bed with David beside her . . . the longing to have him with her was suddenly overwhelming. She just wanted to hear his voice, feel the reassuring strength of his presence, anything . . .

"Your husband is really amazing in bed," Deven said suddenly. "I love that thing he does with his tongue—"

"Shut up!" Miranda snapped, her attention whipping back to center, and with it, the realization that she was on the verge of cracking. Now was no time to pine herself to death—she had to act. "You're such a bastard," she said, though she was almost grinning as she spoke.

Deven managed a smile. "Better. Now get up . . . or I'll give you the play-by-play of the night with the handcuffs—"

"Like you're really into bondage," she muttered half-heartedly, focusing her energy on moving back to the corner of her cell. The farther she could get Ovaska in, the more room she'd have to take her down. Miranda fought hard to ignore the pain in her hand and shoulder, the slow creeping madness of being cut off from David, the burning in veins that needed blood, badly, to help her recover from her injuries and the poison . . . soon she'd have time to rest, and she could feed and sleep. But now she had to focus.

"Okay," she said. "Try to look dead."

"No . . . problem . . ."

Miranda tucked the stake out of sight under her arm, took a deep breath . . . and screamed at the top of her lungs.

"This way!"

Faith held her phone out in front of her, gesturing with her free arm for the rest of the team to follow her around the corner and up the street. The green line that marked Ovaska's trail glowed in the moonless night, leading them miles from where they had originally thought Ovaska was hiding, back to the industrial warehouse neighborhood where Sophie had once lived.

Fifteen Southern Elite and twelve from the West converged on the trail's end, Faith in the lead, all of them out for blood and under orders to take Ovaska down by any means necessary. Jonathan and David were right behind them, but David was still woozy from the aftereffects of the poison, and he had sent the Elite ahead instead of making them waste precious minutes waiting for their Prime.

"Here!" Faith announced, looking up from her phone.

They were in the middle of the street.

"Goddamn it!" Faith exclaimed. "What went wrong?"

*"Something is degrading the trail,"* David said over the coms. *"Fan out and search every building on the intersection from sub-basement to roof."*

"You have your orders, Elite!" Faith called. "Go!"

Faith turned in a circle, watching the Elite disperse in teams to kick down doors, her heart sinking—there had to be a dozen buildings surrounding the intersection, some of them huge. They didn't have time to canvass the whole neighborhood. The Queen and Prime might have only minutes to live.

David and Jonathan appeared by her side. "Whatever she's using to shield them must be interfering with the readings," David told her, panting just a little from exertion. "I don't think I can narrow it down any further without taking more time than we have."

"You said this was Sophie's old neighborhood?" Jonathan asked. "Which building was she in?"

Faith shook her head. "I don't remember—hang on—" She accessed her e-mail and searched for the message Sophie had sent her with her address, months and months ago when Faith had asked her to train Miranda. She double-checked the street names again. "That one over there, the red one on the corner. But Ovaska wouldn't use her building, would she? That would be too obvious."

"Yes," Jonathan agreed, "and that's exactly why she'd use it. It would be the last place you'd look, especially if you'd already searched it before."

David turned to Jonathan. "Do you know if Ovaska was strongly gifted?"

"No," Jonathan replied. "She wasn't—she had some telepathy, but nothing outstanding."

David nodded once and took off for Sophie's building.

Faith ran to catch up with him. "What is it?"

"She has to be keeping Miranda and Deven in a shielded room like the one where I taught Miranda to use her empathy. Proximity to a room like the one at the Haven could disrupt the readings that led us here—that would explain why the trail ended. It takes time and power to create a room like that. Ovaska had neither—but Sophie might have, and Ovaska would have known about it."

"What if she's got some other kind of magic, or more amulets, and not a shielded room?"

David reached the building and angled left, looking for an entrance. "Then Ovaska just happened to choose another building in the exact same block as Sophie's. Which do you think is more likely?"

Faith nodded and lifted her wrist. "Report!"

*"No luck so far,"* one of the team leaders answered. *"We've only been through three buildings. They could be anywhere."*

"No they couldn't," Faith said. "I need all Elite to 2421 Buckland."

"I can't Mist inside," David told Jonathan. "I'm still too scattered. Can you?"

Jonathan closed his eyes briefly, then shook his head and opened them. "Whatever's interfering with the signal is making it impossible to Mist—it's like I can't see clearly enough to get a lock on the destination. We're going to need a good old-fashioned door like normal people."

Faith stepped back to look at the building's walls, trying to figure out where the entrance was. "I'll call Mitchell with the city planning office and get a schematic. It'll take two minutes—"

No sooner were the words out of her mouth than she heard David say, "Oh, God . . ."

The Prime had gone pale, and a second later Faith knew why; faintly, somewhere inside the building, a woman was screaming.

Miranda heard the door opening, heard Ovaska demand, "What in hell is going on in here?"

She kept screaming, doubled over in the cell corner, until she heard the jingle of keys and the clank of the cell door opening.

"Shut up!" Ovaska yelled. "Shut up or I'll dose you again!"

Miranda let her get one foot closer, gathering all the strength she could into her body, then clamped her mouth shut and twisted around toward Ovaska, ramming the stake as hard as she could into the woman's thigh.

Now it was Ovaska's turn to scream.

Miranda threw herself at the assassin, knocking her into the side of the cell, but Ovaska was hardly amateur enough to let a stake wound stop her. She grabbed Miranda's arms and flung her aside, firing off a string of curses at the Queen.

Miranda wasn't an amateur either. Adrenaline surged through her, hot and bloody. She caught herself and used the back wall as leverage, flying into Ovaska and tackling her, and they rolled across the floor, both snarling like animals, trying to pin each other, too well matched in strength to do so.

Miranda reached down and pushed on the stake that was still in Ovaska's leg, driving it deeper and eliciting a cry of pain. Unyielding, Ovaska shoved her and struggled to her feet, running for the cell door, no doubt intending to lock her in again.

This time Miranda was fast enough; she wedged her body in the doorway as Ovaska tried to slam it shut, knocking the breath out of Miranda but not trapping her. Ovaska ran for the outer door, and Miranda ignored the pain in her chest and followed.

The cells were in a basement room—the outer door led to a stairwell. Miranda sprinted up after Ovaska's retreating form.

Miranda threw the door at the head of the stairs open and dove out, aiming low, anticipating that Ovaska would have doubled back to ambush her as she came out. She barely avoided the sword that whistled through the air inches from her neck, and then she hit the ground rolling, coming up onto her feet in time to leap back from another swipe.

She didn't have time to look around, but she knew

immediately where they were. She knew this room, had fought in it a hundred times; she remembered where all the weapons had once hung on the walls. The Elite had taken Sophie's arsenal, so the walls should have been bare, but two swords and several other blades were hanging up—hers, Miranda realized, and Deven's.

Miranda raced for the wall, and just as she got her hand around one of the swords she felt the sting of Ovaska's blade slicing into her left arm. Miranda forced herself to ignore the pain and the blood and spun around, bringing the sword up to meet Ovaska's.

They stared at each other for a few seconds. Ovaska was bleeding profusely from her thigh, and her face was disfigured with bruises from their struggle on the floor. The stake was still in her leg.

"Who are you working for?" the Queen demanded.

Ovaska laughed. "Your death," she said simply, and attacked.

Distantly Miranda heard something pounding on the wall, but neither she nor Ovaska allowed herself to be distracted. This time, with both of them injured, it was a more evenly matched fight. They fought across the broad expanse of Sophie's studio, Miranda backflipping out of her reach then diving back in again, Ovaska spinning in midair to add more momentum to her arm. Miranda felt the sword almost alive in her hand, as if her entire body were a weapon, and she let herself slip into the space that Sophie had shown her, between present and future, drawing on a strength beyond herself until she almost knew what Ovaska would do next—

Miranda dropped low, swiping out with her foot, knocking Ovaska off balance as Miranda struck her injured leg. Ovaska tumbled backward, wheeling her arms to regain her equilibrium, but she lost her guard just long enough for Miranda to kick her again, this time in the stomach, sending her to the ground.

The Queen sprang back up and went in for the kill.

Ovaska scooted back, and instead of beheading her,

Miranda's blade opened her chest, blood gushing out in its wake. Ovaska pushed herself backward again, and as Miranda brought the blade down a second time Ovaska reached down and pulled the stake from her leg, using all her remaining will to thrust it upward.

Miranda felt the wood penetrate her rib cage, but she, too, had one last burst of strength to give, and as Ovaska fell down onto the ground again, Miranda's sword flashed, and Ovaska's neck parted, her body striking the concrete floor . . . followed by her head.

Ovaska's arm fell outstretched, her sword landing beside her with a loud clang.

For just a second Miranda heard nothing but the hoarse sound of her own breath, and the world was held suspended, the Queen's eyes on the fallen body of Marja Ovaska, the floor stained with their mingled blood.

Miranda heard another thunderous pounding, and it shook her enough to make her remember . . . she wasn't finished yet.

She bent over Ovaska's body and stuck her hand in the assassin's pants pocket, retrieving the ring with the keys to the basement room and cell doors.

Miranda stumbled back the way she had come, her entire body begging her to fall, her strength finally failing her, in so much pain she couldn't think—but she didn't need to think. She just had to walk.

She held on to the rail as she half fell down the stairs, her vision swimming black and gray, her breath nothing but wheezes; the stake had collapsed her lung. She absently reached up and pulled it, but she didn't even feel the wood leaving her body. She had to keep going. In just a minute . . . in just a minute she could lie down . . .

The Queen fell against the cell door, swinging with it into the cell itself. Her fingers were numb around the keys, but she used the bars to support herself and put one foot in front of the other, forcing herself to keep going.

"Sweet Jesus," she heard someone whisper. "Miranda, sit down . . . you're going to kill yourself . . ."

Stubbornly she shook her head and sagged into the back wall, trying to focus her gaze on the keys enough to figure out which one went to the shackles.

"Miranda—stop."

She could barely move, but she lifted her head and met Deven's eyes.

"Put your hand on my shoulder," he said softly.

She started to protest, but he held her eyes. She could see how tired he was . . . so tired . . . she understood . . . she just wanted to sleep . . .

"Put your hand on my shoulder, Miranda," he repeated.

Shaking too violently to speak, she obeyed.

"It's all right," she heard him say. "I'm ready."

Miranda felt power, more than she would have believed he still had, lifted into her, a gentle current of energy that stemmed the flow of blood from her wounds, eased her pain, and helped her slide slowly to the floor instead of falling.

The keys fell out of her left hand, the sword out of her right.

"There," he whispered. "We can both rest now."

Miranda smiled, nodded, and closed her eyes.


Before the Elite even had the door open all the way, David and Jonathan both raced inside the building, into a scene of blood and death, Ovaska's headless body sprawled on the ground, her lifeless face caught in a moment of eternal shock.

David had been able to feel Miranda for a few minutes, but she was gone again—back into the shielded room, he knew. She was hurt . . . badly hurt . . . dying . . .

So was Deven. Jonathan faltered, gasping, his hand flying up to his Signet. "Dev . . . no, baby, don't . . ."

"Over here!"

Faith was pointing at an open door in the corner. David grabbed Jonathan's arm and hauled him along into the stairwell.

Prime and Consort burst into the room, and David made it to Miranda's side in a heartbeat, falling to his knees beside her and pulling her into his arms, knocking Deven's sword out of her lap.

David was already weakened, but he didn't care; he opened himself to her fully, letting the energy between them return to balance, giving her everything he could spare to heal her at least enough to make it home safely . . . but to his surprise she wasn't as bad off as he had felt she was even a moment ago, and her wounds had already stopped bleeding.

He looked up in time to see Jonathan lowering Deven's body from the wall where he had been chained, the two of them sinking to the floor together.

It didn't look like Deven was breathing . . . but Jonathan was still alive. There had to be some hope . . .

He felt the same tide of power between the Pair that had passed between him and Miranda. Jonathan held Deven close, breathing hard, his eyes full of anguish, waiting . . . but Deven hadn't just given all his energy to Miranda, he'd given her everything, even his life force, the base energy that held the body and soul together . . . and Jonathan simply wasn't strong enough to replenish that.

Desperate, David extended the connection between himself and Miranda to Jonathan. He wasn't sure if the Consort would know what to do with it the way Deven would, but Jonathan seemed to have learned a few things from his lover; he "caught" the line of energy and drew from it, his gratitude echoing along the line to David. Then, with the four of them joined as they had been that night to heal Kat, Jonathan poured the energy into Deven as gingerly as he could . . . and again they waited, afraid to even breathe, afraid to disturb the fragile equilibrium they'd managed to cobble together for the Prime.

Finally, finally, David saw the Prime's lip tremble. Deven's eyes fluttered open, pupils dilating until they focused on his Consort.

Jonathan smiled, so relieved he half sobbed, and kissed

Deven everywhere he could that wasn't covered in bruises or blood.

Deven returned the smile weakly and murmured something in Gaelic too low for David to interpret, but that made Jonathan laugh; then, with a sigh, Deven turned his face into his Consort's chest and passed out.

David withdrew from the connection, shielding himself and Miranda off again. He felt Miranda stir in his arms and looked down into her face. Blood had run down her forehead from a cut and was drying on her cheek, but her skin was unmarred, and her eyes were exhausted but full of life as she blinked up at him.

She started to cry. She could barely speak, but she was determined to be heard as she whispered raggedly, "David . . . Deven . . . he's . . ."

"Shh . . ." He laid a finger on her lips. "He's alive, beloved. He's alive."

Miranda was still crying, but she broke out into a smile and nodded with relief.

Then she said, "Blood. Shower. Chocolate. You. Now."

He laughed quietly, kissed her, and replied, "As you will it, my Lady."

# Nineteen

Texas didn't have much of a winter, but what it had was wet and bitter, and autumn was already headed that way, a line of storms from the north driving freezing rain into the Hill Country with a vengeance.

Esther had built a roaring fire for the Queen, clucking over her still-pale cheeks like a mother hen before leaving the suite warm and cozy and smelling faintly of herbs and candle wax.

Miranda leaned her chin on her guitar and stared into the flames, absently plucking a string here and there. Despite Esther's worries, she was feeling better tonight, just shaky and tired; for the past three days she'd slept more than she'd been awake, and she hadn't left the Haven even though she was due back at the Bat Cave for a follow-up session to rerecord a couple of problematic tracks.

She had told Grizzly she had the flu. Because it was going around in this nasty weather, he had no reason to doubt her.

She paused and reached up to touch her Signet. Part of her wanted to cancel the entire project and give up on the idea of performing. So many people had been hurt . . . but in the end, she couldn't be anyone but who she was, and as she had told Faith, music was a part of her she wouldn't surrender unless there was no other choice. She'd find a way to make it work . . . tomorrow.

Tonight, she just wanted to be warm and safe and comfortable, with the rain falling outside and the firelight soothing her inside. But her heart still ached, and her body still ached, and it was hard to feel comforted knowing how many of her friends had suffered at the hands of Marja Ovaska. It was hard not to feel guilty—for not stopping Marja sooner, for letting Sophie get killed, for a hundred things Miranda couldn't have anticipated and couldn't change even if she had. There were still questions that needed answering—chief among them, who was Ovaska working for? What did that client want with a Signet? Miranda was afraid to even contemplate that.

There was a knock at the door.

"Come in," she called.

When she looked up, she was surprised, and said, "Deven."

The Prime closed the door quietly behind him. He, too, was still drawn and tired looking, moving a little more slowly than usual. He hadn't even regained consciousness until last night. Even Jonathan's power combined with David's and Miranda's almost hadn't been enough to save him—Jonathan wasn't a healer and didn't have Deven's skill to direct the raw power as a healer could. He could only push the energy into Deven and hope it kept him alive. It was something of a miracle Deven had survived at all. It would take a while to fully recover from that, even as strong as he had been.

David had apologized to Miranda a half-dozen times for taking the liberty of offering their energy . . . before she reminded him that Deven had given his own life to save her and had been the one to shield her from the explosion before that. She had no regrets about having to sleep an extra day or two if it meant that Deven was still alive . . . and that was something she'd never expected to hear herself say.

Deven came to the couch where she was sitting and held something out to her.

Miranda frowned. "What is this?"

He smiled. "It's a sword, Miranda."

"I know that. But why are you giving it to me?"

"Because she's yours."

Miranda set aside her guitar and took the blade he offered; it was the one he had worn here, the one David had said was new. Her fingers wrapped around the hilt, and she felt a stab of recognition—she had fought Ovaska with it, not with Sophie's sword. This one felt natural in her grip and was perfectly balanced, as if it had been created for her arm.

"I had her made for you," Deven explained. "Not by Volundr, though, don't worry. Call her a wedding gift, or perhaps a peace offering."

She drew the blade partway from the sheath, admiring the carving along the steel. "It's . . . she's beautiful . . . thank you."

He nodded and took a step back, intending to leave, but she said, "I've been thinking."

"About?"

Miranda went on. "I was thinking that . . . maybe you and David should see each other again."

He didn't bother—or perhaps didn't have the energy—to hide his surprise. "What?"

"I don't want to be the reason that David is unhappy," she said. "He loves you. So maybe you could meet sometimes, like a weekend every couple of months, no questions asked. We could make some kind of arrangement that would work for all four of us."

Deven stared at her for a long moment. Then he smiled and shook his head. "No."

"Wait . . . *you're* saying no?"

"That's right."

"But . . . why?"

Again, the smile; a touch rueful, a touch enigmatic, a touch wry. "Because I don't want to be the reason you're unhappy."

"But . . ."

He reached over and touched her head as if in benediction. She felt a light energetic pulse, as if he had stroked her hair, though his hand didn't move, and it made her feel warm and safe . . . the way she had craved to feel for days. "It's time for him to be with you, Miranda. You have the right to grow together as a Pair without me interfering. Life is going to be hard enough for you already in the next few years. Perhaps one day later on we can talk about it. But for now . . . Jonathan and I are going home, where we belong."

This time he did walk away, but as he opened the door, she glanced down at the sword in her hands, then looked back up and called, "Deven."

He paused in the doorway without looking at her. "Yes?"

She held up the blade. "David said you name your swords, and that's what this carving is."

"It is indeed."

"Well . . . who is she? What do I call her?"

Deven smiled at her over his shoulder. "Shadowflame."


The stables were heated, of course, but David still fretted over the horses' comfort in such ghastly weather, so he visited them every night for at least a few minutes. As far as he could tell, neither one was at all perturbed at being cooped up inside—the forecast called for a few days' clearing before the next front, so he hoped he could take them both out tomorrow night, but in the meantime both seemed content to be coddled.

He ran his hand down Osiris's nose. The Friesian flicked his ears toward David and whuffled his hair affectionately.

"Here you go," David said to the stallion, offering him a cookie from his pocket.

Osiris munched contentedly on the cookie and nosed David for more, but David shook his head and chuckled, admonishing the horse. "Don't be greedy."

"He can't help it," came a voice. "You're irresistible."

David turned toward the sound; he hadn't felt anyone approaching, but it wasn't that surprising given who it was.

"You should be in bed . . . and certainly not walking through the cold to get here."

Deven shrugged. He was bundled up in his coat, with a scarf and gloves; he looked a hundred times better than he had even the night before, but still weary, even with his usual wardrobe, jewelry, and eyeliner perfectly in place. For once Deven looked older than a teenager, and it made David want to drag him into the house and tuck him back into bed whether Dev liked it or not.

"Our steward called," Deven said. "The jet's been cleared to leave tonight. There's a car on the way to pick us up."

"You're . . . you're leaving? Now?"

"We've been away too long." When he saw the uncertainty in David's expression, he added, "I'm fine to travel, dear one. I need a few days' rest yet, but I'll sleep much more soundly in my own bed."

"With your own Consort," David said—almost blurted—before he could stop himself.

Deven gave him a searching look. "So that's why you were angry at me," he mused. "It wasn't just for keeping the Red Shadow secret from you . . . it was for keeping it from you but telling Jonathan."

David started to make the expected denial but couldn't. He also couldn't meet Deven's eyes. "You're right."

"He's my Consort, David. I don't say that to rub it in your face . . . it's just the way things are. He knows me, and loves me, in a way you can't . . . and vice versa. Each of you is a part of me, and that will never change."

David noted the careful distance Deven was keeping— but that might be as much about Osiris as about David. Deven had never been comfortable around horses. Experimentally, David moved away from the stall, toward the Prime, who stood his ground.

They faced each other, eyes holding for a while, before Deven said, "I suppose I'll see you at Council."

"Right . . . I suppose."

Another pause. "Any luck figuring out how those amulets worked?"

David didn't remark on the change of subject. "Novotny's analyzing the one we found on the body as well as looking for other evidence. We didn't find anything else in the building—nothing at all, not even personal effects."

"So Sophie's warehouse wasn't where Ovaska was living. It was just a holding pen for us. She might have other artifacts at her real home base."

"It looks that way. We're working on finding her hideout. There's not much to go on so far, but . . . Novotny's people are smarter than the FBI and have better equipment. They'll find something."

"What about her client?"

"There were no other vampires in the area that night, at least none that showed up on the sensors. I had Elite canvass the neighborhood. Witnesses we questioned that night saw a limo traveling down Buckland, but it didn't stop at the building. Either her client has a shielding device of his or her own, or her client is a human."

Deven nodded. "I'd wager it's a human."

"Why do you say that?"

"Because the Shadow only hires out to humans. Her leaving her victims' left hands behind indicates she was still following standard Shadow protocol, so it stands to reason she was working for a human."

"She didn't cut off Miranda's hand."

"Her client wanted Miranda alive and unspoiled."

"But we can't know for sure the client is human."

"Perhaps you can't. But I know my agents."

David asked what had been on his mind for days. "Did you mean it when you said you didn't try to recruit me because we were sleeping together?"

Deven sighed, looking down at the hay-scattered ground, then back up at David. "As I said . . . Sophie was the only agent I was ever attached to. I knew better, even as I let her keep working for me. Caring about them compromises my ability to send them into certain death. There was no way I could have done it to you."

"Do you enjoy being the Alpha? Killing people for money?"

The Prime gave him a mischievous grin. "I don't kill people for money, David. I pay other people to kill people for money. I'm a murder pimp."

David laughed. "That's one way to put it."

"And to answer your question . . . I enjoy training warriors. I enjoy the satisfaction of knowing that they're the best in the world. And it's not all about vengeance and greed. More than half of our contracts are for governments that need something done that the human military can't accomplish. Many of my people have stopped wars before they started, brought down dictators, taken out spies. I'm not ashamed of what I do . . . or of what I've done."

They met each other's eyes again, and David understood what he was saying. Despite the consequences, despite almost dying, Deven would do it all again if it meant bringing Miranda to David . . . and not only had Sophie taught David's Queen, she had fought in the battle of the Haven and had a hand in ending the Blackthorn war. Deven had no regrets about that . . . and, in the end, neither did David.

Finally, Deven nodded. "It's time for me to go," he said. "Take care of yourself . . . and take care of each other."

"You, too."

Deven reached out and took David's hand, lifting it to his lips, squeezing it, and then letting go. "Good-bye, David."

David didn't expect to feel his heart breaking as Deven walked away, and yet . . . there it was. No matter what, no matter how much time or distance came between them, some part of him would always be at Deven's side, and part of Deven would always reside in David's heart.

David crossed the stable to catch up to Deven, laying a hand on his shoulder. Deven stopped and turned toward him, and David saw the pain in his eyes, pain he had intended to keep hidden until he was safely twenty-five thousand feet above Texas and long gone from here.

David slid his hand up to Deven's face, tipping the Prime's chin and kissing him softly. He felt Deven's arms move around him, and they held on to each other for a moment, eyes closed, memorizing the smell and taste of each other, the sound of each other's breathing.

"I love you," David said into Deven's ear.

Holding on to his hands, Deven stepped back, his smile remarkably like the one that David had seen on his face after he had healed Kat that night in the city: a smile of peace and happiness, untouched by the sorrow that he wore habitually beneath his coat.

"I love you, too," Deven replied.

Then he released David's hands and walked away.


Once again, a car was waiting to take Deven and Jonathan to the airport; and once again, Faith was waiting, but this time she was standing inside the Haven's enormous front doors. Protocol be damned—it was cold outside.

The Pair emerged from the hallway with their honor guard. The rest of their Elite were already on the way back to California, but their bodyguards would travel on the jet with them.

David and Miranda had said their good-byes to the Pair in private. They were trying to keep as much of the story under wraps as possible to avoid causing gossip about Ovaska's intentions or origins, so they had all agreed not to make a dramatic production of the farewell; but this time no one was slinking away, just observing tradition in truth instead of hiding behind it. This time there were no furtive glances, and Deven and Jonathan were side by side.

Faith was just glad to have a chance to hug them both.

She smiled to herself. Jonathan gave his Prime a kiss on the forehead, and Deven looked up at him with an indulgent sparkle in his eyes. Yes, this time things were different. Thank God for that.

"I'm sorry about Lalita," Deven told her.

Faith nodded. "So am I . . . you lost her, too."

"Thank you for not being pissed off about that," Jonathan added. "Like Dev said . . . her commitment to her post was genuine."

"I know." Faith raised an eyebrow at Deven and said, "But we'll be changing our employee screening methods from here on out."

The Prime smiled. "Don't worry, Faith. She was the only agent I had here."

Now she gave him a look. "Please, Sire. Surely you know that nothing you say is ever going to go without question again."

The smile widened. "Good."

Jonathan winked at her. "Take care, Faith. And keep an eye on those two."

"As always."

Their guards started to open the door, but Faith asked, "Can I ask you something, Sire?"

Deven turned back to her, lifting his chin inquisitively.

Faith moved close enough that her voice wouldn't carry through the hall. "Why didn't you ever try to recruit me for the Shadow? Was I not a good enough warrior? Not trustworthy enough?"

Deven regarded her silently for a moment, considering her question. "You are an excellent warrior, Faith. You would have made a superlative agent."

"Then why . . ."

Deven's gaze traveled up the stairs, to where Faith realized David was standing at the balcony rail. He smiled and gave Deven a little wave before walking on toward his workroom.

When Faith looked back down, Deven was watching her face carefully, and he said with equal care, "Because I demand absolute loyalty from my agents, Faith . . . and I knew that you were already devoted to someone else."

Faith frowned. "What does that—"

Deven shook his head, smiling. "Don't insult your own

intelligence, Faith, or mine. We both know why you're really here."

She started to stammer a rebuttal, but he gave her a knowing look that silenced her; then he turned back toward the door, took Jonathan's arm, and left Faith standing in the doorway with her face turning scarlet and her heart in her throat.

"It's over."

Kat looked up from the box of books she was taping, unsurprised to see Miranda standing in the doorway, resplendent in her long black coat. "Good."

Miranda didn't ask what Kat was doing; she didn't protest or try to change Kat's mind. She offered no apologies. She simply sat down on the arm of the couch, silent, and watched Kat pack.

"I'm going to stay with my mom until the baby's born," Kat said. "I don't know exactly what I'll do after that. I might do private counseling. Or teach."

No reply.

Kat wrote *BOOKS* on the box with a fat Sharpie, then capped the marker and looked at Miranda. "I can't do this anymore."

Miranda nodded. "I understand."

Kat looked down at the pile of books that had to go in the next box. The one on top was an old Robert Jordan hardcover. It had been Drew's. She rested her hand on the dust jacket for a moment, then said, "Tell me this is all a nightmare, Miranda. Tell me I'm going to wake up a year ago, before any of this happened."

She raised her eyes to Miranda, whose expression was strange: not disdainful, exactly, but distant, perhaps detached . . . no, that wasn't it. There was plenty of emotion in Miranda's face, but there was something else as well . . . and it wasn't human.

The woman sitting on her couch wasn't human. She might look like one to most people. She might pass for one onstage. She might drink a beer or eat an ice cream sundae. But everything about her, from the tumble of her dark red hair to the almost predatory grace in her posture, was carved out of something ancient and alien . . . something that, Kat had finally realized, was going to kill everything mortal she touched.

Something in Miranda had changed, and it would continue to change long after Kat had died of old age. Slowly, the darkness within her was unfolding, its tendrils curling around Miranda's soul, giving her strength, but also stealing her away, the way children in fairy tales had been stolen by elves in the night, leaving a changeling in the cradle.

This was a woman with work to do, and that work had no room in it for pregnant best friends, or anything that would bind her to the world she had left behind. She had killed people, had beheaded a woman, would probably kill more, in the name of law and order and justice in a world so far beyond Kat's grasp it might as well be the gilded halls of the gods themselves.

Suddenly Kat couldn't look at her. She stared, instead, at the door to the guest bathroom . . . where Miranda had turned into a vampire. "Aren't you going to say anything?"

A sigh. "I said I understand."

"And that's it?"

Miranda's fingers absently touched the stone of her Signet. "You have to do what you think is best for you and your daughter. I don't blame you for being afraid, or tired, or wanting to run. You've lost so much because of me . . . and the truth is, you will probably lose more if you stay."

Kat took a deep breath. "Are there any vampires in West Oak?"

Miranda smiled slightly. "Not that we know of."

Kat nodded, swallowing. She wanted to say she'd e-mail or call. But she knew—they both knew—it wasn't true.

Still, Miranda made the effort. "If you or the baby need anything, ever . . ."

"Yeah. I'll call."

Silence stretched out between them, but finally Miranda said in a soft, sad voice, "Thank you for being my friend, Kat."

Kat felt tears burn her eyes, and she started to say something, looking up at Miranda . . .

. . . but the Queen was already gone.


Miranda closed the front door of Kat's house behind her. She leaned back against the door for a moment, eyes shut tightly, and took a deep breath.

It was raining, slow and steady, a quiet rain that seemed to blur everything, make it softer and gentler, even emotions that were hard and jagged and felt like teeth ripping through her heart. She tried to breathe in the softness, to release the pain.

When she opened her eyes again David was standing by the curb, hands in his coat pockets, watching her silently.

She reached up and wiped impatiently at her eyes. David sighed and opened his arms.

Miranda walked down the steps and into his embrace, and they held on to each other for a long time, her face buried in his shoulder, his hand stroking her hair.

When she drew back, she didn't speak, and he didn't expect her to. He simply took her hand and walked with her down the street away from Kat's house, into a cold and rainy night at the receding edge of autumn, one year turning slowly into the next, one season at its end, another just beginning.

# Epilogue

She watched from the roof as the dark red-haired figure ran down the street, her leather coat flying out behind her, her boots striking the pavement with deadly purpose. Behind the Queen a cadre of black-clad warriors followed at speed.

They chased the man almost to the end of the block before the Queen drew up short, her hand shooting out in a quick flicking gesture, and a trash can flew from the side of the building onto the sidewalk, right into the path of her prey.

The man hit the trash can hard and fell over it, landing in a sprawl. He tried to get to his feet and run again, but by the time he got up he was surrounded. Rough hands grabbed his shoulders and hauled him to the red-haired woman, whose green eyes were those of a serpent, coiled, hungry.

The Queen removed something from her coat. "Do you know why we came for you, Mr. Shikai?"

The man stammered something. His eyes were huge and he was drenched in cold sweat.

"Weeks ago we showed you this sketch, Mr. Shikai, and asked if you had ever seen this woman before. You said no."

"Don't know her," he panted. "I swear, I don't."

The Queen tilted her head to one side, considering the man before her dispassionately. "Trace evidence found on her corpse links her to your building, Mr. Shikai. We know she lived there. We searched the building and found nothing, so I have to ask you: What did you do with her belongings?"

"Nothing! She didn't leave anything!"

"Ah, but we know you're lying," she replied, stepping closer. "We tracked a particular artifact to that building—an amulet that gave off a very distinct energy signature. It was there yesterday, long after she was dead. It was gone tonight. What did you do with her things, Mr. Shikai?"

"Nothing! I swear, I—"

"Do you remember the night your wife died a hundred years ago?" the Queen cut in coldly, moving so close she was inches from his ashen face. "Do you remember the pain you felt holding her lifeless body in your arms?"

"How did you know—"

"I can make you relive that night over and over again," she said, lowering her voice until the moment felt almost intimate. "I can trap your mind in a loop of grief and agony that never ends. I can go through your memories and find every hurt you've ever caused, every one you've ever felt, and you'll spend the rest of your immortality there."

He was shaking, staring at her, her power gradually amplifying the fear he already felt until he was so petrified he could think of nothing but escape—and the only way to escape was to give the Queen what she wanted.

"I moved them," he said in a hoarse whisper. "Storage unit. Number eighty-five. Victory Storage on Burnet."

She stared at him a moment longer, ascertaining whether he was telling the truth, and then took a step back.

The man's relief was immense, and his knees seemed to give out. He knelt on the sidewalk panting.

The Queen gestured for the others to move back out of the man's way, saying, "Next time my Elite question you, Mr. Shikai, I suggest you simply tell the truth. Ovaska may have terrified you into keeping her secrets, but I was the one who took her head . . . and if you lie to me again, I'll take yours."

He said something that was either gratitude or an apology, then lurched to his feet, staggering away as fast as he could.

The Queen spoke quietly into the band on her wrist, and her warriors began to melt back into the night that had created them.

Then, as if she'd sensed something, perhaps some movement on the roof above, or perhaps someone watching her, the redhead looked up at the building's roof, eyes narrowed, her gaze penetrating.

All she saw were shadows.

Lydia smiled from the darkness.

Let her wonder . . .

The Queen would know her soon enough.